ADVENTURES

Full of Stories a Lifetime Shouldn't Miss

ADVENTURES
PEOPLE AND STORIES THAT SHOULD NOT BE FORGOTTEN

Spring 2025

WWW.ADVENTURESBOOKZINE.COM

ADVENTURES

FULL OF STORIES A LIFETIME SHOULDN'T MISS

SPRING 2025   **ISSUE #15**

WHAT

WHERE

Editor's Note

FOR MOST OF US, WINTER IS A TIME TO RELAX, TO STAY INSIDE AND STAY WARM and "hibernate" until spring arrives with its promise of sunnier, warmer days. And when those first warm spring-like days arrive, it almost feels like we're experiencing the world again, like we've been rejuvenated. So we thought, what better time for "Adventures" to share a classic story by H.G. Wells that takes place after a long "hibernation"?

"When the Sleeper Wakes" - also known as "The Sleeper Awakes" - is the story of a man who sleeps for 203 years and wakes up in a dystopian future. He's reborn into a vastly different world. Those of you familiar with Washington Irving's "Rip Van Winkle" or even the Matt Groening cartoon show "Futurama" will note some similarities in the premise, but Wells goes darker. Much darker.

In this tale, our hero finds that he has become the richest man in the world, but a group called the White Council has been using his funds to establish a plutarchy (which is similar to an oligarchy, a word that has been bandied about recently). Without giving away too much, let's just say the awakened man now must decide which side he is on, the rich minority or the rebels.

It's a wonderful story, and it pairs well with the Wells story we ran in our winter edition, "A Story of the Days to Come." (Head to our website to order that if you missed it!)

In this edition, you'll also find a new original story by speculative fiction writer Murray Eiland, a poem by Conrad Aiken, a "fairy tale" by W.W. Tarn and more.

I don't know about you, but we're more than ready for spring and warm days when one can read "Adventures" outside. Here's hoping spring has sprung where you live, and cheers to making it through another hibernation!

Michael Brian

Michael Brian

Letters to the editor:

Comments/Questions are accepted. Put *Letter to Editor* in Subject and send to: OffBeatReads@pm.me
*Email content could be published in future *Adventures To Go*.

THEY STAYED TOO LONG
BY MURRAY EILAND

A New Original Story

Ennis did his usual walk around the big windows overlooking the yard. Was he just killing time, or was he waiting for something? At this point, he supposed it made little difference what he did or did not do. The nurse said good morning, gave him his pills, and told him to go to the dining hall for breakfast. As Ennis watched, a man and a woman in formal attire—black, straight tunics with seamless pockets—emerged from a gray Rover with tinted windows. In his time, the government issued Rovers to its police workers. Ennis decided it was as good a time as any to get something to eat.

Ennis hoped it wouldn't be a standard morning at the St. John's Psychiatric Unit.

The nurse called him and interrupted his breakfast. It had taken decades, but maybe he would finally be heard.

The woman offered her hand. She was tall, dark-skinned, and had stern eyes. "Good morning, Mr. Lomings. I'm Erica," she said.

"You may call me Ted." The man next to her offered his hand.

He was short but well-built, with pale skin and blond hair. Ennis noticed him studying in the room, then focused on Ennis, looking into his eyes for too long. Ennis couldn't help but smile. Someone in the world realized he was rational, sane, and, most importantly, out of place in a nut house.

Ennis, in turn, studied how much they blinked and breathed and their facial expressions. He relaxed after a minute; *they were fully human.*

"Why don't you have a seat," Erica said. "I am sure you are curious about us. Ted and I are journalists for the Washington Post, and we're working on an article about retired members of the force who ended up in some kind of institution, whether for physical or mental therapy."

"I understand you ended up at St John's due to PTSD-induced delusions."

Ennis took a deep breath before explaining, "Contrary to what my former employers and current doctors here might think, the event that caused the delusions was *not* imaginary. But you already know that, right?"

Though Erica maintained her composure, Ted said, "Well—Mr. Lomings, we're merely—"

"That new Rover you came in was unmarked, both outside and inside. A special bureau was created for a newly discovered problem, correct? The bureau is too new to have had time to mark its cars with fictitious names."

The two supposed "journalists" looked somewhat embarrassed and did not reply.

"Which means," Ennis continued," that the problem has become too grave for you to control. I'll tell you what you want, but let me advise you that you might as well try to enjoy the rest of your life."

Again, they stayed silent. Ennis took this as confirmation.

Erica smiled after an awkward amount of time had passed, though her eyes betrayed tension. She removed a sleek device from her tunic pocket and set it on the table. It was a recorder.

"As I've said, Mr. Lomings, we're just journalists looking into retired members of the police force." Erica looked at him, nodding. "What can you tell us concerning the incident you claim caused your issues?"

Ennis leaned back on his chair. He'd told this story dozens of times over the past twenty-five years. Was he now truly crazy for thinking these people would listen?

He began, "Twenty-five years ago, I caught the Cornfield Killer. I should have retired before I took the case that sent me here….."

THE HEAD OF HIS DEPARTMENT DROPPED A FILE ON HIS DESK AND ASKED ENNIS to see him in the briefing room as soon as possible.

His department head, the Chief of National Security, and an unknown woman in an expensive suit waited for him in the briefing room. The woman turned out to be the head of security at ARGONAUT, one of the biggest mining companies in the solar system.

The new case was top-secret. Details would only be disclosed to the people in the briefing room and the civilians involved.

Workers aboard an atmospheric-mining station, Uranus Station, had disappeared for over a year. The previous detective assigned to the case had taken a few days' leave, and when he returned, he vanished without a trace.

Two curious points stood out in the notes. Despite the harsh conditions of a miner's job, Uranus Station's manager, Beth Lee, did her best to ensure everyone was healthy and well-rested. Mining station managers were rarely easygoing people. The notes also highlighted a janitor named George Harrington, whose records were vague and incomplete, a rarity in this digital age.

Ennis left for Uranus in one of ARGONAUT's shuttles the next day. The security process was meticulous.

"Rachel," as he called the AI planted on his earbud, "delineate the security process for me, please."

"Sure thing, Ennis," she replied. Rachel reviewed the infrared cameras and other sensors that monitored everything inside a shuttle. It was on the cusp of breaking existing privacy laws. Indeed, no contraband would be coming or going from the station.

Just like that, Ennis was on the job.

"Rachel, do me a favor and send a formal request to ARGONAUT asking for all non-regular logs from every shuttle." A perk of having a government AI was how much-privileged network access she had. "Then, dig through those logs to see if you can find anything unexpected."

"Of course, Ennis," Rachel said. Ennis snuggled against his seat as the shuttle shot off into space. "Now, relax. I'll wake you up when we reach Uranian orbit."

"WE'RE HERE," RACHEL SOUNDED PLEASED. MAYBE IT WAS JUST HIS IMAGI-nation.

Ennis opened his eyes, and his sight was full of stars—white, blue, red, yellow, and orange. The shuttle turned slowly, and the bright blue-green of Uranus filled the window.

"That's marvelous," Ennis said.

"Your vital signs show excitement," said Rachel.

The shuttle dove into Uranus, taking him through the opaque clouds, until the shape of the Uranus Station morphed from a hazy bubble into a gargantuan construction, floating in the upper layers of the planet's atmosphere. Enormous tubes stuck out from everywhere, like a tangle of hair, sucking out hydrogen and helium.

The shuttle entered the station's bay, docked, and finally, the airlock opened with a hiss.

A small entourage was there to receive him, and Ennis recognized them all from images assembled by Rachel. Two were human resources trainees, one was the man in charge of the station's guest quarters, and the two figures just in front of the airlock were the station manager, Beth Lee, and the chief engineer, Missy Johnson. Despite their high status, both women wore workers' uniforms.

"Welcome to Uranus Station, Detective Lomings," Ms. Lee said.

The entry bay was cramped and crisscrossed with wires. The station was practical, not aesthetic.

"Please, call me Ennis."

"And you may call me Beth," she said. Beth had dark bags under her eyes and a smile that wanted to collapse in exhaustion." We are sad to hear that the search for your colleague— the previous detective —failed. You will have constant video coverage on you; there are cameras everywhere. We have three security guards waiting to help."

Ennis wanted no hindrances. "That won't be necessary, but thank you."

"As you'll understand, we are like one big family here, so we're all open to cooperating and answering your questions." She clapped her hands to signal she was finished.

The chief engineer coughed twice.

"Right, I almost forgot," Beth continued, grabbing a card from her vest's pocket. She handed it to Ennis. "This will permit you to go anywhere you want, except for a few restricted passages that may compromise Uranus Stations' engineering functions. If you wish to visit those compartments, please call Ms. Johnson here, and she'll accompany you. This is more to safeguard your—"

"My safety. I'm well aware," Ennis replied.

"I'll need access to the station's system," Rachel said in his ear.

Ennis repeated that message from his AI. Ms. Johnson took a tablet from her pocket, opened it, and approved Rachel's electronic request.

"Got it," Rachel said. She added quietly," You saw it, too, didn't you?"

Ennis tapped his earbud with his finger while eying a vent. Someone had been there just now.

"Want me to scan the logs and try to catch who that was?" Rachel asked.

Ennis whispered after he took a few steps back and turned around to face the wall. "It can probably go around cameras and sensors." He turned to Beth to finish his public conversation. "I'll review logs and the stored video feeds in my room. Thank you."

THE THROB AND HUM OF PUMPS REACHED EVEN THE CUBICLE THAT SERVED AS his room. He gradually acclimatized to the white noise and reviewed all his information so far.

One clip stood out. It showed one of the first workers to disappear, a woman named Mary, walking down a corridor, turning a corner. The next passage's camera feed showed nothing. No one had passed by, and Mary had not gone anywhere. She'd turned the corner and vanished.

His first hypothesis was that the feed had been tampered with. Someone with advanced AI could have edited it. Another theory was that someone was waiting in a blind spot not covered by cameras and could have taken Mary and then covered their tracks.

"How's your part going, Rachel?" Ennis asked.

"Still running through logs," she replied.

"Keep me up to date." Ennis jotted down a list of six blind spots to check. The corner where Mary vanished was not far from him. He pulled up his visor, used the live map provided by ARGONAUT, and guided himself through the passages Mary traversed.

All the while he was walking, it felt like someone was watching. He warned Rachel to be on guard.

He got to the corner where Mary had disappeared and looked around. He noted the two cameras and how this corner was the only blind spot. Ennis saw no vents or openings except next to the cameras. There were not even access ducts to electrical components or plumbing. Whoever had—

Ennis slowly stepped up to a vent next to one of the cameras, drew his gun, and slowly pointed it at the vent. "Who the hell are you? No sudden moves, or I'll shoot."

Ennis had expected the person to run. Instead, he heard a high-pitched laugh.

"Come on! Seriously?" someone said. "I was *so* quiet. You've got ears like a dog's—not that I've ever seen one."

"Come on out," Ennis said, relieved but not letting his guard or gun down.

"Fine, fine, but don't shoot. The funny thing about living is that dying kinda sucks."

The grate on the vent fell forward with a clang. A young woman, perhaps in her early twenties, jumped out of the duct and spun around to face Ennis. She had auburn hair, was short and razor-thin, and wore an engineer's tool belt.

"Aren't you a little young to be using an engineering belt?" Ennis asked.

"Name's Sylvie. I'm an apprentice engineer."

"You know who I am, right?"

"Yes, up to speed on that, Ennis. Oh, and say hi to Rachel for me."

Ennis did not appreciate the unseriousness and tried to get back to the investigation.

"You know a lot about the station's alleyways for an apprentice."

"I know a *lot*, period," she smiled mischievously, putting the vent's grate back in place.

Ennis grinned. Sylvie had all the skills necessary to kill without being seen on Uranus Station. Should he consider her a potentially dangerous suspect, or should he use her to explore the farthest corners of the station?

The answer was simple—keep her close and keep watching.

"Why don't you show me where someone could hide?"

"Follow me." She pranced around the corner. "Do you have many movies on Earth? The network here kinda sucks, but I manage to catch a few movies here and there. What's your favorite one? I bet it's some lame police story; that'd be just your type."

Ennis sighed. It was going to be a long evening.

"I'm finished," said Rachel.

Ennis was halfway to sleep on the bed in his room/office. Uranus Station's constant whirring was surprisingly calming.

"Okay, shoot," he said.

"About the shuttle logs, I found just one *slightly* suspicious entry from seven years ago. A cavity in the shuttle showed cold in the infrared sensors, while the scales showed more weight than expected."

"That sounds like someone was masking a body. Was the shuttle coming to or from the station?"

"The shuttle was headed from Earth to Uranus Station."

Ennis paused. "Hmm. A dead body coming here, perhaps. I'll keep that in mind. What about the patterns common to the victims? You find any interesting ones?"

"All were medicated with inflammatory pills and painkillers at some point in their lives."

Ennis sat up in his bed. "At the same time?"

"Yup."

"Which brand?"

"Mostly Synapse," Rachel said.

Taking both medications, mainly Synapse, could mean all the victims had implants. Implants were widely used for bodily repair, performance enhancement, or fashion accessories.

"Can you check if these people had implants?"

The previous detective got a knee implant before returning to duty. But why would that be an essential factor? Implants were personalized for every patient, so they were not profitable on the black market. Thus, the quintessential question: why?

"I'll have to access medical records." Rachel's voice became mechanical," The current system will need special permission to log into the International Medical Database."

"Yes, yes, I give you permission. Check the records, Rachel."

"On it."

Forty-five minutes later, Rachel pinged. "Every single one of them had some kind of cybernetic or prosthetic enhancement."

There was his first clue.

"Prepare me a list of every person on board who has implants. And show it to me in the morning. I need to sleep."

"Sure thing, Ennis," Rachel said before logging off.

Ennis suddenly opened his eyes. "Rachel, come back. Let me review the medical records."

ENNIS HAD NO IDEA WHEN HE EVENTUALLY FELL ASLEEP, SO HE WAS SURPRISED to hear footfalls outside his door.

He jerked awake, grabbed his gun, and slammed the red open button next to the door. It slowly ground open, and he saw Sylvie, who was happy for some reason.

"Good morning!" She chirped.

Ennis started to mumble something and stopped when he thought better of it.

"I bet you've got a lot to do. Ms. Lee told me I could accompany you if I did not bother you. Can I? I know this station like the palm of my hand. I can help you. And I'll behave! Sir, yes, sir! I can help. I'm not a bother, am I?"

"Not at all," Ennis said. He closed the door, put on some clothes, and followed Sylvie to the dining hall for breakfast. After a quick meal, Ennis realized that duty called.

"I'm just going to stay by the dining hall and interview those who come and go."

Sylvie nodded, appearing somewhat deflated. "That's efficient but boring."

Ennis ignored his new helper and went on to do his job. One particular employee caught his attention: Alice Lee, Beth Lee's mother. Alice claimed she'd seen strange shadows around, and no one—she said—was talking about them for fear of being called crazy. Those who were called crazy were not kept on the payroll for long.

Ennis mentally noted how silent Sylvie became as she listened to Alice Lee.

At the end of the day, Ennis decided to question one of the previous detective's main suspects: the janitor named George Harrington.

Mr. Harrington had yet to stop by the dining hall. Sylvie described him as brooding but otherwise nice. However, she described everyone as nice, so that wasn't much help.

Ennis intercepted him as he was getting to his cubicle.

Ennis and Mr. Harrington exchanged pleasantries, and after Ennis threw his standard questions at Mr. Harrington, he began to exert some pressure.

"Were you aware, Mr. Harrington," Ennis said, "that my colleague also went missing?"

Mr. Harrington's shoulders sagged. "Oh, Christ, you think I had something to do with it."

"I have not implied that *yet*."

"I bet your colleague left some notes that didn't exactly put me in a good light," Mr. Harrington said. "I tried to tell him that he was wasting time focusing his energies on ex-cons like me."

"And why do you say that?"

"Because the ex-cons Ms. Lee has been kind enough to employ, they must be solid. The opportunity Ms. Lee provided is one we cannot afford to throw away. She gave us fair work and wages. Look, son, I'm rehabilitated. That's what prison is for. I'm just savin' up some money for my grandkids. I have never caused any problems since getting out. Hell, I've never shown up late. Not even once."

That was true.

"If you ask me, the people you can trust the most up here are the ex-cons who owe their livelihoods to Ms. Lee," Mr. Harrington said. "Ms. Lee is an angel. None of us would do anything to bring shame to her."

Ennis couldn't get much more out of the man. He decided to make his way to Beth's office and called Sylvie to help him through the maze.

"STOP," SAID SYLVIE.

"What? Beth's office is just over—"

"Stop," she repeated. Sylvie grabbed a remote from her tool belt and selected a green square on her screen. Sylvie touched a part of the wall, and a vent opened. It was wide enough to fit two people. Sylvie went in and called back, "Come on."

"I'm not going in there." And then, Ennis heard steps approaching. "This better be worth it," he said, then jumped into the dark. Sylvie pressed another button on her controller, and the vent closed.

Right on cue, two miners hurried through the corridor, talking in whispers easily audible from the vent.

"—telling you I saw something," the taller miner said.

"We can't be raising hell. Ms. Lee's bosses will fire her if we start raising hell. Then, we'll be screwed."

"And what do I do about what I saw? They were dark and thin—and no, I do not believe in little green men from Mars."

"We may be screwing our jobs."

"Better fired than dead!"

And then they were out of earshot.

"What was that about?" Ennis asked Sylvie while stepping out of the vent. "Do Beth's superiors hate her?"

"They hate what she does. They call her "Robin Hood" behind her back."

"Because she helps ex-cons?"

"Because she helps, period."

ENNIS KNOCKED ON BETH'S DOOR.

"Come in," she said from inside.

He and Sylvie went in and sat in two comfortable chairs before a wide desk. Sylvie swung her legs and gazed around. Beth's office, like the rest of the station, was cramped. It looked like a messy workshop and computer lab. Beth's career had started as a roboticist, and she still tested miniatures of her miners' machines.

"So, how can I help you, or should I say you two?" Beth asked amiably. Are you making good progress?"

"I'm not sure yet." Ennis was honest. He pointed to the AI in his ear. "Mind if I record?"

"Not at all! Shoot your questions. I'll be happy to answer them."

"Thank you. Rachel, record." Ennis loved direct people like Beth. "Why do so many of your employees have criminal or socially deviant pasts?"

"Recording stopped," Rachel said in an unusually mechanical tone. Ennis was surprised but repeated the command.

"Rachel, record. And stay recording," Ennis said.

"And stay recording," Rachel mimicked him. This was not a typical response, but at least it was recording, so Ennis pressed on and waited for an answer.

"These people are more than criminals," Beth began after consideration. "They have all had hard pasts, but that doesn't mean they aren't good people."

Rachel said quietly in his ear, "Ennis, I advise you to be more sympathetic."

Ennis took a breath and continued in a softer tone: "I really am happy for you. But right now, people are disappearing. I'm here to find the reason. And I'm sorry to say, the people most likely to engage in crime have participated in it before, which is most of your employees, Beth."

Rachel pinged, signaling she was busy. What was up with her?

"I don't think the problem is Beth's people, Ennis," Sylvie said.

"They aren't," Beth went on. "They really—"

"Ennis," Rachel thundered. "There's something you've got to see. One of the disappeared miners has appeared on Earth. He's now being held in your bureau."

"What!"

"What's wrong?" Sylvie and Beth asked.

"Wait a moment," he told them. "Rachel, give me the details."

Rachel forwarded images to Ennis's tablet. It included a video feed of the man, Louis Truman, waiting in a questioning room. Rachel fast-forwarded the video. The detective working on Louis was none other than the Chief of Security. "He doesn't know how he ended up on Earth," Rachel explained. "He claims he feels fine and drank too much and must have fallen into a shuttle by accident."

"That sounds awfully convenient," Ennis said. "Rachel, play the video feed on Beth's screen."

Rachel took control of the largest screen in the office and spoke through its speakers. "His body was scanned. He's healthy. Even his implant is where it is supposed to be. Nothing's missing."

Beth gasped. "That's Louis! He was one of the first to disappear."

Sylvie was quiet, eyes intent on the screen. "Slow the video to normal speed, please." Rachel did as asked. Sylvie went silent again.

"Sylvie, what's wrong?" Ennis asked.

"That's—that's not Louis."

"What do you mean?" Beth asked.

"That's *not* Louis. Louis had a slightly lazy eye. Slight but very much noticeable. The man on the video doesn't have a lazy eye."

"Rachel, pull up the man's scans from when he was first hired and the scan we have now."

"Working," Rachel said.

The AI set both scans on the large screen. The old scan showed Louis's brain implant in a light tone. The implant was on. In the new scan, the implant was off. It wasn't even in the exact same spot; it was a little lower. Just a little, but enough to know something was wrong.

Something was very wrong.

Ennis grimaced and asked for more information.

"Rachel, play me the security camera clip when Louis was kidnapped."

The screen changed to Louis walking down the hall, turning a corner, and never appearing in the next hall. He vanished, but, of course, people do not just disappear.

"Rachel, has the video log been altered?"

Rachel replied quickly, "The security camera logs are immaculate."

There was silence in the room as if no one wanted to speak." Wait, I've got something," Rachel said. The AI put a time stamp on the screen and used the highest magnification setting possible. The video showed that for six seconds, the dust motes were suspended—completely stationary.

That was impossible in the well-ventilated hall. Rachel played the clip several times, and again, the room was silent. Everyone was thinking the same thing.

This was good hacking. Whoever the culprit was, they had ultra-fine control over the security software used aboard the station.

Ennis' mind immediately jumped. He realized that whatever happened to Louis could happen to him.

Damn it. He was in danger, and now Sylvie was dragged into it. Beth *had* had something to do with the kidnappings, and Ennis had stumbled right into it.

Ennis suddenly took notice of how silent everyone was. Sylvie was motionless. Usually, she was constantly shaking her legs or chewing her nails.

"Sylvie?" Ennis said.

She whispered, "Look. Ms. Lee is blinking. Oddly. In a rhythm. She looks like she is struggling with something."

Christ, how had he not noticed it before? Beth's eyes were strange, and it was because she blinked about every two seconds without fail.

Beth stared at Ennis. Then, at Sylvie. Then, Beth let an empty smile glide across her glassy face. It was almost as if, when under stress, something else took over her consciousness that made her blinks regular. Too regular.

Something was sliding outside Beth's door. It was fast, and it was slowly prying the door open. Ennis's heart was now pounding, and his mind was racing. He wasn't ready to deal with whatever this was. It was hard to develop a rational hypothesis with Beth staring at him like that as if she were not made of flesh but of metal.

Sylvie jumped on Beth's desk, pressed the controller in her tool belt, and a vent opened on the ceiling. Sylvie punched it, trying to pry it open. The noise outside the door stopped. Sylvie's movements grew frantic.

Beth got up and grabbed Sylvie's leg. Ennis, by pure instinct, rose and pushed Beth away from Sylvie. Sylvie held onto the vent and climbed inside.

Just then, as Sylvie crawled in, Ennis saw a horror. It was a tentacled monster, dark, with bright electric blue lights around it. The tentacles surrounded a face that was pure light. The creature was studying Ennis. It was dark and thin yet heavy.

Ennis jumped back to draw his gun, and the creature lunged and struck him.

Ennis's mind went dark.

Dark. Lights. Sound. Someone breathing. Head heavy, hurting, throbbing. Under him, hard floor, cold. It was so dark. So blurry.

Ennis groaned and tried to rise but fell and felt a wall against his back. He touched his hands, his arms, his face. He was alive.

His vision cleared, and he saw he was in some sort of cell with bars on one wall. It was dark, but even so, he recognized the soldering on the floor and walls. He was still inside Uranus Station. But where?

Wires with strange masses on their shielding ran around the cell and through the corridor in front of it. The only illumination sources were the masses on the cables, which shone weak blue light.

"You okay, man?" A woman asked suddenly. Ennis turned and saw two people—two workers— hunched in a corner. Ennis recognized them as Paul and Joanne, the two last miners to be abducted.

"Yeah, yeah. Damn it. This is bad. Someone took my AI earbud and phone."

At that moment, they heard something coming. It was getting closer.

"No, no, no, no, no," Paul whimpered. Joanne was stoical—no, she was just empty—staring forward.

One of the monsters appeared in front of the cage. It was much bigger than a human, and its body was like a snake. Its face was some kind of light source, and a wheel of tentacled arms surrounded it.

"It's not carrying food," Joanne said in a cold monotone.

It opened a door through the bars, and one of its arms slithered forward. Ennis recoiled and hugged the wall, praying he could melt into it, pass through it, and escape all this.

Paul was screaming, eyes shut, palms against his ears. Joanne was catatonic. She almost appeared calm as the tentacle reached her, wrapped around her waist, and dragged her out.

"God, no!" Paul cried. A tear rolled down Joanne's cheek, but she kept her silence. The cell door closed behind the monster, and everything was dark again.

It took a while, but Paul finally calmed down. He explained how Joanna had arrived three days ago. He arrived a day ago. Or, at least, what felt like a day. It was impossible to be sure. He explained how Joanne had met a woman who spent three weeks in the cell before being taken.

Something prowled outside the cell.

"God!" Paul whispered, but the noise was different. It wasn't coming from the halls. It seemed like it was coming from the ceiling. They heard a click, and a vent dropped open, held by its hinges.

"Ennis?" a small voice called.

"Sylvie?" he asked, incredulous.

Sylvie's head popped out of the vent. "My goodness! You're alive," she whispered.

"Where are we?"

"Just a moment. Get up here first before that thing passes through again. Come on, let's go. Hey, is that Paul?"

"You shouldn't have come here, girl," Paul scolded her.

"Screw that," she said. She helped Ennis climb up, and then Ennis helped Paul up.

Ennis glanced at Sylvie's tablet. The red dot—her location—was on a black spot in the middle of nowhere.

"Where are we, Sylvie?" he asked. The strange wires proliferated in the vents as well.

"The very center of the station. This is snuggled right at the station's core, which I had read was metallic for equilibrium. This part is completely closed off from everywhere except for lots of old ducts connected to the station's network. No one has stepped into this place since the station entered Uranus."

"Christ," Ennis muttered. This could mean ARGONAUT was involved in the conspiracy. Was Beth even human? Was Louis? What was happening? There were so many unknown variables and so much danger coming from everywhere. He wasn't concerned with the truth anymore. Ennis wanted to survive. "Show us the way out, Sylvie."

They crawled through the ducts as silently as possible, carefully avoiding touching the bulbous wires. Sylvie had no maps of these vents, so they had to guess where to turn. It'd be hard to tell whether they were crawling in circles if it weren't for the fact that every duct Sylvie encountered only took an instant to sync with her tablet and appear on the map in green.

Suddenly, Sylvie's tablet beeped. One of the vents in a green duct turned blue. It had been opened. The ducts shook like something large was on its way.

"Hurry up," was all Sylvie said as she picked up the pace. They moved through ducts, and Sylvie closed them behind her, yet whatever pursued them kept getting closer.

Then, they reached a dead end. A loading bar popped up on Sylvie's tablet.

"Please, please, please," she prayed, shaking the remote. "Please!"

They heard a click. A vent opened. Sylvie kicked it open and jumped. Paul went next, and then Ennis. He closed the vent before looking at where he was.

THE ROOM THEY'D COME TO HAD A LARGE WINDOW THAT OCCUPIED MOST OF the wall and overlooked a small exterior platform. A hidden port. The strange wires led to that room and connected to even stranger machines. Arrays of the luminous masses formed what looked like a control panel near the window. The masses functioned to hide what was going on.

"These robots, or whatever they are, had to hack deep into the security system to build that port without being seen," Sylvie said. Now that Ennis noticed, the port was made of a different material than the rest of the station. It was cleaner and of a lighter, almost smoky tone.

Strange tools lined the walls. The instruments seemed glued to the walls with a petroleum-like goo.

This wasn't human technology. It couldn't be. ARGONAUT wasn't responsible. Something else was.

An intense light flashed outside, out on the port. Ennis, Sylvie, and Paul hid behind barrels of the goo-like material.

A swirling blue mass was on the port. It wasn't large but seemed to have depth—it was infinitely and unfathomably deep. Even its blue color wasn't what it seemed. A portal? The more Ennis stared at it, the more he realized it wasn't a color fully perceptible to the human eye. Ennis was slick with sweat and breathless and couldn't look away.

A white pyramid stretched out of the portal. A door on it opened. One of the robots jumped out, its tentacles going wild. The robot entered Uranus Station through a small hidden door while the pyramid-shaped ship retreated into the portal. Then, the portal vanished.

That robot suddenly entered the room. Somehow, knowing it was not from Earth, it seemed more sinister. Ennis and Sylvie hid behind the barrels, clamping their mouths shut to avoid crying out in fear. They could hear the thing prowling around, grabbing tools from the walls. Finally, it moved away. Ennis removed his hand and breathed through his mouth for a moment.

Then, the screams began. It was Joanne.

"Please!"

Something whirred.

"Oh God, *Please!*"

And then she screamed in a way that Ennis hadn't known humans could. It was a scream that went beyond pain, horror, and the certainty of death.

And then, Joanne went quiet.

Something moved behind them.

Ennis had been so focused on Joanne that he hadn't heard the other robot. It grabbed Paul with one arm and struck his head with two other tentacles. He went limp.

It lunged for Ennis, but Ennis jumped away in time, grabbed Sylvie's hand, and sprinted away.

They glanced into the room where the second robot was dissecting Joanne. Ennis caught a glimpse of her and flinched, yet he didn't lose speed. A corridor led out of wherever they were, and its door was open.

"There!" Sylvie cried and led the way. The robot followed, apparently in no real hurry. Ennis needed more time to think it through.

"Please, find a way out," he asked Sylvie in between breaths.

The hall had two doors, one closed and the other wide open, though it was too dark to see if either led anywhere. Ennis and Sylvie went inside.

Sylvie turned on a flashlight to look for a way out, but all the flashlight showed was an empty room. It was a plain room—no windows, no vents, empty.

"Do you have any implants?" Ennis asked quickly.

"Yes!" she cried. "Too many."

Ennis poked his head slowly out of the room. He glanced at the far end of the corridor, where they had come from. It was empty. He looked at the other side—

And the robot lunged at him again. Ennis fell back and scrambled away, but the robot blocked their only exit. Sylvie yelled. Ennis tried to escape while the flashlight lit the thing's metal feet and slithering body.

Its luminous face shone right in Ennis's eyes. It opened its tentacles wide.

The tentacles descended on Ennis, but they didn't hurt him. The tentacles bound his arms and legs and did the same to Sylvie.

"Ennis!" she called. "Please, Ennis!"

"Someone! Help!" Ennis yelled.

Then Ennis felt a sharp sting on his neck, and his conscience left him.

He woke up but did not open his eyes. Ennis knew precisely where he was and what had happened before he was sedated. Then, he opened his eyes, slow and easy. His vision was blurry, but he could just see the two robots by the lights on their tentacles. They were circling a figure hanging by the wrists. It was Sylvie.

Slowly, Ennis. Careful and slow, he told himself as he took a deep breath and exhaled through his nostrils. He moved his hands and feet. They were not bound. The robots had left him in a corner, perhaps confident their sedative would work. Why hadn't it?

Sylvie, too, was awake. The robots kept circling her, using multiple instruments to examine her. The bastards were planning something.

"—please please please please please—" she whimpered.

She glanced at something every chance she got. Ennis looked in that direction and saw her tablet lying near the door.

One of the robot's arms started to glow red-hot. Its shape changed, thinning, and it became a red-hot blade, cutting into Sylvie's arm.

And she screamed.

"Help me, Ennis. Please help me!"

Her voice was interrupted by sobs. But as much as it wrenched his heart, what could he do?

Sylvie lost consciousness. Seconds later, she woke up, and the alien robots cut into her leg. She cried and vomited. Ennis used the noise to get up without being heard and grabbed the tablet.

"Please, Ennis, don't leave me here! Please!"

Ennis held on to the tablet, entered the other room, and found the vent from which they had come. His mind raced; he had to be innovative. He couldn't just run and make lots of noise; they'd hear him.

So, he went straight, going only where there were open doors. He did his best to follow the corners, which appeared to have fewer strange wires.

"Ennis, come back!" Sylvie's voice echoed. He was getting closer again. Ennis turned and crawled in the opposite direction. He was a bat, and Sylvie's pleas were his sonar.

"Ennis, please, don't leave me alone." He wouldn't have heard her if he hadn't been so quiet. He guessed he had come far enough now.

Ennis began to open all the vents that appeared as dots on Sylvie's remote, closing all the vents in the general direction of the station's center. Now, he crawled in a sprint. He hurried, hearing distant sounds like the robots were no longer attending Sylvie.

The things were looking for him, but he had given them too large an area to search. The station's daunting size and complexity were the only things keeping Ennis safe.

In his frantic dance to escape the robots, he didn't realize the vents now lacked those wires, nor could he hear Sylvie. He kept going, opening all the closed doors in his path until he came to a vent, punched it open so hard his knuckles bled, and fell on a table.

He crawled away from the hands reaching for him, then saw they were human. Flesh. Apart from his sweat, Ennis smelled food.

The dining hall. He'd arrived in the dining hall.

"Robots!" he screamed, panicked. Damn it, but people had to know." There are alien robots in the center of the ship. They've been taking people. We've got to get away from here. Everyone to the shuttles, *now!*"

"Hey, Detective Lomings." A reassuring hand fell on his shoulder. He looked up to see Alice Lee. Did she know her daughter was not her daughter anymore?

"No, no, no, you're not getting it! They're turning us into their puppets, into their—Christ, they're turning us into their cyborgs!"

"Is everything alright?" Ennis lifted his head to see Beth Lee walking calmly toward the confusion. "Is he okay, Mom?"

"I think he's in shock, sweetie," Alice Lee said.

"Get her away from me!" Ennis yelled. *"Get her away from me!"*

Ennis scrambled again, stumbled over a bench, fell, and then crawled away from everyone. Anyone could be unsafe. *Anyone* could be compromised.

The dining hall doors opened, and two figures walked in. There was no mistaking it.

Sylvie and Joanne.

They stopped, turned to him, smiled, and waved.

Ennis let out a yell that startled everyone in the hall.

AGENT TED SIGHED AND LEANED HIS CHAIR BACK. AGENT ERICA, ON THE OTHer hand, stood rigidly still. As she absorbed his story, her eyes focused on the tranquilized old man sitting before them. They believed him, but his was an old story from decades past.

"You ran to the emergency shuttle while holding a knife and departed for Earth. You took eight people with you. Correct, Mr. Lomings?" Erica asked.

"That's correct, yes."

"What about everyone else aboard Uranus Station? Dozens of miners and technicians, ten senior bureaucrats," Ted said. "What happened to those who stayed?"

Ennis shrugged. "You already know. Those who stayed are not those who arrived at Uranus Station. At least, not wholly. They became something else. Human, but not quite. They gradually made it back to Earth. It is like a parasite laying one egg at a time."

He got up and went to the window. He looked out over the courtyard and the small garden of tulips he spent his evenings caring for. Ted and Erica joined him. Ennis nodded toward a patient sitting on a bench near the tulip garden. The patient was staring intently at Ennis.

"One, two," said Ennis, and the man blinked. "One, two," and he blinked again. "One, two," blink. "One, two," blink. "One, two," blink. "One, two—"

"Okay, okay! We get it," Erica said, abandoning her journalist facade. "We've encountered them before. There's got to be some way of turning this around."

But Ennis just looked down and smiled. "There could have been." Two other patients joined the man. Then came another patient. And another. They stood around the bench, staring at Ennis with blank expressions. While some were from Uranus Station, some were from other stations. "But not anymore."

One, two, blink. One, two, blink.

All Ennis could do was count seconds between blinks and gaze at those who had returned transformed. They stayed too long.

END

Eiland is a speculative fiction (particularly from the 1940s) enthusiast and an archaeologist. This is the second time he has published with Adventures BookZine. His Facebook site is:

https://www.facebook.com/p/Science-Fiction-Eiland-61555246300627

RED IS THE COLOR OF BLOOD

BY CONRAD AIKEN

Red is the color of blood, and I will seek it:
I have sought it in the grass.
It is the color of steep sun seen through eyelids.

It is hidden under the suave flesh of women—
Flows there, quietly flows.
It mounts from the heart to the temples, the singing mouth—
As cold sap climbs to the rose.
I am confused in webs and knots of scarlet
Spun from the darkness;
Or shuttled from the mouths of thirsty spiders.

Madness for red! I devour the leaves of autumn.
I tire of the green of the world.
I am myself a mouth for blood ...

Here, in the golden haze of the late slant sun,
Let us walk, with the light in our eyes,
To a single bench from the outset predetermined.
Look: there are seagulls in these city skies,
Kindled against the blue.
But I do not think of the seagulls, I think of you.

Your eyes, with the late sun in them,
Are like blue pools dazzled with yellow petals.
This pale green suits them well.

Here is your finger, with an emerald on it:
The one I gave you. I say these things politely—
But what I think beneath them, who can tell?

For I think of you, crumpled against a whiteness;
Flayed and torn, with a dulled face.
I think of you, writing, a thing of scarlet,
And myself, rising red from that embrace.

November sun is sunlight poured through honey:
Old things, in such a light, grow subtle and fine.
Bare oaks are like still fire.
Talk to me: now we drink the evening's wine.
Look, how our shadows creep along the grave!—
And this way, how the gravel begins to shine!

This is the time of day for recollections,
For sentimental regrets, oblique allusions,
Rose-leaves, shrivelled in a musty jar.
Scatter them to the wind! There are tempests coming.
It is dark, with a windy star.

If human mouths were really roses, my dear,—
(Why must we link things so?—)
I would tear yours petal by petal with slow murder.
I would pluck the stamens, the pistils,
The gold and the green,—
Spreading the subtle sweetness that was your breath
On a cold wave of death....

Now let us walk back, slowly, as we came.
We will light the room with candles; they may shine
Like rows of yellow eyes.
Your hair is like spun fire, by candle-flame.
You smile at me—say nothing. You are wise.

For I think of you, flung down brutal darkness;
Crushed and red, with pale face.
I think of you, with your hair disordered and dripping.
And myself, rising red from that embrace.

A Still from the 1921 film, "Sowing the Wind"

Southwest Scenarios

COMMENTARIES FROM RURAL ARIZONA
BY DARRYLE PURCELL

Nutty idea becomes a swinging success

from July 11, 2001

IN 1997 I WROTE A COLUMN ABOUT A NEW PRODUCT ON THE MARKET. A KANsas City candy maker had come up with the idea of testicular implants to ease the suffering of male pets going through "post-neutering trauma." He called them Neuticles.

Now, four years later, with a slightly flaccid economy, the Neuticles market is still quite potent. An Associated Press story in Friday's Mohave Valley Daily News, "'Neuticles' boost dogs' self-image," updates us on the masculine canine falsies.

Dr. Thomas Allen, veterinarian, pointed out how the product helps dogs' "self-image" and went on to say it also makes the owners feel better about sterilization. "It's a pretty common thing for a family to be in a squabble when the wife wants to do it and the husband is against it. This could be a compromise," he said.

I don't want to doubt the good doctor's philosophy, but, if I thought my wife's idea of a compromise was the implantation of artificial nuts anywhere, I'd be somewhere in the Sierra Nevada Mountains by now. It's not a good precedent to set in one's relationship.

The story went on to describe the "standard model" implants as being made of polypropylene. But for a few more bucks one can purchase the Cadillac of artificial dog testicles, which are made of silicone. The AP story says the silicone Neuticles have a "more natural feel." Now how did the reporter find that out? I know that some AP reporters will go to all ends to get a story, but this one worries me.

One pet owner quoted in the story remarks about her English bulldog who had recently had the procedure, "He's got the cutest rear end I've ever seen." Where do they get these people?

Neuticles are offered in sizes ranging from Chihuahua to Great Dane and are more popular, according to the 1997 information, with shorthaired dogs where they can be noticed (by people like the above mentioned pet owner, I assume). Cat Neuticles are also available. (Why? How could you tell? And who's gonna check?)

This is the kind of procedure that one would believe only Hollywood dog stars like Benji or My Dog Skip would go through. But, apparently, many preppie suburban canines are profiling the product as well. And, obviously, there must be quite a market for this product throughout modern America or it would not have survived the last four years.

Perhaps Mohave County *(Arizona)* Economic Development Authority (MCEDA) could get back into the County Supervisors' good graces by getting a Neuticles plant built along the I-40 industrial corridor. It wouldn't take as much electricity as a steel mill. It certainly wouldn't use as much water as a power plant, and, unlike Griffith Energy, if it sells its entire product out of area, no one will be shortchanged.

With the right marketing and economic development assistance, other competing product manufacturers could be lured to the I-40 industrial corridor. MCEDA could exonerate its image and get the last laugh on its detractors by making Mohave County the artificial dog testicle capital of the world.

But perhaps I'm being too optimistic. It's quite possible that, over time, recipients of silicone Neuticles could develop certain medical problems like warm noses and misshapen doohickeys. If that begins to happen, hordes of lawyers will join in class-action suits to take a bite out of the industry, and our county could be subject to some liability in the case.

Maybe we should be a little more conservative and keep an eye out for other more positive and profitable clean industries such as manufacturers of desert tortoise Speedos or birth control devices for rabbits.

Southwest Scenarios

The commentaries here and in future issues were originally published by *The Mohave Valley Daily News between 1993 & 2013--and* in many ways they apply to today. We are grateful to republish these commentaries written by Darryle Purcell in full and unedited. His own brand of humor and style can deliver insight, provoke thought, and even boil blood.

WHEN THE SLEEPER WAKES
BY H.G. WELLS

Original Illustrations by Henry Lanos

A NEW SERIAL, BY H. G. WELLS, BEGINS THIS WEEK

HARPER'S WEEKLY

JOURNAL OF CIVILIZATION

NEW YORK, SATURDAY, JANUARY 7, 1899

TEN CENTS A COPY
FOUR DOLLARS A YEAR

ICE-YACHTING—HARD-A-LEE!

DRAWN BY W. P. SNYDER.

WHEN THE SLEEPER AWAKES WAS FIRST PUBLISHED AS A SERIAL
BEGINNING IN THIS 1899 HARPER'S WEEKLY ISSUE.

CHAPTER I
INSOMNIA

One afternoon, at low water, Mr. Isbister, a young artist lodging at Boscastle, walked from that place to the picturesque cove of Pentargen, desiring to examine the caves there. Halfway down the precipitous path to the Pentargen beach he came suddenly upon a man sitting in an attitude of profound distress beneath a projecting mass of rock. The hands of this man hung limply over his knees, his eyes were red and staring before him, and his face was wet with tears.

He glanced round at Isbister's footfall. Both men were disconcerted, Isbister the more so, and, to override the awkwardness of his involuntary pause, he remarked, with an air of mature conviction, that the weather was hot for the time of year.

"Very," answered the stranger shortly, hesitated a second, and added in a colourless tone, "I can't sleep."

Isbister stopped abruptly. "No?" was all he said, but his bearing conveyed his helpful impulse.

"It may sound incredible," said the stranger, turning weary eyes to Isbister's face and emphasizing his words with a languid hand, "but I have had no sleep—no sleep at all for six nights."

"Had advice?"

"Yes. Bad advice for the most part. Drugs. My nervous system.... They are all very well for the run of people. It's hard to explain. I dare not take... sufficiently powerful drugs."

"That makes it difficult," said Isbister.

He stood helplessly in the narrow path, perplexed what to do. Clearly the man wanted to talk. An idea natural enough under the circumstances, prompted him to keep the conversation going. "I've never suffered from sleeplessness myself," he said in a tone of commonplace gossip, "but in those cases I have known, people have usually found something—"

"I dare make no experiments."

He spoke wearily. He gave a gesture of rejection, and for a space both men were silent.

"Exercise?" suggested Isbister diffidently, with a glance from his interlocutor's face of wretchedness to the touring costume he wore.

"That is what I have tried. Unwisely perhaps. I have followed the coast, day after day—from New Quay. It has only added muscular fatigue to the mental. The cause of this unrest was overwork—trouble. There was something—"

He stopped as if from sheer fatigue. He rubbed his forehead with a lean hand. He resumed speech like one who talks to himself.

"I am a lone wolf, a solitary man, wandering through a world in which I have no part. I am wifeless—childless—who is it speaks of the childless as the dead twigs on the tree of life? I am wifeless, I childless—I could find no duty to do. No desire even in my heart. One thing at last I set myself to do.

"I said, I will do this, and to do it, to overcome the inertia of this dull body, I resorted to drugs. Great God, I've had enough of drugs! I don't know if _you_ feel the heavy inconvenience of the body, its exasperating demand of time from the mind—time—life! Live! We only live in patches. We have to eat, and then comes the dull digestive complacencies—or irritations. We have to take the air or else our thoughts grow sluggish, stupid, run into gulfs and blind alleys. A thousand distractions arise from within and without, and then comes drowsiness and sleep. Men seem to live for sleep. How little of a man's day is his own—even at the best! And then come those false friends, those Thug helpers, the alkaloids that stifle natural fatigue and kill rest—black coffee, cocaine—"

"I see," said Isbister.

"I did my work," said the sleepless man with a querulous intonation.

"And this is the price?"

"Yes."

For a little while the two remained without speaking.

"You cannot imagine the craving for rest that I feel—a hunger and thirst. For six long days, since my work was done, my mind has been a whirlpool, swift, unprogressive and incessant, a torrent of thoughts leading nowhere, spinning round swift and steady—"

He paused. "Towards the gulf."

"You must sleep," said Isbister decisively, and with an air of a remedy discovered. "Certainly you must sleep."

"My mind is perfectly lucid. It was never clearer. But I know I am drawing towards the vortex. Presently—"

"Yes?"

"You have seen things go down an eddy? Out of the light of the day, out of this sweet world of sanity—down—"

"But," expostulated Isbister.

The man threw out a hand towards him, and his eyes were wild, and his voice suddenly high. "I shall kill myself. If in no other way—at the foot of yonder dark precipice there, where the waves are green, and the white surge lifts and falls, and that little thread of water trembles down. There at any rate is ... sleep."

"That's unreasonable," said Isbister, startled at the man's hysterical gust of emotion. "Drugs are better than that."

"There at any rate is sleep," repeated the stranger, not heeding him.

Isbister looked at him and wondered transitorily if some complex Providence had indeed brought them together that afternoon. "It's not a cert, you know," he remarked. "There's a cliff like that at Lulworth Cove— as high, anyhow—and a little girl fell from top to bottom. And lives to-day—sound and well."

"But those rocks there?"

"One might lie on them rather dismally through a cold night, broken bones grating as one shivered, chill water splashing over you. Eh?"

Their eyes met. "Sorry to upset your ideals," said Isbister with a sense of devil-may-careish brilliance.

"But a suicide over that cliff (or any cliff for the matter of that), really, as an artist—" He laughed. "It's so damned amateurish."

"But the other thing," said the sleepless man irritably, "the other thing. No man can keep sane if night after night—"

"Have you been walking along this coast alone?"

"Yes."

"Silly sort of thing to do. If you'll excuse my saying so. Alone! As you say; body fag is no cure for brain fag. Who told you to? No wonder; walking! And the sun on your head, heat, fag, solitude, all the day long, and then, I suppose, you go to bed and try very hard—eh?"

Isbister stopped short and looked at the sufferer doubtfully.

"Look at these rocks!" cried the seated man with a sudden force of gesture. "Look at that sea that has shone and quivered there for ever! See the white spume rush into darkness under that great cliff. And this blue vault, with the blinding sun pouring from the dome of it. It is your world. You accept it, you rejoice in it. It warms and supports and delights you. And for me—"

He turned his head and showed a ghastly face, bloodshot pallid eyes and bloodless lips. He spoke almost in a whisper. "It is the garment of my misery. The whole world... is the garment of my misery."

Isbister looked at all the wild beauty of the sunlit cliffs about them and back to that face of despair. For a moment he was silent.

He started, and made a gesture of impatient rejection. "You get a night's sleep," he said, "and you won't see much misery out here. Take my word for it."

He was quite sure now that this was a providential encounter. Only half an hour ago he had been feeling horribly bored. Here was employment the bare thought of which was righteous self-applause. He took possession forthwith. It seemed to him that the first need of this exhausted being was companionship He flung himself down on the steeply sloping turf beside the motionless seated figure, and deployed forthwith into a skirmishing line of gossip.

His hearer seemed to have lapsed into apathy; he stared dismally seaward, and spoke only in answer to Isbister's direct questions—and not to all of those. But he made no sign of objection to this benevolent intrusion upon his despair.

In a helpless way he seemed even grateful, and when presently Isbister, feeling that his unsupported talk was losing vigour, suggested that they should reascend the steep and return towards Boscastle, alleging the view into Blackapit, he submitted quietly. Halfway up he began talking to himself, and abruptly turned a ghastly face on his helper. "What can be happening?" he asked with a gaunt illustrative hand. "What can be happening? Spin, spin, spin, spin. It goes round and round, round and round for evermore."

He stood with his hand circling

"It's all right, old chap," said Isbister with the air of an old friend. "Don't worry yourself. Trust to me."

The man dropped his hand and turned again. They went over the brow in single file and to the headland beyond Penally, with the sleepless man gesticulating ever and again, and speaking fragmentary things concerning his whirling brain. At the headland they stood for a space by the seat that looks into the dark mysteries of Blackapit, and then he sat down. Isbister had resumed his talk whenever the path had widened sufficiently for them to walk abreast. He was enlarging upon the complex difficulty of making Boscastle Harbour in bad weather, when suddenly and quite irrelevantly his companion interrupted him again.

"My head is not like what it was," he said, gesticulating for want of expressive phrases. "It's not like what it was. There is a sort of oppression, a weight. No—not drowsiness, would God it were! It is like a shadow, a deep shadow falling suddenly and swiftly across something busy. Spin, spin into the darkness. The tumult of thought, the confusion, the eddy and eddy. I can't express it. I can hardly keep my mind on it—steadily enough to tell you."

He stopped feebly.

"Don't trouble, old chap," said Isbister. "I think I can understand. At any rate, it don't matter very much just at present about telling me, you know."

The sleepless man thrust his knuckles into his eyes and rubbed them. Isbister talked for awhile while this rubbing continued, and then he had a fresh idea. "Come down to my room," he said, "and try a pipe. I can show you some sketches of this Blackapit. If you'd care?"

The other rose obediently and followed him down the steep.

Several times Isbister heard him stumble as they came down, and his movements were slow and hesitating. "Come in with me," said Isbister, "and try some cigarettes and the blessed gift of alcohol. If you take alcohol?"

The stranger hesitated at the garden gate. He seemed no longer clearly aware of his actions. "I don't drink," he said slowly, coming up the garden path, and after a moment's interval repeated absently, "No—I don't drink. It goes round. Spin, it goes—spin—"

He stumbled at the doorstep and entered the room with the bearing of one who sees nothing.

Then he sat down abruptly and heavily in the easy chair, seemed almost to fall into it. He leant forward with his brows on his hands and became motionless.

Presently he made a faint sound in his throat. Isbister moved about the room with the nervousness of an inexperienced host, making little remarks that scarcely required answering. He crossed the room to his portfolio, placed it on the table and noticed the mantel clock.

"I don't know if you'd care to have supper with me," he said with an unlighted cigarette in his hand—his mind troubled with a design of the furtive administration of chloral. "Only cold mutton, you know, but passing sweet. Welsh. And a tart, I believe." He repeated this after momentary silence.

The seated man made no answer. Isbister stopped, match in hand, regarding him.

The stillness lengthened. The match went out, the cigarette was put down unlit. The man was certainly very still. Isbister took up the portfolio, opened it, put it down, hesitated, seemed about to speak. "Perhaps," he whispered doubtfully. Presently he glanced at the door and back to the figure. Then he stole on tiptoe out of the room, glancing at his companion after each elaborate pace.

He closed the door noiselessly. The house door was standing open, and he went out beyond the porch, and stood where the monkshood rose at the corner of the garden bed. From this point he could see the stranger through the open window, still and dim, sitting head on hand. He had not moved.

A number of children going along the road stopped and regarded the artist curiously. A boatman exchanged civilities with him. He felt that possibly his circumspect attitude and position seemed peculiar and unaccountable. Smoking, perhaps, might seem more natural. He drew pipe and pouch from his pocket, filled the pipe slowly.

"I wonder,"... he said, with a scarcely perceptible loss of complacency. "At any rate we must give him a chance." He struck a match in the virile way, and proceeded to light his pipe.

Presently he heard his landlady behind him, coming with his lamp lit from the kitchen. He turned, gesticulating with his pipe, and stopped her at the door of his sitting-room. He had some difficulty in explaining the situation in whispers, for she did not know he had a visitor. She retreated again with the lamp, still a little mystified to judge from her manner, and he resumed his hovering at the corner of the porch, flushed and less at his ease.

Long after he had smoked out his pipe, and when the bats were abroad, his curiosity dominated his complex hesitations, and he stole back into his darkling sitting-room. He paused in the doorway. The stranger was still in the same attitude, dark against the window. Save for the singing of some sailors aboard one of the little slate-carrying ships in the harbour, the evening was very still. Outside, the spikes of monkshood and delphinium stood erect and motionless against the shadow of the hillside. Something flashed into Isbister's mind; he started, and leaning over the table, listened. An unpleasant suspicion grew stronger; became conviction. Astonishment seized him and became—dread!

No sound of breathing came from the seated figure!

He crept slowly and noiselessly round the table, pausing twice to listen. At last he could lay his hand on the back of the armchair. He bent down until the two heads were ear to ear.

Then he bent still lower to look up at his visitor's face. He started violently and uttered an exclamation. The eyes were void spaces of white.

He looked again and saw that they were open and with the pupils rolled under the lids. He was suddenly afraid. Overcome by the strangeness of the man's condition, he took him by the shoulder and shook him. "Are you asleep?" he said, with his voice jumping into alto, and again, "Are you asleep?"

A conviction took possession of his mind that this man was dead. He suddenly became active and noisy, strode across the room, blundering against the table as he did so, and rang the bell.

"Please bring a light at once," he said in the passage. "There is something wrong with my friend."

Then he returned to the motionless seated figure, grasped the shoulder, shook it, and shouted. The room was flooded with yellow glare as his astonished landlady entered with the light. His face was white as he turned blinking towards her. "I must fetch a doctor at once," he said. "It is either death or a fit. Is there a doctor in the village? Where is a doctor to be found?"

CHAPTER II
THE TRANCE

The state of cataleptic rigour into which this man had fallen, lasted for an unprecedented length of time, and then he passed slowly to the flaccid state, to a lax attitude suggestive of profound repose. Then it was his eyes could be closed.

He was removed from the hotel to the Boscastle surgery, and from the surgery, after some weeks, to London. But he still resisted every attempt at reanimation. After a time, for reasons that will appear later, these attempts were discontinued. For a great space he lay in that strange condition, inert and still neither dead nor living but, as it were, suspended, hanging midway between nothingness and existence. His was a darkness unbroken by a ray of thought or sensation, a dreamless inanition, a vast space of peace. The tumult of his mind had swelled and risen to an abrupt climax of silence. Where was the man? Where is any man when insensibility takes hold of him?

"It seems only yesterday," said Isbister. "I remember it all as though it happened yesterday—clearer perhaps, than if it had happened yesterday."

It was the Isbister of the last chapter, but he was no longer a young man. The hair that had been brown and a trifle in excess of the fashionable length, was iron grey and clipped close, and the face that had been pink and white was buff and ruddy. He had a pointed beard shot with grey. He talked to an elderly man who wore a summer suit of drill (the summer of that year was unusually hot). This was Warming, a London solicitor and next of kin to Graham, the man who had fallen into the trance. And the two men stood side by side in a room in a house in London regarding his recumbent figure.

It was a yellow figure lying lax upon a water-bed and clad in a flowing shirt, a figure with a shrunken face and a stubby beard, lean limbs and lank nails, and about it was a case of thin glass. This glass seemed to mark off the sleeper from the reality of life about him, he was a thing apart, a strange, isolated abnormality. The two men stood close to the glass, peering in.

"The thing gave me a shock," said Isbister "I feel a queer sort of surprise even now when I think of his white eyes. They were white, you know, rolled up. Coming here again brings it all back to me."

"Have you never seen him since that time?" asked Warming.

"Often wanted to come," said Isbister; "but business nowadays is too serious a thing for much holiday keeping. I've been in America most of the time."

"If I remember rightly," said Warming, "you were an artist?"

"Was. And then I became a married man. I saw it was all up with black and white, very soon—at least for a mediocre man, and I jumped on to process. Those posters on the Cliffs at Dover are by my people."

"Good posters," admitted the solicitor, "though I was sorry to see them there."

"Last as long as the cliffs, if necessary," exclaimed Isbister with satisfaction. "The world changes. When he fell asleep, twenty years ago, I was down at Boscastle with a box of water-colours and a noble, old-fashioned ambition. I didn't expect that some day my pigments would glorify the whole blessed coast of England, from Land's End round again to the Lizard. Luck comes to a man very often when he's not looking."

Warming seemed to doubt the quality of the luck. "I just missed seeing you, if I recollect aright."

"You came back by the trap that took me to Camelford railway station. It was close on the Jubilee, Victoria's Jubilee, because I remember the seats and flags in Westminster, and the row with the cabman at Chelsea."

"The Diamond Jubilee, it was," said Warming; "the second one."

"Ah, yes! At the proper Jubilee—the Fifty Year affair—I was down at Wookey—a boy. I missed all that.... What a fuss we had with him! My landlady wouldn't take him in, wouldn't let him stay—he looked so queer when he was rigid. We had to carry him in a chair up to the hotel. And the Boscastle doctor—it wasn't the present chap, but the G.P. before him—was at him until nearly two, with, me and the landlord holding lights and so forth."

"It was a cataleptic rigour at first, wasn't it?"

"Stiff!—wherever you bent him he stuck. You might have stood him on his head and he'd have stopped. I never saw such stiffness. Of course this"—he indicated the prostrate figure by a movement of his head—"is quite different. And, of course, the little doctor—what was his name?"

"Smithers?"

"Smithers it was—was quite wrong in trying to fetch him round too soon, according to all accounts. The things he did. Even now it makes me feel all—ugh! Mustard, snuff, pricking. And one of those beastly little things, not dynamos—"

"Induction coils."

"Yes. You could see his muscles throb and jump, and he twisted about. There was just two flaring yellow candles, and all the shadows were shivering, and the little doctor nervous and putting on side, and him—stark and squirming in the most unnatural ways. Well, it made me dream."

Pause.

"It's a strange state," said Warming.

"It's a sort of complete absence," said Isbister.

"Here's the body, empty. Not dead a bit, and yet not alive. It's like a seat vacant and marked 'engaged.' No feeling, no digestion, no beating of the heart—not a flutter. _That_ doesn't make me feel as if there was a man present. In a sense it's more dead than death, for these doctors tell me that even the hair has stopped growing. Now with the proper dead, the hair will go on growing—"

"I know," said Warming, with a flash of pain in his expression.

They peered through the glass again. Graham was indeed in a strange state, in the flaccid phase of a trance, but a trance unprecedented in medical history. Trances had lasted for as much as a year before—but at the end of that time it had ever been waking or a death; sometimes first one and then the other. Isbister noted the marks the physicians had made in injecting nourishment, for that device had been resorted to to postpone collapse; he pointed them out to Warming, who had been trying not to see them.

"And while he has been lying here," said Isbister, with the zest of a life freely spent, "I have changed my plans in life; married, raised a family, my eldest lad—I hadn't begun to think of sons then—is an American citizen, and looking forward to leaving Harvard. There's a touch of grey in my hair. And this man, not a day older nor wiser (practically) than I was in my downy days. It's curious to think of."

Warming turned. "And I have grown old too. I played cricket with him when I was still only a lad. And he looks a young man still. Yellow perhaps. But that is a young man nevertheless."

"And there's been the War," said Isbister.

"From beginning to end."

"And these Martians."

"I've understood," said Isbister after a pause, "that he had some moderate property of his own?"

"That is so," said Warming. He coughed primly. "As it happens—have charge of it."

"Ah!" Isbister thought, hesitated and spoke: "No doubt—his keep here is not expensive—no doubt it will have improved—accumulated?"

"It has. He will wake up very much better off—if he wakes—than when he slept."

"As a business man," said Isbister, "that thought has naturally been in my mind. I have, indeed, sometimes thought that, speaking commercially, of course, this sleep may be a very good thing for him. That he knows what he is about, so to speak, in being insensible so long. If he had lived straight on—"

"I doubt if he would have premeditated as much," said Warming. "He was not a far-sighted man. In fact—"

"Yes?"

"We differed on that point. I stood to him somewhat in the relation of a guardian. You have probably seen enough of affairs to recognise that occasionally a certain friction—. But even if that was the case, there is a doubt whether he will ever wake. This sleep exhausts slowly, but it exhausts. Apparently he is sliding slowly, very slowly and tediously, down a long slope, if you can understand me?"

"It will be a pity to lose his surprise. There's been a lot of change these twenty years. It's Rip Van Winkle come real."

"It's Bellamy," said Warming. "There has been a lot of change certainly. And, among other changes, I have changed. I am an old man."

Isbister hesitated, and then feigned a belated surprise. "I shouldn't have thought it."

"I was forty-three when his bankers—you remember you wired to his bankers—sent on to me."

"I got their address from the cheque book in his pocket," said Isbister.

"Well, the addition is not difficult," said Warming.

There was another pause, and then Isbister gave way to an unavoidable curiosity. "He may go on for years yet," he said, and had a moment of hesitation. "We have to consider that. His affairs, you know, may fall some day into the hands of—someone else, you know."

"That, if you will believe me, Mr. Isbister, is one of the problems most constantly before my mind. We happen to be—as a matter of fact, there are no very trustworthy connections of ours. It is a grotesque and unprecedented position."

"It is," said Isbister. "As a matter of fact, it's a case for a public trustee, if only we had such a functionary."

"It seems to me it's a case for some public body, some practically undying guardian. If he really is going on living—as the doctors, some of them, think. As a matter of fact, I have gone to one or two public men about it. But, so far, nothing has been done."

"It wouldn't be a bad idea to hand him over to some public body—the British Museum Trustees, or the Royal College of Physicians. Sounds a bit odd, of course, but the whole situation is odd."

"The difficulty is to induce them to take him."

"Red tape, I suppose?"

"Partly."

Pause. "It's a curious business, certainly," said Isbister. "And compound interest has a way of mounting up."

"It has," said Warming. "And now the gold supplies are running short there is a tendency towards ... appreciation."

"I've felt that," said Isbister with a grimace. "But it makes it better for him."

"If he wakes."

"If he wakes," echoed Isbister. "Do you notice the pinched-ill look of his nose, and the way in which his eyelids sink?"

Warming looked and thought for a space. "I doubt if he will wake," he said at last.

"I never properly understood," said Isbister, "what it was brought this on. He told me something about overstudy. I've often been curious."

"He was a man of considerable gifts, but spasmodic, emotional. He had grave domestic troubles, divorced his wife, in fact, and it was as a relief from that, I think, that he took up politics of the rabid sort. He was a fanatical Radical—a Socialist—or typical Liberal, as they used to call themselves, of the advanced school. Energetic—flighty—undisciplined. Overwork upon a controversy did this for him. I remember the pamphlet he wrote—a curious production. Wild, whirling stuff. There were one or two prophecies. Some of them are already exploded, some of them are established facts. But for the most part to read such a thesis is to realise how full the world is of unanticipated things. He will have much to learn, much to unlearn, when he wakes. If ever a waking comes."

"I'd give anything to be there," said Isbister, "just to hear what he would say to it all."

"So would I," said Warming. "Aye! so would I," with an old man's sudden turn to self pity. "But I shall never see him wake."

He stood looking thoughtfully at the waxen figure. "He will never wake," he said at last. He sighed "He will never wake again."

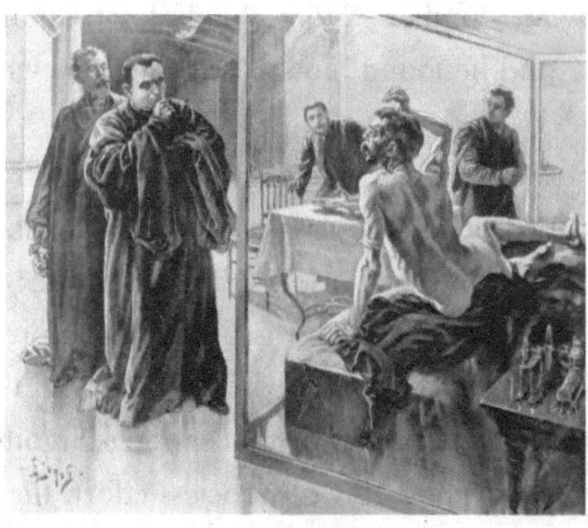

CHAPTER III
THE AWAKENING

But Warming was wrong in that. An awakening came.

What a wonderfully complex thing! this simple seeming unity—the self! Who can trace its reintegration as morning after morning we awaken, the flux and confluence of its countless factors interweaving, rebuilding, the dim first stirrings of the soul, the growth and synthesis of the unconscious to the subconscious, the sub-conscious to dawning consciousness, until at last we recognise ourselves again. And as it happens to most of us after the night's sleep, so it was with Graham at the end of his vast slumber. A dim cloud of sensation taking shape, a cloudy dreariness, and he found himself vaguely somewhere, recumbent, faint, but alive.

The pilgrimage towards a personal being seemed to traverse vast gulfs, to occupy epochs. Gigantic dreams that were terrible realities at the time, left vague perplexing memories, strange creatures, strange scenery, as if from another planet. There was a distinct impression, too, of a momentous conversation, of a name—he could not tell what name—that was subsequently to recur, of some queer long-forgotten sensation of vein and muscle, of a feeling of vast hopeless effort, the effort of a man near drowning in darkness. Then came a panorama of dazzling unstable confluent scenes.

Graham became aware his eyes were open and regarding some unfamiliar thing.

It was something white, the edge of something, a frame of wood. He moved his head slightly, following the contour of this shape. It went up beyond the top of his eyes. He tried to think where he might be. Did it matter, seeing he was so wretched? The colour of his thoughts was a dark depression. He felt the featureless misery of one who wakes towards the hour of dawn. He had an uncertain sense of whispers and footsteps hastily receding.

The movement of his head involved a perception of extreme physical weakness. He supposed he was in bed in the hotel at the place in the valley—but he could not recall that white edge. He must have slept. He remembered now that he had wanted to sleep. He recalled the cliff and waterfall again, and then recollected something about talking to a passer-by.

How long had he slept? What was that sound of pattering feet? And that rise and fall, like the murmur of breakers on pebbles? He put out a languid hand to reach his watch from the chair whereon it was his habit to place it, and touched some smooth hard surface like glass. This was so unexpected that it startled him extremely. Quite suddenly he rolled over, stared for a moment, and struggled into a sitting position. The effort was unexpectedly difficult, and it left him giddy and weak—and amazed.

He rubbed his eyes. The riddle of his surroundings was confusing but his mind was quite clear—evidently his sleep had benefited him. He was not in a bed at all as he understood the word, but lying naked on a very soft and yielding mattress, in a trough of dark glass. The mattress was partly transparent, a fact he observed with a strange sense of insecurity, and below it was a mirror reflecting him greyly. About his arm—and he saw with a shock that his skin was strangely dry and yellow—was bound a curious apparatus of rubber, bound so cunningly that it seemed to pass into his skin above and below. And this strange bed was placed in a case of greenish coloured glass (as it seemed to him), a bar in the white framework of which had first arrested his attention. In the corner of the case was a stand of glittering and delicately made apparatus, for the most part quite strange appliances, though a maximum and minimum thermometer was recognisable.

The slightly greenish tint of the glass-like substance which surrounded him on every hand obscured what lay behind, but he perceived it was a vast apartment of splendid appearance, and with a very large and simple white archway facing him. Close to the walls of the cage were articles of furniture, a table covered with a silvery cloth, silvery like the side of a fish, a couple of graceful chairs, and on the table a number of dishes with substances piled on them, a bottle and two glasses. He realised that he was intensely hungry.

He could see no human being, and after a period of hesitation scrambled off the translucent mattress and tried to stand on the clean white floor of his little apartment. He had miscalculated his strength, however, and staggered and put his hand against the glasslike pane before him to steady himself. For a moment it resisted his hand, bending outward like a distended bladder, then it broke with a slight report and vanished—a pricked bubble. He reeled out into the general space of the hall, greatly astonished. He caught at the table to save himself, knocking one of the glasses to the floor—it rang but did not break—and sat down in one of the armchairs.

When he had a little recovered he filled the remaining glass from the bottle and drank—a colourless liquid it was, but not water, with a pleasing faint aroma and taste and a quality of immediate support and stimulus. He put down the vessel and looked about him.

The apartment lost none of its size and magnificence now that the greenish transparency that had intervened was removed. The archway he saw led to a flight of steps, going downward without the intermediation of a door, to a spacious transverse passage. This passage ran between polished pillars of some white-veined substance of deep ultramarine, and along it came the sound of human movements and voices and a deep undeviating droning note. He sat, now fully awake, listening alertly, forgetting the viands in his attention.

Then with a shock he remembered that he was naked, and casting about him for covering, saw a long black robe thrown on one of the chairs beside him. This he wrapped about him and sat down again, trembling.

His mind was still a surging perplexity. Clearly he had slept, and had been removed in his sleep. But here? And who were those people, the distant crowd beyond the deep blue pillars? Boscastle? He poured out and partially drank another glass of the colourless fluid.

What was this place?—this place that to his senses seemed subtly quivering like a thing alive? He looked about him at the clean and beautiful form of the apartment, unstained by ornament, and saw that the roof was broken in one place by a circular shaft full of light, and, as he looked, a steady, sweeping shadow blotted it out and passed, and came again and passed. "Beat, beat," that sweeping shadow had a note of its own in the subdued tumult that filled the air.

He would have called out, but only a little sound came into his throat. Then he stood up, and, with the uncertain steps of a drunkard, made his way towards the archway. He staggered down the steps, tripped on the corner of the black cloak he had wrapped about himself, and saved himself by catching at one of the blue pillars.

The passage ran down a cool vista of blue and purple, and ended remotely in a railed space like a balcony, brightly lit and projecting into a space of haze, a space like the interior of some gigantic building. Beyond and remote were vast and vague architectural forms. The tumult of voices rose now loud and clear, and on the balcony and with their backs to him, gesticulating and apparently in animated conversation, were three figures, richly dressed in loose and easy garments of bright soft colourings. The noise of a great multitude of people poured up over the balcony, and once it seemed the top of a banner passed, and once some brightly coloured object, a pale blue cap or garment thrown up into the air perhaps, flashed athwart the space and fell. The shouts sounded like English, there was a reiteration of "Wake!" He heard some indistinct shrill cry, and abruptly the three men began laughing.

"Ha, ha, ha!" laughed one—a red-haired man in a short purple robe. "When the Sleeper wakes——_When!_"

He turned his eyes full of merriment along the passage. His face changed, the whole man changed, became rigid. The other two turned swiftly at his exclamation and stood motionless. Their faces assumed an expression of consternation, an expression that deepened into awe.

Suddenly Graham's knees bent beneath him, his arm against the pillar collapsed limply, he staggered forward and fell upon his face.

CHAPTER IV
THE SOUND OF A TUMULT

Graham's last impression before he fainted was of a clamorous ringing of bells. He learnt afterwards that he was insensible, hanging between life and death, for the better part of an hour. When he recovered his senses, he was back on his translucent couch, and there was a stirring warmth at heart and throat. The dark apparatus, he perceived, had been removed from his arm, which was bandaged. The white framework was still about him, but the greenish transparent substance that had filled it was altogether gone. A man in a deep violet robe, one of those who had been on the balcony, was looking keenly into his face.

Remote but insistent was a clamour of bells and confused sounds, that suggested to his mind the picture of a great number of people shouting together. Something seemed to fall across this tumult, a door suddenly closed.

Graham moved his head. "What does this all mean?" he said slowly. "Where am I?"

He saw the red-haired man who had been first to discover him. A voice seemed to be asking what he had said, and was abruptly stilled.

The man in violet answered in a soft voice, speaking English with a slightly foreign accent, or so at least it seemed to the Sleeper's ears, "You are quite safe. You were brought hither from where you fell asleep. It is quite safe. You have been here some time—sleeping. In a trance."

He said something further that Graham could not hear, and a little phial was handed across to him. Graham felt a cooling spray, a fragrant mist played over his forehead for a moment, and his sense of refreshment increased. He closed his eyes in satisfaction.

"Better?" asked the man in violet, as Graham's eyes reopened. He was a pleasant-faced man of thirty, perhaps, with a pointed flaxen beard, and a clasp of gold at the neck of his violet robe.

"Yes," said Graham.

"You have been asleep some time. In a cataleptic trance. You have heard? Catalepsy? It may seem strange to you at first, but I can assure you everything is well."

Graham did not answer, but these words served their reassuring purpose. His eyes went from face to face of the three people about him. They were regarding him strangely. He knew he ought to be somewhere in Cornwall, but he could not square these things with that impression.

A matter that had been in his mind during his last waking moments at Boscastle recurred, a thing resolved upon and somehow neglected. He cleared his throat.

"Have you wired my cousin?" he asked. "E. Warming, 27, Chancery Lane?"

They were all assiduous to hear. But he had to repeat it. "What an odd _blurr_ in his accent!" whispered the red-haired man. "Wire, sir?" said the young man with the flaxen beard, evidently puzzled.

"He means send an electric telegram," volunteered the third, a pleasant-faced youth of nineteen or twenty. The flaxen-bearded man gave a cry of comprehension. "How stupid of me! You may be sure everything shall be done, sir," he said to Graham. "I am afraid it would be difficult to—wire to your cousin. He is not in London now. But don't trouble about arrangements yet; you have been asleep a very long time and the important thing is to get over that, sir." (Graham concluded the word was sir, but this man pronounced it "Sire.")

"Oh!" said Graham, and became quiet.

It was all very puzzling, but apparently these people in unfamiliar dress knew what they were about. Yet they were odd and the room was odd. It seemed he was in some newly established place. He had a sudden flash of suspicion. Surely this wasn't some hall of public exhibition! If it was he would give Warming a piece of his mind. But it scarcely had that character. And in a place of public exhibition he would not have discovered himself naked.

Then suddenly, quite abruptly, he realised what had happened. There was no perceptible interval of suspicion, no dawn to his knowledge. Abruptly he knew that his trance had lasted for a vast interval; as if by some processes of thought reading he interpreted the awe in the faces that peered into his. He looked at them strangely, full of intense emotion. It seemed they read his eyes. He framed his lips to speak and could not. A queer impulse to hide his knowledge came into his mind almost at the moment of his discovery. He looked at his bare feet, regarding then silently. His impulse to speak passed. He was trembling exceedingly.

They gave him some pink fluid with a greenish fluorescence and a meaty taste, and the assurance of returning strength grew.

"That—that makes me feel better," he said hoarsely, and there were murmurs of respectful approval. He knew now quite clearly. He made to speak again, and again he could not.

He pressed his throat and tried a third time.

"How long?" he asked in a level voice. "How long have I been asleep?"

"Some considerable time," said the flaxen-bearded man, glancing quickly at the others.

"How long?"

"A very long time."

"Yes—yes," said Graham, suddenly testy. "But I want—Is it—it is—some years? Many years? There was something—I forget what. I feel—confused. But you—" He sobbed. "You need not fence with me. How long—?"

He stopped, breathing irregularly. He squeezed his eyes with his knuckles and sat waiting for an answer.

They spoke in undertones.

"Five or six?" he asked faintly. "More?"

"Very much more than that."

"More!"

"More."

He looked at them and it seemed as though imps were twitching the muscles of his face. He looked his question.

"Many years," said the man with the red beard.

Graham struggled into a sitting position. He wiped a rheumy tear from his face with a lean hand. "Many years!" he repeated. He shut his eyes tight, opened them, and sat looking about him, from one unfamiliar thing to another.

"How many years?" he asked.

"You must be prepared to be surprised."

"Well?"

"More than a gross of years."

He was irritated at the strange word. "More than a what?"

Two of them spoke together. Some quick remarks that were made about "decimal" he did not catch.

"How long did you say?" asked Graham. "How long? Don't look like that. Tell me."

Among the remarks in an undertone, his ear caught six words: "More than a couple of centuries."

"What?" he cried, turning on the youth who he thought had spoken. "Who says—? What was that? A couple of centuries!"

"Yes," said the man with the red beard. "Two hundred years."

Graham repeated the words. He had been prepared to hear of a vast repose, and yet these concrete centuries defeated him.

"Two hundred years," he said again, with the figure of a great gulf opening very slowly in his mind; and then, "Oh, but—!"

They said nothing.

"You—did you say—?"

"Two hundred years. Two centuries of years," said the man with the red beard.

There was a pause. Graham looked at their faces and saw that what he had heard was indeed true.

"But it can't be," he said querulously. "I am dreaming. Trances. Trances don't last. That is not right—this is a joke you have played upon me! Tell me—some days ago, perhaps, I was walking along the coast of Cornwall—?"

His voice failed him.

The man with the flaxen beard hesitated. "I'm not very strong in history, sir," he said weakly, and glanced at the others.

"That was it, sir," said the youngster. "Boscastle, in the old Duchy of Cornwall—it's in the southwest country beyond the dairy meadows. There is a house there still. I have been there."

"Boscastle!" Graham turned his eyes to the youngster. "That was it—Boscastle. Little Boscastle. I fell asleep—somewhere there. I don't exactly remember. I don't exactly remember."

He pressed his brows and whispered, "More than two hundred years!"

He began to speak quickly with a twitching face, but his heart was cold within him. "But if it is two hundred years, every soul I know, every human being that ever I saw or spoke to before I went to sleep, must be dead."

They did not answer him.

"The Queen and the Royal Family, her Ministers, of Church and State. High and low, rich and poor, one with another—"

"Is there England still?"

"That's a comfort! Is there London? Eh?" "This _is_ London, eh? And you are my assistant—custodian; assistant-custodian. And these—? Eh? Assistant-custodians to?"

He sat with a gaunt stare on his face. "But why am I here? No! Don't talk. Be quiet. Let me—"

He sat silent, rubbed his eyes, and, uncovering them, found another little glass of pinkish fluid held towards him. He took the dose. It was almost immediately sustaining. Directly he had taken it he began to weep naturally and refreshingly.

Presently he looked at their faces, suddenly laughed through his tears, a little foolishly. "But—two—hun—dred—years!" he said. He grimaced hysterically and covered up his face again.

After a space he grew calm. He sat up, his hands hanging over his knees in almost precisely the same attitude in which Isbister had found him on the cliff at Pentargen. His attention was attracted by a thick domineering voice, the footsteps of an advancing personage. "What are you doing? Why was I not warned? Surely you could tell? Someone will suffer for this. The man must be kept quiet. Are the doorways closed? All the doorways? He must be kept perfectly quiet. He must not be told. Has he been told anything?"

The man with the fair beard made some inaudible remark, and Graham looking over his shoulder saw approaching a very short, fat, and thickset beardless man, with aquiline nose and heavy neck and chin. Very thick black and slightly sloping eyebrows that almost met over his nose and overhung deep grey eyes, gave his face an oddly formidable expression. He scowled momentarily at Graham and then his regard returned to the man with the flaxen beard. "These others," he said in a voice of extreme irritation. "You had better go."

"Go?" said the red-bearded man.

"Certainly—go now. But see the doorways are closed as you go."

The two men addressed turned obediently, after one reluctant glance at Graham, and instead of going through the archway as he expected, walked straight to the dead wall of the apartment opposite the archway. And then came a strange thing; a long strip of this apparently solid wall rolled up with a snap, hung over the two retreating men and fell again, and immediately Graham was alone with the new comer and the purple-robed man with the flaxen beard.

For a space the thickset man took not the slightest notice of Graham, but proceeded to interrogate the other—obviously his subordinate—upon the treatment of their charge. He spoke clearly, but in phrases only partially intelligible to Graham. The awakening seemed not only a matter of surprise but of consternation and annoyance to him. He was evidently profoundly excited.

"You must not confuse his mind by telling him things," he repeated again and again. "You must not confuse his mind."

His questions answered, he turned quickly and eyed the awakened sleeper with an ambiguous expression.

"Feel queer?" he asked.

"Very."

"The world, what you see of it, seems strange to you?"

"I suppose I have to live in it, strange as it seems."

"I suppose so, now."

"In the first place, hadn't I better have some clothes?"

"They——" said the thickset man and stopped, and the flaxen-bearded man met his eye and went away. "You will very speedily have clothes," said the thickset man.

"Is it true indeed, that I have been asleep two hundred——?" asked Graham.

"They have told you that, have they? Two hundred and three, as a matter of fact."

Graham accepted the indisputable now with raised eyebrows and depressed mouth. He sat silent for a moment, and then asked a question, "Is there a mill or dynamo near here?" He did not wait for an answer. "Things have changed tremendously, I suppose?" he said.

"What is that shouting?" he asked abruptly.

"Nothing," said the thickset man impatiently. "It's people. You'll understand better later—perhaps. As you say, things have changed." He spoke shortly, his brows were knit, and he glanced about him like a man trying to decide in an emergency. "We must get you clothes and so forth, at any rate. Better wait here until some can come. No one will come near you. You want shaving."

Graham rubbed his chin.

The man with the flaxen beard came back towards them, turned suddenly, listened for a moment, lifted his eyebrows at the older man, and hurried off through the archway towards the balcony. The tumult of shouting grew louder, and the thickset man turned and listened also. He cursed suddenly under his breath, and turned his eyes upon Graham with an unfriendly expression. It was a surge of many voices, rising and falling, shouting and screaming, and once came a sound like blows and sharp cries, and then a snapping like the crackling of dry sticks. Graham strained his ears to draw some single thread of sound from the woven tumult.

Then he perceived, repeated again and again, a certain formula. For a time he doubted his ears. But surely these were the words: "Show us the Sleeper! Show us the Sleeper!"

The thickset man rushed suddenly to the archway.

"Wild!" he cried, "How do they know? Do they know? Or is it guessing?"

There was perhaps an answer.

"I can't come," said the thickset man; "I have _him_ to see to. But shout from the balcony."

There was an inaudible reply.

"Say he is not awake. Anything! I leave it to you."

He came hurrying back to Graham. "You must have clothes at once," he said. "You cannot stop here—and it will be impossible to—"

He rushed away, Graham shouting unanswered questions after him. In a moment he was back.

"I can't tell you what is happening. It is too complex to explain. In a moment you shall have your clothes made. Yes—in a moment. And then I can take you away from here. You will find out our troubles soon enough."

"But those voices. They were shouting—?"

"Something about the Sleeper—that's you. They have some twisted idea. I don't know what it is. I know nothing."

A shrill bell jetted acutely across the indistinct mingling of remote noises, and this brusque person sprang to a little group of appliances in the corner of the room. He listened for a moment, regarding a ball of crystal, nodded, and said a few indistinct words; then he walked to the wall through which the two men had vanished. It rolled up again like a curtain, and he stood waiting.

Graham lifted his arm and was astonished to find what strength the restoratives had given him. He thrust one leg over the side of the couch and then the other. His head no longer swam. He could scarcely credit his rapid recovery. He sat feeling his limbs.

The man with the flaxen beard re-entered from the archway, and as he did so the cage of a lift came sliding down in front of the thickset man, and a lean, grey-bearded man, carrying a roll, and wearing a tightly-fitting costume of dark green, appeared therein.

"This is the tailor," said the thickset man with an introductory gesture. "It will never do for you to wear that black. I cannot understand how it got here. But I shall. I shall. You will be as rapid as possible?" he said to the tailor.

The man in green bowed, and, advancing, seated himself by Graham on the bed. His manner was calm, but his eyes were full of curiosity. "You will find the fashions altered, Sire," he said. He glanced from under his brows at the thickset man.

He opened the roller with a quick movement, and a confusion of brilliant fabrics poured out over his knees. "You lived, Sire, in a period essentially cylindrical—the Victorian. With a tendency to the hemisphere in hats. Circular curves always. Now—" He flicked out a little appliance the size and appearance of a keyless watch, whirled the knob, and behold—a little figure in white appeared kinetoscope fashion on the dial, walking and turning. The tailor caught up a pattern of bluish white satin. "That is my conception of your immediate treatment," he said.

The thickset man came and stood by the shoulder of Graham.

"We have very little time," he said.

"Trust me," said the tailor. "My machine follows. What do you think of this?"

"What is that?" asked the man from the nineteenth century.

"In your days they showed you a fashion-plate," said the tailor, "but this is our modern development See here." The little figure repeated its evolutions, but in a different costume. "Or this," and with a click another small figure in a more voluminous type of robe marched on to the dial. The tailor was very quick in his movements, and glanced twice towards the lift as he did these things.

It rumbled again, and a crop-haired anaemic lad with features of the Chinese type, clad in coarse pale blue canvas, appeared together with a complicated machine, which he pushed noiselessly on little castors into the room. Incontinently the little kinetoscope was dropped, Graham was invited to stand in front of the machine and the tailor muttered some instructions to the crop-haired lad, who answered in guttural tones and with words Graham did not recognise. The boy then went to conduct an incomprehensible monologue in the corner, and the tailor pulled out a number of slotted arms terminating in little discs, pulling them out until the discs were flat against the body of Graham, one at each shoulder blade, one at the elbows, one at the neck and so forth, so that at last there were, perhaps, two score of them upon his body and limbs. At the same time, some other person entered the room by the lift, behind Graham. The tailor set moving a mechanism that initiated a faint-sounding rhythmic movement of parts in the machine, and in another moment he was knocking up the levers and Graham was released. The tailor replaced his cloak of black, and the man with the flaxen beard proffered him a little glass of some refreshing fluid. Graham saw over the rim of the glass a pale-faced young man regarding him with a singular fixity.

The thickset man had been pacing the room fretfully, and now turned and went through the archway towards the balcony, from which the noise of a distant crowd still came in gusts and cadences. The cropheaded lad handed the tailor a roll of the bluish satin and the two began fixing this in the mechanism in a manner reminiscent of a roll of paper in a nineteenth century printing machine. Then they ran the entire thing on its easy, noiseless bearings across the room to a remote corner where a twisted cable looped rather gracefully from the wall. They made some connexion and the machine became energetic and swift.

"What is that doing?" asked Graham, pointing with the empty glass to the busy figures and trying to ignore the scrutiny of the new comer. "Is that—some sort of force—laid on?"

"Yes," said the man with the flaxen beard.

"Who is that?" He indicated the archway behind him.

The man in purple stroked his little beard, hesitated, and answered in an undertone, "He is Howard, your chief guardian. You see, Sire,—it's a little difficult to explain. The Council appoints a guardian and assistants. This hall has under certain restrictions been public. In order that people might satisfy themselves. We have barred the doorways for the first time. But I think—if you don't mind, I will leave him to explain."

"Odd" said Graham. "Guardian? Council?" Then turning his back on the new comer, he asked in an undertone, "Why is this man glaring at me? Is he a mesmerist?"

"Mesmerist! He is a capillotomist."

"Capillotomist!"

"Yes—one of the chief. His yearly fee is sixdoz lions."

It sounded sheer nonsense. Graham snatched at the last phrase with an unsteady mind. "Sixdoz lions?" he said.

"Didn't you have lions? I suppose not. You had the old pounds? They are our monetary units."

"But what was that you said—sixdoz?"

"Yes. Six dozen, Sire. Of course things, even these little things, have altered. You lived in the days of the decimal system, the Arab system— tens, and little hundreds and thousands. We have eleven numerals now. We have single figures for both ten and eleven, two figures for a dozen, and a dozen dozen makes a gross, a great hundred, you know, a dozen gross a dozand, and a dozand dozand a myriad. Very simple?"

"I suppose so," said Graham. "But about this cap—what was it?"

The man with the flaxen beard glanced over his shoulder.

"Here are your clothes!" he said. Graham turned round sharply and saw the tailor standing at his elbow smiling, and holding some palpably new garments over his arm. The crop-headed boy, by means of one finger, was impelling the complicated machine towards the lift by which he had arrived. Graham stared at the completed suit. "You don't mean to say—!"

"Just made," said the tailor. He dropped the garments at the feet of Graham, walked to the bed on which Graham had so recently been lying, flung out the translucent mattress, and turned up the looking glass. As he did so a furious bell summoned the thickset man to the corner. The man with the flaxen beard rushed across to him and then hurried out by the archway.

The tailor was assisting Graham into a dark purple combination garment, stockings, vest, and pants in one, as the thickset man came back from the corner to meet the man with the flaxen beard returning from the balcony. They began speaking quickly in an undertone, their bearing had an unmistakable quality of anxiety. Over the purple under-garment came a complex but graceful garment of bluish white, and I Graham was clothed in the fashion once more and saw himself, sallow-faced, unshaven and shaggy still, but at least naked no longer, and in some indefinable unprecedented way graceful.

"I must shave," he said regarding himself in the glass.

"In a moment," said Howard.

The persistent stare ceased. The young man closed his eyes, reopened them, and with a lean hand extended, advanced on Graham. Then he stopped, with his hand slowly gesticulating, and looked about him.

"A seat," said Howard impatiently, and in a moment the flaxen-bearded man had a chair behind Graham. "Sit down, please," said Howard.

Graham hesitated, and in the other hand of the wildeyed man he saw the glint of steel.

"Don't you understand, Sire?" cried the flaxen-bearded man with hurried politeness. "He is going to cut your hair."

"Oh!" cried Graham enlightened. "But you called him—

"A capillotomist—precisely! He is one of the finest artists in the world."

Graham sat down abruptly. The flaxen-bearded man disappeared. The capillotomist came forward with graceful gestures, examined Graham's ears and surveyed him, felt the back of his head, and would have sat down again to regard him but for Howard's audible impatience. Forthwith with rapid movements and a succession of deftly handled implements he shaved Graham's chin, clipped his moustache, and cut and arranged his hair. All this he did without a word, with something of the rapt air of a poet inspired. And as soon as he had finished Graham was handed a pair of shoes.

Suddenly a loud voice shouted—it seemed from a piece of machinery in the corner—"At once—at once. The people know all over the city. Work is being stopped. Work is being stopped. Wait for nothing, but come."

This shout appeared to perturb Howard exceedingly. By his gestures it seemed to Graham that he hesitated between two directions. Abruptly he went towards the corner where the apparatus stood about the little crystal ball. As he did so the undertone of tumultuous shouting from the archway that had continued during all these occurrences rose to a mighty sound, roared as if it were sweeping past, and fell again as if receding swiftly. It drew Graham after it with an irresistible attraction. He glanced at the thickset man, and then obeyed his impulse. In two strides he was down the steps and in the passage, and, in a score he was out upon the balcony upon which the three men had been standing.

CHAPTER V
THE MOVING WAYS

He went to the railings of the balcony and stared upward. An exclamation of surprise at his appearance, and the movements of a number of people came from the spacious area below.

His first impression was of overwhelming architecture. The place into which he looked was an aisle of Titanic buildings, curving spaciously in either direction. Overhead mighty cantilevers sprang together across the huge width of the place, and a tracery of translucent material shut out the sky. Gigantic globes of cool white light shamed the pale sunbeams that filtered down through the girders and wires. Here and there a gossamer suspension bridge dotted with foot passengers flung across the chasm and the air was webbed with slender cables. A cliff of edifice hung above him, he perceived as he glanced upward, and the opposite facade was grey and dim and broken by great archings, circular perforations, balconies, buttresses, turret projections, myriads of vast windows, and an intricate scheme of architectural relief. Athwart these ran inscriptions horizontally and obliquely in an unfamiliar lettering. Here and there close to the roof cables of a peculiar stoutness were fastened, and drooped in a steep curve to circular openings on the opposite side of the space, and even as Graham noted these a remote and tiny figure of a man clad in pale blue arrested his attention. This little figure was far overhead across the space beside the higher fastening of one of these festoons, hanging forward from a little ledge of masonry and handling some well-nigh invisible strings dependent from the line. Then suddenly, with a swoop that sent Graham's heart into his mouth, this man had rushed down the curve and vanished through a round opening on the hither side of the way. Graham had been looking up as he came out upon the balcony, and the things he saw above and opposed to him had at first seized his attention to the exclusion of anything else. Then suddenly he discovered the roadway! It was not a roadway at all, as Graham understood such things, for in the nineteenth century the only roads and streets were beaten tracks of motionless earth, jostling rivulets of vehicles between narrow footways. But this roadway was three hundred feet across, and it moved; it moved, all save the middle, the lowest part. For a moment, the motion dazzled his mind. Then he understood.

Under the balcony this extraordinary roadway ran swiftly to Graham's right, an endless flow rushing along as fast as a nineteenth century express train, an endless platform of narrow transverse overlapping slats with little interspaces that permitted it to follow the curvatures of the street. Upon it were seats, and here and there little kiosks, but they swept by too swiftly for him to see what might be therein. From this nearest and swiftest platform a series of others descended to the centre of the space. Each moved to the right, each perceptibly slower than the one above it, but the difference in pace was small enough to permit anyone to step from any platform to the one adjacent, and so walk uninterruptedly from the swiftest to the motionless middle way. Beyond this middle way was another series of endless platforms rushing with varying pace to Graham's left. And seated in crowds upon the two widest and swiftest platforms, or stepping from one to another down the steps, or swarming over the central space, was an innumerable and wonderfully diversified multitude of people.

"You must not stop here," shouted Howard suddenly at his side. "You must come away at once."

Graham made no answer. He heard without hearing. The platforms ran with a roar and the people were shouting. He perceived women and girls with flowing hair, beautifully robed, with bands crossing between the breasts. These first came out of the confusion. Then he perceived that the dominant note in that kaleidoscope of costume was the pale blue that the tailor's boy had worn. He became aware of cries of "The Sleeper. What has happened to the Sleeper?" and it seemed as though the rushing platforms before him were suddenly spattered with the pale buff of human faces, and then still more thickly. He saw pointing fingers. He perceived that the motionless central area of this huge arcade just opposite to the balcony was densely crowded with blue-clad people. Some sort of struggle had sprung into life. People seemed to be pushed up the running platforms on either side, and carried away against their will. They would spring off so soon as they were beyond the thick of the confusion, and run back towards the conflict.

"It is the Sleeper. Verily it is the Sleeper," shouted voices. "That is never the Sleeper," shouted others. More and more faces were turned to him. At the intervals along this central area Graham noted openings, pits, apparently the heads of staircases going down with people ascending out of them and descending into them. The struggle it seemed centred about the one of these nearest to him. People were running down the moving platforms to this, leaping dexterously from platform to platform. The clustering people on the higher platforms seemed to divide their interest between this point and the balcony. A number of sturdy little figures clad in a uniform of bright red, and working methodically together, were employed it seemed in preventing access to this descending staircase. About them a crowd was rapidly accumulating. Their brilliant colour contrasted vividly with the whitish-blue of their antagonists, for the struggle was indisputable.

He saw these things with Howard shouting in his ear and shaking his arm. And then suddenly Howard was gone and he stood alone.

He perceived that the cries of "The Sleeper" grew in volume, and that the people on the nearer platform were standing up. The nearer swifter platform he perceived was empty to the right of him, and far across the space the platform running in the opposite direction was coming crowded and passing away bare. With incredible swiftness a vast crowd had gathered in the central space before his eyes; a dense swaying mass of people, and the shouts grew from a fitful crying to a voluminous incessant clamour: "The Sleeper! The Sleeper!" and yells and cheers, a waving of garments and cries of "Stop the ways!" They were also crying another name strange to Graham. It sounded like "Ostrog." The slower platforms were soon thick with active people, running against the movement so as to keep themselves opposite to him.

"Stop the ways," they cried. Agile figures ran up swiftly from the centre to the swift road nearest to him, were borne rapidly past him, shouting strange, unintelligible things, and ran back obliquely to the central way. One thing he distinguished: "It is indeed the Sleeper. It is indeed the Sleeper," they testified.

For a space Graham stood without a movement. Then he became vividly aware that all this concerned him. He was pleased at his wonderful popularity, he bowed, and, seeking a gesture of longer range, waved his arm. He was astonished at the violence of uproar that this provoked. The tumult about the descending stairway rose to furious violence. He became aware of crowded balconies, of men sliding along ropes, of men in trapeze-like seats hurling athwart the space. He heard voices behind him, a number of people descending the steps through the archway; he suddenly perceived that his guardian Howard was back again and gripping his arm painfully, and shouting inaudibly in his ear.

He turned, and Howard's face was white. "Come back," he heard. "They will stop the ways. The whole city will be in confusion."

He perceived a number of men hurrying along the passage of blue pillars behind Howard, the red-haired man, the man with the flaxen beard, a tall man in vivid vermilion, a crowd of others in red carrying staves, and all these people had anxious eager faces.

"Get him away," cried Howard.

"But why?" said Graham. "I don't see—"

"You must come away!" said the man in red in a resolute voice. His face and eyes were resolute, too. Graham's glances went from face to face, and he was suddenly aware of that most disagreeable flavour in life, compulsion. Some one gripped his arm.... He was being dragged away. It seemed as though the tumult suddenly became two, as if half the shouts that had come in from this wonderful roadway had sprung into the passages of the great building behind him. Marvelling and confused, feeling an impotent desire to resist, Graham was half led, half thrust, along the passage of blue pillars, and suddenly he found himself alone with Howard in a lift and moving swiftly upward.

CHAPTER VI
THE HALL OF THE ATLAS

From the moment when the tailor had bowed his farewell to the moment when Graham found himself in the lift, was altogether barely five minutes. And as yet the haze of his vast interval of sleep hung about him, as yet the initial strangeness of his being alive at all in this remote age touched everything with wonder, with a sense of the irrational, with something of the quality of a realistic dream. He was still detached, an astonished spectator, still but half involved in life. What he had seen, and especially the last crowded tumult, framed in the setting of the balcony, had a spectacular turn, like a thing witnessed from the box of a theatre. "I don't understand," he said. "What was the trouble? My mind is in a whirl. Why were they shouting? What is the danger?"

"We have our troubles," said Howard. His eyes avoided Graham's enquiry. "This is a time of unrest. And, in fact, your appearance, your waking just now, has a sort of connexion—"

He spoke jerkily, like a man not quite sure of his breathing. He stopped abruptly.

"I don't understand," said Graham.

"It will be clearer later," said Howard.

He glanced uneasily upward, as though he found the progress of the lift slow.

"I shall understand better, no doubt, when I have seen my way about a little," said Graham puzzled. "It will be—it is bound to be perplexing. At present it is all so strange. Anything seems possible. Anything. In the details even. Your counting, I understand, is different."

The lift stopped, and they stepped out into a narrow but very long passage between high walls, along which ran an extraordinary number of tubes and big cables.

"What a huge place this is!" said Graham. "Is it all one building? What place is it?"

"This is one of the city ways for various public services. Light and so forth."

"Was it a social trouble—that—in the great roadway place? How are you governed? Have you still a police?" "Several," said Howard.

"Several?"

"About fourteen."

"I don't understand."

"Very probably not. Our social order will probably seem very complex to you. To tell you the truth, I don't understand it myself very clearly. Nobody does. You will, perhaps—bye and bye. We have to go to the Council."

Graham's attention was divided between the urgent necessity of his inquiries and the people in the passages and halls they were traversing. For a moment his mind would be concentrated upon Howard and the halting answers he made, and then he would lose the thread in response to some vivid unexpected impression. Along the passages, in the halls, half the people seemed to be men in the red uniform. The pale blue canvas that had been so abundant in the aisle of moving ways did not appear. Invariably these men looked at him, and saluted him and Howard as they passed.

He had a clear vision of entering a long corridor, and there were a number of girls sitting on low seats and as though in a class. He saw no teacher, but only a novel apparatus from which he fancied a voice proceeded. The girls regarded him and his conductor, he thought, with curiosity and astonishment. But he was hurried on before he could form a clear idea of the gathering. He judged they knew Howard and not himself, and that they wondered who he was. This Howard, it seemed, was a person of importance. But then he was also merely Graham's guardian. That was odd.

There came a passage in twilight, and into this passage a footway hung so that he could see the feet and ankles of people going to and fro thereon, but no more of them. Then vague impressions of galleries and of casual astonished passers-by turning round to stare after the two of them with their red-clad guard.

The stimulus of the restoratives he had taken was only temporary. He was speedily fatigued by this excessive haste. He asked Howard to slacken his speed. Presently he was in a lift that had a window upon the great street space, but this was glazed and did not open, and they were too high for him to see the moving platforms below. But he saw people going to and fro along cables and along strange, frail-looking ridges.

And thence they passed across the street and at a vast height above it. They crossed by means of a narrow bridge closed in with glass, so clear that it made him giddy even to remember it. The floor of it also was of glass. From his memory of the cliffs between New Quay and Boscastle, so remote in time, and so recent in his experience, it seemed to him that they must be near four hundred feet above the moving ways. He stopped, looked down between his legs upon the swarming blue and red multitudes, minute and fore-shortened, struggling and gesticulating still towards the little balcony far below, a little toy balcony, it seemed, where he had so recently been standing. A thin haze and the glare of the mighty globes of light obscured everything. A man seated in a little open-work cradle shot by from some point still higher than the little narrow bridge, rushing down a cable as swiftly almost as if he were falling. Graham stopped involuntarily to watch this strange passenger vanish in a great circular opening below, and then his eyes went back to the tumultuous struggle.

Along one of the swifter ways rushed a thick crowd of red spots. This broke up into individuals as it approached the balcony, and went pouring down the slower ways towards the dense struggling crowd on the central area. These men in red appeared to be armed with sticks or truncheons; they seemed to be striking and thrusting. A great shouting, cries of wrath, screaming, burst out and came up to Graham, faint and thin. "Go on," cried Howard, laying hands on him.

Another man rushed down a cable. Graham suddenly glanced up to see whence he came, and beheld through the glassy roof and the network of cables and girders, dim rhythmically passing forms like the vans of windmills, and between them glimpses of a remote and pallid sky. Then Howard had thrust him forward across the bridge, and he was in a little narrow passage decorated with geometrical patterns.

"I want to see more of that," cried Graham, resisting.

"No, no," cried Howard, still gripping his arm.

"This way. You must go this way." And the men in red following them seemed ready to enforce his orders.

Some negroes in a curious wasp-like uniform of black and yellow appeared down the passage, and one hastened to throw up a sliding shutter that had seemed a door to Graham, and led the way through it. Graham found himself in a gallery overhanging the end of a great chamber. The attendant in black and yellow crossed this, thrust up a second shutter and stood waiting.

This place had the appearance of an ante-room. He saw a number of people in the central space, and at the opposite end a large and imposing doorway at the top of a flight of steps, heavily curtained but giving a glimpse of some still larger hall beyond. He perceived white men in red and other negroes in black and yellow standing stiffly about those portals.

As they crossed the gallery he heard a whisper from below, "The Sleeper," and was aware of a turning of heads, a hum of observation. They entered another little passage in the wall of this ante-chamber, and then he found himself on an iron-railed gallery of metal that passed round the side of the great hall he had already seen through the curtains. He entered the place at the corner, so that he received the fullest impression of its huge proportions. The black in the wasp uniform stood aside like a well-trained servant, and closed the valve behind him.

Compared with any of the places Graham had see thus far, this second hall appeared to be decorate with extreme richness. On a pedestal at the remote end, and more brilliantly lit than any other object, was a gigantic white figure of Atlas, strong and strenuous, the globe upon his bowed shoulders. It was the first thing to strike his attention, it was so vast, so patiently and painfully real, so white and simple. Save for this figure and for a dais in the centre, the wide floor of the place was a shining vacancy. The dais was remote in the greatness of the area; it would have looked a mere slab of metal had it not been for the group of seven men who stood about a table on it, and gave an inkling of its proportions. They were all dressed in white robes, they seemed to have arisen that moment from their seats, and they were regarding Graham steadfastly. At the end of the table he perceived the glitter of some mechanical appliances.

Howard led him along the end gallery until they were opposite this mighty labouring figure. Then he stopped. The two men in red who had followed them into the gallery came and stood on either hand of Graham.

"You must remain here," murmured Howard, "for a few moments," and, without waiting for a reply, hurried away along the gallery.

"But, why?" began Graham.

He moved as if to follow Howard, and found his path obstructed by one of the men in red. "You have to wait here, Sire," said the man in red.

"Why?"

"Orders, Sire."

"Whose orders?"

"Our orders, Sire."

Graham looked his exasperation.

"What place is this?" he said presently. "Who are those men?"

"They are the lords of the Council, Sire."

"What Council?"

"The Council."

"Oh!" said Graham, and after an equally ineffectual attempt at the other man, went to the railing and stared at the distant men in white, who stood watching him and whispering together.

The Council? He perceived there were now eight, though how the newcomer had arrived he had not observed. They made no gestures of greeting; they stood regarding him as in the nineteenth century a group of men might have stood in the street regarding a distant balloon that had suddenly floated into view. What council could it be that gathered there, that little body of men beneath the significant white Atlas, secluded from every eavesdropper in this impressive spaciousness? And why should he be brought to them, and be looked at strangely and spoken of inaudibly?

Howard appeared beneath, walking quickly across the polished floor towards them. As he drew near he bowed and performed certain peculiar movements, apparently of a ceremonious nature. Then he ascended the steps of the dais, and stood by the apparatus at the end of the table.

Graham watched that visible inaudible conversation. Occasionally, one of the white-robed men would glance towards him. He strained his ears in vain. The gesticulation of two of the speakers became animated. He glanced from them to the passive faces of his attendants.... When he looked again Howard was extending his hands and moving his head like a man who protests. He was interrupted, it seemed, by one of the white-robed men rapping the table.

The conversation lasted an interminable time to Graham's sense. His eyes rose to the still giant at whose feet the Council sat. Thence they wandered at last to the walls of the hall. It was decorated in long painted panels of a quasi-Japanese type, many of them very beautiful. These panels were grouped in a great and elaborate framing of dark metal, which passed into the metallic caryatidae of the galleries, and the great structural lines of the interior. The facile grace of these panels enhanced the mighty white effort that laboured in the centre of the scheme. Graham's eyes came back to the Council, and Howard was descending the steps. As he drew nearer his features could be distinguished, and Graham saw that he was flushed and blowing out his cheeks. His countenance was still disturbed when presently he reappeared along the gallery.

"This way," he said concisely, and they went on in silence to a little door that opened at their approach. The two men in red stopped on either side of this door. Howard and Graham passed in, and Graham, glancing back, saw the white-robed Council still standing in a close group and looking at him. Then the door closed behind him with a heavy thud, and for the first time since his awakening he was in silence. The floor, even, was noiseless to his feet.

Howard opened another door, and they were in the first of two contiguous chambers furnished in white and green. "What Council was that?" began Graham. "What were they discussing? What have they to do with me?" Howard closed the door carefully, heaved a huge sigh, and said something in an undertone. He walked slanting ways across the room and turned, blowing out his cheeks again. "Ugh!" he grunted, a man relieved.

Graham stood regarding him.

"You must understand," began Howard abruptly, avoiding Graham's eyes, "that our social order is very complex. A half explanation, a bare unqualified statement would give you false impressions. As a matter of fact—it is a case of compound interest partly—your small fortune, and the fortune of your cousin Warming which was left to you—and certain other beginnings—have become very considerable. And in other ways that will be hard for you to understand, you have become a person of significance— of very considerable significance—involved in the world's affairs."

He stopped.

"Yes?" said Graham.

"We have grave social troubles."

"Yes?"

"Things have come to such a pass that, in fact, is advisable to seclude you here."

"Keep me prisoner!" exclaimed Graham.

"Well—to ask you to keep in seclusion."

Graham turned on him. "This is strange!" he said.

"No harm will be done you."

"No harm!"

"But you must be kept here—"

"While I learn my position, I presume."

"Precisely."

"Very well then. Begin. Why harm?"

"Not now."

"Why not?"

"It is too long a story, Sire."

"All the more reason I should begin at once. You say I am a person of importance. What was that shouting I heard? Why is a great multitude shouting and excited because my trance is over, and who are the men in white in that huge council chamber?"

"All in good time, Sire," said Howard. "But not crudely, not crudely. This is one of those flimsy times when no man has a settled mind. Your awakening. No one expected your awakening. The Council is consulting."

"What council?"

"The Council you saw."

Graham made a petulant movement. "This is not right," he said. "I should be told what is happening."

"You must wait. Really you must wait."

Graham sat down abruptly. "I suppose since I have waited so long to resume life," he said, "that I must wait a little longer."

"That is better," said Howard. "Yes, that is much better. And I must leave you alone. For a space. While I attend the discussion in the Council. I am sorry."

He went towards the noiseless door, hesitated and vanished.

Graham walked to the door, tried it, found it securely fastened in some way he never came to understand, turned about, paced the room restlessly, made the circuit of the room, and sat down. He remained sitting for some time with folded arms and knitted brow, biting his finger nails and trying to piece together the kaleidoscopic impressions of this first hour of awakened life; the vast mechanical spaces, the endless series of chambers and passages, the great struggle that roared and splashed through these strange ways, the little group of remote unsympathetic men beneath the colossal Atlas, Howard's mysterious behaviour. There was an inkling of some vast inheritance already in his mind—a vast inheritance perhaps misapplied—of some unprecedented importance and opportunity. What had he to do? And this room's secluded silence was eloquent of imprisonment!

It came into Graham's mind with irresistible conviction that this series of magnificent impressions was a dream. He tried to shut his eyes and succeeded, but that time-honoured device led to no awakening.

Presently he began to touch and examine all the unfamiliar appointments of the two small rooms in which he found himself.

In a long oval panel of mirror he saw himself and stopped astonished. He was clad in a graceful costume of purple and bluish white, with a little greyshot beard trimmed to a point, and his hair, its blackness streaked now with bands of grey, arranged over his forehead in an unfamiliar but graceful manner. He seemed a man of five-and-forty perhaps. For a moment he did not perceive this was himself.

A flash of laughter came with the recognition. "To call on old Warming like this!" he exclaimed, "and make him take me out to lunch!"

Then he thought of meeting first one and then another of the few familiar acquaintances of his early manhood, and in the midst of his amusement realised that every soul with whom he might jest had died many score of years ago. The thought smote him abruptly and keenly; he stopped short, the expression of his face changed to a white consternation.

The tumultuous memory of the moving platforms and the huge facade of that wonderful street reasserted itself. The shouting multitudes came back clear and vivid, and those remote, inaudible, unfriendly councilors in white. He felt himself a little figure, very small and ineffectual, pitifully conspicuous. And all about him, the world was—strange.

CHAPTER VII
IN THE SILENT ROOMS

Presently Graham resumed his examination of his apartments. Curiosity kept him moving in spite of his fatigue. The inner room, he perceived, was high, and its ceiling dome shaped, with an oblong aperture in the centre, opening into a funnel in which a wheel of broad fans seemed to be rotating, apparently driving the air up the shaft. The faint humming note of its easy motion was the only clear sound in that quiet place. As these vans sprang up one after the other, Graham could get transient glimpses of the sky. He was surprised to see a star.

This drew his attention to the fact that the bright lighting of these rooms was due to a multitude of very faint glow lamps set about the cornices. There were no windows. And he began to recall that along all the vast chambers and passages he had traversed with Howard he had observed no windows at all. Had there been windows? There were windows on the street indeed, but were they for light? Or was the whole city lit day and night for evermore, so that there was no night there?

And another thing dawned upon him. There was no fireplace in either room. Was the season summer, and were these merely summer apartments, or was the whole City uniformly heated or cooled? He became interested in these questions, began examining the smooth texture of the walls, the simply constructed bed, the ingenious arrangements by which the labour of bedroom service was practically abolished. And over everything was a curious absence of deliberate ornament, a bare grace of form and colour, that he found very pleasing to the eye. There were several very comfortable chairs, a light table on silent runners carrying several bottles of fluids and glasses, and two plates bearing a clear substance like jelly. Then he noticed there were no books, no newspapers, no writing materials. "The world has changed indeed," he said.

He observed one entire side of the outer room was set with rows of peculiar double cylinders inscribed with green lettering on white that harmonized with the decorative scheme of the room, and in the centre of this side projected a little apparatus about a yard square and having a white smooth face to the room. A chair faced this. He had a transitory idea that these cylinders might be books, or a modern substitute for books, but at first it did not seem so.

The lettering on the cylinders puzzled him. At first sight it seemed like Russian. Then he noticed a suggestion of mutilated English about certain of the words.

"oi Man huwdbi Kin"

forced itself on him as "The Man who would be King." "Phonetic spelling," he said. He remembered reading a story with that title, then he recalled the story vividly, one of the best stories in the world. But this thing before him was not a book as he understood it. He puzzled out the titles of two adjacent cylinders. 'The Heart of Darkness,' he had never heard of before nor 'The Madonna of the Future'—no doubt if they were indeed stories, they were by post Victorian authors.

He puzzled over this peculiar cylinder for some time and replaced it. Then he turned to the square apparatus and examined that. He opened a sort of lid and found one of the double cylinders within, and on the upper edge a little stud like the stud of an electric bell. He pressed this and a rapid clicking began and ceased. He became aware of voices and music, and noticed a play of colour on the smooth front face. He suddenly realised what this might be, and stepped back to regard it.

On the flat surface was now a little picture, very vividly coloured, and in this picture were figures that moved. Not only did they move, but they were conversing in clear small voices. It was exactly like reality viewed through an inverted opera glass and heard through a long tube. His interest was seized at once by the situation, which presented a man pacing up and down and vociferating angry things to a pretty but petulant woman. Both were in the picturesque costume that seemed so strange to Graham. "I have worked," said the man, "but what have you been doing?"

"Ah!" said Graham. He forgot everything else, and sat down in the chair. Within five minutes he heard himself named, heard "when the Sleeper wakes," used jestingly as a proverb for remote postponement, and passed himself by, a thing remote and incredible. But in a little while he knew those two people like intimate friends.

At last the miniature drama came to an end, and the square face of the apparatus was blank again.

It was a strange world into which he had been permitted to see, unscrupulous, pleasure seeking, energetic, subtle, a world too of dire economic struggle; there were allusions he did not understand, incidents that conveyed strange suggestions of altered moral ideals, flashes of dubious enlightenment. The blue canvas that bulked so largely in his first impression of the city ways appeared again and again as the costume of the common people. He had no doubt the story was contemporary, and its intense realism was undeniable. And the end had been a tragedy that oppressed him. He sat staring at the blankness.

He started and rubbed his eyes. He had been so absorbed in the latter-day substitute for a novel, that he awoke to the little green and white room with more than a touch of the surprise of his first awakening.

He stood up, and abruptly he was back in his own wonderland. The clearness of the kinetoscope drama passed, and the struggle in the vast place of streets, the ambiguous Council, the swift phases of his waking hour, came back. These people had spoken of the Council with suggestions of a vague universality of power. And they had spoken of the Sleeper; it had not really struck him vividly at the time that he was the Sleeper. He had to recall precisely what they had said.

He walked into the bedroom and peered up through the quick intervals of the revolving fan. As the fan swept round, a dim turmoil like the noise of machinery came in rhythmic eddies. All else was silence.

Though the perpetual day still irradiated his apartments, he perceived the little intermittent strip of sky was now deep blue—black almost, with a dust of little stars.

He resumed his examination of the rooms. He could find no way of opening the padded door, no bell nor other means of calling for attendance. His feeling of wonder was in abeyance; but he was curious, anxious for information. He wanted to know exactly how he stood to these new things. He tried to compose himself to wait until someone came to him. Presently he became restless and eager for information, for distraction, for fresh sensations.

He went back to the apparatus in the other room, and had soon puzzled out the method of replacing the cylinders by others. As he did so, it came into his mind that it must be these little appliances had fixed the language so that it was still clear and understandable after two hundred years. The haphazard cylinders he substituted displayed a musical fantasia. At first it was beautiful, and then it was sensuous. He presently recognized what appeared to him to be an altered version of the story of Tannhauser. The music was unfamiliar. But the rendering was realistic, and with a contemporary unfamiliarity. Tannhauser did not go to a Venusberg, but to a Pleasure City. What was a Pleasure City? A dream, surely, the fancy of a fantastic, voluptuous writer.

He became interested, curious. The story developed with a flavour of strangely twisted sentimentality. Suddenly he did not like it. He liked it less as it proceeded.

He had a revulsion of feeling. These were no pictures, no idealisations, but photographed realities. He wanted no more of the twenty-second century Venusberg. He forgot the part played by the model in nineteenth century art, and gave way to an archaic indignation. He rose, angry and half ashamed at himself for witnessing this thing even in solitude. He pulled forward the apparatus, and with some violence sought for a means of stopping its action. Something snapped. A violet spark stung and convulsed his arm and the thing was still. When he attempted next day to replace these Tannhauser cylinders by another pair, he found the apparatus broken....

He struck out a path oblique to the room and paced to and fro, struggling with intolerable vast impressions. The things he had derived from the cylinders and the things he had seen, conflicted, confused him. It seemed to him the most amazing thing of all that in his thirty years of life he had never tried to shape a picture of these coming times. "We were making the future," he said, "and hardly any of us troubled to think what future we were making. And here it is!"

"What have they got to, what has been done? How do I come into the midst of it all?" The vastness of street and house he was prepared for, the multitudes of people. But conflicts in the city ways! And the systematised sensuality of a class of rich men!

He thought of Bellamy, the hero of whose Socialistic Utopia had so oddly anticipated this actual experience. But here was no Utopia, no Socialistic state. He had already seen enough to realise that the ancient antithesis of luxury, waste and sensuality on the one hand and abject poverty on the other, still prevailed. He knew enough of the essential factors of life to understand that correlation. And not only were the buildings of the city gigantic and the crowds in the street gigantic, but the voices he had heard in the ways, the uneasiness of Howard, the very atmosphere spoke of gigantic discontent. What country was he in? Still England it seemed, and yet strangely "un-English." His mind glanced at the rest of the world, and saw only an enigmatical veil.

He prowled about his apartment, examining everything as a caged animal might do. He felt very tired, felt that feverish exhaustion that does not admit of rest. He listened for long spaces under the ventilator to catch some distant echo of the tumults he felt must be proceeding in the city.

He began to talk to himself. "Two hundred and three years!" he said to himself over and over again, laughing stupidly. "Then I am two hundred and thirty-three years old! The oldest inhabitant. Surely they haven't reversed the tendency of our time and gone back to the rule of the oldest. My claims are indisputable. Mumble, mumble. I remember the Bulgarian atrocities as though it was yesterday. 'Tis a great age! Ha ha!" He was surprised at first to hear himself laughing, and then laughed again deliberately and louder. Then he realised that he was behaving foolishly. "Steady," he said. "Steady!"

His pacing became more regular. "This new world," he said. "I don't understand it. _Why?_... But it is all _why!_"

"I suppose they can fly and do all sorts of things Let me try and remember just how it began."

He was surprised at first to find how vague the memories of his first thirty years had become. He remembered fragments, for the most part trivial moments, things of no great importance that he had observed. His boyhood seemed the most accessible at first, he recalled school books and certain lessons in mensuration. Then he revived the more salient features of his life, memories of the wife long since dead, her magic influence now gone beyond corruption, of his rivals and friends and betrayers, of the swift decision of this issue and that, and then of his, last years of misery, of fluctuating resolves, and at last of his strenuous studies. In a little while he perceived he had it all again; dim perhaps, like metal long laid aside, but in no way defective or injured, capable of re-polishing. And the hue of it was a deepening misery. Was it worth re-polishing? By a miracle he had been lifted out of a life that had become intolerable.

He reverted to his present condition. He wrestled with the facts in vain. It became an inextricable tangle. He saw the sky through the ventilator pink with dawn. An old persuasion came out of the dark recesses of his memory. "I must sleep," he said. It appeared as a delightful relief from this mental distress and from the growing pain and heaviness of his limbs. He went to the strange little bed, lay down and was presently asleep.

He was destined to become very familiar indeed with these apartments before he left them, for he remained imprisoned for three days. During that time no one, except Howard, entered his prison. The marvel of his fate mingled with and in some way minimised the marvel of his survival. He had awakened to mankind it seemed only to be snatched away into this unaccountable solitude. Howard came regularly with subtly sustaining and nutritive fluids, and light and pleasant foods, quite strange to Graham. He always closed the door carefully as he entered. On matters of detail he was increasingly obliging, but the bearing of Graham on the great issues that were evidently being contested so closely beyond the soundproof walls that enclosed him, he would not elucidate. He evaded, as politely as possible, every question on the position of affairs in the outer world.

And in those three days Graham's incessant thoughts went far and wide. All that he had seen, all this elaborate contrivance to prevent him seeing, worked together in his mind. Almost every possible interpretation of his position he debated—even as it chanced, the right interpretation. Things that presently happened to him, came to him at last credible, by virtue of this seclusion. When at length the moment of his release arrived, it found him prepared.

Howard's bearing went far to deepen Graham's impression of his own strange importance; the door between its opening and closing seemed to admit with him a breath of momentous happening. His enquiries became more definite and searching. Howard retreated through protests and difficulties. The awakening was unforeseen, he repeated; it happened to have fallen in with the trend of a social convulsion.

"To explain it I must tell you the history of a gross and a half of years," protested Howard.

"The thing is this," said Graham. "You are afraid of something I shall do. In some way I am arbitrator—I might be arbitrator."

"It is not that. But you have—I may tell you this much—the automatic increase of your property puts great possibilities of interference in your hands. And in certain other ways you have influence, with your eighteenth century notions."

"Nineteenth century," corrected Graham.

"With your old world notions, anyhow, ignorant as you are of every feature of our State."

"Am I a fool?"

"Certainly not."

"Do I seem to be the sort of man who would act rashly?"

"You were never expected to act at all. No one counted on your awakening. No one dreamt you would ever awake. The Council had surrounded you with antiseptic conditions. As a matter of fact, we thought that you were dead—a mere arrest of decay. And—but it is too complex. We dare not suddenly—while you are still half awake."

"It won't do," said Graham. "Suppose it is as you say—why am I not being crammed night and day with facts and warnings and all the wisdom of the time to fit me for my responsibilities? Am I any wiser now than two days ago, if it is two days, when I awoke?"

Howard pulled his lip.

"I am beginning to feel—every hour I feel more clearly—a sense of complex concealment of which you are the salient point. Is this Council, or committee, or whatever they are, cooking the accounts of my estate? Is that it?"

"That note of suspicion——" said Howard.

"Ugh!" said Graham. "Now, mark my words, it will be ill for those who have put me here. It will be ill. I am alive. Make no doubt of it, I am alive. Every day my pulse is stronger and my mind clearer and more vigorous. No more quiescence. I am a man come back to life. And I want to live——"

"Live!"

Howard's face lit with an idea. He came towards Graham and spoke in an easy confidential tone.

"The Council secludes you here for your good. You are restless. Naturally—an energetic man! You find it dull here. But we are anxious that everything you may desire—every desire—every sort of desire... There may be something. Is there any sort of company?"

He paused meaningly.

"Yes," said Graham thoughtfully. "There is."

"Ah! Now! We have treated you neglectfully."

"The crowds in yonder streets of yours."

"That," said Howard, "I am afraid——. But——"

Graham began pacing the room. Howard stood near the door watching him. The implication of Howard's suggestion was only half evident to Graham Company? Suppose he were to accept the proposal, demand some sort of _company_? Would there be any possibilities of gathering from the conversation of this additional person some vague inkling of the struggle that had broken out so vividly at his waking moment? He meditated again, and the suggestion took colour. He turned on Howard abruptly.

"What do you mean by company?"

Howard raised his eyes and shrugged his shoulders. "Human beings," he said, with a curious smile on his heavy face.

"Our social ideas," he said, "have a certain increased liberality, perhaps, in comparison with your times. If a man wishes to relieve such a tedium as this—by feminine society, for instance. We think it no scandal. We have cleared our minds of formulae. There is in our city a class, a necessary class, no longer despised—discreet——"

Graham stopped dead.

"It would pass the time," said Howard. "It is a thing I should perhaps have thought of before, but, as a matter of fact, so much is happening—"

He indicated the exterior world.

Graham hesitated. For a moment the figure of a possible woman that his imagination suddenly created dominated his mind with an intense attraction. Then he flashed into anger.

"No!" he shouted.

He began striding rapidly up and down the room.

"Everything you say, everything you do, convinces me—of some great issue in which I am concerned. I do not want to pass the time, as you call it. Yes, I know. Desire and indulgence are life in a sense—and Death! Extinction! In my life before I slept I had worked out that pitiful question. I will not begin again. There is a city, a multitude—. And meanwhile I am here like a rabbit in a bag."

His rage surged high. He choked for a moment and began to wave his clenched fists. He gave way to an anger fit, he swore archaic curses. His gestures had the quality of physical threats.

"I do not know who your party may be. I am in the dark, and you keep me in the dark. But I know this, that I am secluded here for no good purpose. For no good purpose. I warn you, I warn you of the consequences. Once I come at my power—"

He realised that to threaten thus might be a danger to himself. He stopped. Howard stood regarding him with a curious expression.

"I take it this is a message to the Council," said Howard.

Graham had a momentary impulse to leap upon the man, fell or stun him. It must have shown upon his face; at any rate Howard's movement was quick. In a second the noiseless door had closed again, and the man from the nineteenth century was alone.

For a moment he stood rigid, with clenched hands half raised. Then he flung them down. "What a fool I have been!" he said, and gave way to his anger again, stamping about the room and shouting curses. For a long time he kept himself in a sort of frenzy, raging at his position, at his own folly, at the knaves who had imprisoned him. He did this because he did not want to look calmly at his position. He clung to his anger—because he was afraid of Fear.

Presently he found himself reasoning with himself This imprisonment was unaccountable, but no doubt the legal forms—new legal forms—of the time permitted it. It must, of course, be legal. These people were two hundred years further on in the march of civilisation than the Victorian generation. It was not likely they would be less—humane. Yet they had cleared their minds of formulae! Was humanity a formula as well as chastity?

His imagination set to work to suggest things that might be done to him. The attempts of his reason to dispose of these suggestions, though for the most part logically valid, were quite unavailing. "Why should anything be done to me?"

"If the worst comes to the worst," he found himself saying at last, "I can give up what they want. But what do they want? And why don't they ask me for it instead of cooping me up?"

He returned to his former preoccupation with the Council's possible intentions. He began to reconsider the details of Howard's behaviour, sinister glances, inexplicable hesitations. Then, for a time, his mind circled about the idea of escaping from these rooms; but whither could he escape into this vast, crowded world? He would be worse off than a Saxon yeoman suddenly dropped into nineteenth century London. And besides, how could anyone escape from these rooms?

"How can it benefit anyone if harm should happen to me?"

He thought of the tumult, the great social trouble of which he was so unaccountably the axis. A text, irrelevant enough and yet curiously insistent, came floating up out of the darkness of his memory. This also a Council had said:

"It is expedient for us that one man should die for the people."

CHAPTER VIII

THE ROOF SPACES

As the fans in the circular aperture of the inner room rotated and permitted glimpses of the night, dim sounds drifted in thereby. And Graham, standing underneath, wrestling darkly with the unknown powers that imprisoned him, and which he had now deliberately challenged, was startled by the sound of a voice.

He peered up and saw in the intervals of the rotation, dark and dim, the face and shoulders of a man regarding him. When a dark hand was extended, the swift fan struck it, swung round and beat on with a little brownish patch on the edge of its thin blade, and something began to fall therefrom upon the floor, dripping silently.

Graham looked down, and there were spots of blood at his feet. He looked up again in a strange excitement. The figure had gone.

He remained motionless—his every sense intent upon the flickering patch of darkness, for outside it was high night. He became aware of some faint, remote, dark specks floating lightly through the outer air. They came down towards him, fitfully, eddyingly, and passed aside out of the uprush from the fan. A gleam of light flickered, the specks flashed white, and then the darkness came again. Warmed and lit as he was, he perceived that it was snowing within a few feet of him.

Graham walked across the room and came back to the ventilator again. He saw the head of a man pass near. There was a sound of whispering. Then a smart blow on some metallic substance, effort, voices, and the vans stopped. A gust of snowflakes whirled into the room, and vanished before they touched the floor. "Don't be afraid," said a voice.

Graham stood under the fan. "Who are you?" he whispered.

For a moment there was nothing but a swaying of the fan, and then the head of a man was thrust cautiously into the opening. His face appeared nearly inverted to Graham; his dark hair was wet with dissolving flakes of snow upon it. His arm went up into the darkness holding something unseen. He had a youthful face and bright eyes, and the veins of his forehead were swollen. He seemed to be exerting himself to maintain his position.

For several seconds neither he nor Graham spoke.

"You were the Sleeper?" said the stranger at last.

"Yes," said Graham. "What do you want with me?"

"I come from Ostrog, Sire."

"Ostrog?"

The man in the ventilator twisted his head round so that his profile was towards Graham. He appeared to be listening. Suddenly there was a hasty exclamation, and the intruder sprang back just in time to escape the sweep of the released fan. And when Graham peered up there was nothing visible but the slowly falling snow.

It was perhaps a quarter of an hour before anything returned to the ventilator. But at last came the same metallic interference again; the fans stopped and the face reappeared. Graham had remained all this time in the same place, alert and tremulously excited.

"Who are you? What do you want?" he said.

"We want to speak to you, Sire," said the intruder.

"We want—I can't hold the thing. We have been trying to find a way to you these three days."

"Is it rescue?" whispered Graham. "Escape?"

"Yes, Sire. If you will."

"You are my party—the party of the Sleeper?"

"Yes, Sire."

"What am I to do?" said Graham.

There was a struggle. The stranger's arm appeared, and his hand was bleeding. His knees came into view over the edge of the funnel. "Stand away from me," he said, and he dropped rather heavily on his hands and one shoulder at Graham's feet. The released ventilator whirled noisily. The stranger rolled over, sprang up nimbly and stood panting, hand to a bruised shoulder, and with his bright eyes on Graham.

"You are indeed the Sleeper," he said. "I saw you asleep. When it was the law that anyone might see you."

"I am the man who was in the trance," said Graham. "They have imprisoned me here. I have been here since I awoke—at least three days."

The intruder seemed about to speak, heard something, glanced swiftly at the door, and suddenly left Graham and ran towards it, shouting quick incoherent words. A bright wedge of steel flashed in his hand, and he began tap, tap, a quick succession of blows upon the hinges. "Mind!" cried a voice. "Oh!" The voice came from above.

Graham glanced up, saw the soles of two feet, ducked, was struck on the shoulder by one of them, and a heavy weight bore him to the earth. He fell on his knees and forward, and the weight went over his head. He knelt up and saw a second man from above seated before him.

"I did not see you, Sire," panted the man. He rose and assisted Graham to arise. "Are you hurt, Sire?" he panted. A succession of heavy blows on the ventilator began, something fell close to Graham's face, and a shivering edge of white metal danced, fell over, and lay flat upon the floor.

"What is this?" cried Graham, confused and looking at the ventilator. "Who are you? What are you going to do? Remember, I understand nothing."

"Stand back," said the stranger, and drew him from under the ventilator as another fragment of metal fell heavily.

"We want you to come, Sire," panted the newcomer, and Graham glancing at his face again, saw a new cut had changed from white to red on his forehead, and a couple of little trickles of blood starting therefrom. "Your people call for you."

"Come where? My people?"

"To the hall about the markets. Your life is in danger here. We have spies. We learned but just in time. The Council has decided—this very day—either to drug or kill you. And everything is ready. The people are drilled, the wind-vane police, the engineers, and half the way-gearers are with us. We have the halls crowded—shouting. The whole city shouts against the Council. We have arms." He wiped the blood with his hand. "Your life here is not worth—" "But why arms?"

"The people have risen to protect you, Sire. What?"

He turned quickly as the man who had first come down made a hissing with his teeth. Graham saw the latter start back, gesticulate to them to conceal themselves, and move as if to hide behind the opening door.

As he did so Howard appeared, a little tray in one hand and his heavy face downcast. He started, looked up, the door slammed behind him, the tray tilted sideways, and the steel wedge struck him behind the ear. He went down like a felled tree, and lay as he fell athwart the floor of the outer room. The man who had struck him bent hastily, studied his face for a moment, rose, and returned to his work at the door.

"Your poison!" said a voice in Graham's ear.

Then abruptly they were in darkness. The innumerable cornice lights had been extinguished. Graham saw the aperture of the ventilator with ghostly snow whirling above it and dark figures moving hastily. Three knelt on the fan. Some dim thing—a ladder was being lowered through the opening, and a hand appeared holding a fitful yellow light.

He had a moment of hesitation. But the manner of these men, their swift alacrity, their words, marched so completely with his own fears of the Council, with his idea and hope of a rescue, that it lasted not a moment. And his people awaited him!

"I do not understand," he said, "I trust. Tell me what to do."

The man with the cut brow gripped Graham's arm.

"Clamber up the ladder," he whispered. "Quick. They will have heard—"

Graham felt for the ladder with extended hands, put his foot on the lower rung, and, turning his head, saw over the shoulder of the nearest man, in the yellow flicker of the light, the first-comer astride over Howard and still working at the door. Graham turned to the ladder again, and was thrust by his conductor and helped up by those above, and then he was standing on something hard and cold and slippery outside the ventilating funnel.

He shivered. He was aware of a great difference in the temperature. Half a dozen men stood about him, and light flakes of snow touched hands and face and melted. For a moment it was dark, then for a flash a ghastly violet white, and then everything was dark again.

He saw he had come out upon the roof of the vast city structure which had replaced the miscellaneous houses, streets and open spaces of Victorian London. The place upon which he stood was level, with huge serpentine cables lying athwart it in every direction. The circular wheels of a number of windmills loomed indistinct and gigantic through the darkness and snowfall, and roared with a varying loudness as the fitful white light smote up from below, touched the snow eddies with a transient glitter, and made an evanescent spectre in the night; and here and there, low down! some vaguely outlined wind-driven mechanism flickered with livid sparks.

All this he appreciated in a fragmentary manner as his rescuers stood about him. Someone threw a thick soft cloak of fur-like texture about him, and fastened it by buckled straps at waist and shoulders. Things were said briefly, decisively. Someone thrust him forward.

Before his mind was yet clear a dark shape gripped his arm. "This way," said this shape, urging him along, and pointed Graham across the flat roof in the direction of a dim semicircular haze of light. Graham obeyed.

"Mind!" said a voice, as Graham stumbled against a cable. "Between them and not across them," said the voice. And, "We must hurry."

"Where are the people?" said Graham. "The people you said awaited me?"

The stranger did not answer. He left Graham's arm as the path grew narrower, and led the way with rapid strides. Graham followed blindly. In a minute he found himself running. "Are the others coming?" he panted, but received no reply. His companion glanced back and ran on. They came to a sort of pathway of open metal-work, transverse to the direction they had come, and they turned aside to follow this. Graham looked back, but the snowstorm had hidden the others.

"Come on!" said his guide. Running now, they drew near a little windmill spinning high in the air. "Stoop," said Graham's guide, and they avoided an endless band running roaring up to the shaft of the vane. "This way!" and they were ankle deep in a gutter full of drifted thawing snow, between two low walls of metal that presently rose waist high. "I will go first," said the guide. Graham drew his cloak about him and followed. Then suddenly came a narrow abyss across which the gutter leapt to the snowy darkness of the further side. Graham peeped over the side once and the gulf was black. For a moment he regretted his flight. He dared not look again, and his brain spun as he waded through the half liquid snow.

Then out of the gutter they clambered and hurried across a wide flat space damp with thawing snow, and for half its extent dimly translucent to lights that went to and fro underneath. He hesitated at this unstable looking substance, but his guide ran on unheeding, and so they came to and clambered up slippery steps to the rim of a great dome of glass. Round this they went. Far below a number of people seemed to be dancing, and music filtered through the dome.... Graham fancied he heard a shouting through the snowstorm, and his guide hurried him on with a new spurt of haste. They clambered panting to a space of huge windmills, one so vast that only the lower edge of its vans came rushing into sight and rushed up again and was lost in the night and the snow. They hurried for a time through the colossal metallic tracery of its supports, and came at last above a place of moving platforms like the place into which Graham had looked from the balcony. They crawled across the sloping transparency that covered this street of platforms, crawling on hands and knees because of the slipperiness of the snowfall.

For the most part the glass was bedewed, and Graham saw only hazy suggestions of the forms below, but near the pitch of the transparent roof the glass was clear, and he found himself looking sheerly down upon it all. For awhile, in spite of the urgency of his guide, he gave way to vertigo and lay spread-eagled on the glass, sick and paralysed. Far below, mere stirring specks and dots, went the people of the unsleeping city in their perpetual daylight, and the moving platforms ran on their incessant journey. Messengers and men on unknown businesses shot along the drooping cables and the frail bridges were crowded with men. It was like peering into a gigantic glass hive, and it lay vertically below him with only a tough glass of unknown thickness to save him from a fall. The street showed warm and lit, and Graham was wet now to the skin with thawing snow, and his feet were numbed with cold. For a space he could not move.

"Come on!" cried his guide, with terror in his voice. "Come on!"

Graham reached the pitch of the roof by an effort.

Over the ridge, following his guide's example, he turned about and slid backward down the opposite slope very swiftly, amid a little avalanche of snow While he was sliding he thought of what would happen if some broken gap should come in his way. At the edge he stumbled to his feet ankle deep in slush thanking heaven for an opaque footing again. His guide was already clambering up a metal screen to a level expanse.

Through the spare snowflakes above this loomed another line of vast windmills, and then suddenly the amorphous tumult of the rotating wheels was pierced with a deafening sound. It was a mechanical shrilling of extraordinary intensity that seemed to come simultaneously from every point of the compass.

"They have missed us already!" cried Graham's guide in an accent of terror, and suddenly, with a blinding flash, the night became day.

Above the driving snow, from the summits of the wind-wheels, appeared vast masts carrying globes of livid light. They receded in illimitable vistas in every direction. As far as his eye could penetrate the snowfall they glared.

"Get on this," cried Graham's conductor, and thrust him forward to a long grating of snowless metal that ran like a band between two slightly sloping expanses of snow. It felt warm to Graham's benurrled feet, and a faint eddy of steam rose from it.

"Come on!" shouted his guide ten yards off, and, without waiting, ran swiftly through the incandescent glare towards the iron supports of the next range of wind-wheels. Graham, recovering from his astonishment, followed as fast, convinced of his imminent capture.

In a score of seconds they were within a tracery of glare and black shadows shot with moving bars beneath the monstrous wheels. Graham's conductor ran on for some time, and suddenly darted sideways and vanished into a black shadow in the corner of the foot of a huge support. In another moment Graham was beside him.

They cowered panting and stared out.

The scene upon which Graham looked was very wild and strange. The snow had now almost ceased; only a belated flake passed now and again across the picture. But the broad stretch of level before them was a ghastly white, broken only by gigantic masses and moving shapes and lengthy strips of impenetrable darkness, vast ungainly Titans of shadow. All about them, huge metallic structures, iron girders, inhumanly vast as it seemed to him, interlaced, and the edges of wind-wheels, scarcely moving in the lull, passed in great shining curves steeper and steeper up into a luminous haze. Wherever the snow-spangled light struck down, beams and girders, and incessant bands running with a halting, indomitable resolution passed upward and downward into the black. And with all that mighty activity, with an omnipresent sense of motive and design, this snow-clad desolation of mechanism seemed void of all human presence save themselves, seemed as trackless and deserted and unfrequented by men as some inaccessible Alpine snowfield.

"They will be chasing us," cried the leader. "We are scarcely halfway there yet. Cold as it is we must hide here for a space—at least until it snows more thickly again."

His teeth chattered in his head.

"Where are the markets?" asked Graham staring out. "Where are all the people?"

The other made no answer.

"Look!" whispered Graham, crouched close, and became very still.

The snow had suddenly become thick again, and sliding with the whirling eddies out of the black pit of the sky came something, vague and large and very swift. It came down in a steep curve and swept round, wide wings extended and a trail of white condensing steam behind it, rose with an easy swiftness and went gliding up the air, swept horizontally forward in a wide curve, and vanished again in the steaming specks of snow. And, through the ribs of its body, Graham saw two little men, very minute and active, searching the snowy areas about him, as it seemed to him, with field glasses. For a second they were clear, then hazy through a thick whirl of snow, then small and distant, and in a minute they were gone.

"Now!" cried his companion. "Come!"

He pulled Graham's sleeve, and incontinently the two were running headlong down the arcade of ironwork beneath the wind-wheels. Graham, running blindly, collided with his leader, who had turned back on him suddenly. He found himself within a dozen yards of a black chasm. It extended as far as he could see right and left. It seemed to cut off their progress in either direction.

"Do as I do," whispered his guide. He lay down and crawled to the edge, thrust his head over and twisted until one leg hung. He seemed to feel for something with his foot, found it, and went sliding over the edge into the gulf. His head reappeared. "It is a ledge," he whispered. "In the dark all the way along. Do as I did."

Graham hesitated, went down upon all fours, crawled to the edge, and peered into a velvety blackness. For a sickly moment he had courage neither to go on nor retreat, then he sat and hung his leg down, felt his guide's hands pulling at him, had a horrible sensation of sliding over the edge into the unfathomable, splashed, and felt himself in a slushy gutter, impenetrably dark.

"This way," whispered the voice, and he began crawling along the gutter through the trickling thaw, pressing himself against the wall. They continued along it for some minutes. He seemed to pass through a hundred stages of misery, to pass minute after minute through a hundred degrees of cold, damp, and exhaustion. In a little while he ceased to feel his hands and feet.

The gutter sloped downwards. He observed that they were now many feet below the edge of the buildings. Rows of spectral white shapes like the ghosts of blind-drawn windows rose above them. They came to the end of a cable fastened above one of these white windows, dimly visible and dropping into impenetrable shadows. Suddenly his hand came against his guide's.

"Still!" whispered the latter very softly.

He looked up with a start and saw the huge wings of the flying machine gliding slowly and noiselessly overhead athwart the broad band of snow-flecked grey-blue sky. In a moment it was hidden again.

"Keep still; they were just turning."

For awhile both were motionless, then Graham's companion stood up, and reaching towards the fastenings of the cable fumbled with some indistinct tackle.

"What is that?" asked Graham.

The only answer was a faint cry. The man crouched motionless. Graham peered and saw his face dimly. He was staring down the long ribbon of sky, and Graham, following his eyes, saw the flying machine small and faint and remote. Then he saw that the wings spread on either side, that it headed towards them, that every moment it grew larger. It was following the edge of the chasm towards them.

The man's movements became convulsive. He thrust two cross bars into Graham's hand. Graham could not see them, he ascertained their form by feeling. They were slung by thin cords to the cable. On the cord were hand grips of some soft elastic substance. "Put the cross between your legs," whispered the guide hysterically, "and grip the holdfasts. Grip tightly, grip!"

Graham did as he was told.

"Jump," said the voice. "In heaven's name, jump!"

For one momentous second Graham could not speak. He was glad afterwards that darkness hid his face. He said nothing. He began to tremble violently. He looked sideways at the swift shadow that swallowed up the sky as it rushed upon him.

"Jump! Jump—in God's name! Or they will have us," cried Graham's guide, and in the violence of his passion thrust him forward.

Graham tottered convulsively, gave a sobbing cry, a cry in spite of himself, and then, as the flying machine swept over them, fell forward into the pit of that darkness, seated on the cross wood and holding the ropes with the clutch of death. Something cracked, something rapped smartly against a wall. He heard the pulley of the cradle hum on its rope. He heard the aeronauts shout. He felt a pair of knees digging into his back.... He was sweeping headlong through the air, falling through the air. All his strength was in his hands. He would have screamed but he had no breath.

He shot into a blinding light that made him grip the tighter. He recognised the great passage with the running ways, the hanging lights and interlacing girders. They rushed upward and by him. He had a momentary impression of a great circular aperture yawning to swallow him up.

He was in the dark again, falling, falling, gripping with aching hands, and behold! a clap of sound, a burst of light, and he was in a brightly lit hall with a roaring multitude of people beneath his feet. The people! His people! A proscenium, a stage rushed up towards him, and his cable swept down to a circular aperture to the right of this. He felt he was travelling slower, and suddenly very much slower. He distinguished shouts of "Saved! The Master. He is safe!" The stage rushed up towards him with rapidly diminishing swiftness. Then—

He heard the man clinging behind him shout as if suddenly terrified, and this shout was echoed by a shout from below. He felt that he was no longer gliding along the cable but falling with it. There was a tumult of yells, screams and cries. He felt something soft against his extended hand, and the impact of a broken fall quivering through his arm...

He wanted to be still and the people were lifting him. He believed afterwards he was carried to the platform and given some drink, but he was never sure. He did not notice what became of his guide. When his mind was clear again he was on his feet; eager hands were assisting him to stand. He was in a big alcove, occupying the position that in his previous experience had been devoted to the lower boxes. If this was indeed a theatre.

A mighty tumult was in his ears, a thunderous roar, the shouting of a countless multitude. "It is the Sleeper! The Sleeper is with us!"

"The Sleeper is with us! The Master—the Owner! The Master is with us. He is safe."

Graham had a surging vision of a great hall crowded with people. He saw no individuals, he was conscious of a froth of pink faces, of waving arms and garments, he felt the occult influence of a vast crowd pouring over him, buoying him up. There were balconies, galleries, great archways giving remoter perspectives, and everywhere people, a vast arena of people, densely packed and cheering. Across the nearer space lay the collapsed cable like a huge snake. It had been cut by the men of the flying machine at its upper end, and had crumpled down into the hall. Men seemed to be hauling this out of the way. But the whole effect was vague, the very buildings throbbed and leapt with the roar of the voices.

He stood unsteadily and looked at those about him. Someone supported him by one arm. "Let me go into a little room," he said, weeping; "a little room," and could say no more. A man in black stepped forward, took his disengaged arm. He was aware of officious men opening a door before him. Someone guided him to a seat. He staggered. He sat down heavily and covered his face with his hands; he was trembling violently, his nervous control was at an end. He was relieved of his cloak, he could not remember how; his purple hose he saw were black with wet. People were running about him, things were happening, but for some time he gave no heed to them.

He had escaped. A myriad of cries told him that. He was safe. These were the people who were on his side. For a space he sobbed for breath, and then he sat still with his face covered. The air was full of the shouting of innumerable men.

CHAPTER IX

THE PEOPLE MARCH

He became aware of someone urging a glass of clear fluid upon his attention, looked up and discovered this was a dark young man in a yellow garment. He took the dose forthwith, and in a moment he was glowing. A tall man in a black robe stood by his shoulder, and pointed to the half open door into the hall. This man was shouting close to his ear and yet what was said was indistinct because of the tremendous uproar from the great theatre. Behind the man was a girl in a silvery grey robe, whom Graham, even in this confusion, perceived to be beautiful. Her dark eyes, full of wonder and curiosity, were fixed on him, her lips trembled apart. A partially opened door gave a glimpse of the crowded hall, and admitted a vast uneven tumult, a hammering, clapping and shouting that died away and began again, and rose to a thunderous pitch, and so continued intermittently all the time that Graham remained in the little room. He watched the lips of the man in black and gathered that he was making some clumsy explanation.

He stared stupidly for some moments at these things and then stood up abruptly; he grasped the arm of this shouting person.

"Tell me!" he cried. "Who am I? Who am I?"

The others came nearer to hear his words. "Who am I?" His eyes searched their faces.

"They have told him nothing!" cried the girl.

"Tell me, tell me!" cried Graham.

"You are the Master of the Earth. You are owner of half the world."

He did not believe he heard aright. He resisted the persuasion. He pretended not to understand, not to hear. He lifted his voice again. "I have been awake three days—a prisoner three days. I judge there is some struggle between a number of people in this city—it is London?"

"Yes," said the younger man.

"And those who meet in the great hall with the white Atlas? How does it concern me? In some way it has to do with me. Why, I don't know. Drugs? It seems to me that while I have slept the world has gone mad. I have gone mad."

"Who are those Councillors under the Atlas? Why should they try to drug me?"

"To keep you insensible," said the man in yellow.

"To prevent your interference."

"But _why?_"

"Because _you_ are the Atlas, Sire," said the man in yellow. "The world is on your shoulders. They rule it in your name."

The sounds from the hall had died into a silence threaded by one monotonous voice. Now suddenly, trampling on these last words, came a deafening tumult, a roaring and thundering, cheer crowded on cheer, voices hoarse and shrill, beating, overlapping, and while it lasted the people in the little room could not hear each other shout.

Graham stood, his intelligence clinging helplessly to the thing he had just heard. "The Council," he repeated blankly, and then snatched at a name that had struck him. "But who is Ostrog?" he said.

"He is the organiser—the organiser of the revolt. Our Leader—in your name."

"In my name?—And you? Why is he not here?"

"He—has deputed us. I am his brother—his half-brother, Lincoln. He wants you to show yourself to these people and then come on to him. That is why he has sent. He is at the wind-vane offices directing. The people are marching."

"In your name," shouted the younger man. "They have ruled, crushed, tyrannised. At last even—"

"In my name! My name! Master?"

The younger man suddenly became audible in a pause of the outer thunder, indignant and vociferous, a high penetrating voice under his red aquiline nose and bushy moustache. "No one expected you to wake. No one expected you to wake. They were cunning. Damned tyrants! But they were taken by surprise. They did not know whether to drug you, hypnotise you, kill you."

Again the hall dominated everything.

"Ostrog is at the wind-vane offices ready—. Even now there is a rumour of fighting beginning."

The man who had called himself Lincoln came close to him. "Ostrog has it planned. Trust him. We have our organisations ready. We shall seize the flying stages—. Even now he may be doing that. Then—"

"This public theatre," bawled the man in yellow, "is only a contingent. We have five myriads of drilled men—"

"We have arms," cried Lincoln. "We have plans. A leader. Their police have gone from the streets and are massed in the—" (inaudible). "It is now or never. The Council is rocking—They cannot trust even their drilled men—"

"Hear the people calling to you!"

Graham's mind was like a night of moon and swift clouds, now dark and hopeless, now clear and ghastly. He was Master of the Earth, he was a man sodden with thawing snow. Of all his fluctuating impressions the dominant ones presented an antagonism; on the one hand was the White Council, powerful, disciplined, few, the White Council from which he had just escaped; and on the other, monstrous crowds, packed masses of indistinguishable people clamouring his name, hailing him Master. The other side had imprisoned him, debated his death. These shouting thousands beyond the little doorway had rescued him. But why these things should be so he could not understand.

The door opened, Lincoln's voice was swept away and drowned, and a rush of people followed on the heels of the tumult. These intruders came towards him and Lincoln gesticulating. The voices without explained their soundless lips. "Show us the Sleeper, show us the Sleeper!" was the burden of the uproar Men were bawling for "Order! Silence!"

Graham glanced towards the open doorway, and saw a tall, oblong picture of the hall beyond, a waving, incessant confusion of crowded, shouting faces, men and women together, waving pale blue garments, extended hands. Many were standing, one man in rags of dark brown, a gaunt figure, stood on the seat and waved a black cloth. He met the wonder and expectation of the girl's eyes. What did these people expect from him. He was dimly aware that the tumult outside had changed its character, was in some way beating, marching. His own mind, too, changed for a space he did not recognise the influence that was transforming him. But a moment that was near to panic passed. He tried to make audible inquiries of what was required of him.

Lincoln was shouting in his ear, but Graham was deafened to that. All the others save the woman gesticulated towards the hall. He perceived what had happened to the uproar. The whole mass of people was chanting together. It was not simply a song, the voices were gathered together and upborne by a torrent of instrumental music, music like the music of an organ, a woven texture of sounds, full of trumpets, full of flaunting banners, full of the march and pageantry of opening war. And the feet of the people were beating time—tramp, tramp.

He was urged towards the door. He obeyed mechanically. The strength of that chant took hold of him, stirred him, emboldened him. The hall opened to him, a vast welter of fluttering colour swaying to the music.

"Wave your arm to them," said Lincoln. "Wave your arm to them."

"This," said a voice on the other side, "he must have this." Arms were about his neck detaining him in the doorway, and a black subtly-folding mantle hung from his shoulders. He threw his arm free of this and followed Lincoln. He perceived the girl in grey close to him, her face lit, her gesture onward. For the instant she became to him, flushed and eager as she was, an embodiment of the song. He emerged in the alcove again. Incontinently the mounting waves of the song broke upon his appearing, and flashed up into a foam of shouting. Guided by Lincoln's hand he marched obliquely across the centre of the stage facing the people.

The hall was a vast and intricate space—galleries, balconies, broad spaces of amphitheatral steps, and great archways. Far away, high up, seemed the mouth of a huge passage full of struggling humanity. The whole multitude was swaying in congested masses. Individual figures sprang out of the tumult, impressed him momentarily, and lost definition again. Close to the platform swayed a beautiful fair woman, carried by three men, her hair across her face and brandishing a green staff. Next this group an old careworn man in blue canvas maintained his place in the crush with difficulty, and behind shouted a hairless face, a great cavity of toothless mouth. A voice called that enigmatical word "Ostrog." All his impressions were vague save the massive emotion of that trampling song. The multitude were beating time with their feet—marking time, tramp, tramp, tramp, tramp. The green weapons waved, flashed and slanted. Then he saw those nearest to him on a level space before the stage were marching in front of him, passing towards a great archway, shouting "To the Council!" Tramp, tramp, tramp, tramp. He raised his arm, and the roaring was redoubled. He remembered he had to shout "March!" His mouth shaped inaudible heroic words. He waved his arm again and pointed to the archway, shouting "Onward!" They were no longer marking time, they were marching; tramp, tramp, tramp, tramp. In that host were bearded men, old men, youths, fluttering robed bare-armed women, girls. Men and women of the new age! Rich robes, grey rags fluttered together in the whirl of their movement amidst the dominant blue. A monstrous black banner jerked its way to the right. He perceived a blue-clad negro, a shrivelled woman in yellow, then a group of tall fair-haired, white-faced, blue-clad men pushed theatrically past him. He noted two Chinamen. A tall, sallow, dark-haired, shining-eyed youth, white clad from top to toe, clambered up towards the platform shouting loyally, and sprang down again and receded, looking backward. Heads, shoulders, hands clutching weapons, all were swinging with those marching cadences.

Faces came out of the confusion to him as he stood there, eyes met his and passed and vanished. Men gesticulated to him, shouted inaudible personal things. Most of the faces were flushed, but many were ghastly white. And disease was there, and many a hand that waved to him was gaunt and lean. Men and women of the new age! Strange and incredible meeting! As the broad stream passed before him to the right, tributary gangways from the remote uplands of the hall thrust downward in an incessant replacement of people; tramp, tramp, tramp, tramp. The unison of the song was enriched and complicated by the massive echoes of arches and passages. Men and women mingled in the ranks; tramp, tramp, tramp, tramp. The whole world seemed marching. Tramp, tramp, tramp, tramp; his brain was tramping. The garments waved onward, the faces poured by more abundantly.

Tramp, tramp, tramp, tramp; at Lincoln's pressure he turned towards the archway, walking unconsciously in that rhythm, scarcely noticing his movement for the melody and stir of it. The multitude, the gesture and song, all moved in that direction, the flow of people smote downward until the upturned faces were below the level of his feet. He was aware of a path before him, of a suite about him, of guards and dignities, and Lincoln on his right hand. Attendants intervened, and ever and again blotted out the sight of the multitude to the left. Before him went the backs of the guards in black—three and three and three. He was marched along a little railed way, and crossed above the archway, with the torrent dipping to flow beneath, and shouting up to him. He did not know whither he went; he did not want to know. He glanced back across a flaming spaciousness of hall. Tramp, tramp, tramp, tramp.

CHAPTER X
THE BATTLE OF THE DARKNESS

He was no longer in the hall. He was marching along a gallery overhanging one of the great streets of the moving platforms that traversed the city. Before him and behind him tramped his guards. The whole concave of the moving ways below was a congested mass of people marching, tramping to the left, shouting, waving hands and arms, pouring along a huge vista, shouting as they came into view, shouting as they passed, shouting as they receded, until the globes of electric light receding in perspective dropped down it seemed and hid the swarming bare heads. Tramp, tramp, tramp, tramp.

The song roared up to Graham now, no longer upborne by music, but coarse and noisy, and the beating of the marching feet, tramp, tramp, tramp, tramp, interwove with a thunderous irregularity of footsteps from the undisciplined rabble that poured along the higher ways.

Abruptly he noted a contrast. The buildings on the opposite side of the way seemed deserted, the cables and bridges that laced across the aisle were empty and shadowy. It came into Graham's mind that these also should have swarmed with people.

He felt a curious emotion—throbbing—very fast! He stopped again. The guards before him marched on; those about him stopped as he did.

He saw the direction of their faces. The throbbing had something to do with the lights. He too looked up.

At first it seemed to him a thing that affected the lights simply, an isolated phenomenon, having no bearing on the things below. Each huge globe of blinding whiteness was as it were clutched, compressed in a systole that was followed by a transitory diastole, and again a systole like a tightening grip, darkness, light, darkness, in rapid alternation.

Graham became aware that this strange behaviour of the lights had to do with the people below. The appearance of the houses and ways, the appearance of the packed masses changed, became a confusion of vivid lights and leaping shadows. He saw a multitude of shadows had sprung into aggressive existence, seemed rushing up, broadening, widening, growing with steady swiftness—to leap suddenly back and return reinforced. The song and the tramping had ceased. The unanimous march, he discovered, was arrested, there were eddies, a flow sideways, shouts of "The lights!" Voices were crying together one thing. "The lights!" cried these voices. "The lights!" He looked down. In this dancing death of the lights the area of the street had suddenly become a monstrous struggle. The huge white globes became purple-white, purple with a reddish glow, flickered, flickered faster and faster, fluttered between light and extinction, ceased to flicker and became mere fading specks of glowing red in a vast obscurity. In ten seconds the extinction was accomplished, and there was only this roaring darkness, a black monstrosity that had suddenly swallowed up those glittering myriads of men.

He felt invisible forms about him; his arms were gripped. Something rapped sharply against his shin. A voice bawled in his ear, "It is all right— all right."

Graham shook off the paralysis of his first astonishment. He struck his forehead against Lincoln's and bawled, "What is this darkness?"

"The Council has cut the currents that light the city. We must wait— stop. The people will go on. They will—"

His voice was drowned. Voices were shouting, "Save the Sleeper. Take care of the Sleeper." A guard stumbled against Graham and hurt his hand by an inadvertent blow of his weapon. A wild tumult tossed and whirled about him, growing, as it seemed, louder, denser, more furious each moment. Fragments of recognisable sounds drove towards him, were whirled away from him as his mind reached out to grasp them. Voices seemed to be shouting conflicting orders, other voices answered. There were suddenly a succession of piercing screams close beneath them.

A voice bawled in his ear, "The red police," and receded forthwith beyond his questions.

A crackling sound grew to distinctness, and there with a leaping of faint flashes along the edge of the further ways. By their light Graham saw the heads and bodies of a number of men, armed with weapons like those of his guards, leap into an instant's dim visibility. The whole area began to crackle, to flash with little instantaneous streaks of light, and abruptly the darkness rolled back like a curtain.

A glare of light dazzled his eyes, a vast seething expanse of struggling men confused his mind. A shout, a burst of cheering, came across the ways. He looked up to see the source of the light. A man hung far overhead from the upper part of a cable, holding by a rope the blinding star that had driven the darkness back. He wore a red uniform.

Graham's eyes fell to the ways again. A wedge of red a little way along the vista caught his eye. He saw it was a dense mass of red-clad men jammed the higher further way, their backs against the pitiless cliff of building, and surrounded by a dense crowd of antagonists. They were fighting. Weapons flashed and rose and fell, heads vanished at the edge of the contest, and other heads replaced them, the little flashes from the green weapons became little jets of smoky grey while the light lasted.

Abruptly the flare was extinguished and the ways were an inky darkness once more, a tumultuous mystery.

He felt something thrusting against him. He was being pushed along the gallery. Someone was shouting—it might be at him. He was too confused to hear. He was thrust against the wall, and a number of people blundered past him. It seemed to him that his guards were struggling with one another.

Suddenly the cable-hung star-holder appeared again, and the whole scene was white and dazzling. The band of red-coats seemed broader and nearer; its apex was half-way down the ways towards the central aisle. And raising his eyes Graham saw that a number of these men had also appeared now in the darkened lower galleries of the opposite building, and were firing over the heads of their fellows below at the boiling confusion of people on the lower ways. The meaning of these things dawned upon him. The march of the people had come upon an ambush at the very outset. Thrown into confusion by the extinction of the lights they were now being attacked by the red police. Then he became aware that he was standing alone, that his guards and Lincoln were along the gallery in the direction along which he had come before the darkness fell. He saw they were gesticulating to him wildly, running back towards him. A great shouting came from across the ways. Then it seemed as though the whole face of the darkened building opposite was lined and speckled with red-clad men. And they were pointing over to him and shouting. "The Sleeper! Save the Sleeper!" shouted a multitude of throats.

Something struck the wall above his head. He looked up at the impact and saw a star-shaped splash of silvery metal. He saw Lincoln near him. Felt his arm gripped. Then, pat, pat; he had been missed twice.

For a moment he did not understand this. The street was hidden, everything was hidden, as he looked. The second flare had burned out.

Lincoln had gripped Graham by the arm, was lugging him along the gallery. "Before the next light!" he cried. His haste was contagious. Graham's instinct of self-preservation overcame the paralysis of his incredulous astonishment. He became for a time the blind creature of the fear of death. He ran, stumbling because of the uncertainty of the darkness, blundered into his guards as they turned to run with him. Haste was his one desire, to escape this perilous gallery upon which he was exposed. A third glare came close on its predecessors. With it came a great shouting across the ways, an answering tumult from the ways. The red-coats below, he saw, had now almost gained the central passage. Their countless faces turned towards him, and they shouted. The white facade opposite was densely stippled with red. All these wonderful things concerned him, turned upon him as a pivot. These were the guards of the Council attempting to recapture him.

Lucky it was for him that these shots were the first fired in anger for a hundred and fifty years. He heard bullets whacking over his head, felt a splash of molten metal sting his ear, and perceived without looking that the whole opposite facade, an unmasked ambuscade of red police, was crowded and bawling and firing at him.

Down went one of his guards before him, and Graham, unable to stop, leapt the writhing body.

In another second he had plunged, unhurt, into a black passage, and incontinently someone, coming, it may be, in a transverse direction, blundered violently into him. He was hurling down a staircase in absolute darkness. He reeled, and was struck again, and came against a wall with his hands. He was crushed by a weight of struggling bodies, whirled round, and thrust to the right. A vast pressure pinned him. He could not breathe, his ribs seemed cracking. He felt a momentary relaxation, and then the whole mass of people moving together, bore him back towards the great theatre from which he had so recently come.

There were moments when his feet did not touch the ground. Then he was staggering and shoving. He heard shouts of "They are coming!" and a muffled cry close to him. His foot blundered against something soft, he heard a hoarse scream under foot. He heard shouts of "The Sleeper!" but he was too confused to speak. He heard the green weapons crackling. For a space he lost his individual will, became an atom in a panic, blind, unthinking, mechanical. He thrust and pressed back and writhed in the pressure, kicked presently against a step, and found himself ascending a slope. And abruptly the faces all about him leapt out of the black, visible, ghastly-white and astonished, terrified, perspiring, in a livid glare. One face, a young man's, was very near to him, not twenty inches away. At the time it was but a passing incident of no emotional value, but afterwards it came back to him in his dreams. For this young man, wedged upright in the crowd for a time, had been shot and was already dead.

A fourth white star must have been lit by the man on the cable. Its light came glaring in through vast windows and arches and showed Graham that he was now one of a dense mass of flying black figures pressed back across the lower area of the great theatre. This time the picture was livid and fragmentary slashed and barred with black shadows. He saw that quite near to him the red guards were fighting their way through the people. He could not tell whether they saw him. He looked for Lincoln and his guards. He saw Lincoln near the stage of the theatre surrounded in a crowd of black-badged revolutionaries, lifted up and staring to and fro as if seeking him. Graham perceived that he himself was near the opposite edge of the crowd, that behind him, separated by a barrier, sloped the now vacant seats of the theatre. A sudden idea came to him, and he began fighting his way towards the barrier. As he reached it the glare came to an end.

In a moment he had thrown off the great cloak that not only impeded his movements but made him conspicuous, and had slipped it from his shoulders. He heard someone trip in its folds. In another he was scaling the barrier and had dropped into the blackness on the further side. Then feeling his way he came to the lower end of an ascending gangway. In the darkness the sound of firing ceased and the roar of feet and voices lulled. Then suddenly he came to an unexpected step and tripped and fell. As he did so pools and islands amidst the darkness about him leapt to vivid light again, the uproar surged louder and the glare of the fifth white star shone through the vast fenestrations of the theatre walls.

He rolled over among some seats, heard a shouting and the whirring rattle of weapons, struggled up and was knocked back again, perceived that a number of black-badged men were all about him firing at the rebels below, leaping from seat to seat, crouching among the seats to reload. Instinctively he crouched amidst the seats, as stray shots ripped the pneumatic cushions and cut bright slashes on their soft metal frames. Instinctively he marked the direction of the gangways, the most plausible way of escape for him so soon as the veil of darkness fell again.

A young man in faded blue garments came vaulting over the seats. "Hullo!" he said, with his flying feet within six inches of the crouching Sleeper's face.

He stared without any sign of recognition, turned to fire, fired, and, shouting, "To hell with the Council!" was about to fire again. Then it seemed to Graham that the half of this man's neck had vanished. A drop of moisture fell on Graham's cheek. The green weapon stopped half raised. For a moment the man stood still with his face suddenly expressionless, then he began to slant forward. His knees bent. Man and darkness fell together. At the sound of his fall Graham rose up and ran for his life until a step down to the gangway tripped him. He scrambled to his feet, turned up the gangway and ran on.

When the sixth star glared he was already close to the yawning throat of a passage. He ran on the swifter for the light, entered the passage and turned a corner into absolute night again. He was knocked sideways, rolled over, and recovered his feet. He found himself one of a crowd of invisible fugitives pressing in one direction. His one thought now was their thought also; to escape out of this fighting. He thrust and struck, staggered, ran, was wedged tightly, lost ground and then was clear again.

For some minutes he was running through the darkness along a winding passage, and then he crossed some wide and open space, passed down a long incline, and came at last down a flight of steps to a level place. Many people were shouting, "They are coming! The guards are coming. They are firing. Get out of the fighting. The guards are firing. It will be safe in Seventh Way. Along here to Seventh Way!" There were women and children in the crowd as well as men. Men called names to him. The crowd converged on an archway, passed through a short throat and emerged on a wider space again, lit dimly. The black figures about him spread out and ran up what seemed in the twilight to be a gigantic series of steps. He followed. The people dispersed to the right and left.... He perceived that he was no longer in a crowd. He stopped near the highest step. Before him, on that level, were groups of seats and a little kiosk. He went up to this and, stopping in the shadow of its eaves, looked about him panting.

Everything was vague and gray, but he recognised that these great steps were a series of platforms of the "ways," now motionless again. The platform slanted up on either side, and the tall buildings rose beyond, vast dim ghosts, their inscriptions and advertisements indistinctly seen, and up through the girders and cables was a faint interrupted ribbon of pallid sky. A number of people hurried by. From their shouts and voices, it seemed they were hurrying to join the fighting. Other less noisy figures flitted timidly among the shadows.

From very far away down the street he could hear the sound of a struggle. But it was evident to him that this was not the street into which the theatre opened. That former fight, it seemed, had suddenly dropped out of sound and hearing. And—grotesque thought!—they were fighting for him!

For a space he was like a man who pauses in the reading of a vivid book, and suddenly doubts what he has been taking unquestioningly. At that time he had little mind for details; the whole effect was a huge astonishment. Oddly enough, while the flight from the Council prison, the great crowd in the hall, and the attack of the red police upon the swarming people were clearly present in his mind, it cost him an effort to piece in his awakening and to revive the meditative interval of the Silent Rooms. At first his memory leapt these things and took him back to the cascade at Pentargen quivering in the wind, and all the sombre splendours of the sunlit Cornish coast. The contrast touched everything with unreality. And then the gap filled, and he began to comprehend his position.

It was no longer absolutely a riddle, as it had been in the Silent Rooms. At least he had the strange, bare outline now. He was in some way the owner of half the world, and great political parties were fighting to possess him. On the one hand was the White Council, with its red police, set resolutely, it seemed, on the usurpation of his property and perhaps his murder; on the other, the revolution that had liberated him, with this unseen "Ostrog" as its leader. And the whole of this gigantic city was convulsed by their struggle. Frantic development of his world! "I do not understand," he cried. "I do not understand!"

He had slipped out between the contending parties into this liberty of the twilight. What would happen next? What was happening? He figured the redclad men as busily hunting him, driving the blackbadged revolutionists before them.

At any rate chance had given him a breathing space. He could lurk unchallenged by the passers-by, and watch the course of things. His eye followed up the intricate dim immensity of the twilight buildings, and it came to him as a thing infinitely wonderful, that above there the sun was rising, and the world was lit and glowing with the old familiar light of day. In a little while he had recovered his breath. His clothing had already dried upon him from the snow.

He wandered for miles along these twilight ways, speaking to no one, accosted by no one—a dark figure among dark figures—the coveted man out of the past, the inestimable unintentional owner of half the world. Wherever there were lights or dense crowds, or exceptional excitement he was afraid of recognition, and watched and turned back or went up and down by the middle stairways, into some transverse system of ways at a lower or higher level. And though he came on no more fighting, the whole city stirred with battle. Once he had to run to avoid a marching multitude of men that swept the street. Everyone abroad seemed involved. For the most part they were men, and they carried what he judged were weapons. It seemed as though the struggle was concentrated mainly in the quarter of the city from which he came. Ever and again a distant roaring, the remote suggestion of that conflict, reached his ears. Then his caution and his curiosity struggled together. But his caution prevailed, and he continued wandering away from the fighting—so far as he could judge. He went unmolested, unsuspected through the dark. After a time he ceased to hear even a remote echo of the battle, fewer and fewer people passed him, until at last the Titanic streets became deserted. The frontages of the buildings grew plain and harsh; he seemed to have come to a district of vacant warehouses. Solitude crept upon him—his pace slackened.

He became aware of a growing fatigue. At times he would turn aside and seat himself on one of the numerous seats of the upper ways. But a feverish restlessness, the knowledge of his vital implication in his struggle, would not let him rest in any place for long. Was the struggle on his behalf alone?

And then in a desolate place came the shock of an earthquake—a roaring and thundering—a mighty wind of cold air pouring through the city, the smash of glass, the slip and thud of falling masonry—a series of gigantic concussions. A mass of glass and ironwork fell from the remote roofs into the middle gallery, not a hundred yards away from him, and in the distance were shouts and running. He, too, was startled to an aimless activity, and ran first one way and then as aimlessly back.

A man came running towards him. His self-control returned. "What have they blown up?" asked the man breathlessly. "That was an explosion," and before Graham could speak he had hurried on.

The great buildings rose dimly, veiled by a perplexing twilight, albeit the rivulet of sky above was now bright with day. He noted many strange features, understanding none at the time; he even spelt out many of the inscriptions in Phonetic lettering. But what profits it to decipher a confusion of odd-looking letters resolving itself, after painful strain of eye and mind, into "Here is Eadhamite," or, "Labour Bureau—Little Side?" Grotesque thought, that in all probability some or all of these cliff-like houses were his!

The perversity of his experience came to him vividly. In actual fact he had made such a leap in time as romancers have imagined again and again. And that fact realised, he had been prepared, his mind had, as it were, seated itself for a spectacle. And no spectacle, but a great vague danger, unsympathetic shadows and veils of darkness. Somewhere through the labyrinthine obscurity his death sought him. Would he, after all, be killed before he saw? It might be that even at the next shadowy corner his destruction ambushed. A great desire to see, a great longing to know, arose in him.

He became fearful of corners. It seemed to him that there was safety in concealment. Where could he hide to be inconspicuous when the lights returned? At last he sat down upon a seat in a recess on one of the higher ways, conceiving he was alone there.

He squeezed his knuckles into his weary eyes. Suppose when he looked again he found the dark through of parallel ways and that intolerable altitude of edifice, gone? Suppose he were to discover the whole story of these last few days, the awakening, the shouting multitudes, the darkness and the fighting, a phantasmagoria, a new and more vivid sort of dream. It must be a dream; it was so inconsecutive, so reasonless. Why were the people fighting for him? Why should this saner world regard him as Owner and Master?

So he thought, sitting blinded, and then he looked again, half hoping in spite of his ears to see some familiar aspect of the life of the nineteenth century, to see, perhaps, the little harbour of Boscastle about him, the cliffs of Pentargen, or the bedroom of his home. But fact takes no heed of human hopes. A squad of men with a black banner tramped athwart the nearer shadows, intent on conflict, and beyond rose that giddy wall of frontage, vast and dark, with the dim incomprehensible lettering showing faintly on its face.

"It is no dream," he said, "no dream." And he bowed his face upon his hands.

CHAPTER XI
THE OLD MAN WHO KNEW EVERYTHING

He was startled by a cough close at hand.

He turned sharply, and peering, saw a small, hunched-up figure sitting a couple of yards off in the shadow of the enclosure.

"Have ye any news?" asked the high-pitched wheezy voice of a very old man.

Graham hesitated. "None," he said.

"I stay here till the lights come again," said the old man. "These blue scoundrels are everywhere—everywhere."

Graham's answer was inarticulate assent. He tried to see the old man but the darkness hid his face. He wanted very much to respond, to talk, but he did not know how to begin.

"Dark and damnable," said the old man suddenly. "Dark and damnable. Turned out of my room among all these dangers."

"That's hard," ventured Graham. "That's hard on you."

"Darkness. An old man lost in the darkness. And all the world gone mad. War and fighting. The police beaten and rogues abroad. Why don't they bring some negroes to protect us?... No more dark passages for me. I fell over a dead man."

"You're safer with company," said the old man, "if it's company of the right sort," and peered frankly. He rose suddenly and came towards Graham.

Apparently the scrutiny was satisfactory. The old man sat down as if relieved to be no longer alone. "Eh!" he said, "but this is a terrible time! War and fighting, and the dead lying there—men, strong men, dying in the dark. Sons! I have three sons. God knows where they are tonight."

The voice ceased. Then repeated quavering: "God knows where they are tonight."

Graham stood revolving a question that should not betray his ignorance. Again the old man's voice ended the pause.

"This Ostrog will win," he said. "He will win. And what the world will be like under him no one can tell. My sons are under the wind-vanes, all three. One of my daughters-in-law was his mistress for a while. His mistress! We're not common people. Though they've sent me to wander tonight and take my chance.... I knew what was going on. Before most people. But this darkness! And to fall over a dead body suddenly in the dark!"

His wheezy breathing could be heard.

"Ostrog!" said Graham.

"The greatest Boss the world has ever seen," said the voice.

Graham ransacked his mind. "The Council has few friends among the people," he hazarded.

"Few friends. And poor ones at that. They've had their time. Eh! They should have kept to the clever ones. But twice they held election. And Ostrog. And now it has burst out and nothing can stay it, nothing can stay it. Twice they rejected Ostrog—Ostrog the Boss. I heard of his rages at the time—he was terrible. Heaven save them! For nothing on earth can now, he has raised the Labour Companies upon them. No one else would have dared. All the blue canvas armed and marching! He will go through with it. He will go through."

He was silent for a little while. "This Sleeper," he said, and stopped.

"Yes," said Graham. "Well?"

The senile voice sank to a confidential whisper, the dim, pale face came close. "The real Sleeper—"

"Yes," said Graham.

"Died years ago."

"What?" said Graham, sharply.

"Years ago. Died. Years ago."

"You don't say so!" said Graham.

"I do. I do say so. He died. This Sleeper who's woke up—they changed in the night. A poor, drugged insensible creature. But I mustn't tell all I know. I mustn't tell all I know."

For a little while he muttered inaudibly. His secret was too much for him. "I don't know the ones that put him to sleep—that was before my time—but I know the man who injected the stimulants and woke him again. It was ten to one—wake or kill. Wake or kill. Ostrog's way."

Graham was so astonished at these things that he had to interrupt, to make the old man repeat his words, to re-question vaguely, before he was sure of the meaning and folly of what he heard. And his awakening had not been natural! Was that an old man's senile superstition, too, or had it any truth in it? Feeling in the dark corners of his memory, he presently came on something that might conceivably be an impression of some such stimulating effect. It dawned upon him that he had happened upon a lucky encounter, that at last he might learn something of the new age. The old man wheezed a while and spat, and then the piping, reminiscent voice resumed:

"The first time they rejected him. I've followed it all."

"Rejected whom?" said Graham. "The Sleeper?"

"Sleeper? No. Ostrog. He was terrible—terrible! And he was promised then, promised certainly the next time. Fools they were—not to be more afraid of him. Now all the city's his millstone, and such as we dust ground upon it. Dust ground upon it. Until he set to work—the workers cut each other's throats, and murdered a Chinaman or a Labour policeman at times, and left the rest of us in peace. Dead bodies! Robbing! Darkness! Such a thing hasn't been this gross of years. Eh!—but 'tis ill on small folks when the great fall out! It's ill."

"Did you say—there had not been what?—for a gross of years?"

"Eh?" said the old man.

The old man said something about clipping his words, and made him repeat this a third time. "Fighting and slaying, and weapons in hand, and fools bawling freedom and the like," said the old man. "Not in all my life has there been that. These are like the old days—for sure—when the Paris people broke out—three gross of years ago. That's what I mean hasn't been. But it's the world's way. It had to come back. I know. I know. This five years Ostrog has been working, and there has been trouble and trouble, and hunger and threats and high talk and arms. Blue canvas and murmurs. No one safe. Everything sliding and slipping. And now here we are! Revolt and fighting, and the Council come to its end."

"You are rather well-informed on these things," said Graham.

"I know what I hear. It isn't all Babble Machine with me."

"No," said Graham, wondering what Babble Machine might be. "And you are certain this Ostrog—you are certain Ostrog organised this rebellion and arranged for the waking of the Sleeper? Just to assert himself—because he was not elected to the Council?

"Everyone knows that, I should think," said the old man. "Except—just fools. He meant to be master somehow. In the Council or not. Everyone who knows anything knows that. And here we are with dead bodies lying in the dark! Why, where have you been if you haven't heard all about the trouble between Ostrog and the Verneys? And what do you think the troubles are about? The Sleeper? Eh? You think the Sleeper's real and woke of his own accord—eh?"

"I'm a dull man, older than I look, and forgetful," said Graham. "Lots of things that have happened—especially of late years—. If I was the Sleeper, to tell you the truth, I couldn't know less about them."

"Eh!" said the voice. "Old, are you? You don't sound so very old! But its not everyone keeps his memory to my time of life—truly. But these notorious things! But you're not so old as me—not nearly so old as me. Well! I ought not to judge other men by myself, perhaps. I'm young—for so old a man. Maybe you're old for so young."

"That's it," said Graham. "And I've a queer history. I know very little. And history! Practically I know no history. The Sleeper and Julius Caesar are all the same to me. It's interesting to hear you talk of these things."

"I know a few things," said the old man. "I know a thing or two. But—. Hark!"

The two men became silent, listening. There was heavy thud, a concussion that made their seat shiver. The passers-by stopped, shouted to one another. The old man was full of questions; he shouted to a man who passed near. Graham, emboldened by his example, got up and accosted others. None knew what had happened.

He returned to the seat and found the old man muttering vague interrogations in an undertone. For a while they said nothing to one another.

The sense of this gigantic struggle, so near and yet so remote oppressed Graham's imagination. Was this old man right, was the report of the people right, and were the revolutionaries winning? Or were they all in error, and were the red guards driving all before them? At any time the flood of warfare might pour into this silent quarter of the city and seize upon him again. It behooved him to learn all he could while there was time. He turned suddenly to the old man with a question and left it unsaid. But his motion moved the old man to speech again.

"Eh! but how things work together!" said the old man. "This Sleeper that all the fools put their trust in! I've the whole history of it—I was always a good one for histories. When I was a boy—I'm that old—I used to read printed books. You'd hardly think it. Likely you've seen none—they rot and dust so—and the Sanitary Company burns them to make ashlarite. But they were convenient in their dirty way. Oh I learnt a lot. These new-fangled Babble Machines—they don't seem new-fangled to you, eh?— they're easy to hear, easy to forget. But I've traced all the Sleeper business from the first."

"You will scarcely believe it," said Graham slowly, "I'm so ignorant— I've been so preoccupied in my own little affairs, my circumstances have been so odd—I know nothing of this Sleeper's history. Who was he?"

"Eh!" said the old man. "I know. I know. He was a poor nobody, and set on a playful woman, poor soul! And he fell into a trance. There's the old things they had, those brown things—silver photographs—still showing him as he lay, a gross and a half years ago—a gross and a half of years."

"Set on a playful woman, poor soul," said Graham softly to himself, and then aloud, "Yes—well! go on."

"You must know he had a cousin named Warming a solitary man without children, who made a big fortune speculating in roads—the first Eadhamite roads. But surely you've heard? No? Why? He bought all the patent rights and made a big company. In those days there were grosses of grosses of separate businesses and business companies. Grosses of grosses! His roads killed the railroads—the old things—in two dozen years; he bought up and Eadhamited the tracks. And because he didn't want to break up his great property or let in shareholders, he left it all to the Sleeper, and put it under a Board of Trustees that he had picked and trained. He knew then the Sleeper wouldn't wake, that he would go on sleeping, sleeping till he died. He knew that quite well! And plump! a man in the United States, who had lost two sons in a boat accident, followed that up with another great bequest. His trustees found themselves with a dozen myriads of lions'-worth or more of property at the very beginning."

"What was his name?"

"Graham."

"No, I mean—that American's."

"Isbister."

"Isbister!" cried Graham. "Why, I don't even know the name."

"Of course not," said the old man. "Of course not. People don't learn much in the schools nowadays. But I know all about him. He was a rich American who went from England, and he left the Sleeper even more than Warming. How he made it? That I don't know. Something about pictures by machinery. But he made it and left it, and so the Council had its start. It was just a council of trustees at first."

"And how did it grow?"

"Eh!—but you're not up to things. Money attracts money—and twelve brains are better than one. They played it cleverly. They worked politics with money, and kept on adding to the money by working currency and tariffs. They grew—they grew. And for years the twelve trustees hid the growing of the Sleeper's estate, under double names and company titles and all that. The Council spread by title deed, mortgage, share, every political party, every newspaper, they bought. If you listen to the old stories you will see the Council growing and growing. Billions and billions of lions at last—the Sleeper's estate. And all growing out of a whim—out of this Warming's will, and an accident to Isbister's sons.

"Men are strange," said the old man. "The strange, thing to me is how the Council worked together so long. As many as twelve. But they worked in cliques from the first. And they've slipped back. In my young days speaking of the Council was like an ignorant man speaking of God.

We didn't think they could do wrong. We didn't know of their women and all that! Or else I've got wiser.

"Men are strange," said the old man. "Here are you, young and ignorant, and me—sevendy years old, and I might reasonably be forgetting—explaining it all to you short and clear.

"Sevendy," he said, "sevendy, and I hear and see—hear better than I see. And reason clearly, and keep myself up to all the happenings of things. Sevendy!

"Life is strange. I was twaindy before Ostrog was a baby. I remember him long before he'd pushed his way to the head of the Wind Vanes Control. I've seen many changes. Eh! I've worn the blue. And at last I've come to see this crush and darkness and tumult and dead men carried by in heaps on the ways. And all his doing! All his doing!"

His voice died away in scarcely articulate praises of Ostrog.

Graham thought. "Let me see," he said, "if I have it right."

He extended a hand and ticked off points upon his fingers. "The Sleeper has been asleep—"

"Changed," said the old man.

"Perhaps. And meanwhile the Sleeper's property grew in the hands of Twelve Trustees, until it swallowed up nearly all the great ownership of the world. The Twelve Trustees—by virtue of this property have become virtually masters of the world. Because they are the paying power—just as the old English Parliament used to be—"

"Eh!" said the old man. "That's so—that's a good comparison. You're not so—"

"And now this Ostrog—has suddenly revolutionised the world by waking the Sleeper—whom no one but the superstitious, common people had ever dreamt would wake again—raising the Sleeper to claim his property from the Council, after all these years."

The old man endorsed this statement with a cough. "It's strange," he said, "to meet a man who learns these things for the first time tonight."

"Aye," said Graham, "it's strange."

"Have you been in a Pleasure City?" said the old man. "All my life I've longed—" He laughed. "Even now," he said, "I could enjoy a little fun. Enjoy seeing things, anyhow." He mumbled a sentence Graham did not understand.

"The Sleeper—when did he awake?" said Graham suddenly.

"Three days ago."

"Where is he?"

"Ostrog has him. He escaped from the Council not four hours ago. My dear sir, where were you at the time? He was in the hall of the markets—where the fighting has been. All the city was screaming about it. All the Babble Machines! Everywhere it was shouted. Even the fools who speak for the Council were admitting it. Everyone was rushing off to see him—everyone was getting arms. Were you drunk or asleep? And even then! But you're joking! Surely you're pretending. It was to stop the shouting of the Babble Machines and prevent the people gathering that they turned off the electricity—and put this damned darkness upon us. Do you mean to say—?"

"I had heard the Sleeper was rescued," said Graham. "But—to come back a minute. Are you sure Ostrog has him?"

"He won't let him go," said the old man.

"And the Sleeper. Are you sure he is not genuine? I have never heard—"

"So all the fools think. So they think. As if there wasn't a thousand things that were never heard. I know Ostrog too well for that. Did I tell you? In a way I'm a sort of relation of Ostrog's. A sort of relation. Through my daughter-in-law."

"I suppose—"

"Well?"

"I suppose there's no chance of this Sleeper asserting himself. I suppose he's certain to be a puppet—in Ostrog's hands or the Council's, as soon as the struggle is over."

"In Ostrog's hands—certainly. Why shouldn't he be a puppet? Look at his position. Everything done for him, every pleasure possible. Why should he want to assert himself?"

"What are these Pleasure Cities?" said Graham, abruptly.

The old man made him repeat the question. When at last he was assured of Graham's words, he nudged him violently. "That's too much," said he. "You're poking fun at an old man. I've been suspecting you know more than you pretend."

"Perhaps I do," said Graham. "But no! why should I go on acting? No, I do not know what a Pleasure City is."

The old man laughed in an intimate way.

"What is more, I do not know how to read your letters, I do not know what money you use, I do not know what foreign countries there are. I do not know where I am. I cannot count. I do not know where to get food, nor drink, nor shelter."

"Come, come," said the old man, "if you had a glass of drink, now, would you put it in your ear or your eye?"

"I want you to tell me all these things."

"He, he! Well, gentlemen who dress in silk must have their fun." A withered hand caressed Graham's arm for a moment. "Silk. Well, well! But, all the same, I wish I was the man who was put up as the Sleeper. He'll have a fine time of it. All the pomp and pleasure. He's a queer looking face. When they used to let anyone go to see him, I've got tickets and been. The image of the real one, as the photographs show him, this substitute used to be. Yellow. But he'll get fed up. It's a queer world. Think of the luck of it. The luck of it. I expect he'll be sent to Capri. It's the best fun for a greener."

His cough overtook him again. Then he began mumbling enviously of pleasures and strange delights. "The luck of it, the luck of it! All my life I've been in London, hoping to get my chance."

"But you don't know that the Sleeper died," said Graham, suddenly.

The old man made him repeat his words.

"Men don't live beyond ten dozen. It's not in the order of things," said the old man. "I'm not a fool. Fools may believe it, but not me."

Graham became angry with the old man's assurance. "Whether you are a fool or not," he said, "it happens you are wrong about the Sleeper."

"Eh?"

"You are wrong about the Sleeper. I haven't told you before, but I will tell you now. You are wrong about the Sleeper."

"How do you know? I thought you didn't know anything—not even about Pleasure Cities."

Graham paused.

"You don't know," said the old man. "How are you to know? It's very few men—"

"I _am_ the Sleeper."

He had to repeat it.

There was a brief pause. "There's a silly thing to say, sir, if you'll excuse me. It might get you into trouble in a time like this," said the old man. Graham, slightly dashed, repeated his assertion.

"I was saying I was the Sleeper. That years and years ago I did, indeed, fall asleep, in a little stonebuilt village, in the days when there were hedgerows, and villages, and inns, and all the countryside cut up into little pieces, little fields. Have you never heard of those days? And it is I—I who speak to you—who awakened again these four days since."

"Four days since!—the Sleeper! But they've got the Sleeper. They have him and they won't let him go. Nonsense! You've been talking sensibly enough up to now. I can see it as though I was there. There will be Lincoln like a keeper just behind him; they won't let him go about alone. Trust them. You're a queer fellow. One of these fun pokers. I see now why you have been clipping your words so oddly, but—"

He stopped abruptly, and Graham could see his gesture.

"As if Ostrog would let the Sleeper run about alone! No, you're telling that to the wrong man altogether. Eh! as if I should believe. What's your game? And besides, we've been talking of the Sleeper."

Graham stood up. "Listen," he said. "I am the Sleeper."

"You're an odd man," said the old man, "to sit here in the dark, talking clipped, and telling a lie of that sort. But—"

Graham's exasperation fell to laughter. "It is preposterous," he cried. "Preposterous. The dream must end. It gets wilder and wilder. Here am I—in this damned twilight—I never knew a dream in twilight before—an anachronism by two hundred years and trying to persuade an old fool that I am myself, and meanwhile—Ugh!"

He moved in gusty irritation and went striding. In a moment the old man was pursuing him. "Eh! but don't go!" cried the old man. "I'm an old fool, I know. Don't go. Don't leave me in all this darkness."

Graham hesitated, stopped. Suddenly the folly of telling his secret flashed into his mind.

"I didn't mean to offend you—disbelieving you," said the old man coming near. "It's no manner of harm. Call yourself the Sleeper if it pleases you. 'Tis a foolish trick."

Graham hesitated, turned abruptly and went on his way.

For a time he heard the old man's hobbling pursuit and his wheezy cries receding. But at last the darkness swallowed him, and Graham saw him no more.

CHAPTER XII

OSTROG

Graham could now take a clearer view of his position. For a long time yet he wandered, but after the talk of the old man his discovery of this Ostrog was clear in his mind as the final inevitable decision. One thing was evident, those who were at the headquarters of the revolt had succeeded very admirably in suppressing the fact of his disappearance. But every moment he expected to hear the report of his death or of his recapture by the Council.

Presently a man stopped before him. "Have you heard?" he said.

"No!" said Graham starting.

"Near a dozand," said the man, "a dozand men!" and hurried on.

A number of men and a girl passed in the darkness, gesticulating and shouting: "Capitulated! Given up!" "A dozand of men." "Two dozand of men." "Ostrog, Hurrah! Ostrog, Hurrah!" These cries receded, became indistinct.

Other shouting men followed. For a time his attention was absorbed in the fragments of speech he heard. He had a doubt whether all were speaking English. Scraps floated to him, scraps like Pigeon English, like 'nigger' dialect, blurred and mangled distortions. He dared accost no one with questions. The impression the people gave him jarred altogether with his preconceptions of the struggle and confirmed the old man's faith in Ostrog. It was only slowly he could bring himself to believe that all these people were rejoicing at the defeat of the Council, that the Council which had pursued him with such power and vigour was after all the weaker of the two sides in conflict. And if that was so, how did it affect him? Several times he hesitated on the verge of fundamental questions. Once he turned and walked for a long way after a little man of rotund inviting outline, but he was unable to master confidence to address him.

It was only slowly that it came to him that he might ask for the "wind-vane offices," whatever the "wind-vane offices" might be. His first enquiry simply resulted in a direction to go on towards Westminster. His second led to the discovery of a short cut in which he was speedily lost. He was told to leave the ways to which he had hitherto confined himself knowing no other means of transit—and to plunge down one of the middle staircases into the blackness of a crossway. Thereupon came some trivial adventures; chief of these an ambiguous encounter with a gruff-voiced invisible creature speaking in a strange dialect that seemed at first a strange tongue, a thick flow of speech with the drifting corpses of English words therein, the dialect of the latter-day vile. Then another voice drew near, a girl's voice singing, "tralala tralala." She spoke to Graham, her English touched with something of the same quality. She professed to have lost her sister, she blundered needlessly into him he thought, caught hold of him and laughed. But a word of vague remonstrance sent her into the unseen again.

The sounds about him increased. Stumbling people passed him, speaking excitedly. "They have surrendered!" "The Council! Surely not the Council!" "They are saying so in the Ways." The passage seemed wider. Suddenly the wall fell away. He was in a great space and people were stirring remotely. He inquired his way of an indistinct figure. "Strike straight across," said a woman's voice. He left his guiding wall, and in a moment had stumbled against a little table on which were utensils of glass. Graham's eyes, now attuned to darkness, made out a long vista with pallid tables on either side. He went down this. At one or two of the tables he heard a clang of glass and a sound of eating. There were people then cool enough to dine, or daring enough to steal a meal in spite of social convulsion and darkness. Far off and high up he presently saw a pallid light of a semi-circular shape. As he approached this, a black edge came up and hid it. He stumbled at steps and found himself in a gallery. He heard a sobbing, and found two scared little girls crouched by a railing. These children became silent at the near sound of feet. He tried to console them, but they were very still until he left them. Then as he receded he could hear them sobbing again.

Presently he found himself at the foot of a staircase and near a wide opening. He saw a dim twilight above this and ascended out of the blackness into a street of moving Ways again. Along this a disorderly swarm of people marched shouting. They were singing snatches of the song of the revolt, most of them out of tune. Here and there torches flared creating brief hysterical shadows. He asked his way and was twice puzzled by that same thick dialect. His third attempt won an answer he could understand. He was two miles from the wind-vane offices in Westminster, but the way was easy to follow.

When at last he did approach the district of the wind-vane offices it seemed to him, from the cheering processions that came marching along the Ways, from the tumult of rejoicing, and finally from the restoration of the lighting of the city, that the overthrow of the Council must already be accomplished. And still no news of his absence came to his ears.

The re-illumination of the city came with startling abruptness. Suddenly he stood blinking, all about him men halted dazzled, and the world was incandescent. The light found him already upon the outskirts of the excited crowds that choked the Ways near the wind-vane offices, and the sense of visibility and exposure that came with it turned his colourless intention of joining Ostrog to a keen anxiety.

For a time he was jostled, obstructed, and endangered by men hoarse and weary with cheering his name, some of them bandaged and bloody in his cause. The frontage of the wind-vane offices was illuminated by some moving picture, but what it was he could not see, because in spite of his strenuous attempts the density of the crowd prevented his approaching it. From the fragments of speech he caught, he judged it conveyed news of the fighting about the Council House. Ignorance and indecision made him slow and ineffective in his movements. For a time he could not conceive how he was to get within the unbroken facade of this place. He made his way slowly into the midst of this mass of people, until he realised that the descending staircase of the central Way led to the interior of the buildings.

This gave him a goal, but the crowding in the central path was so dense that it was long before he could reach it. And even then he encountered intricate obstruction, and had an hour of vivid argument first in this guard room and then in that before he could get a note taken to the one man of all men who was most eager to see him. His story was laughed to scorn at one place, and wiser for that, when at last he reached a second stairway he professed simply to have news of extraordinary importance for Ostrog. What it was he would not say. They sent his note reluctantly. For a long time he waited in a little room at the foot of the lift shaft, and thither at last came Lincoln, eager, apologetic, astonished. He stopped in the doorway scrutinising Graham, then rushed forward effusively.

"Yes," he cried. "It is you. And you are not dead!"

Graham made a brief explanation.

"My brother is waiting," explained Lincoln. "He is alone in the wind-vane offices. We feared you had been killed in the theatre. He doubted—and things are very urgent still in spite of what we are telling them _there_—or he would have come to you."

They ascended a lift, passed along a narrow passage, crossed a great hall, empty save for two hurrying messengers, and entered a comparatively little room, whose only furniture was a long settee and a large oval disc of cloudy, shifting grey, hung by cables from the wall. There Lincoln left Graham for a space, and he remained alone without understanding the shifting smoky shapes that drove slowly across this disc.

His attention was arrested by a sound that began abruptly. It was cheering, the frantic cheering of a vast but very remote crowd, a roaring exultation. This ended as sharply as it had begun, like a sound heard between the opening and shutting of a door. In the outer room was a noise of hurrying steps and a melodious clinking as if a loose chain was running over the teeth of a wheel.

Then he heard the voice of a woman, the rustle of unseen garments. "It is Ostrog!" he heard her say. A little bell rang fitfully, and then everything was still again.

Presently came voices, footsteps and movement without. The footsteps of some one person detached itself from the other sounds and drew near, firm, evenly measured steps. The curtain lifted slowly. A tall, white-haired man, clad in garments of cream coloured silk, appeared, regarding Graham from under his raised arm.

For a moment the white form remained holding the curtain, then dropped it and stood before it. Graham's first impression was of a very broad forehead, very pale blue eyes deep sunken under white brows, an aquiline nose, and a heavily-lined resolute mouth. The folds of flesh over the eyes, the drooping of the corners of the mouth contradicted the upright bearing, and said the man was old. Graham rose to his feet instinctively, and for a moment the two men stood in silence, regarding each other.

"You are Ostrog?" said Graham.

"I am Ostrog."

"The Boss?"

"So I am called."

Graham felt the inconvenience of the silence. "I have to thank you chiefly, I understand, for my safety," he said presently.

"We were afraid you were killed," said Ostrog.

"Or sent to sleep again—for ever. We have been doing everything to keep our secret—the secret of your disappearance. Where have you been? How did you get here?"

Graham told him briefly.

Ostrog listened in silence.

He smiled faintly. "Do you know what I was doing when they came to tell me you had come?"

"How can I guess?"

"Preparing your double."

"My double?"

"A man as like you as we could find. We were going to hypnotise him, to save him the difficulty of acting. It was imperative. The whole of this revolt depends on the idea that you are awake, alive, and with us. Even now a great multitude of people has gathered in the theatre clamouring to see you. They do not trust... You know, of course—something of your position?"

"Very little," said Graham.

"It is like this." Ostrog walked a pace or two into the room and turned. "You are absolute owner," he said, "of more than half the world. As a result of that you are practically King. Your powers are limited in many intricate ways, but you are the figure head, the popular symbol of government. This White Council, the Council of Trustees as it is called."

"I have heard the vague outline of these things."

"I wondered."

"I came upon a garrulous old man."

"I see... Our masses—the word comes from your days—you know of course, that we still have masses—regard you as our actual ruler. Just as a great number of people in your days regarded the Crown as the ruler. They are discontented—the masses all over the earth—with the rule of your Trustees. For the most part it is the old discontent, the old quarrel of the common man with his commonness—the misery of work and discipline and unfitness. But your Trustees have ruled ill. In certain matters, in the administration of the Labour Companies, for example, they have been unwise. They have given endless opportunities. Already we of the popular party were agitating for reforms—when your waking came. Came! If it had been contrived it could not have come more opportunity." He smiled. "The public mind, making no allowance for your years of quiescence, had already hit on the thought of waking you and appealing to you, and—Flash!"

He indicated the outbreak by a gesture, and Graham moved his head to show that he understood.

"The Council muddled—quarreled. They always do. They could not decide what to do with you. You know how they imprisoned you?"

"I see. I see. And now—we win?"

"We win. Indeed we win. Tonight, in five swift hours. Suddenly we struck everywhere. The windvane people, the Labour Company and its millions, burst the bonds. We got the pull of the aeropiles."

He paused. "Yes," said Graham, guessing that aeropile meant flying machine.

"That was, of course, essential. Or they could have got away. All the city rose, every third man almost was in it! All the blue, all the public services, save only just a few aeronauts and about half the red police. You were rescued, and their own police of the Ways—not half of them could be massed at the Council House—have been broken up, disarmed or killed. All London is ours—now. Only the Council House remains.

"Half of those who remain to them of the red police were lost in that foolish attempt to recapture you. They lost their heads when they lost you. They flung all they had at the theatre. We cut them off from the Council House there. Truly tonight has been a night of victory. Everywhere your star has blazed. A day ago—the White Council ruled as it has ruled for a gross of years, for a century and a half of years, and then, with only a little whispering, a covert arming here and there, suddenly—So!"

"I am very ignorant," said Graham. "I suppose—. I do not clearly understand the conditions of this fighting. If you could explain. Where is the Council? Where is the fight?"

Ostrog stepped across the room, something clicked, and suddenly, save for an oval glow, they were in darkness. For a moment Graham was puzzled.

Then he saw that the cloudy grey disc had taken depth and colour, had assumed the appearance of an oval window looking out upon a strange unfamiliar scene.

At the first glance he was unable to guess what this scene might be. It was a daylight scene, the daylight of a wintry day, grey and clear. Across the picture and halfway as it seemed between him and the remoter view, a stout cable of twisted white wire stretched vertically. Then he perceived that the rows of great windwheels he saw, the wide intervals, the occasional gulfs of darkness, were akin to those through which he had fled from the Council House. He distinguished an orderly file of red figures marching across an open space between files of men in black, and realised before Ostrog spoke that he was looking down on the upper surface of latter-day London. The overnight snows had gone. He judged that this mirror was some modern replacement of the camera obscura, but that matter was not explained to him. He saw that though the file of red figures was trotting from left to right, yet they were passing out of the picture to the left. He wondered momentarily, and then saw that the picture was passing slowly, panorama fashion, across the oval.

"In a moment you will see the fighting," said Ostrog at his elbow. "Those fellows in red you notice are prisoners. This is the roof space of London—all the houses are practically continuous now. The streets and public squares are covered in. The gaps and chasms of your time have disappeared."

Something out of focus obliterated half the picture. Its form suggested a man. There was a gleam of metal, a flash, something that swept across the oval, as the eyelid of a bird sweeps across its eye, and the picture was clear again. And now Graham beheld men running down among the wind-wheels, pointing weapons from which jetted out little smoky flashes. They swarmed thicker and thicker to the right, gesticulating—it might be they were shouting, but of that the picture told nothing. They and the windwheels passed slowly and steadily across the field of the mirror.

"Now," said Ostrog, "comes the Council House," and slowly a black edge crept into view and gathered Graham's attention. Soon it was no longer an edge but a cavity, a huge blackened space amidst the clustering edifices, and from it thin spires of smoke rose into the pallid winter sky. Gaunt ruinous masses of the building, mighty truncated piers and girders, rose dismally out of this cavernous darkness. And over these vestiges of some splendid place, countless minute men were clambering, leaping, swarming.

"This is the Council House," said Ostrog. "Their last stronghold. And the fools wasted enough ammunition to hold out for a month in blowing up the buildings all about them—to stop our attack. You heard the smash? It shattered half the brittle glass in the city."

And while he spoke, Graham saw that beyond this sea of ruins, overhanging it and rising to a great height, was a ragged mass of white building. This mass had been isolated by the ruthless destruction of its surroundings. Black gaps marked the passages the disaster had torn apart; big halls had been slashed open and the decoration of their interiors showed dismally in the wintry dawn, and down the jagged wall hung festoons of divided cables and twisted ends of lines and metallic rods. And amidst all the vast details moved little red specks, the red-clothed defenders of the Council. Every now and then faint flashes illuminated the bleak shadows. At the first sight it seemed to Graham that an attack upon this isolated white building was in progress, but then he perceived that the party of the revolt was not advancing, but sheltered amidst the colossal wreckage that encircled this last ragged stronghold of the red-garbed men, was keeping up a fitful firing.

And not ten hours ago he had stood beneath the ventilating fans in a little chamber within that remote building wondering what was happening in the world!

Looking more attentively as this warlike episode moved silently across the centre of the mirror, Graham saw that the white building was surrounded on every side by ruins, and Ostrog proceeded to describe in concise phrases how its defenders had sought by such destruction to isolate themselves from a storm. He spoke of the loss of men that huge downfall had entailed in an indifferent tone. He indicated an improvised mortuary among the wreckage showed ambulances swarming like cheese-mites along a ruinous groove that had once been a street of moving ways. He was more interested in pointing out the parts of the Council House, the distribution of the besiegers. In a little while the civil contest that had convulsed London was no longer a mystery to Graham. It was no tumultuous revolt had occurred that night, no equal warfare, but a splendidly organised _coup d'etat_. Ostrog's grasp of details was astonishing; he seemed to know the business of even the smallest knot of black and red specks that crawled amidst these places.

He stretched a huge black arm across the luminous picture, and showed the room whence Graham had escaped, and across the chasm of ruins the course of his flight. Graham recognised the gulf across which the gutter ran, and the wind-wheels where he had crouched from the flying machine. The rest of his path had succumbed to the explosion. He looked again at the Council House, and it was already half hidden, and on the right a hillside with a cluster of domes and pinnacles, hazy, dim and distant, was gliding into view.

"And the Council is really overthrown?" he said.

"Overthrown," said Ostrog.

"And I—. Is it indeed true that I?"

"You are Master of the World."

"But that white flag—"

"That is the flag of the Council—the flag of the Rule of the World. It will fall. The fight is over. Their attack on the theatre was their last frantic struggle. They have only a thousand men or so, and some of these men will be disloyal. They have little ammunition. And we are reviving the ancient arts. We are casting guns."

"But—help. Is this city the world?"

"Practically this is all they have left to them of their empire. Abroad the cities have either revolted with us or wait the issue. Your awakening has perplexed them, paralysed them."

"But haven't the Council flying machines? Why is there no fighting with them?"

"They had. But the greater part of the aeronauts were in the revolt with us. They wouldn't take the risk of fighting on our side, but they would not stir against us. We had to get a pull with the aeronauts. Quite half were with us, and the others knew it. Directly they knew you had got away, those looking for you dropped. We killed the man who shot at you—an hour ago. And we occupied the flying stages at the outset in every city we could, and so stopped and captured the airplanes, and as for the little flying machines that turned out—for some did—we kept up too straight and steady a fire for them to get near the Council House. If they dropped they couldn't rise again, because there's no clear space about there for them to get up. Several we have smashed, several others have dropped and surrendered, the rest have gone off to the Continent to find a friendly city if they can before their fuel runs out. Most of these men were only too glad to be taken prisoner and kept out of harm's way. Upsetting in a flying machine isn't a very attractive prospect. There's no chance for the Council that way. Its days are done."

He laughed and turned to the oval reflection again to show Graham what he meant by flying stages. Even the four nearer ones were remote and obscured by a thin morning haze. But Graham could perceive they were very vast structures, judged even by the standard of the things about them.

And then as these dim shapes passed to the left there came again the sight of the expanse across which the disarmed men in red had been marching. And then the black ruins, and then again the beleaguered white fastness of the Council. It appeared no longer a ghostly pile, but glowing amber in the sunlight, for a cloud shadow had passed. About it the pigmy struggle still hung in suspense, but now the red defenders were no longer firing.

So, in a dusky stillness, the man from the nineteenth century saw the closing scene of the great revolt, the forcible establishment of his rule. With a quality of startling discovery it came to him that this was his world, and not that other he had left behind; that this was no spectacle to culminate and cease; that in this world lay whatever life was still before him, lay all his duties and dangers and responsibilities. He turned with fresh questions. Ostrog began to answer them, and then broke off abruptly. "But these things I must explain more fully later. At present there are—duties. The people are coming by the moving ways towards this ward from every part of the city—the markets and theatres are densely crowded. You are just in time for them. They are clamouring to see you. And abroad they want to see you. Paris, New York, Chicago, Denver, Capri—thousands of cities are up and in a tumult, undecided, and clamouring to see you. They have clamoured that you should be awakened for years, and now it is done they will scarcely believe—"

"But surely—I can't go..."

Ostrog answered from the other side of the room, and the picture on the oval disc paled and vanished as the light jerked back again. "There are kinetotele-photographs," he said. "As you bow to the people here—all over the world myriads of myriads of people, packed and still in darkened halls, will see you also. In black and white, of course—not like this. And you will hear their shouts reinforcing the shouting in the hall.

"And there is an optical contrivance we shall use," said Ostrog, "used by some of the posturers and women dancers. It may be novel to you. You stand in a very bright light, and they see not you but a magnified image of you thrown on a screen—so that even the furtherest man in the remotest gallery can, if he chooses, count your eyelashes."

Graham clutched desperately at one of the questions in his mind. "What is the population of London?"

"Eight and twaindy myriads."

"Eight and what?"

"More than thirty-three millions."

These figures went beyond Graham's imagination "You will be expected to say something," said Ostrog. "Not what you used to call a Speech, but what our people call a Word—just one sentence, six or seven words. Something formal. If I might suggest—'I have awakened and my heart is with you.' That is the sort of thing they want."

"What was that?" asked Graham.

"'I am awakened and my heart is with you.' And bow—bow royally. But first we must get you black robes—for black is your colour. Do you mind? And then they will disperse to their homes."

Graham hesitated. "I am in your hands," he said.

Ostrog was clearly of that opinion. He thought for a moment, turned to the curtain and called brief directions to some unseen attendants. Almost immediately a black robe, the very fellow of the black robe Graham had worn in the theatre, was brought. And as he threw it about his shoulders there came from the room without the shrilling of a high-pitched bell. Ostrog turned in interrogation to the attendant, then suddenly seemed to change his mind, pulled the curtain aside and disappeared.

For a moment Graham stood with the deferential attendant listening to Ostrog's retreating steps. There was a sound of quick question and answer and of men running. The curtain was snatched back and Ostrog reappeared, his massive face glowing with excitement. He crossed the room in a stride, clicked the room into darkness, gripped Grahams arm and pointed to the mirror.

"Even as we turned away," he said.

Graham saw his index finger, black and colossal, above the mirrored Council House. For a moment he did not understand. And then he perceived that the flagstaff that had carried the white banner was bare.

"Do you mean—?" he began.

"The Council has surrendered. Its rule is at an end for evermore."

"Look!" and Ostrog pointed to a coil of black that crept in little jerks up the vacant flagstaff, unfolding as it rose.

The oval picture paled as Lincoln pulled the curtain aside and entered.

"They are clamourous," he said.

Ostrog kept his grip of Graham's arm.

"We have raised the people," he said. "We have given them arms. For today at least their wishes must be law."

Lincoln held the Curtain open for Graham and Ostrog to pass through.

On his way to the markets Graham had a transitory glance of a long narrow white-walled room in which men in the universal blue canvas were carrying covered things like biers, and about which men in medical purple hurried to and fro. From this room came groans and wailing. He had an impression of an empty blood-stained couch, of men on other couches, bandaged and blood-stained. It was just a glimpse from a railed footway and then a buttress hid the place and they were going on towards the markets.

The roar of the multitude was near now: it leapt to thunder. And, arresting his attention, a fluttering of black banners, the waving of blue canvas and brown rags, and the swarming vastness of the theatre near the public markets came into view down a long passage. The picture opened out. He perceived they were entering the great theatre of his first appearance, the great theatre he had last seen as a chequer-work of glare and blackness in his flight from the red police. This time he entered it along a gallery at a level high above the stage. The place was now brilliantly lit again. He sought the gangway up which he had fled, but he could not tell it from among its dozens of fellows; nor could he see anything of the smashed seats, deflated cushions, and such like traces of the fight because of the density of the people. Except the stage the whole place was closely packed. Looking down the effect was a vast area of stippled pink, each dot a still upturned face regarding him. At his appearance with Ostrog the cheering died away, the singing died away, a common interest stilled and unified the disorder. It seemed as though every individual of those myriads was watching him.

CHAPTER XIII

THE END OF THE OLD ORDER

So far as Graham was able to judge, it was near midday when the white banner of the Council fell. But some hours had to elapse before it was possible to effect the formal capitulation, and so after he had spoken his "Word" he retired to his new apartments in the wind-vane offices. The continuous excitement of the last twelve hours had left him inordinately fatigued, even his curiosity was exhausted; for a space he sat inert and passive with open eyes, and for a space he slept. He was roused by two medical attendants, come prepared with stimulants to sustain him through the next occasion. After he had taken their drugs and bathed by their advice in cold water, he felt a rapid return of interest and energy, and was presently able and willing to accompany Ostrog through several miles (as it seemed) of passages, lifts, and slides to the closing scene of the White Council's rule.

The way ran deviously through a maze of buildings. They came at last to a passage that curved about, and showed broadening before him an oblong opening, clouds hot with sunset, and the ragged skyline of the ruinous Council House. A tumult of shouts came drifting up to him. In another moment they had come out high up on the brow of the cliff of torn buildings that overhung the wreckage. The vast area opened to

Graham's eyes, none the less strange and wonderful for the remote view he had had of it in the oval mirror.

This rudely amphitheatral space seemed now the better part of a mile to its outer edge. It was gold lit on the left hand, catching the sunlight, and below and to the right clear and cold in the shadow. Above the shadowy grey Council House that stood in the midst of it, the great black banner of the surrender still hung in sluggish folds against the blazing sunset. Severed rooms, halls and passages gaped strangely, broken masses of metal projected dismally from the complex wreckage, vast masses of twisted cable dropped like tangled seaweed, and from its base came a tumult of innumerable voices, violent concussions, and the sound of trumpets. All about this great white pile was a ring of desolation; the smashed and blackened masses, the gaunt foundations and ruinous lumber of the fabric that had been destroyed by the Council's orders, skeletons of girders, Titanic masses of wall, forests of stout pillars. Amongst the sombre wreckage beneath, running water flashed and glistened, and far away across the space, out of the midst of a vague vast mass of buildings, there thrust the twisted end of a water-main, two hundred feet in the air, thunderously spouting a shining cascade. And everywhere great multitudes of people.

Wherever there was space and foothold, people swarmed, little people, small and minutely clear, except where the sunset touched them to indistinguishable gold. They clambered up the tottering walls, they clung in wreaths and groups about the high-standing pillars. They swarmed along the edges of the circle of ruins. The air was full of their shouting, and were pressing and swaying towards the central space.

The upper storeys of the Council House seemed deserted, not a human being was visible. Only the drooping banner of the surrender hung heavily against the light. The dead were within the Council House, or hidden by the swarming people, or carried away. Graham could see only a few neglected bodies in gaps and corners of the ruins, and amidst the flowing water.

"Will you let them see you, Sire?" said Ostrog. "They are very anxious to see you."

Graham hesitated, and then walked forward to where the broken verge of wall dropped sheer. He I stood looking down, a lonely, tall, black figure against the sky.

Very slowly the swarming ruins became aware of him. And as they did so little bands of black-uniformed men appeared remotely, thrusting through the crowds towards the Council House. He saw little black heads become pink, looking at him, saw by that means a wave of recognition sweep across the space. It occurred to him that he should accord them some recognition. He held up his arm, then pointed to the Council House and dropped his hand. The voices below became unanimous, gathered volume, came up to him as multitudinous wavelets of cheering.

The western sky was a pallid bluish green, and Jupiter shone high in the south, before the capitulation was accomplished. Above was a slow insensible change, the advance of night serene and beautiful; below was hurry, excitement, conflicting orders, pauses, spasmodic developments of organisation, a vast ascending clamour and confusion. Before the Council came out, toiling perspiring men, directed by a conflict of shouts, carried forth hundreds of those who had perished in the hand-to-hand conflict within those long passages and chambers.

Guards in black lined the way that the Council would come, and as far as the eye could reach into the hazy blue twilight of the ruins, and swarming now at every possible point in the captured Council House and along the shattered cliff of its circumadjacent buildings, were innumerable people, and their voices even when they were not cheering, were as the soughing of the sea upon a pebble beach. Ostrog had chosen a huge commanding pile of crushed and overthrown masonry, and on this a stage of timbers and metal girders was being hastily constructed. Its essential parts were complete, but humming and clangorous machinery still glared fitfully in the shadows beneath this temporary edifice.

The stage had a small higher portion on which Graham stood with Ostrog and Lincoln close beside him, a little in advance of a group of minor officers. A broader lower stage surrounded this quarter deck, and on this were the black-uniformed guards of the revolt armed with the little green weapons whose very names Graham still did not know. Those standing about him perceived that his eyes wandered perpetually from the swarming people in the twilight ruins about him to the darkling mass of the White Council House, whence the Trustees would presently come, and to the gaunt cliffs of ruin that encircled him, and so back to the people. The voices of the crowd swelled to a deafening tumult.

He saw the Councillors first afar off in the glare of one of the temporary lights that marked their path, a little group of white figures blinking in a black archway. In the Council House they had been in darkness. He watched them approaching, drawing nearer past first this blazing electric star and then that; the minatory roar of the crowd over whom their power had lasted for a hundred and fifty years marched along beside them. As they drew still nearer their faces came out weary, white and anxious. He saw them blinking up through the glare about him and Ostrog. He contrasted their strange cold looks in the Hall of Atlas.... Presently he could recognise several of them; the man who had rapped the table at Howard, a burly man with a red beard, and one delicate-featured, short, dark man with a peculiarly long skull. He noted that two were whispering together and looking behind him at Ostrog. Next there came a tall, dark and handsome man, walking downcast. Abruptly he glanced up, his eyes touched Graham for a moment, and passed beyond him to Ostrog. The way that had been made for them was so contrived that they had to march past and curve about before they came to the sloping path of planks that ascended to the stage where their surrender was to be made.

"The Master, the Master! God and the Master," shouted the people. "To hell with the Council!" Graham looked at their multitudes, receding beyond counting into a shouting haze, and then at Ostrog beside him, white and steadfast and still. His eye went again to the little group of White Councillors. And then he looked up at the familiar quiet stars overhead. The marvellous element in his fate was suddenly vivid. Could that be his indeed, that little life in his memory two hundred years gone by—and this as well?

CHAPTER XIV
FROM THE CROW'S NEST

And so after strange delays and through an avenue of doubt and battle, this man from the nineteenth century came at last to his position at the head of that complex world.

At first when he rose from the long deep sleep that followed his rescue and the surrender of the Council, he did not recognise his surroundings. By an effort he gained a clue in his mind, and all that had happened came back to him, at first with a quality of insincerity like a story heard, like something read out of a book. And even before his memories were clear, the exultation of his escape, the wonder of his prominence were back in his mind. He was owner of half the world; Master of the Earth. This new great age was in the completest sense his. He no longer hoped to discover his experiences a dream; he became anxious now to convince himself that they were real.

An obsequious valet assisted him to dress under the direction of a dignified chief attendant, a little man whose face proclaimed him Japanese, albeit he spoke English like an Englishman. From the latter he learnt something of the state of affairs. Already the revolution was an accepted fact; already business was being resumed throughout the city. Abroad the downfall of the Council had been received for the most part with delight.

Nowhere was the Council popular, and the thousand cities of Western America, after two hundred years still jealous of New York, London, and the East, had risen almost unanimously two days before at the news of Graham's imprisonment. Paris was fighting within itself. The rest of the world hung in suspense.

While he was breaking his fast, the sound of a telephone bell jetted from a corner, and his chief attendant called his attention to the voice of Ostrog making polite enquiries. Graham interrupted his refreshment to reply. Very shortly Lincoln arrived, and Graham at once expressed a strong desire to talk to people and to be shown more of the new life that was opening before him. Lincoln informed him that in three hours' time a representative gathering of officials and their wives would be held in the state apartments of the wind-vane Chief. Graham's desire to traverse the ways of the city was, however, at present impossible, because of the enormous excitement of the people. It was, however, quite possible for him to take a bird's eye view of the city from the crow's nest of the windvane keeper. To this accordingly Graham was conducted by his attendant. Lincoln, with a graceful compliment to the attendant, apologised for not accompanying them, on account of the present pressure of administrative work.

Higher even than the most gigantic wind-wheels hung this crow's nest, a clear thousand feet above the roofs, a little disc-shaped speck on a spear of metallic filigree, cable stayed. To its summit Graham was drawn in a little wire-hung cradle. Halfway down the frail-seeming stem was a light gallery about which hung a cluster of tubes—minute they looked from above—rotating slowly on the ring of its outer rail. These were the specula, _en rapport_ with the wind-vane keeper's mirrors, in one of which Ostrog had shown him the coming of his rule. His Japanese attendant ascended before him and they spent nearly an hour asking and answering questions.

It was a day full of the promise and quality of spring. The touch of the wind warmed. The sky was an intense blue and the vast expanse of London shone dazzling under the morning sun. The air was clear of smoke and haze, sweet as the air of a mountain glen.

Save for the irregular oval of ruins about the House of the Council and the black flag of the surrender that fluttered there, the mighty city seen from above showed few signs of the swift revolution that had, to his imagination, in one night and one day, changed the destinies of the world. A multitude of people still swarmed over these ruins, and the huge openwork stagings in the distance from which started in times of peace the service of aeroplanes to the various great cities of Europe and America, were also black with the victors. Across a narrow way of planking raised on trestles that crossed the ruins a crowd of workmen were busy restoring the connection between the cables and wires of the Council House and the rest of the city, preparatory to the transfer thither of Ostrog's headquarters from the Wind-Vane buildings.

For the rest the luminous expanse was undisturbed. So vast was its serenity in comparison with the areas of disturbance, that presently Graham, looking beyond them, could almost forget the thousands of men lying out of sight in the artificial glare within the quasi-subterranean labyrinth, dead or dying of the overnight wounds, forget the improvised wards with the hosts of surgeons, nurses, and bearers feverishly busy, forget, indeed, all the wonder, consternation and novelty under the electric lights. Down there in the hidden ways of the anthill he knew that the revolution triumphed, that black everywhere carried the day, black favours, black banners, black festoons across the streets. And out here, under the fresh sunlight, beyond the crater of the fight, as if nothing had happened to the earth, the forest of Wind Vanes that had grown from one or two while the Council had ruled, roared peacefully upon their incessant duty.

Far away, spiked, jagged and indented by the wind vanes, the Surrey Hills rose blue and faint; to the north and nearer, the sharp contours of Highgate and Muswell Hill were similarly jagged. And all over the countryside, he knew, on every crest and hill, where once the hedges had interlaced, and cottages, churches, inns, and farmhouses had nestled among their trees, wind wheels similar to those he saw and bearing like vast advertisements, gaunt and distinctive symbols of the new age, cast their whirling shadows and stored incessantly the energy that flowed away incessantly through all the arteries of the city. And underneath these wandered the countless flocks and herds of the British Food Trust with their lonely guards and keepers.

Not a familiar outline anywhere broke the cluster of gigantic shapes below. St. Paul's he knew survived, and many of the old buildings in Westminster, embedded out of sight, arched over and covered in among the giant growths of this great age. The Themes, too, made no fall and gleam of silver to break the wilderness of the city; the thirsty water mains drank up every drop of its waters before they reached the walls. Its bed and estuary scoured and sunken, was now a canal of sea water and a race of grimy bargemen brought the heavy materials of trade from the Pool thereby beneath the very feet of the workers. Faint and dim in the eastward between earth and sky hung the clustering masts of the colossal shipping in the Pool. For all the heavy traffic, for which there was no need of haste, came in gigantic sailing ships from the ends of the earth, and the heavy goods for which there was urgency in mechanical ships of a smaller swifter sort.

And to the south over the hills, came vast aqueducts with sea water for the sewers and in three separate directions, ran pallid lines—the roads, stippled with moving grey specks. On the first occasion that offered he was determined to go out and see these roads. That would come after the flying ship he was presently to try. His attendant officer described them as a pair of gently curving surfaces a hundred yards wide, each one for the traffic going in one direction, and made of a substance called Eadhamite—an artificial substance, so far as he could gather, resembling toughened glass. Along this shot a strange traffic of narrow rubber-shod vehicles, great single wheels, two and four wheeled vehicles, sweeping along at velocities of from one to six miles a minute. Railroads had vanished; a few embankments remained as rust-crowned trenches here and there. Some few formed the cores of Eadhamite ways.

Among the first things to strike his attention had been the great fleets of advertisement balloons and kites that receded in irregular vistas northward and southward along the lines of the aeroplane journeys. No aeroplanes were to be seen. Their passages had ceased, and only one little-seeming aeropile circled high in the blue distance above the Surrey Hills, an unimpressive soaring speck.

A thing Graham had already learnt, and which he found very hard to imagine, was that nearly all the towns in the country, and almost all the villages, had disappeared. Here and there only, he understood, some gigantic hotel-like edifice stood amid square miles of some single cultivation and preserved the name of a town—as Bournemouth, Wareham, or Swanage. Yet the officer had speedily convinced him how inevitable such a change had been. The old order had dotted the country with farmhouses, and every two or three miles was the ruling landlord's estate, and the place of the inn and cobbler, the grocer's shop and church—the village. Every eight miles or so was the country town, where lawyer, corn merchant, woolstapler, saddler, veterinary surgeon, doctor, draper, milliner and so forth lived. Every eight miles—simply because that eight mile marketing journey, four there and back, was as much as was comfortable for the farmer. But directly the railways came into play, and after them the light railways, and all the swift new motor cars that had replaced waggons and horses, and so soon as the high roads began to be made of wood, and rubber, and Eadhamite, and all sorts of elastic durable substances—the necessity of having such frequent market towns disappeared. And the big towns grew. They drew the worker with the gravitational force of seemingly endless work, the employer with their suggestions of an infinite ocean of labour.

And as the standard of comfort rose, as the complexity of the mechanism of living increased life in the country had become more and more costly, or narrow and impossible. The disappearance of vicar and squire, the extinction of the general practitioner by the city specialist, had robbed the village of its last touch of culture. After telephone, kinematograph and phonograph had replaced newspaper, book, schoolmaster, and letter, to live outside the range of the electric cables was to live an isolated savage. In the country were neither means of being clothed nor fed (according to the refined conceptions of the time), no efficient doctors for an emergency, no company and no pursuits.

Moreover, mechanical appliances in agriculture made one engineer the equivalent of thirty labourers. So, inverting the condition of the city clerk in the days when London was scarce inhabitable because of the coaly foulness of its air, the labourers now came hurrying by road or air to the city and its life and delights at night to leave it again in the morning. The city had swallowed up humanity; man had entered upon a new stage in his development. First had come the nomad, the hunter, then had followed the agriculturist of the agricultural state, whose towns and cities and ports were but the headquarters and markets of the countryside. And now, logical consequence of an epoch of invention, was this huge new aggregation of men. Save London, there were only four other cities in Britain— Edinburgh, Portsmouth, Manchester and Shrewsbury. Such things as these, simple statements of fact though they were to contemporary men, strained Graham's imagination to picture. And when he glanced "over beyond there" at the strange things that existed on the Continent, it failed him altogether.

He had a vision of city beyond city, cities on great plains, cities beside great rivers, vast cities along the sea margin, cities girdled by snowy mountains. Over a great part of the earth the English tongue was spoken; taken together with its Spanish American and Hindoo and Negro and "Pidgin" dialects, it was the everyday language of two-thirds of the people of the earth. On the Continent, save as remote and curious survivals, three other languages alone held sway—German, which reached to Antioch and Genoa and jostled Spanish-English at Gdiz, a Gallicised Russian which met the Indian English in Persia and Kurdistan and the "Pidgin" English in Pekin, and French still clear and brilliant, the language of lucidity, which shared the Mediterranean with the Indian English and German and reached through a negro dialect to the Congo.

And everywhere now, through the city-set earth, save in the administered "black belt" territories of the tropics, the same cosmopolitan social organisation prevailed, and everywhere from Pole to Equator his property and his responsibilities extended. The whole world was civilised; the whole world dwelt in cities; the whole world was property. Over the British Empire and throughout America his ownership was scarcely disguised, Congress and Parliament were usually regarded as antique, curious gatherings. And even in the two Empires of Russia and Germany, the influence of his wealth was conceivably of enormous weight. There, of course, came problems—possibilities, but, uplifted as he was, even Russia and Germany seemed sufficiently remote. And of the quality of the black belt administration, and of what that might mean for him he thought, after the fashion of his former days, not at all. That it should hang like a threat over the spacious vision before him could not enter his nineteenth century mind. But his mind turned at once from the scenery to the thought of a vanished dread. "What of the yellow peril?" he asked and Asano made him explain. The Chinese spectre had vanished. Chinaman and European were at peace. The twentieth century had discovered with reluctant certainty that the average Chinaman was as civilised, more moral, and far more intelligent than the average European serf, and had repeated on a gigantic scale the fraternisation of Scot and Englishman that happened in the seventeenth century. As Asano put it; "They thought it over. They found we were white men after all." Graham turned again to the view and his thoughts took a new direction.

Out of the dim south-west, glittering and strange, voluptuous, and in some way terrible, shone those Pleasure Cities, of which the kinematograph-phonograph and the old man in the street had spoken. Strange places reminiscent of the legendary Sybaris, cities of art and beauty, mercenary art and mercenary beauty, sterile wonderful cities of motion and music, whither repaired all who profited by the fierce, inglorious, economic struggle that went on in the glaring labyrinth below.

Fierce he knew it was. How fierce he could judge from the fact that these latter-day people referred back to the England of the nineteenth century as the figure of an idyllic easy-going life. He turned his eyes to the scene immediately before him again, trying to conceive the big factories of that intricate maze.

Northward he knew were the potters, makers not only of earthenware and china, but of the kindred pastes and compounds a subtler mineralogical chemistry had devised; there were the makers of statuettes and wall ornaments and much intricate furniture; there too were the factories where feverishly competitive authors devised their phonograph discourses and advertisements and arranged the groupings and developments for their perpetually startling and novel kinematographic dramatic works. Thence, too, flashed the world-wide messages, the world-wide falsehoods of the news-tellers, the chargers of the telephonic machines that had replaced the newspapers of the past.

To the westward beyond the smashed Council House were the voluminous offices of municipal control and government; and to the eastward, towards the port, the trading quarters, the huge public markets, the theatres, houses of resort, betting palaces, miles of billiard saloons, baseball and football circuses, wild beast rings and the innumerable temples of the Christian and quasi-Christian sects, the Mahomedans, Buddhists, Gnostics, Spook Worshippers, the Incubus Worshippers, the Furniture Worshippers, and so forth; and to the south again a vast manufacture of textiles, pickles, wines and condiments. And from point to point tore the countless multitudes along the roaring mechanical ways. A gigantic hive, of which the winds were tireless servants, and the ceaseless wind-vanes an appropriate crown and symbol.

He thought of the unprecedented population that had been sucked up by this sponge of halls and galleries—the thirty-three million lives that were playing out each its own brief ineffectual drama below him, and the complacency that the brightness of the day and the space and splendour of the view, and above all the sense of his own importance had begotten, dwindled and perished. Looking down from this height over the city it became at last possible to conceive this overwhelming multitude of thirty-three millions, the reality of the responsibility he would take upon himself, the vastness of the human Maelstrom over which his slender kingship hung.

He tried to figure the individual life. It astonished him to realise how little the common man had changed in spite of the visible change in his conditions. Life and property, indeed, were secure from violence almost all over the world, zymotic diseases, bacterial diseases of all sorts had practically vanished, everyone had a sufficiency of food and clothing, was warmed in the city ways and sheltered from the weather—so much the almost mechanical progress of science and the physical organisation of society had accomplished. But the crowd, he was already beginning to discover, was a crowd still, helpless in the hands of demagogue and organiser, individually cowardly, individually swayed by appetite, collectively incalculable. The memory of countless figures in pale blue canvas came before his mind. Millions of such men and women below him, he knew, had never been out of the city, had never seen beyond the little round of unintelligent grudging participation in the world's business, and unintelligent dissatisfied sharing in its tawdrier pleasures. He thought of the hopes of his vanished contemporaries, and for a moment the dream of London in Morris's quaint old _News from Nowhere_, and the perfect land of Hudson's beautiful _Crystal Age_—appeared before him in an atmosphere of infinite loss. He thought of his own hopes.

For in the latter days of that passionate life that lay now so far behind him, the conception of a free and equal manhood had become a very real thing to him. He had hoped, as indeed his age had hoped, rashly taking it for granted, that the sacrifice of the many to the few would some day cease, that a day was near when every child born of woman should have a fair and assured chance of happiness. And here, after two hundred years, the same hope, still unfulfilled, cried passionately through the city. After two hundred years, he knew, greater than ever, grown with the city to gigantic proportions, were poverty and helpless labour and all the sorrows of his time.

Already he knew something of the history of the intervening years. He had heard now of the moral decay that had followed the collapse of supernatural religion in the minds of ignoble man, the decline of public honour, the ascendency of wealth. For men who had lost their belief in God had still kept their faith in property, and wealth ruled a venial world.

His Japanese attendant, Asano, in expounding the political history of the intervening two centuries, drew an apt image from a seed eaten by insect parasites. First there is the original seed, ripening vigorously enough. And then comes some insect and lays an egg under the skin, and behold! in a little while the seed is a hollow shape with an active grub inside that has eaten out its substance. And then comes some secondary parasite, some ichneumon fly, and lays an egg within this grub, and behold! that, too, is a hollow shape, and the new living thing is inside its predecessor's skin which itself is snug within the seed coat. And the seed coat still keeps its shape, most people think it a seed still, and for all one knows it may still think itself a seed, vigorous and alive. "Your Victorian kingdom," said Asano, "was like that—kingship with the heart eaten out. The landowners—the barons and gentry—began ages ago with King John; there were lapses, but they beheaded King Charles, and ended practically with King George mere husk of a king... the real power in the hands of their parliament. But the Parliament—the organ of the land-holding tenant-ruling gentry—did not keep its power long. The change had already come in the nineteenth century. The franchises had been broadened until it included masses of ignorant men, 'urban myriads,' who went in their featureless thousands to vote together. And the natural consequence of a swarming constituency is the rule of the party organisation. Power was passing even in the Victorian time to the party machinery, secret, complex, and corrupt. Very speedily power was in the hands of great men of business who financed the machines. A time came when the real power and interest of the Empire rested visibly between the two party councils, ruling by newspapers and electoral organisations—two small groups of rich and able men, working at first in opposition, then presently together."

There was a reaction of a genteel ineffectual sort. There were numberless books in existence, Asano said, to prove that—the publication of some of them was as early as Graham's sleep—a whole literature of reaction in fact. The party of the reaction seems to have locked itself into its study and rebelled with unflinching determination—on paper. The urgent necessity of either capturing or depriving the party councils of power is a common suggestion underlying all the thoughtful work of the early twentieth century, both in America and England. In most of these things America was a little earlier than England, though both countries drove the same way.

That counter-revolution never came. It could never organise and keep pure. There was not enough of the old sentimentality, the old faith in righteousness, left among men. Any organisation that became big enough to influence the polls became complex enough to be undermined, broken up, or bought outright by capable rich men. Socialistic and Popular, Reactionary and Purity Parties were all at last mere Stock Exchange counters, selling their principles to pay for their electioneering. And the great concern of the rich was naturally to keep property intact, the board clear for the game of trade. Just as the feudal concern had been to keep the board clear for hunting and war. The whole world was exploited, a battle field of businesses; and financial convulsions, the scourge of currency manipulation, tariff wars, made more human misery during the twentieth century—because the wretchedness was dreary life instead of speedy death—than had war, pestilence and famine, in the darkest hours of earlier history.

His own part in the development of this time he now knew clearly enough. Through the successive phases in the development of this mechanical civilisation, aiding and presently directing its development, there had grown a new power, the Council, the board of his trustees. At first it had been a mere chance union of the millions of Isbister and Warming, a mere property holding company, the creation of two childless testators' whims, but the collective talent of its first constitution had speedily guided it to a vast influence, until by title deed, loan and share, under a hundred disguises and pseudonyms it had ramified through the fabric of the American and English States.

Wielding an enormous influence and patronage, the Council had early assumed a political aspect; and in its development it had continually used its wealth to tip the beam of political decisions and its political advantages to grasp yet more and more wealth. At last the party organisations of two hemispheres were in its hands; it became an inner council of political control. Its last struggle was with the tacit alliance of the great Jewish families. But these families were linked only by a feeble sentiment, at any time inheritance might fling a huge fragment of their resources to a minor, a woman or a fool, marriages and legacies alienated hundreds of thousands at one blow. The Council had no such breach in its continuity. Steadily, steadfastly it grew.

The original Council was not simply twelve men of exceptional ability; they fused, it was a council of genius. It struck boldly for riches, for political influence, and the two subserved each other. With amazing foresight it spent great sums of money on the art of flying, holding that invention back against an hour foreseen. It used the patent laws, and a thousand half-legal expedients, to hamper all investigators who refused to work with it. In the old days it never missed a capable man. It paid his price. Its policy in those days was vigorous—unerring, and against it as it grew steadily and incessantly was only the chaotic selfish rule of the casually rich. In a hundred years Graham had become almost exclusive owner of Africa, of South America, of France, of London, of England and all its influence— for all practical purposes, that is—a power in North America—then the dominant power in America. The Council bought and organised China, drilled Asia, crippled the Old World empires, undermined them financially, fought and defeated them.

And this spreading usurpation of the world was so dexterously performed—a proteus—hundreds of banks, companies, syndicates, masked the Council's operations—that it was already far advanced before common men suspected the tyranny that had come. The Council never hesitated, never faltered. Means of communication, land, buildings, governments, municipalities, the territorial companies of the tropics, every human enterprise, it gathered greedily. And it drilled and marshalled its men, its railway police, its roadway police, its house guards, and drain and cable guards, its hosts of land-workers. Their unions it did not fight, but it undermined and betrayed and bought them. It bought the world at last. And, finally, its culminating stroke was the introduction of flying.

When the Council, in conflict with the workers in some of its huge monopolies, did something flagrantly illegal and that without even the ordinary civility of bribery, the old Law, alarmed for the profits of its complaisance, looked about it for weapons. But there were no more armies, no fighting navies; the age of Peace had come. The only possible war ships were the great steam vessels of the Council's Navigation Trust. The police forces they controlled; the police of the railways, of the ships, of their agricultural estates, their time-keepers and order-keepers, outnumbered the neglected little forces of the old country and municipal organisations ten to one. And they produced flying machines. There were men alive still who could remember the last great debate in the London House of Commons—the legal party, the party against the Council was in a minority, but it made a desperate fight—and how the members came crowding out upon the terrace to see these great unfamiliar winged shapes circling quietly overhead. The Council had soared to its power. The last sham of a democracy that had permitted unlimited irresponsible property was at an end.

Within one hundred and fifty years of Graham's falling asleep, his Council had thrown off its disguises and ruled openly, supreme in his name. Elections had become a cheerful formality, a septennial folly, an ancient unmeaning custom; a social Parliament as ineffectual as the convocation of the Established Church in Victorian times assembled now and then; and a legitimate King of England, disinherited, drunken and witless, played foolishly in a second-rate music-hall. So the magnificent dream of the nineteenth century, the noble project of universal individual liberty and universal happiness, touched by a disease of honour, crippled by a superstition of absolute property, crippled by the religious feuds that had robbed the common citizens of education, robbed men of standards of conduct, and brought the sanctions of morality to utter contempt, had worked itself out in the face of invention and ignoble enterprise, first to a warring plutocracy, and finally to the rule of a supreme plutocrat. His Council at last had ceased even to trouble to have its decrees endorsed by the constitutional authorities, and he a motionless, sunken, yellow-skinned figure had lain, neither dead nor living, recognisably and immediately

Master of the Earth. And awoke at last to find himself—Master of that inheritance! Awoke to stand under the cloudless empty sky and gaze down upon the greatness of his dominion.

To what end had he awakened? Was this city, this hive of hopeless toilers, the final refutation of his ancient hopes? Or was the fire of liberty, the fire that had blazed and waned in the years of his past life, still smouldering below there? He thought of the stir and impulse of the song of the revolution. Was that song merely the trick of a demagogue, to be forgotten when its purpose was served? Was the hope that still stirred within him only the memory of abandoned things, the vestige of a creed outworn? Or had it a wider meaning, an import interwoven with the destiny of man? To what end had he awakened, what was there for him to do? Humanity was spread below him like a map. He thought of the millions and millions of humanity following each other unceasingly for ever out of the darkness of non-existence into the darkness of death. To what end? Aim there must be, but it transcended his power of thought. He saw for the first time clearly his own infinite littleness, saw stark and terrible the tragic contrast of human strength and the craving of the human heart. For that little while he knew himself for the petty accident he was, and knew therewith the greatness of his desire. And suddenly his littleness was intolerable, his aspiration was intolerable, and there came to him an irresistible impulse to pray. And he prayed. He prayed vague, incoherent, contradictory things, his soul strained up through time and space and all the fleeting multitudinous confusion of being, towards something—he scarcely knew what—towards something that could comprehend his striving and endure.

A man and a woman were far below on a roof space to the southward enjoying the freshness of the morning air. The man had brought out a perspective glass to spy upon the Council House and he was showing her how to use it. Presently their curiosity was satisfied, they could see no traces of bloodshed from their position, and after a survey of the empty sky she came round to the crow's nest. And there she saw two little black figures, so small it was hard to believe they were men, one who watched and one who gesticulated with hands outstretched to the silent emptiness of Heaven.

She handed the glass to the man. He looked and exclaimed:

"I believe it is the Master. Yes. I am sure. It is the Master!"

He lowered the glass and looked at her. "Waving his hands about almost as if he was praying. I wonder what he is up to. Worshipping the sun? There weren't Parses in this country in his time, were there?"

He looked again. "He's stopped it now. It was a chance attitude, I suppose." He put down the glass and became meditative. "He won't have anything to do but enjoy himself—just enjoy himself. Ostrog will boss the show of course. Ostrog will have to, because of keeping all these Labourer fools in bounds. Them and their song! And got it all by sleeping, dear eyes—just sleeping. It's a wonderful world."

CHAPTER XV
PROMINENT PEOPLE

The state apartments of the Wind Vane Keeper would have seemed astonishingly intricate to Graham had he entered them fresh from his nineteenth century life, but already he was growing accustomed to the scale of the new time. They can scarcely be described as halls and rooms, seeing that a complicated system of arches, bridges, passages and galleries divided and united every part of the great space. He came out through one of the now familiar sliding panels upon a. plateau of landing at the head of a flight of very broad and gentle steps, with men and women far more brilliantly dressed than any he had hitherto seen ascending and descending. From this position he looked down a vista of intricate ornament in lustreless white and mauve and purple, spanned by bridges that seemed wrought of porcelain and filigree, and terminating far off in a cloudy mystery of perforated screens.

Glancing upward, he saw tier above tier of ascending galleries with faces looking down upon him. The air was full of the babble of innumerable voices and of a music that descended from above, a gay and exhilarating music whose source he never discovered.

The central aisle was thick with people, but by no means uncomfortably crowded; altogether that assembly must have numbered many thousands.

They were brilliantly, even fantastically dressed, the men as fancifully as the women, for the sobering influence of the Puritan conception of dignity upon masculine dress had long since passed away. The hair of the men, too, though it was rarely worn long, was commonly curled in a manner that suggested the barber, and baldness had vanished from the earth. Frizzy straight-cut masses that would have charmed Rossetti abounded, and one gentleman, who was pointed out to Graham under the mysterious title of an "amorist", wore his hair in two becoming plaits a la Marguerite. The pigtail was in evidence; it would seem that citizens of Chinese extraction were no longer ashamed of their race. There was little uniformity of fashion apparent in the forms of clothing worn. The more shapely men displayed their symmetry in trunk hose, and here were puffs and slashes, and there a cloak and there a robe. The fashions of the days of Leo the Tenth were perhaps the prevailing influence, but the aesthetic conceptions of the far east were also patent. Masculine embonpoint, which, in Victorian times, would have been subjected to the tightly buttoned perils, the ruthless exaggeration of tight-legged tight-armed evening dress, now formed but the basis of a wealth of dignity and drooping folds. Graceful slenderness abounded also. To Graham, a typically stiff man from a typically stiff period, not only did these men seem altogether too graceful in person, but altogether too expressive in their vividly expressive faces. They gesticulated, they expressed surprise, interest, amusement, above all, they expressed the emotions excited in their minds by the ladies about them with astonishing frankness. Even at the first glance it was evident that women were in a great majority.

The ladies in the company of these gentlemen displayed in dress, bearing and manner alike, less emphasis and more intricacy. Some affected a classical simplicity of robing and subtlety of fold, after the fashion of the First French Empire, and flashed conquering arms and shoulders as Graham passed. Others had closely-fitting dresses without seam or belt at the waist, sometimes with long folds falling from the shoulders. The delightful confidences of evening dress had not been diminished by the passage of two centuries.

Everyone's movements seemed graceful. Graham remarked to Lincoln that he saw men as Raphael's cartoons walking, and Lincoln told him that the attainment of an appropriate set of gestures was part of every rich person's education. The Master's entry was greeted with a sort of tittering applause, but these people showed their distinguished manners by not crowding upon him nor annoying him by any persistent scrutiny, as he descended the steps towards the floor of the aisle.

He had already learnt from Lincoln that these were the leaders of existing London society; almost every person there that night was either a powerful official or the immediate connexion of a powerful official. Many had returned from the European Pleasure Cities expressly to welcome him. The aeronautic authorities, whose defection had played a part in the overthrow of the Council only second to Graham's were very prominent, and so, too, was the Wind Vane Control. Amongst others there were several of the more prominent officers of the Food Trust; the controller of the European Piggeries had a particularly melancholy and interesting countenance and a daintily cynical manner. A bishop in full canonicals passed athwart Graham's vision, conversing with a gentleman dressed exactly like the traditional Chaucer, including even the laurel wreath.

"Who is that?" he asked almost involuntarily

"The Bishop of London," said Lincoln.

"No—the other, I mean."

"Poet Laureate."

"You still?"

"He doesn't make poetry, of course. He's a cousin of Wotton—one of the Councillors. But he's one of the Red Rose Royalists—a delightful club—and they keep up the tradition of these things."

"Asano told me there was a King."

"The King doesn't belong. They had to expel him. It's the Stuart blood, I suppose; but really—"

"Too much?"

"Far too much."

Graham did not quite follow all this, but it seemed part of the general inversion of the new age. He bowed condescendingly to his first introduction. It was evident that subtle distinctions of class prevailed even in this assembly, that only to a small proportion of the guests, to an inner group, did Lincoln consider it appropriate to introduce him. This first introduction was the Master Aeronaut, a man whose suntanned face contrasted oddly with the delicate complexions about him. Just at present his critical defection from the Council made him a very important person indeed.

His manner contrasted very favourably, according to Graham's ideas, with the general bearing. He made a few commonplace remarks, assurances of loyalty and frank inquiries about the Master's health. His manner was breezy, his accent lacked the easy staccato of latter-day English. He made it admirably clear to Graham that he was a bluff "aerial dog"—he used that phrase—that there was no nonsense about him, that he was a thoroughly manly fellow and old-fashioned at that, that he didn't profess to know much, and that what he did not know was not worth knowing He made a manly bow, ostentatiously free from obsequiousness and passed.

"I am glad to see that type endures," said Graham

"Phonographs and kinematographs," said Lincoln, a little spitefully. "He has studied from the life." Graham glanced at the burly form again. It was oddly reminiscent.

"As a matter of fact we bought him," said Lincoln. "Partly. And partly he was afraid of Ostrog. Everything rested with him."

He turned sharply to introduce the Surveyor-General of the Public School Trust. This person was a willowy figure in a blue-grey academic gown, he beamed down upon Graham through _pince-nez_ of a Victorian pattern, and illustrated his remarks by gestures of a beautifully manicured hand. Graham was immediately interested in this gentleman's functions, and asked him a number of singularly direct questions. The Surveyor-General seemed quietly amused at the Master's fundamental bluntness. He was a little vague as to the monopoly of education his Company possessed; it was done by contract with the syndicate that ran the numerous London Municipalities, but he waxed enthusiastic over educational progress since the Victorian times. "We have conquered Cram," he said, "completely conquered Cram—there is not an examination left in the world. Aren't you glad?"

"How do you get the work done?" asked Graham.

"We make it attractive—as attractive as possible. And if it does not attract then—we let it go. We cover an immense field."

He proceeded to details, and they had a lengthy conversation. The Surveyor-General mentioned the names of Pestalozzi and Froebel with profound respect, although he displayed no intimacy with their epoch-making works. Graham learnt that University Extension still existed in a modified form. "There is a certain type of girl, for example," said the Surveyor-General, dilating with a sense of his usefulness, "with a perfect passion for severe studies—when they are not too difficult you know. We cater for them by the thousand. At this moment," he said with a Napoleonic touch, "nearly five hundred phonographs are lecturing in different parts of London on the influence exercised by Plato and Swift on the love affairs of Shelley, Hazlitt, and Burns. And afterwards they write essays on the lectures, and the names in order of merit are put in conspicuous places. You see how your little germ has grown? The illiterate middle-class of your days has quite passed away."

"About the public elementary schools," said Graham. "Do you control them?"

The Surveyor-General did, "entirely." Now, Graham, in his later democratic days, had taken a keen interest in these and his questioning quickened. Certain casual phrases that had fallen from the old man with whom he had talked in the darkness recurred to him. The Surveyor-General, in effect, endorsed the old man's words. "We have abolished Cram," he said, a phrase Graham was beginning to interpret as the abolition of all sustained work. The Surveyor-General became sentimental. "We try and make the elementary schools very pleasant for the little children. They will have to work so soon. Just a few simple principles—obedience—industry."

"You teach them very little?"

"Why should we? It only leads to trouble and discontent. We amuse them. Even as it is—there are troubles—agitations. Where the labourers get the ideas, one cannot tell. They tell one another. There are socialistic dreams—anarchy even! Agitators will get to work among them. I take it—I have always taken it—that my foremost duty is to fight against popular discontent. Why should people be made unhappy?"

"I wonder," said Graham thoughtfully. "But there are a great many things I want to know."

Lincoln, who had stood watching Graham's face throughout the conversation, intervened. "There are others," he said in an undertone.

The Surveyor-General of schools gesticulated himself away. "Perhaps," said Lincoln, intercepting a casual glance, "you would like to know some of these ladies?"

The daughter of the Manager of the Piggeries of the European Food Trust was a particularly charming little person with red hair and animated blue eyes. Lincoln left him awhile to converse with her, and she displayed herself as quite an enthusiast for the "dear old times," as she called them, that had seen the beginning of his trance. As she talked she smiled, and her eyes smiled in a manner that demanded reciprocity.

"I have tried," she said, "countless times—to imagine those old romantic days. And to you they are memories. How strange and crowded the world must seem to you! I have seen photographs and pictures of the old times, the little isolated houses built of bricks made out of burnt mud and all black with soot from your fires, the railway bridges, the simple advertisements, the solemn savage Puritanical men in strange black coats and those tall hats of theirs, iron railway trains on iron bridges overhead, horses and cattle, and even dogs running half wild about the streets. And suddenly, you have come into this!"

"Into this," said Graham.

"Out of your life—out of all that was familiar."

"The old life was not a happy one," said Graham. "I do not regret that."

She looked at him quickly. There was a brief pause. She sighed encouragingly. "No?"

"No," said Graham. "It was a little life—and unmeaning. But this—. We thought the world complex and crowded and civilised enough. Yet I see—although in this world I am barely four days old—looking back on my own time, that it was a queer, barbaric time—the mere beginning of this new order. The mere beginning of this new order. You will find it hard to understand how little I know."

"You may ask me what you like," she said, smiling at him.

"Then tell me who these people are. I'm still very much in the dark about them. It's puzzling. Are there any Generals?"

"Men in hats and feathers?"

"Of course not. No. I suppose they are the men who control the great public businesses. Who is that distinguished looking man?"

"That? He's a most important officer. That is Morden. He is managing director of the Antibilious Pill Company. I have heard that his workers sometimes turn out a myriad myriad pills a day in the twenty-four hours. Fancy a myriad myriad!"

"A myriad myriad. No wonder he looks proud," said Graham. "Pills! What a wonderful time it is! That man in purple?"

"He is not quite one of the inner circle, you know. But we like him. He is really clever and very amusing. He is one of the heads of the Medical Faculty of our London University. All medical men, you know, are shareholders in the Medical Faculty Company, and wear that purple. You have to be—to be qualified. But of course, people who are paid by fees for doing something—" She smiled away the social pretensions of all such people.

"Are any of your great artists or authors here?"

"No authors. They are mostly such queer people—and so preoccupied about themselves. And they quarrel so dreadfully! They will fight, some of them, for precedence on staircases! Dreadful isn't it? But I think Wraysbury, the fashionable capillotomist, is here. From Capri."

"Capillotomist," said Graham. "Ah! I remember. An artist! Why not?"

"We have to cultivate him," she said apologetically. "Our heads are in his hands." She smiled.

Graham hesitated at the invited compliment, but his glance was expressive. "Have the arts grown with the rest of civilised things?" he said. "Who are your great painters?"

She looked at him doubtfully. Then laughed. "For a moment," she said, "I thought you meant—" She laughed again. "You mean, of course, those good men you used to think so much of because they could cover great spaces of canvas with oil-colours? Great oblongs. And people used to put the things in gilt frames and hang them up in rows in their square rooms. We haven't any. People grew tired of that sort of thing."

"But what did you think I meant?"

She put a finger significantly on a cheek whose glow was above suspicion, and smiled and looked very arch and pretty and inviting. "And here," and she indicated her eyelid.

Graham had an adventurous moment. Then a grotesque memory of a picture he had somewhere seen of Uncle Toby and the Widow flashed across his mind. An archaic shame came upon him. He became acutely aware that he was visible to a great number of interested people. "I see," he remarked inadequately. He turned awkwardly away from her, fascinating facility. He looked about him to meet a number of eyes that immediately occupied themselves with other things. Possibly he coloured a little. "Who is that talking with the lady in saffron?" he asked, avoiding her eyes.

The person in question he learnt was one of the great organisers of the American theatres just fresh from a gigantic production at Mexico. His face reminded Graham of a bust of Caligula. Another striking looking man was the Black Labour Master. The phrase at the time made no deep impression, but afterwards it recurred;—the Black Labour Master? The little lady, in no degree embarrassed, pointed out to him a charming little woman as one of the subsidiary wives of the Anglican Bishop of London. She added encomiums on the episcopal courage—hitherto there had been a rule of clerical monogamy—"neither a natural nor an expedient condition of things. Why should the natural development of the affections be dwarfed and restricted because a man is a priest?"

"And, bye the bye," she added, "are you an Anglican?" Graham was on the verge of hesitating inquiries about the status of a "subsidiary wife," apparently an euphemistic phrase, when Lincoln's return broke off this very suggestive and interesting conversation. They crossed the aisle to where a tall man in crimson, and two charming persons in Burmese costume (as it seemed to him) awaited him diffidently. From their civilities he passed to other presentations.

In a little while his multitudinous impressions began to organise themselves into a general effect. At first the glitter of the gathering had raised all the democrat in Graham; he had felt hostile and satirical. But it is not in human nature to resist an atmosphere of courteous regard. Soon the music, the light, the play of colours, the shining arms and shoulders about him, the touch of hands, the transient interest of smiling faces, the frothing sound of skillfully modulated voices, the atmosphere of compliment, interest and respect, had woven together into a fabric of indisputable pleasure. Graham for a time forgot his spacious resolutions. He gave way insensibly to the intoxication of the position that was conceded him, his manner became less conscious, more convincingly regal, his feet walked assuredly, the black robe fell with a bolder fold and pride ennobled his voice. After all this was a brilliant interesting world.

His glance went approvingly over the shifting colours of the people, it rested here and there in kindly criticism upon a face. Presently it occurred to him that he owed some apology to the charming little person with the red hair and blue eyes. He felt guilty of a clumsy snub. It was not princely to ignore her advances, even if his policy necessitated their rejection. He wondered if he should see her again. And suddenly a little thing touched all the glamour of this brilliant gathering and changed its quality.

He looked up and saw passing across a bridge of porcelain and looking down upon him, a face that was almost immediately hidden, the face of the girl he had seen overnight in the little room beyond the theatre after his escape from the Council. And she was looking with much the same expression of curious expectation, of uncertain intentness, upon his proceedings. For the moment he did not remember when he had seen her, and then with recognition came a vague memory of the stirring emotions of their first encounter. But the dancing web of melody about him kept the air of that great marching song from his memory.

The lady to whom he was talking repeated her remark, and Graham recalled himself to the quasiregal flirtation upon which he was engaged.

But from that moment a vague restlessness, a feeling that grew to dissatisfaction, came into his mind. He was troubled as if by some half forgotten duty, by the sense of things important slipping from him amidst this light and brilliance. The attraction that these bright ladies who crowded about him were beginning to exercise ceased. He no longer made vague and clumsy responses to the subtly amorous advances that he was now assured were being made to him, and his eyes wandered for another sight of that face that had appealed so strongly to his sense of beauty. But he did not see her again until he was awaiting Lincoln's return to leave this assembly. In answer to his request Lincoln had promised that an attempt should be made to fly that afternoon, if the weather permitted. He had gone to make certain necessary arrangements.

Graham was in one of the upper galleries in conversation with a bright-eyed lady on the subject of Eadhamite—the subject was his choice and not hers. He had interrupted her warm assurances of personal devotion with a matter-of-fact inquiry. He found her, as he had already found several other latter-day women that night, less well informed than charming. Suddenly, struggling against the eddying drift of nearer melody, the song of the Revolt, the great song he had heard in the Hall, hoarse and massive, came beating down to him.

He glanced up startled, and perceived above him an _oeil de boeuf_ through which this song had come, and beyond, the upper courses of cable, the blue haze, and the pendant fabric of the lights of the public ways. He heard the song break into a tumult of voices and cease. But now he perceived quite clearly the drone and tumult of the moving platforms and a murmur of many people. He had a vague persuasion that he could not account for, a sort of instinctive feeling that outside in the ways a huge crowd must be watching this place in which their Master amused himself. He wondered what they might be thinking.

Though the song had stopped so abruptly, though the special music of this gathering reasserted itself, the motif of the marching song, once it had begun, lingered in his mind.

The bright-eyed lady was still struggling with the mysteries of Eadhamite when he perceived the girl he had seen in the theatre again. She was coming now along the gallery towards him; he saw her first before she saw him. She was dressed in a faintly luminous grey, her dark hair about her brows was like a cloud, and as he saw her the cold light from the circular opening into the ways fell upon her downcast face.

The lady in trouble about the Eadhamite saw the change in his expression, and grasped her opportunity to escape. "Would you care to know that girl, Sire?" she asked boldly. "She is Helen Wotton—a niece of Ostrog's. She knows a great many serious things. She is one of the most serious persons alive. I am sure you will like her."

In another moment Graham was talking to the girl, and the bright-eyed lady had fluttered away.

"I remember you quite well," said Graham. "You were in that little room. When all the people were singing and beating time with their feet. Before I walked across the Hall."

Her momentary embarrassment passed. She looked up at him, and her face was steady. "It was wonderful," she said, hesitated, and spoke with a sudden effort. "All those people would have died for you, Sire. Countless people did die for you that night."

Her face glowed. She glanced swiftly aside to see that no other heard her words.

Lincoln appeared some way off along the gallery, making his way through the press towards them. She saw him and turned to Graham strangely eager, with a swift change to confidence and intimacy. "Sire," she said quickly, "I cannot tell you now and here. But the common people are very unhappy; they are oppressed—they are misgoverned. Do not forget the people, who faced death—death that you might live."

"I know nothing—" began Graham.

"I cannot tell you now."

Lincoln's face appeared close to them. He bowed an apology to the girl.

"You find the new world pleasant, Sire?" asked Lincoln, with smiling deference, and indicating the space and splendour of the gathering by one comprehensive gesture. "At any rate, you find it changed."

"Yes," said Graham, "changed. And yet, after all, not so greatly changed."

"Wait till you are in the air," said Lincoln. "The wind has fallen; even now an aeropile awaits you."

The girl's attitude awaited dismissal.

Graham glanced at her face, was on the verge of a question, found a warning in her expression, bowed to her and turned to accompany Lincoln.

CHAPTER XVI
THE AEROPHILE

For a while, as Graham went through the passages of the Wind-Vane offices with Lincoln, he was preoccupied. But, by an effort, he attended to the things which Lincoln was saying. Soon his preoccupation vanished. Lincoln was talking of flying. Graham had a strong desire to know more of this new human attainment. He began to ply Lincoln with questions. He had followed the crude beginnings of aerial navigation very keenly in his previous life; he was delighted to find the familiar names of Maxim and Pilcher, Langley and Chanute, and, above all, of the aerial proto-martyr Lillienthal, still honoured by men.

Even during his previous life two lines of investigation had pointed clearly to two distinct types of contrivance as possible, and both of these had been realised. On the one hand was the great engine-driven aeroplane, a double row of horizontal floats with a big aerial screw behind, and on the other the nimbler aeropile. The aeroplanes flew safely only in a calm or moderate wind, and sudden storms, occurrences that were now accurately predictable, rendered them for all practical purposes useless. They were built of enormous size—the usual stretch of wing being six hundred feet or more, and the length of the fabric a thousand feet. They were for passenger traffic alone. The lightly swung car they carried was from a hundred to a hundred and fifty feet in length. It Was hung in a peculiar manner in order to minimise the complex vibration that even a moderate wind produced, and for the same reason the little seats within the car—each passenger remained seated during the voyage—were slung with great freedom of movement. The starting of the mechanism was only possible from a gigantic car on the rail of a specially constructed stage. Graham had seen these vast stages, the flying stages, from the crow's nest very well. Six huge blank areas they were, with a giant "carrier" stage on each.

The choice of descent was equally circumscribed, an accurately plane surface being needed for safe grounding. Apart from the destruction that would have been caused by the descent of this great expanse of sail and metal, and the impossibility of its rising again, the concussion of an irregular surface, a tree-set hillside, for instance, or an embankment, would be sufficient to pierce or damage the framework, to smash the ribs of the body, and perhaps kill those aboard.

At first Graham felt disappointed with these cumbersome contrivances, but he speedily grasped the fact that smaller machines would have been unremunerative, for the simple reason that their carrying power would be disproportionately diminished with diminished size. Moreover, the huge size of these things enabled them—and it was a consideration of primary importance—to traverse the air at enormous speeds, and so run no risks of unanticipated weather. The briefest journey performed, that from London to Paris, took about three-quarters of an hour, but the velocity attained was not high; the leap to New York occupied about two hours, and by timing oneself carefully at the intermediate stations it was possible in quiet weather to go around the world in a day.

The little aeropiles (as for no particular reason they were distinctively called) were of an altogether different type. Several of these were going to and fro in the air. They were designed to carry only one or two persons, and their manufacture and maintenance was so costly as to render them the monopoly of the richer sort of people. Their sails, which were brilliantly coloured, consisted only of two pairs of lateral air floats in the same plane, and of a screw behind. Their small size rendered a descent in any open space neither difficult nor disagreeable, and it was possible to attach pneumatic wheels or even the ordinary motors for terrestrial traffic to them, and so carry them to a convenient starting place. They required a special sort of swift car to throw them into the air, but such a car was efficient in any open place clear of high buildings or trees. Human aeronautics, Graham perceived, were evidently still a long way behind the instinctive gift of the albatross or the fly-catcher. One great influence that might have brought the aeropile to a more rapid perfection had been withheld; these inventions had never been used in warfare. The last great international struggle had occurred before the usurpation of the Council.

The Flying Stages of London were collected together in an irregular crescent on the southern side of the river. They formed three groups of two each and retained the names of ancient suburban hills or villages. They were named in order, Roehampton, Wimbledon Park, Streatham, Norwood, Blackheath, and Shooter's Hill. They were uniform structures rising high above the general roof surfaces. Each was about four thousand yards long and a thousand broad, and constructed of the compound of aluminium and iron that had replaced iron in architecture. Their higher tiers formed an openwork of girders through which lifts and staircases ascended. The upper surface was a uniform expanse, with portions—the starting carriers—that could be raised and were then able to run on very slightly inclined rails to the end of the fabric. Save for any aeropiles or aeroplanes that were in port these open surfaces were kept clear for arrivals.

During the adjustment of the aeroplanes it was the custom for passengers to wait in the system of theatres, restaurants, news-rooms, and places of pleasure and indulgence of various sorts that interwove with the prosperous shops below. This portion of London was in consequence commonly the gayest of all its districts, with something of the meretricious gaiety of a seaport or city of hotels. And for those who took a more serious view of aeronautics, the religious quarters had flung out an attractive colony of devotional chapels, while a host of brilliant medical establishments competed to supply physical preparatives for the journey. At various levels through the mass of chambers and passages beneath these, ran, in addition to the main moving ways of the city which laced and gathered here, a complex system of special passages and lifts and slides, for the convenient interchange of people and luggage between stage and stage. And a distinctive feature of the architecture of this section was the ostentatious massiveness of the metal piers and girders that everywhere broke the vistas and spanned the halls and passages, crowding and twining up to meet the weight of the stages and the weighty impact of the aeroplanes overhead.

Graham went to the flying stages by the public ways. He was accompanied by Asano, his Japanese attendant. Lincoln was called away by Ostrog, who was busy with his administrative concerns. A strong guard of the Wind-Vane police awaited the Master outside the Wind-Vane offices, and they cleared a space for him on the upper moving platform. His passage to the flying stages was unexpected, nevertheless a considerable crowd gathered and followed him to his destination. As he went along, he could hear the people shouting his name, and saw numberless men and women and children in blue come swarming up the staircases in the central path, gesticulating and shouting. He could not hear what they shouted. He was struck again by the evident existence of a vulgar dialect among the poor of the city. When at last he descended, his guards were immediately surrounded by a dense excited crowd. Afterwards it occurred to him that some had attempted to reach him with petitions. His guards cleared a passage for him with difficulty.

He found an aeropile in charge of an aeronaut awaiting him on the westward stage. Seen close this mechanism was no longer small. As it lay on its launching carrier upon the wide expanse of the flying stage, its aluminium body skeleton was as big as the hull of a twenty-ton yacht. Its lateral supporting sails braced and stayed with metal nerves almost like the nerves of a bee's wing, and made of some sort of glassy artificial membrane, cast their shadow over many hundreds of square yards. The chairs for the engineer and his passenger hung free to swing by a complex tackle, within the protecting ribs of the frame and well abaft the middle. The passenger's chair was protected by a wind-guard and guarded about with metallic rods carrying air cushions. It could, if desired, be completely closed in, but Graham was anxious for novel experiences, and desired that it should be left open. The aeronaut sat behind a glass that sheltered his face. The passenger could secure himself firmly in his seat, and this was almost unavoidable on landing, or he could move along by means of a little rail and rod to a locker at the stem of the machine, where his personal luggage, his wraps and restoratives were placed, and which also with the seats, served as a makeweight to the parts of the central engine that projected to the propeller at the stern.

The engine was very simple in appearance. Asano, pointing out the parts of this apparatus to him, told him that, like the gas-engine of Victorian days, it was of the explosive type, burning a small drop of a substance called "fomile" at each stroke. It consisted simply of reservoir and piston about the long fluted crank of the propeller shaft. So much Graham saw of the machine.

The flying stage about him was empty save for Asano and their suite of attendants. Directed by the aeronaut he placed himself in his seat. He then drank a mixture containing ergot—a dose, he learnt, invariably administered to those about to fly, and designed to counteract the possible effect of diminished air pressure upon the system. Having done so, he declared himself ready for the journey. Asano took the empty glass from him, stepped through the bars of the hull, and stood below on the stage waving his hand. Suddenly he seemed to slide along the stage to the right and vanish.

The engine was beating, the propeller spinning, and for a second the stage and the buildings beyond were gliding swiftly and horizontally past Graham's eye; then these things seemed to tilt up abruptly. He gripped the little rods on either side of him instinctively. He felt himself moving upward, heard the air whistle over the top of the wind screen. The propeller screw moved round with powerful rhythmic impulses—one, two, three, pause; one, two, three—which the engineer controlled very delicately. The machine began a quivering vibration that continued throughout the flight, and the roof areas seemed running away to starboard very quickly and growing rapidly smaller. He looked from the face of the engineer through the ribs of the machine. Looking sideways, there was nothing very startling in what he saw—a rapid funicular railway might have given the same sensations. He recognised the Council House and the Highgate Ridge. And then he looked straight down between his feet.

For a moment physical terror possessed him, a passionate sense of insecurity. He held tight. For a second or so he could not lift his eyes. Some hundred feet or more sheer below him was one of the big windvanes of south-west London, and beyond it the southernmost flying stage crowded with little black dots. These things seemed to be falling away from him. For a second he had an impulse to pursue the earth. He set his teeth, he lifted his eyes by a muscular effort, and the moment of panic passed.

He remained for a space with his teeth set hard, his eyes staring into the sky. Throb, throb, throb—beat, went the engine; throb, throb, throb,—beat. He gripped his bars tightly, glanced at the aeronaut, and saw a smile upon his sun-tanned face. He smiled in return—perhaps a little artificially. "A little strange at first," he shouted before he recalled his dignity. But he dared not look down again for some time. He stared over the aeronaut's head to where a rim of vague blue horizon crept up the sky. For a little while he could not banish the thought of possible accidents from his mind. Throb, throb, throb—beat; suppose some trivial screw went wrong in that supporting engine! Suppose—! He made a grim effort to dismiss all such suppositions. After a while they did at least abandon the foreground of his thoughts. And up he went steadily, higher and higher into the clear air.

Once the mental shock of moving unsupported through the air was over, his sensations ceased to be unpleasant, became very speedily pleasurable. He had been warned of air sickness. But he found the pulsating movement of the aeropile as it drove up the faint south-west breeze was very little in excess of the pitching of a boat head on to broad rollers in a moderate gale, and he was constitutionally a good sailor. And the keenness of the more rarefied air into which they ascended produced a sense of lightness and exhilaration. He looked up and saw the blue sky above fretted with cirrus clouds. His eye came cautiously down through the ribs and bars to a shining flight of white birds that hung in the lower sky. For a space he watched these. Then going lower and less apprehensively, he saw the slender figure of the Wind-Vane keeper's crow's nest shining golden in the sunlight and growing smaller every moment. As his eye fell with more confidence now, there came a blue line of hills, and then London, already to leeward, an intricate space of roofing. Its near edge came sharp and clear, and banished his last apprehensions in a shock of surprise. For the boundary of London was like a wall, like a cliff, a steep fall of three or four hundred feet, a frontage broken only by terraces here and there, a complex decorative facade.

That gradual passage of town into country through an extensive sponge of suburbs, which was so characteristic a feature of the great cities of the nineteenth century, existed no longer. Nothing remained of it but a waste of ruins here, variegated and dense with thickets of the heterogeneous growths that had once adorned the gardens of the belt, interspersed among levelled brown patches of sown ground, and verdant stretches of winter greens. The latter even spread among the vestiges of houses. But for the most part the reefs and skerries of ruins, the wreckage of suburban villas, stood among their streets and roads, queer islands amidst the levelled expanses of green and brown, abandoned indeed by the inhabitants years since, but too substantial, it seemed', to be cleared out of the way of the wholesale horticultural mechanisms of the time.

The vegetation of this waste undulated and frothed amidst the countless cells of crumbling house walls, and broke along the foot of the city wall in a surf of bramble and holly and ivy and teazle and tall grasses. Here and there gaudy pleasure palaces towered amidst the puny remains of Victorian times, and cable ways slanted to them from the city. That winter day they seemed deserted. Deserted, too, were the artificial gardens among the ruins. The city limits were indeed as sharply defined as in the ancient days when the gates were shut at nightfall and the robber foreman prowled to the very walls. A huge semi-circular throat poured out a vigorous traffic upon the Eadhamite Bath Road. So the first prospect of the world beyond the city flashed on Graham, and dwindled. And when at last he could look vertically downward again, he saw below him the vegetable fields of the Thames valley—innumerable minute oblongs of ruddy brown, intersected by shining threads, the sewage ditches.

His exhilaration increased rapidly, became a sort of intoxication. He found himself drawing deep breaths of air, laughing aloud, desiring to shout. After a time that desire became too strong for him, and he shouted.

The machine had now risen as high as was customary with aeropiles, and they began to curve about towards the south. Steering, Graham perceived, was effected by the opening or closing of one or two thin strips of membrane in one or other of the otherwise rigid wings, and by the movement of the whole engine backward or forward along its supports. The aeronaut set the engine gliding slowly forward along its rail and opened the valve of the leeward wing until the stem of the aeropile was horizontal and pointing southward. And in that direction they drove with a slight list to leeward, and with a slow alternation of movement, first a short, sharp ascent and then a long downward glide that was very swift and pleasing. During these downward glides the propellor was inactive altogether. These ascents gave Graham a glorious sense of successful effort; the descents through the rarefied air were beyond all experience. He wanted never to leave the upper air again.

For a time he was intent upon the minute details of the landscape that ran swiftly northward beneath him. Its minute, clear detail pleased him exceedingly. He was impressed by the ruin of the houses that had once dotted the country, by the vast treeless expanse of country from which all farms and villages had gone, save for crumbling ruins. He had known the thing was so, but seeing it so was an altogether different matter. He tried to make out places he had known within the hollow basin of the world below, but at first he could distinguish no data now that the Thames valley was left behind. Soon, however, they were driving over a sharp chalk hill that he recognised as the Guildford Hog's Back, because of the familiar outline of the gorge at its eastward end, and because of the ruins of the town that rose steeply on either lip of this gorge. And from that he made out other points, Leith Hill, the sandy wastes of Aldershot, and so forth. The Downs escarpment was set with gigantic slow-moving wind-wheels. Save where the broad Eadhamite Portsmouth Road, thickly dotted with rushing shapes, followed the course of the old railway, the gorge of the Wey was choked with thickets.

The whole expanse of the Downs escarpment, so far as the grey haze permitted him to see, was set with wind-wheels to which the largest of the city was but a younger brother. They stirred with a stately motion before the south-west wind. And here and there were patches dotted with the sheep of the British Food Trust, and here and there a mounted shepherd made a spot of black. Then rushing under the stern of the aeropile came the Wealden Heights, the line of Hindhead, Pitch Hill, and Leith Hill, with a second row of wind-wheels that seemed striving to rob the downland whirlers of their share of breeze. The purple heather was speckled with yellow gorse, and on the further side a drove of black oxen stampeded before a couple of mounted men. Swiftly these swept behind, and dwindled and lost colour, and became scarce moving specks that were swallowed up in haze.

And when these had vanished in the distance Graham heard a peewit wailing close at hand. He perceived he was now above the South Downs, and staring over his shoulder saw the battlements of Portsmouth Landing Stage towering over the ridge of Portsdown Hill. In another moment there came into sight a spread of shipping like floating cities, the little white cliffs of the Needles dwarfed and sunlit, and the grey and glittering waters of the narrow sea. They seemed to leap the Solent in a moment, and in a few seconds the Isle of Wight was running past, and then beneath him spread a wider and wide extent of sea, here purple with the shadow of a cloud, here grey, here a burnished mirror, and here a spread of cloudy greenish blue. The Isle of Wight grew smaller and smaller. In a few more minutes a strip of grey haze detached itself from other strips that were clouds, descended out of the sky and became a coastline—sunlit and pleasant—the coast of northern France. It rose, it took colour, became definite and detailed, and the counterpart of the Downland of England was speeding by below.

In a little time, as it seemed, Paris came above the horizon, and hung there for a space, and sank out of sight again as the aeropile circled about to the north again. But he perceived the Eiffel Tower still standing, and beside it a huge dome surmounted by a pinpoint Colossus. And he perceived, too, though he did not understand it at the time, a slanting drift of smoke. The aeronaut said something about "trouble in the underways," that Graham did not heed at the time. But he marked the minarets and towers and slender masses that streamed skyward above the city windvanes, and knew that in the matter of grace at least Paris still kept in front of her larger rival. And even as he looked a pale blue shape ascended very swiftly from the city like a dead leaf driving up before a gale. It curved round and soared towards them growing rapidly larger and larger. The aeronaut was saying something. "What?" said Graham, loath to take his eyes from this. "Aeroplane, Sire," bawled the aeronaut pointing.

They rose and curved about northward as it drew nearer. Nearer it came and nearer, larger and larger. The throb, throb, throb—beat, of the aeropile's flight, that had seemed so potent and so swift, suddenly appeared slow by comparison with this tremendous rush. How great the monster seemed, how swift and steady! It passed quite closely beneath them, driving along silently, a vast spread of wirenetted translucent wings, a thing alive. Graham had a momentary glimpse of the rows and rows of wrapped-up passengers, slung in their little cradles behind wind-screens, of a white-clothed engineer crawling against the gale along a ladder way, of spouting engines beating together, of the whirling wind screw, and of a wide waste of wing. He exulted in the sight. And in an instant the thing had passed.

It rose slightly and their own little wings swayed in the rush of its flight. It fell and grew smaller. Scarcely had they moved, as it seemed, before it was again only a flat blue thing that dwindled in the sky. This was the aeroplane that went to and fro between London and Paris. In fair weather and in peaceful times it came and went four times a day.

They beat across the Channel, slowly as it seemed now, to Graham's enlarged ideas, and Beachy Head rose greyly to the left of them.

"Land," called the aeronaut, his voice small against the whistling of the air over the wind-screen.

"Not yet," bawled Graham, laughing. "Not land yet. I want to learn more of this machine."

"I meant—" said the aeronaut.

"I want to learn more of this machine," repeated Graham.

"I'm coming to you," he said, and had flung himself free of his chair and taken a step along the guarded rail between them. He stopped for a moment, and his colour changed and his hands tightened. Another step and he was clinging close to the aeronaut. He felt a weight on his shoulder, the pressure of the air. His hat was a whirling speck behind. The wind came in gusts over his wind-screen and blew his hair in streamers past his cheek. The aeronaut made some hasty adjustments for the shifting of the centres of gravity and pressure.

"I want to have these things explained," said Graham. "What do you do when you move that engine forward?"

The aeronaut hesitated. Then he answered, "They are complex, Sire."

"I don't mind," shouted Graham. "I don't mind."

There was a moment's pause. "Aeronautics is the secret—the privilege—"

"I know. But I'm the Master, and I mean to know." He laughed, full of this novel realisation of power that was his gift from the upper air.

The aeropile curved about, and the keen fresh wind cut across Graham's face and his garment lugged at his body as the stem pointed round to the west. The two men looked into each other's eyes.

"Sire, there are rules—"

"Not where I am concerned," said Graham. "You seem to forget."

The aeronaut scrutinised his face. "No," he said. "I do not forget, Sire. But in all the earth—no man who is not a sworn aeronaut—has ever a chance. They come as passengers—"

"I have heard something of the sort. But I'm not going to argue these points. Do you know why I have slept two hundred years? To fly!"

"Sire," said the aeronaut, "the rules—if I break the rules—"

Graham waved the penalties aside.

"Then if you will watch me—"

"No," said Graham, swaying and gripping tight as the machine lifted its nose again for an ascent. "That's not my game. I want to do it myself. Do it myself if I smash for it! No! I will. See. I am going to clamber by this to come and share your seat. Steady! I mean to fly of my own accord if I smash at the end of it. I will have something to pay for my sleep. Of all other things—. In my past it was my dream to fly. Now—keep your balance."

"A dozen spies are watching me, Sire!"

Graham's temper was at end. Perhaps he chose it should be. He swore. He swung himself round the intervening mass of levers and the aeropile swayed.

"Am I Master of the earth?" he said. "Or is your Society? Now. Take your hands off those levers, and hold my wrists. Yes—so. And now, how do we turn her nose down to the glide?"

"Sire," said the aeronaut.

"What is it?"

"You will protect me?"

"Lord! Yes! If I have to burn London. Now!"

And with that promise Graham bought his first lesson in aerial navigation. "It's clearly to your advantage, this journey," he said with a loud laugh—for the air was like strong wine—"to teach me quickly and well. Do I pull this? Ah! So! Hullo!"

"Back, Sire! Back!"

"Back—right. One—two—three—good God! Ah! Up she goes! But this is living!"

And now the machine began to dance the strangest figures in the air. Now it would sweep round a spiral of scarcely a hundred yards diameter, now it would rush up into the air and swoop down again, steeply, swiftly, falling like a hawk, to recover in a rushing loop that swept it high again. In one of these descents it seemed driving straight at the drifting park of balloons in the southeast, and only curved about and cleared them by a sudden recovery of dexterity. The extraordinary swiftness and smoothness of the motion, the extraordinary effect of the rarefied air upon his constitution, threw Graham into a careless fury.

But at last a queer incident came to sober him, to send him flying down once more to the crowded life below with all its dark insoluble riddles. As he swooped, came a tap and something flying past, and a drop like a drop of rain. Then as he went on down he saw something like a white rag whirling down in his wake. "What was that?" he asked. "I did not see."

The aeronaut glanced, and then clutched at the lever to recover, for they were sweeping down. When the aeropile was rising again he drew a deep breath and replied. "That," and he indicated the white thing still fluttering down, "was a swan."

"I never saw it," said Graham.

The aeronaut made no answer, and Graham saw little drops upon his forehead.

They drove horizontally while Graham clambered back to the passenger's place out of the lash of the wind. And then came a swift rush down, with the wind-screw whirling to check their fall, and the flying stage growing broad and dark before them. The sun, sinking over the chalk hills in the west, fell with them, and left the sky a blaze of gold.

Soon men could be seen as little specks. He heard a noise coming up to meet him, a noise like the sound of waves upon a pebbly beach, and saw that the roofs about the flying stage were dark with his people rejoicing over his safe return. A dark mass was crushed together under the stage, a darkness stippled with innumerable faces, and quivering with the minute oscillation of waved white handkerchiefs and waving hands.

CHAPTER XVII

THREE DAYS

Lincoln awaited Graham in an apartment beneath the flying stages. He seemed curious to learn all that had happened, pleased to hear of the extraordinary delight and interest which Graham took in flying Graham was in a mood of enthusiasm. "I must learn to fly," he cried. "I must master that. I pity all poor souls who have died without this opportunity. The sweet swift air! It is the most wonderful experience in the world."

"You will find our new times full of wonderful experiences," said Lincoln. "I do not know what you will care to do now. We have music that may seem novel."

"For the present," said Graham, "flying holds me. Let me learn more of that. Your aeronaut was saying there is some trades union objection to one's learning."

"There is, I believe," said Lincoln. "But for you—! If you would' like to occupy yourself with that, we can make you a sworn aeronaut tomorrow."

Graham expressed his wishes vividly and talked of his sensations for a while. "And as for affairs," he asked abruptly. "How are things going on?"

Lincoln waved affairs aside. "Ostrog will tell you that tomorrow," he said. "Everything is settling down. The Revolution accomplishes itself all over the world. Friction is inevitable here and there, of course; but your rule is assured. You may rest secure with things in Ostrog's hands."

"Would it be possible for me to be made a sworn aeronaut, as you call it, forthwith—before I sleep?" said Graham, pacing. "Then I could be at it the very first thing tomorrow again.

"It would be possible," said Lincoln thoughtfully. "Quite possible. Indeed, it shall be done." He laughed. "I came prepared to suggest amusements, but you have found one for yourself. I will telephone to the aeronautical offices from here and we will return to your apartments in the Wind-Vane Control. By the time you have dined the aeronauts will be able to come. You don't think that after you have dined, you might prefer—?" He paused.

"Yes," said Graham.

"We had prepared a show of dancers—they have been brought from the Capri theatre."

"I hate ballets," said Graham, shortly. "Always did. That other—. That's not what I want to see. We had dancers in the old days. For the matter of that, they had them in ancient Egypt. But flying—"

"True," said Lincoln. "Though our dancers—"

"They can afford to wait," said Graham; "they can afford to wait. I know. I'm not a Latin. There's questions I want to ask some expert—about your machinery. I'm keen. I want no distractions."

"You have the world to choose from," said Lincoln; "whatever you want is yours."

Asano appeared, and under the escort of a strong guard they returned through the city streets to Graham's apartments. Far larger crowds had assembled to witness his return than his departure had gathered, and the shouts and cheering of these masses of people sometimes drowned Lincoln's answers to the endless questions Graham's aerial journey had suggested. At first Graham had acknowledged the cheering and cries of the crowd by bows and gestures, but Lincoln warned him that such a recognition would be considered incorrect behaviour. Graham, already a little wearied by rhythmic civilities, ignored his subjects for the remainder of his public progress.

Directly they arrived at his apartments Asano departed in search of kinematographic renderings of machinery in motion, and Lincoln despatched Graham's commands for models of machines and small machines to illustrate the various mechanical advances of the last two centuries. The little group of appliances for telegraphic communication attracted the Master so strongly that his delightfully prepared dinner, served by a number of charmingly dexterous girls, waited for a space. The habit of smoking had almost ceased from the face of the earth, but when he expressed a wish for that indulgence, inquiries were made and some excellent cigars were discovered in Florida, and sent to him by pneumatic dispatch while the dinner was still in progress. Afterwards came the aeronauts, and a feast of ingenious wonders in the hands of a latter-day engineer. For the time, at any rate, the neat dexterity of counting and numbering machines, building machines, spinning engines, patent doorways, explosive motors, grain and water elevators, slaughter-house machines and harvesting appliances, was more fascinating to Graham than any bayadere. "We were savages," was his refrain, "we were savages. We were in the stone age—compared with this.... And what else have you?"

There came also practical psychologists with some very interesting developments in the art of hypnotism. The names of Milne Bramwell, Fechner, Liebault, William James, Myers and Gurney, he found, bore a value now that would have astonished their contemporaries. Several practical applications of psychology were now in general use; it had largely superseded drugs, antiseptics and anaesthetics in medicine; was employed by almost all who had any need of mental concentration. A real enlargement of human faculty seemed to have been effected in this direction. The feats of "calculating boys," the wonders, as Graham had been wont to regard them, of mesmerisers, were now within the range of anyone who could afford the services of a skilled hypnotist. Long ago the old examination methods in education had been destroyed by these expedients. Instead of years of study, candidates had substituted a few weeks of trances, and during the trances expert coaches had simply to repeat all the points necessary for adequate answering, adding a suggestion of the post hypnotic recollection of these points. In process mathematics particularly, this aid had been of singular service, and it was now invariably invoked by such players of chess and games of manual dexterity as were still to be found. In fact, all operations conducted under finite rules, of a quasi-mechanical sort that is, were now systematically relieved from the wanderings of imagination and emotion, and brought to an unexampled pitch of accuracy. Little children of the labouring classes, so soon as they were of sufficient age to be hypnotised, were thus converted into beautifully punctual and trustworthy machine minders, and released forthwith from the long, long thoughts of youth. Aeronautical pupils, who gave way to giddiness, could be relieved from their imaginary terrors. In every street were hypnotists ready to print permanent memories upon the mind. If anyone desired to remember a name, a series of numbers, a song or a speech, it could be done by this method, and conversely memories could be effaced, habits removed, and desires eradicated—a sort of psychic surgery was, in fact, in general use. Indignities, humbling experiences, were thus forgotten, amorous widows would obliterate their previous husbands, angry lovers release themselves from their slavery. To graft desires, however, was still impossible, and the facts of thought transference were yet unsystematised. The psychologists illustrated their expositions with some astounding experiments in mnemonics made through the agency of a troupe of pale-faced children in blue.

Graham, like most of the people of his former time, distrusted the hypnotist, or he might then and there have eased his mind of many painful preoccupations. But in spite of Lincoln's assurances he held to the old theory that to be hypnotised was in some way the surrender of his personality, the abdication of his will. At the banquet of wonderful experiences that was beginning, he wanted very keenly to remain absolutely himself.

The next day, and another day, and yet another day passed in such interests as these. Each day Graham spent many hours in the glorious entertainment of flying. On the third day he soared across middle France, and within sight of the snow-clad Alps. These vigorous exercises gave him restful sleep, and each day saw a great stride in his health from the spiritless anaemia of his first awakening. And whenever he was not in the air, and awake, Lincoln was assiduous in the cause of his amusement; all that was novel and curious in contemporary invention was brought to him, until at last his appetite for novelty was well-nigh glutted. One might fill a dozen inconsecutive volumes with the strange things they exhibited. Each afternoon he held his court for an hour or so. He speedily found his interest in his contemporaries becoming personal and intimate. At first he had been alert chiefly for unfamiliarity and peculiarity; any foppishness in their dress, any discordance with his preconceptions of nobility in their status and manners had jarred upon him, and it was remarkable to him how soon that strangeness and the faint hostility that arose from it, disappeared; how soon he came to appreciate the true perspective of his position, and see the old Victorian days remote and quaint. He found himself particularly amused by the red-haired daughter of the Manager of the European Piggeries. On the second day after dinner he made the acquaintance of a latter-day dancing girl, and found her an astonishing artist. And after that, more hypnotic wonders. On the third day Lincoln was moved to suggest that the Master should repair to a Pleasure City, but this Graham declined, nor would he accept the services of the hypnotists in his aeronautical experiments. The link of locality held him to London; he found a perpetual wonder in topographical identifications that he would have missed abroad. "Here—or a hundred feet below here," he could say, "I used to eat my midday cutlets during my London University days. Underneath here was Waterloo and the perpetual hunt for confusing trains. Often have I stood waiting down there, bag in hand, and stared up into the sky above the forest of signals, little thinking I should walk some day a hundred yards in the air. And now in that very sky that was once a grey smoke canopy, I circle in an aeropile."

During those three days Graham was so occupied with such distractions that the vast political movements in progress outside his quarters had but a small share of his attention. Those about him told him little. Daily came Ostrog, the Boss, his Grand Vizier, his mayor of the palace, to report in vague terms the steady establishment of his rule; "a little trouble" soon to be settled in this city, "a slight disturbance" in that. The song of the social revolt came to him no more; he never learned that it had been forbidden in the municipal limits; and all the great emotions of the crow's nest slumbered in his mind.

But on the second and third of the three days he found himself, in spite of his interest in the daughter of the Pig Manager, or it may be by, reason of the thoughts her conversation suggested, remembering the girl Helen Wotton, who had spoken to him so oddly at the Wind-Vane Keeper's gathering. The impression she had made was a deep one, albeit the incessant surprise of novel circumstances had kept him from brooding upon it for a space. But now her memory was coming to its own. He wondered what she had meant by those broken half-forgotten sentences; the picture of her eyes and the earnest passion of her face became more vivid as his mechanical interests faded. Her beauty came compellingly between him and certain immediate temptations of ignoble passion. But he did not see her again until three full days were past.

CHAPTER XVIII

GRAHAM REMEMBERS

She came upon him at last in a little gallery that ran from the Wind Vane Offices toward his state apartments. The gallery was long and narrow, with a series of recesses, each with an arched fenestration that looked upon a court of palms. He came upon her suddenly in one of these recesses. She was seated. She turned her head at the sound of his footsteps and started at the sight of him. Every touch of colour vanished from her face. She rose instantly, made a step toward him as if to address him, and hesitated. He stopped and stood still, expectant. Then he perceived that a nervous tumult silenced her, perceived too, that she must have sought speech with him to be waiting for him in this place.

He felt a regal impulse to assist her. "I have wanted to see you," he said. "A few days ago you wanted to tell me something—you wanted to tell me of the people. What was it you had to tell me?"

She looked at him with troubled eyes.

"You said the people were unhappy?"

For a moment she was silent still.

"It must have seemed strange to you," she said abruptly.

"It did. And yet—"

"It was an impulse."

"Well?"

"That is all."

She looked at him with a face of hesitation. She spoke with an effort. "You forget," she said, drawing a deep breath.

"What?"

"The people—"

"Do you mean—?"

"You forget the people."

He looked interrogative.

"Yes. I know you are surprised. For you do not understand what you are. You do not know the things that are happening."

"Well?"

"You do not understand."

"Not clearly, perhaps. But—tell me."

She turned to him with sudden resolution. "It is so hard to explain. I have meant to, I have wanted to. And now—I cannot. I am not ready with words. But about you—there is something. It is Wonder. Your sleep— your awakening. These things are miracles. To me at least—and to all the common people. You who lived and suffered and died, you who were a common citizen, wake again, live again, to find yourself Master almost of the earth."

"Master of the earth," he said. "So they tell me. But try and imagine how little I know of it."

"Cities—Trusts—the Labour Company—"

"Principalities, powers, dominions—the power and the glory. Yes, I have heard them shout. I know. I am Master. King, if you wish. With Ostrog, the Boss—"

He paused.

She turned upon him and surveyed his face with a curious scrutiny. "Well?"

He smiled. "To take the responsibility."

"That is what we have begun to fear." For a moment she said no more. "No," she said slowly. "You will take the responsibility. You will take the responsibility. The people look to you."

She spoke softly. "Listen! For at least half the years of your sleep—in every generation—multitudes of people, in every generation greater multitudes of people, have prayed that you might awake—prayed."

Graham moved to speak and did not.

She hesitated, and a faint colour crept back to her cheek. "Do you know that you have been to myriads—King Arthur, Barbarossa—the King who would come in his own good time and put the world right for them?"

"I suppose the imagination of the people—"

"Have you not heard our proverb, 'When the Sleeper wakes?' While you lay insensible and motionless there—thousands came. Thousands. Every first of the month you lay in state with a white robe upon you and the people filed by you. When I was a little girl I saw you like that, with your face white and calm."

She turned her face from him and looked steadfastly at the painted wall before her. Her voice fell. "When I was a little girl I used to look at your face....it seemed to me fixed and waiting, like the patience of God."

"That is what we thought of you," she said. "That is how you seemed to us."

She turned shining eyes to him, her voice was clear and strong. "In the city, in the earth, a myriad myriad men and women are waiting to see what you will do, full of strange incredible expectations."

"Yes?"

"Ostrog—no one—can take that responsibility."

Graham looked at her in surprise, at her face lit with emotion. She seemed at first to have spoken with an effort, and to have fired herself by speaking.

"Do you think," she said, "that you who have lived that little life so far away in the past, you who have fallen into and risen out of this miracle of sleep—do you think that the wonder and reverence and hope of half the world has gathered about you only that you may live another little life?... That you may shift the responsibility to any other man?"

"I know how great this kingship of mine is," he said haltingly. "I know how great it seems. But is it real? It is incredible—dreamlike. Is it real, or is it only a great delusion?"

"It is real," she said; "if you dare."

"After all, like all kingship, my kingship is Belief. It is an illusion in the minds of men."

"If you dare!" she said.

"But—"

"Countless men," she said, "and while it is in their minds—they will obey."

"But I know nothing. That is what I had in mind. I know nothing. And these others—the Councillors, Ostrog. They are wiser, cooler, they know so much, every detail. And, indeed, what are these miseries of which you speak? What am I to know? Do you mean—"

He stopped blankly.

"I am still hardly more than a girl," she said. "But to me the world seems full of wretchedness. The world has altered since your day, altered very strangely. I have prayed that I might see you and tell you these things. The world has changed. As if a canker had seized it—and robbed life of—everything worth having."

She turned a flushed face upon him, moving suddenly. "Your days were the days of freedom. Yes—I have thought. I have been made to think, for my life—has not been happy. Men are no longer free—no greater, no better than the men of your time. That is not all. This city—is a prison. Every city now is a prison. Mammon grips the key in his hand. Myriads, countless myriads, toil from the cradle to the grave. Is that right? Is that to be—for ever? Yes, far worse than in your time. All about us, beneath us, sorrow and pain. All the shallow delight of such life as you find about you, is separated by just a little from a life of wretchedness beyond any telling Yes, the poor know it—they know they suffer. These countless multitudes who faced death for you two nights since—! You owe your life to them."

"Yes," said Graham, slowly. "Yes. I owe my life to them."

"You come," she said, "from the days when this new tyranny of the cities was scarcely beginning. It is a tyranny—a tyranny. In your days the feudal war lords had gone, and the new lordship of wealth had still to come. Half the men in the world still lived out upon the free countryside. The cities had still to devour them. I have heard the stories out of the old books—there was nobility! Common men led lives of love and faithfulness then—they did a thousand things. And you—you come from that time."

"It was not—. But never mind. How is it now—?"

"Gain and the Pleasure Cities! Or slavery—unthanked, unhonoured, slavery."

"Slavery!" he said.

"Slavery."

"You don't mean to say that human beings are chattels."

"Worse. That is what I want you to know, what I want you to see. I know you do not know. They will keep things from you, they will take you presently to a Pleasure City. But you have noticed men and women and children in pale blue canvas, with thin yellow faces and dull eyes?"

"Everywhere."

"Speaking a horrible dialect, coarse and weak."

"I have heard it."

"They are the slaves—your slaves. They are the slaves of the Labour Company you own."

"The Labour Company! In some way—that is familiar. Ah! now I remember. I saw it when I was wandering about the city, after the lights returned, great fronts of buildings coloured pale blue. Do you really mean—?"

"Yes. How can I explain it to you? Of course the blue uniform struck you. Nearly a third of our people wear it—more assume it now every day. This Labour Company has grown imperceptibly."

"What is this Labour Company?" asked Graham.

"In the old times, how did you manage with starving people?"

"There was the workhouse—which the parishes maintained."

"Workhouse! Yes—there was something. In our history lessons. I remember now. The Labour Company ousted the workhouse. It grew—partly—out of something—you, perhaps, may remember it—an emotional religious organisation called the Salvation Army—that became a business company. In the first place it was almost a charity. To save people from workhouse rigours. Now I come to think of it, it was one of the earliest properties your Trustees acquired. They bought the Salvation Army and reconstructed it as this. The idea in the first place was to give work to starving homeless people."

"Yes."

"Nowadays there are no workhouses, no refuges and charities, nothing but that Company. Its offices are everywhere. That blue is its colour. And any man, woman or child who comes to be hungry and weary and with neither home nor friend nor resort, must go to the Company in the end—or seek some way of death. The Euthanasy is beyond their means—for the poor there is no easy death. And at any hour in the day or night there is food, shelter and a blue uniform for all comers—that is the first condition of the Company's incorporation—and in return for a day's shelter the Company extracts a day's work, and then returns the visitor's proper clothing and sends him or her out again."

"Yes?"

"Perhaps that does not seem so terrible to you. In your days men starved in your streets. That was bad. But they died—men. These people in blue—. The proverb runs: 'Blue canvas once and ever.' The Company trades in their labour, and it has taken care to assure itself of the supply. People come to it starving and helpless—they eat and sleep for a night and day, they—work for a day, and at the end of the day they go out again. If they have worked well they have a penny or so—enough for a theatre or a cheap dancing place, or a kinematograph story, or a dinner or a bet. They wander about after that is spent. Begging is prevented by the police of the ways. Besides, no one gives. They come back again the next day or the day after—brought back by the same incapacity that brought them first. At last their proper clothing wears out, or their rags get so shabby that they are ashamed. Then they must work for months to get fresh. If they want fresh. A great number of children are born under the Company's care. The mother owes them a month thereafter—the children they cherish and educate until they are fourteen, and they pay two years' service. You may be sure these children are educated for the blue canvas. And so it is the Company works."

"And none are destitute in the city?"

"None. They are either in blue canvas or in prison."

"If they will not work?"

"Most people will work at that pitch, and the Company has powers. There are stages of unpleasantness in the work—stoppage of food—and a man or woman who has refused to work once is known by a thumb-marking system in the Company's offices all over the world. Besides, who can leave the city poor? To go to Paris costs two Lions. And for insubordination there are the prisons—dark and miserable—out of sight below. There are prisons now for many things."

"And a third of the people wear this blue canvas?"

"More than a third. Toilers, living without pride or delight or hope, with the stories of Pleasure Cities ringing in their ears, mocking their shameful lives, their privations and hardships. Too poor even for the Euthanasy, the rich man's refuge from life. Dumb, crippled millions, countless millions, all the world about, ignorant of anything but limitations and unsatisfied desires. They are born, they are thwarted and they die. That is the state to which we have come."

For a space Graham sat downcast.

"But there has been a revolution," he said. "All these things will be changed." Ostrog—"

"That is our hope. That is the hope of the world. But Ostrog will not do it. He is a politician. To him it seems things must be like this. He does not mind. He takes it for granted. All the rich, all the influential, all who are happy, come at last to take these miseries for granted. They use the people in their politics, they live in ease by their degradation. But you— you who come from a happier age—it is to you the people look. To you."

He looked at her face. Her eyes were bright with unshed tears. He felt a rush of emotion. For a moment he forgot this city, he forgot the race, and all those vague remote voices, in the immediate humanity of her beauty.

"But what am I to do?" he said with his eyes upon her.

"Rule," she answered, bending towards him and speaking in a low tone. "Rule the world as it has never been ruled, for the good and happiness of men. For you might rule it—you could rule it.

"The people are stirring. All over the world the people are stirring. It wants but a word—but a word from you—to bring them all together. Even the middle sort of people are restless unhappy.

"They are not telling you the things that are happening. The people will not go back to their drudgery—they refuse to be disarmed. Ostrog has awakened something greater than he dreamt of—he has awakened hopes."

His heart was beating fast. He tried to seem judicial, to weigh considerations.

"They only want their leader," she said.

"And then?"

"You could do what you would;—the world is yours."

He sat, no longer regarding her. Presently he spoke. "The old dreams, and the thing I have dreamt, liberty, happiness. Are they dreams? Could one man—one man—?" His voice sank and ceased.

"Not one man, but all men—give them only a leader to speak the desire of their hearts."

He shook his head, and for a time there was silence.

He looked up suddenly, and their eyes met. "I have not your faith," he said. "I have not your youth. I am here with power that mocks me. No—let me speak. I want to do—not right—I have not the strength for that—but something rather right than wrong. It will bring no millennium, but I am resolved now that I will rule. What you have said has awakened me.... You are right. Ostrog must know his place. And I will learn—.... One thing I promise you. This Labour slavery shall end."

"And you will rule?"

"Yes. Provided—. There is one thing."

"Yes?"

"That you will help me."

"I!—a girl!"

"Yes. Does it not occur to you I am absolutely alone?"

She started and for an instant her eyes had pity. "Need you ask whether I will help you?" she said.

She stood before him, beautiful, worshipful, and her enthusiasm and the greatness of their theme was like a great gulf fixed between them. To touch her, to clasp her hand, was a thing beyond hope. "Then I will rule indeed," he said slowly. "I will rule-" He paused. "With you."

There came a tense silence, and then the beating a clock striking the hour. She made him no answer. Graham rose.

"Even now," he said, "Ostrog will be waiting." He hesitated, facing her. "When I have asked him certain questions—. There is much I do not know. It may be, that I will go to see with my own eyes the things of which you have spoken. And when I return—?"

"I shall know of your going and coming. I will wait for you here again."

He stood for a moment regarding her.

"I knew," she said, and stopped.

He waited, but she said no more. They regarded one another steadfastly, questioningly, and then he turned from her towards the Wind Vane office.

CHAPTER XIX
OSTROG'S POINT OF VIEW

Graham found Ostrog waiting to give a formal account of his day's stewardship. On previous occasions he had passed over this ceremony as speedily as possible, in order to resume his aerial experiences, but now he began to ask quick short questions. He was very anxious to take up his empire forthwith. Ostrog brought flattering reports of the development of affairs abroad. In Paris and Berlin, Graham perceived that he was saying, there had been trouble, not organised resistance indeed, but insubordinate proceedings. "After all these years," said Ostrog, when Graham pressed enquiries, "the Commune has lifted its head again. That is the real nature of the struggle, to be explicit." But order had been restored in these cities. Graham, the more deliberately judicial for the stirring emotions he felt, asked if there had been any fighting. "A little," said Ostrog. "In one quarter only. But the Senegalese division of our African agricultural police—the Consolidated African Companies have a very well drilled police—was ready, and so were the aeroplanes. We expected a little trouble in the continental cities, and in America. But things are very quiet in America. They are satisfied with the overthrow of the Council. For the time."

"Why should you expect trouble?" asked Graham abruptly.

"There is a lot of discontent—social discontent."

"The Labour Company?"

"You are learning," said Ostrog with a touch of surprise. "Yes. It is chiefly the discontent with the Labour Company. It was that discontent supplied the motive force of this overthrow—that and your awakening."

"Yes?"

Ostrog smiled. He became explicit. "We had to stir up their discontent, we had to revive the old ideals of universal happiness—all men equal—all men happy—no luxury that everyone may not share—ideas that have slumbered for two hundred years. You know that? We had to revive these ideals, impossible as they are—in order to overthrow the Council. And now—"

"Well?"

"Our revolution is accomplished, and the Council is overthrown, and people whom we have stirred up remain surging. There was scarcely enough fighting... We made promises, of course. It is extraordinary how violently and rapidly this vague out-of-date humanitarianism has revived and spread. We who sowed the seed even, have been astonished. In Paris, as I say—we have had to call in a little external help."

"And here?"

"There is trouble. Multitudes will not go back to work. There is a general strike. Half the factories are empty and the people are swarming in the Ways. They are talking of a Commune. Men in silk and satin have been insulted in the streets. The blue canvas is expecting all sorts of things from you.... Of course there is no need for you to trouble. We are setting the Babble Machines to work with counter suggestions in the cause of law and order. We must keep the grip tight; that is all."

Graham thought. He perceived a way of asserting himself. But he spoke with restraint.

"Even to the pitch of bringing a negro police," he said.

"They are useful," said Ostrog. "They are fine loyal brutes, with no wash of ideas in their heads—such as our rabble has. The Council should have had them as police of the Ways, and things might have been different. Of course, there is nothing to fear except rioting and wreckage. You can manage your own wings now, and you can soar away to Capri if there is any smoke or fuss. We have the pull of all the great things; the aeronauts are privileged and rich, the closest trades union in the world, and so are the engineers of the wind vanes. We have the air, and the mastery of the air is the mastery of the earth. No one of any ability is organising against us. They have no leaders—only the sectional leaders of the secret society we organised before your very opportune awakening. Mere busy bodies and sentimentalists they are and bitterly jealous of each other. None of them is man enough for a central figure. The only trouble will be a disorganised upheaval. To be frank—that may happen. But it won't interrupt your aeronautics. The days when the People could make revolutions are past."

"I suppose they are," said Graham. "I suppose they are." He mused. "This world of yours has been full of surprises to me. In the old days we dreamt of a wonderful democratic life, of a time when all men would be equal and happy."

Ostrog looked at him steadfastly. "The day of democracy is past," he said. "Past for ever. That day began with the bowmen of Crecy, it ended when marching infantry, when common men in masses ceased to win the battles of the world, when costly cannon, great ironclads, and strategic railways became the means of power. To-day is the day of wealth. Wealth now is power as it never was power before—it commands earth and sea and sky. All power is for those who can handle wealth.... You must accept facts, and these are facts. The world for the Crowd! The Crowd as Ruler! Even in your days that creed had been tried and condemned. To-day it has only one believer—a multiplex, silly one—the mall in the Crowd."

Graham did not answer immediately. He stood lost in sombre preoccupations.

"No," said Ostrog. "The day of the common man is past. On the open countryside one man is as good as another, or nearly as good. The earlier aristocracy had a precarious tenure of strength and audacity. They were tempered—tempered. There were insurrections, duels, riots. The first real aristocracy, the first permanent aristocracy, came in with castles and armour, and vanished before the musket and bow. But this is the second aristocracy. The real one. Those days of gunpowder and democracy were only an eddy in the stream. The common man now is a helpless unit. In these days we have this great machine of the city, and an organisation complex beyond his understanding."

"Yet," said Graham, "there is something resists, something you are holding down—something that stirs and presses."

"You will see," said Ostrog, with a forced smile that would brush these difficult questions aside. "I have not roused the force to destroy myself—trust me."

"I wonder," said Graham.

Ostrog stared.

"Must the world go this way?" said Graham, with his emotions at the speaking point. "Must it indeed go in this way? Have all our hopes been vain?"

"What do you mean?" said Ostrog. "Hopes?"

"I came from a democratic age. And I find an aristocratic tyranny!"

"Well,—but you are the chief tyrant."

Graham shook his head.

"Well," said Ostrog, "take the general question. It is the way that change has always travelled. Aristocracy, the prevalence of the best—the suffering and extinction of the unfit, and so to better things."

"But aristocracy! those people I met—"

"Oh! not those!" said Ostrog. "But for the most part they go to their death. Vice and pleasure! They have no children. That sort of stuff will die out. If the world keeps to one road, that is, if there is no turning back. An easy road to excess, convenient Euthanasia for the pleasure seekers singed in the flame, that is the way to improve the race!"

"Pleasant extinction," said Graham. "Yet—." He thought for an instant. "There is that other thing—the Crowd, the great mass of poor men. Will that die out? That will not die out. And it suffers, its suffering is a force that even you—"

Ostrog moved impatiently, and when he spoke, he spoke rather less evenly than before.

"Don't you trouble about these things," he said. "Everything will be settled in a few days now. The Crowd is a huge foolish beast. What if it does not die out? Even if it does not die, it can still be tamed and driven. I have no sympathy with servile men. You heard those people shouting and singing two nights ago. They were taught that song. If you had taken any man there in cold blood and asked why he shouted, he could not have told you. They think they are shouting for you, that they are loyal and devoted to you. Just then they were ready to slaughter the Council. To-day—they are already murmuring against those who have overthrown the Council."

"No, no," said Graham. "They shouted because their lives were dreary, without joy or pride, and because in me—in me—they hoped."

"And what was their hope? What is their hope? What right have they to hope? They work ill and they want the reward of those who work well. The hope of mankind—what is it? That some day the Over-man may come, that some day the inferior, the weak and the bestial may be subdued or eliminated. Subdued if not eliminated. The world is no place for the bad, the stupid, the enervated. Their duty—it's a fine duty too!—is to die. The death of the failure! That is the path by which the beast rose to manhood, by which man goes on to higher things."

Ostrog took a pace, seemed to think, and turned on Graham. "I can imagine how this great world state of ours seems to a Victorian Englishman. You regret all the old forms of representative government— their spectres still haunt the world, the voting councils and parliaments and all that eighteenth century tomfoolery You feel moved against our Pleasure Cities. I might have thought of that,—had I not been busy. But you will learn better. The people are mad with envy—they would be in sympathy with you. Even in the streets now, they clamour to destroy the Pleasure Cities. But the Pleasure Cities are the excretory organs of the State, attractive places that year after year draw together all that is weak and vicious, all that is lascivious and lazy, all the easy roguery of the world, to a graceful destruction. They go there, they have their time, they die childless, all the pretty silly lascivious women die childless, and mankind is the better. If the people were sane they would not envy the rich their way of death. And you would emancipate the silly brainless workers that we have enslaved, and try to make their lives easy and pleasant again. Just as they have sunk to what they are fit for." He smiled a smile that irritated Graham oddly. "You will learn better. I know those ideas; in my boyhood I read your Shelley and dreamt of Liberty. There is no liberty, save wisdom and self control. Liberty is within—not without. It is each man's own affair. Suppose—which is impossible—that these swarming yelping fools in blue get the upper hand of us, what then? They will only fall to other masters. So long as there are sheep Nature will insist on beasts of prey. It would mean but a few hundred years' delay. The coming of the aristocrat is fatal and assured. The end will be the Over-man—for all the mad protests of humanity. Let them revolt, let them win and kill me and my like. Others will arise—other masters. The end will be the same."

"I wonder," said Graham doggedly.

For a moment he stood downcast.

"But I must see these things for myself," he said, suddenly assuming a tone of confident mastery. "Only by seeing can I understand. I must learn. That is what I want to tell you, Ostrog. I do not want to be King in a Pleasure City; that is not my, pleasure. I have spent enough time with aeronautics—and those other things. I must learn how people live now, how the common life has developed. Then I shall understand these things better. I must learn how common people live—the labour people more especially—how they work, marry, bear children, die—"

"You get that from our realistic novelists," suggested Ostrog, suddenly preoccupied.

"I want reality," said Graham, "not realism."

"There are difficulties," said Ostrog, and thought.

"On the whole perhaps—

"I did not expect—.

"I had thought—. And yet, perhaps—. You say you want to go through the Ways of the city and see the common people."

Suddenly he came to some conclusion. "You would need to go disguised," he said. "The city is intensely excited, and the discovery of your presence among them might create a fearful tumult. Still this wish of yours to go into this city—this idea of yours—. Yes, now I think the thing over it seems to me not altogether—. It can be contrived. If you would really find an interest in that! You are, of course, Master. You can go soon if you like. A disguise for this excursion Asano will be able to manage. He would go with you. After all it is not a bad idea of yours."

"You will not want to consult me in any matter?" asked Graham suddenly, struck by an odd suspicion.

"Oh, dear no! No! I think you may trust affairs to me for a time, at any rate," said Ostrog, smiling. "Even if we differ—"

Graham glanced; at him sharply.

"There is no fighting likely to happen soon?" he asked abruptly.

"Certainly not."

"I have been thinking about these negroes. I don't believe the people intend any hostility to me, and, after all, I am the Master. I do not want any negroes brought to London. It is an archaic prejudice perhaps, but I have peculiar feelings about Europeans and the subject races. Even about Paris—"

Ostrog stood watching him from under his drooping brows. "I am not bringing negroes to London," he said slowly. "But if—"

"You are not to bring armed negroes to London, whatever happens," said Graham. "In that matter I am quite decided."

Ostrog, after a pause, decided not to speak, and bowed deferentially.

CHAPTER XX

IN THE CITY WAYS

nd that night, unknown and unsuspected, Graham, dressed in the costume of an inferior wind-vane official keeping holiday, and accompanied by Asano in Labour Company canvas, surveyed the city through which he had wandered when it was veiled in darkness. But now he saw it lit and waking, a whirlpool of life. In spite of the surging and swaying of the forces of revolution, in spite of the unusual discontent, the mutterings of the greater struggle of which the first revolt was but the prelude, the myriad streams of commerce still flowed wide and strong. He knew now something of the dimensions and quality of the new age, but he was not prepared for the infinite surprise of the detailed view, for the torrent of colour and vivid impressions that poured past him.

This was his first real contact with the people of these latter days. He realised that all that had gone before, saving his glimpses of the public theatres and markets, had had its element of seclusion, had been a movement within the comparatively narrow political quarter, that all his previous experiences had revolved immediately about the question of his own position. But here was the city at the busiest hours of night, the people to a large extent returned to their own immediate interests, the resumption of the real informal life, he common habits of the new time.

They emerged at first into a street whose opposite ways were crowded with the blue canvas liveries. This swarm Graham saw was a portion of a procession—it was odd to see a procession parading the city seated They carried banners of coarse red stuff with red letters. "No disarmament," said the banners, for the most part in crudely daubed letters and with variant spelling, and "Why should we disarm?" "No disarming." "No disarming." Banner after banner went by, a stream of banners flowing past, and at last at the end, the song of the revolt and a noisy band of strange instruments. "They all ought to be at work," said Asano. "They have had no food these two days, or they have stolen it."

Presently Asano made a detour to avoid the congested crowd that gaped upon the occasional passage of dead bodies from hospital to a mortuary, the gleanings after death's harvest of the first revolt.

That night few people were sleeping, everyone was abroad. A vast excitement, perpetual crowds perpetually changing, surrounded Graham; his mind was confused and darkened by an incessant tumult, by the cries and enigmatical fragments of the social struggle that was as yet only beginning. Everywhere festoons and banners of black and strange decorations, intensified the quality of his popularity. Everywhere he caught snatches of that crude thick dialect that served the illiterate class, the class, that is, beyond the reach of phonograph culture, in their common-place intercourse. Everywhere this trouble of disarmament was in the air, with a quality of immediate stress of which he had no inkling during his seclusion in the Wind-Vane quarter. He perceived that as soon as he returned he must discuss this with Ostrog, this and the greater issues of which it was the expression, in a far more conclusive way than he had so far done. Perpetually that night, even in the earlier hours of their wanderings about the city, the spirit of unrest and revolt swamped his attention, to the exclusion of countless strange things he might otherwise have observed.

This preoccupation made his impressions fragmentary. Yet amidst so much that was strange and vivid, no subject, however personal and insistent, could exert undivided sway. There were spaces when the revolutionary movement passed clean out of his mind, was drawn aside like a curtain from before some startling new aspect of the time. Helen had swayed his mind to this intense earnestness of enquiry, but there came times when she, even, receded beyond his conscious thoughts. At one moment, for example, he found they were traversing the religious quarter, for the easy transit about the city afforded by the moving ways rendered sporadic churches and chapels no longer necessary—and his attention was vividly arrested by the facade of one of the Christian sects.

They were travelling seated on one of the swift upper ways, the place leapt upon them at a bend and advanced rapidly towards them. It was covered with inscriptions from top to base, in vivid white and blue, save where a vast and glaring kinematograph transparency presented a realistic New Testament scene, and where a vast festoon of black to show that the popular religion followed the popular politics, hung across the lettering Graham had already become familiar with the phonotype writing and these inscriptions arrested him, being to his sense for the most part almost incredible blasphemy. Among the less offensive were "Salvation on the First Floor and turn to the Right." "Put your Money on your Maker." "The Sharpest Conversion in London, Expert Operators! Look Slippy!" "What Christ would say to the Sleeper;—Join the Up-to-date Saints!" "Be a Christian—without hindrance to your present Occupation." "All the Brightest Bishops on the Bench to-night and Prices as Usual." "Brisk Blessings for Busy Business Men."

"But this is appalling!" said Graham, as that deafening scream of mercantile piety towered above them.

"What is appalling?" asked his little officer, apparently seeking vainly for anything unusual in this shrieking enamel.

"_This!_ Surely the essence of religion is reverence."

"Oh _that!_" Asano looked at Graham. "Does it shock you?" he said in the tone of one who makes a discovery. "I suppose it would, of course. I had forgotten. Nowadays the competition for attention is so keen, and people simply haven't the leisure to attend to their souls, you know, as they used to do." He smiled. "In the old days you had quiet Sabbaths and the countryside. Though somewhere I've read of Sunday afternoons that—"

"But, _that_," said Graham, glancing back at the receding blue and white. "That is surely not the only—"

"There are hundreds of different ways. But, of course, if a sect doesn't tell it doesn't pay. Worship has moved with the times. There are high class sects with quieter ways—costly incense and personal attentions and all that. These people are extremely popular and prosperous. They pay several dozen lions for those apartments to the Council—to you, I should say."

Graham still felt a difficulty with the coinage, and this mention of a dozen lions brought him abruptly to that matter. In a moment the screaming temples and their swarming touts were forgotten in this new interest. A turn of a phrase suggested, and an answer confirmed the idea that gold and silver were both demonetised, that stamped gold which had begun its reign amidst the merchants of Phoenicia was at last dethroned. The change had been graduated but swift, brought about by an extension of the system of cheques that had even in his previous life already practically superseded gold in all the larger business transactions. The common traffic of the city, the common currency indeed of all the world, was conducted by means of the little brown, green and pink council cheques for small amounts, printed with a blank payee. Asano had several with him, and at the first opportunity he supplied the gaps in his set. They were printed not on tearable paper, but on a semi-transparent fabric of silken, flexibility, interwoven with silk. Across them all sprawled a facsimile of Graham's signature, his first encounter with the curves and turns of that familiar autograph for two hundred and three years.

Some intermediary experiences made no impression sufficiently vivid to prevent the matter of the disarmament claiming his thoughts again; a blurred picture of a Theosophist temple that promised MIRACLES in enormous letters of unsteady fire was least submerged perhaps, but then came the view of the dining hall in Northumberland Avenue. That interested him very greatly.

By the energy and thought of Asano he was able to view this place from a little screened gallery reserved for the attendants of the tables. The building was pervaded by a distant muffled hooting, piping and bawling, of which he did not at first understand the import, but which recalled a certain mysterious leathery voice he had heard after the resumption of the lights on the night of his solitary wandering.

He had grown accustomed now to vastness and great numbers of people, nevertheless this spectacle held him for a long time. It was as he watched the table service more immediately beneath, and interspersed with many questions and answers concerning details, that the realisation of the full significance of the feast of several thousand people came to him.

It was his constant surprise to find that points that one might have expected to strike vividly at the very outset never occurred to him until some trivial detail suddenly shaped as a riddle and pointed to the obvious thing he had overlooked. In this matter, for instance, it had not occurred to him that this continuity of the city, this exclusion of weather, these vast halls and ways, involved the disappearance of the household; that the typical Victorian "home," the little brick cell containing kitchen and scullery, living rooms and bedrooms, had, save for the ruins that diversified the countryside, vanished as surely as the wattle hut. But now he saw what had indeed been manifest from the first, that London, regarded as a living place, was no longer an aggregation of houses but a prodigious hotel, an hotel with a thousand classes of accommodation, thousands of dining halls, chapels, theatres, markets and places of assembly, a synthesis of enterprises, of which he chiefly was the owner. People had their sleeping rooms, with, it might be, antechambers, rooms that were always sanitary at least whatever the degree of comfort and privacy, and for the rest they lived much as many people had lived in the new-made giant hotels of the Victorian days, eating, reading, thinking, playing, conversing, all in places of public resort, going to their work in the industrial quarters of the city or doing business in their offices in the trading section.

He perceived at once how necessarily this state of affairs had developed from the Victorian city. The fundamental reason for the modern city had ever been the economy of co-operation. The chief thing to prevent the merging of the separate households in his own generation was simply the still imperfect civilisation of the people, the strong barbaric pride, passions, and prejudices, the jealousies, rivalries, and violence of the middle and lower classes, which had necessitated the entire separation of contiguous households. But the change, the taming of the people, had been in rapid progress even then. In his brief thirty years of previous life he had seen an enormous extension of the habit of consuming meals from home, the casually patronised horse-box coffee-house had given place to the open and crowded Aerated Bread Shop for instance, women's clubs had had their beginning, and an immense development of reading rooms, lounges and libraries had witnessed to the growth of social confidence. These promises had by this time attained to their complete fulfillment. The locked and barred household had passed away.

These people below him belonged, he learnt, to the lower middle class, the class just above the blue labourers, a class so accustomed in the Victorian period to feed with every precaution of privacy that its members, when occasion confronted them with a public meal, would usually hide their embarrassment under horseplay or a markedly militant demeanour. But these gaily, if lightly dressed people below, albeit vivacious, hurried and uncommunicative, were dexterously mannered and certainly quite at their ease with regard to one another.

He noted a slight significant thing; the table, as far as he could see, was and remained delightfully neat, there was nothing to parallel the confusion, the broadcast crumbs, the splashes of viand and condiment, the overturned drink and displaced ornaments, which would have marked the stormy progress of the Victorian meal. The table furniture was very different. There were no ornaments, no flowers, and the table was without a cloth, being made, he learnt, of a solid substance having the texture and appearance of damask. He discerned that this damask substance was patterned with gracefully designed trade advertisements.

In a sort of recess before each diner was a complete apparatus of porcelain and metal. There was one plate of white porcelain, and by means of taps for hot and cold volatile fluids the diner washed this himself between the courses; he also washed his elegant white metal knife and fork and spoon as occasion required.

Soup and the chemical wine that was the common drink were delivered by similar taps, and the remaining covers travelled automatically in tastefully arranged dishes down the table along silver rails. The diner stopped these and helped himself at his discretion. They appeared at a little door at one end of the table, and vanished at the other. That turn of democratic sentiment in decay, that ugly pride of menial souls, which renders equals loth to wait on one another, was very strong he found among these people. He was so preoccupied with these details that it was only just as he was leaving the place that he remarked the huge advertisement dioramas that marched majestically along the upper walls and proclaimed the most remarkable commodities.

Beyond this place they came into a crowded hall, and he discovered the cause of the noise that had perplexed him. They paused at a turnstile at which a payment was made.

Graham's attention was immediately arrested by a violent, loud hoot, followed by a vast leathery voice. "The Master is sleeping peacefully," it said vociferately. "He is in excellent health. He is going to devote the rest of his life to aeronautics. He says women are more beautiful than ever. Galloop! Wow! Our wonderful civilisation astonishes him beyond measure. Beyond all measure. Galloop. He puts great trust in Boss Ostrog, absolute confidence in Boss Ostrog. Ostrog is to be his chief minister; is authorised to remove or reinstate public officers—all patronage will be in his hands. All patronage in the hands of Boss Ostrog! The Councillors have been sent back to their own prison above the Council House."

Graham stopped at the first sentence, and, looking up, beheld a foolish trumpet face from which this was brayed. This was the General Intelligence Machine. For a space it seemed to be gathering breath, and a regular throbbing from its cylindrical body was audible. Then it trumpeted "Galloop, Galloop," and broke out again.

"Paris is now pacified. All resistance is over. Galloop! The black police hold every position of importance in the city. They fought with great bravery, singing songs written in praise of their ancestors by the poet Kipling. Once or twice they got out of hand, and tortured and mutilated wounded and captured insurgents, men and women. Moral—don't go rebelling. Haha! Galloop, Galloop! They are lively fellows. Lively brave fellows. Let this be a lesson to the disorderly banderlog of this city. Yah! Banderlog! Filth of the earth! Galloop, Galloop!"

The voice ceased. There was a confused murmur of disapproval among the crowd. "Damned niggers." A man began to harangue near them. "Is this the Master's doing, brothers? Is this the Master's doing?"

"Black police!" said Graham. "What is that? You don't mean—"

Asano touched his arm and gave him a warning look, and forthwith another of these mechanisms screamed deafeningly and gave tongue in a shrill voice. "Yahaha, Yahah, Yap! Hear a live paper yelp! Live paper. Yaha! Shocking outrage in Paris. Yahahah! The Parisians exasperated by the black police to the pitch of assassination. Dreadful reprisals. Savage times come again. Blood! Blood! Yaha!" The nearer Babble Machine hooted stupendously, "Galloop, Galloop," drowned the end of the sentence, and proceeded in a rather flatter note than before with novel comments on the horrors of disorder. "Law and order must be maintained," said the nearer Babble Machine.

"But," began Graham.

"Don't ask questions here," said Asano, "or you will be involved in an argument."

"Then let us go on," said Graham, "for I want to know more of this."

As he and his companion pushed their way through the excited crowd that swarmed beneath these voices, towards the exit, Graham conceived more clearly the proportion and features of this room. Altogether, great and small, there must have been nearly a thousand of these erections, piping, hooting, bawling and gabbling in that great space, each with its crowd of excited listeners, the majority of them men dressed in blue canvas. There were all sizes of machines, from the little gossipping mechanisms that chuckled out mechanical sarcasm in odd corners, through a number of grades to such fifty-foot giants as that which had first hooted over Graham.

This place was unusually crowded, because of the intense public interest in the course of affairs in Paris. Evidently the struggle had been much more savage than Ostrog had represented it. All the mechanisms were discoursing upon that topic, and the repetition of the people made the huge hive buzz with such phrases as "Lynched policemen," "Women burnt alive," "Fuzzy Wuzzy." "But does the Master allow such things?" asked a man near him. "Is this the beginning of the Master's rule?"

Is _this_ the beginning of the Master's rule? For a long time after he had left the place, the hooting, whistling and braying of the machines pursued him; "Galloop, Galloop," "Yahahah, Yaha, Yap! Yaha!" Is this the beginning of the Master's rule?

Directly they were out upon the ways he began to question Asano closely on the nature of the Parisian struggle. "This disarmament! What was their trouble? What does it all mean?" Asano seemed chiefly anxious to reassure him that it was "all right." "But these outrages!" "You cannot have an omelette," said Asano, "without breaking eggs. It is only the rough people. Only in one part of the city. All the rest is all right. The Parisian labourers are the wildest in the world, except ours."

"What! the Londoners?"

"No, the Japanese. They have to be kept in order." "But burning women alive!"

"A Commune!" said Asano. "They would rob you of your property. They would do away with property and give the world over to mob rule. You are Master, the world is yours. But there will be no Commune here. There is no need for black police here.

"And every consideration has been shown. It is their own negroes—French speaking negroes. Senegal regiments, and Niger and Timbuctoo."

"Regiments?" said Graham, "I thought there was only one—."

"No," said Asano, and glanced at him. "There is more than one."

Graham felt unpleasantly helpless.

"I did not think," he began and stopped abruptly He went off at a tangent to ask for information about these Babble Machines. For the most part, the crowd present had been shabbily or even raggedly dressed, and Graham learnt that so far as the more prosperous classes were concerned, in all the more comfortable private apartments of the city were fixed Babble Machines that would speak directly a lever was pulled. The tenant of the apartment could connect this with the cables of any of the great News Syndicates that he preferred. When he learnt this presently, he demanded the reason of their absence from his own suite of apartments. Asano stared. "I never thought," he said. "Ostrog must have had them removed."

Graham stared. "How was I to know?" he exclaimed.

"Perhaps he thought they would annoy you," said Asano.

"They must be replaced directly I return," said Graham after an interval.

He found a difficulty in understanding that this news room and the dining hall were not great central places, that such establishments were repeated almost beyond counting all over the city. But ever and again during the night's expedition his ears, in some new quarter would pick out from the tumult of the ways the peculiar hooting of the organ of Boss Ostrog, "Galloop, Galloop!" or the shrill "Yahaha, Yaha, Yap!—Hear a live paper yelp!" of its chief rival.

Repeated, too, everywhere, were such _creches_ as the one he now entered. It was reached by a lift, and by a glass bridge that flung across the dining hall and traversed the ways at a slight upward angle. To enter the first section of the place necessitated the use of his solvent signature under Asano's direction. They were immediately attended to by a man in a violet robe and gold clasp, the insignia of practising medical men. He perceived from this man's manner that his identity was known, and proceeded to ask questions on the strange arrangements of the place without reserve.

On either side of the passage, which was silent and padded, as if to deaden the footfall, were narrow little doors, their size and arrangement suggestive of the cells of a Victorian prison. But the upper portion of each door was of the same greenish transparent stuff that had enclosed him at his awakening, and within, dimly seen, lay, in every case, a very young baby in a little nest of wadding. Elaborate apparatus watched the atmosphere and rang a bell far away in the central office at the slightest departure from the optimum of temperature and moisture. A system of such _creches_ had almost entirely replaced the hazardous adventures of the old-world nursing. The attendant presently called Graham's attention to the wet nurses, a vista of mechanical figures, with arms, shoulders and breasts of astonishingly realistic modelling, articulation, and texture, but mere brass tripods below, and having in the place of features a flat disc bearing advertisements likely to be of interest to mothers.

Of all the strange things that Graham came upon that night, none jarred more upon his habits of thought than this place. The spectacle of the little pink creatures, their feeble limbs swaying uncertainly in vague first movements, left alone, without embrace or endearment, was wholly repugnant to him. The attendant doctor was of a different opinion. His statistical evidence showed beyond dispute that in the Victorian times the most dangerous passage of life was the arms of the mother, that there human mortality had ever been most terrible. On the other hand this _creche_ company, the International Creche Syndicate, lost not one-half per cent of the million babies or so that formed its peculiar care. But Graham's prejudice was too strong even for those figures.

Along one of the many passages of the place they presently came upon a young couple in the usual blue canvas peering through the transparency and laughing hysterically at the bald head of their first-born. Graham's face must have showed his estimate of them, for their merriment ceased and they looked abashed. But this little incident accentuated his sudden realisation of the gulf between his habits of thought and the ways of the new age. He passed on to the crawling rooms and the Kindergarten, perplexed and distressed. He found the endless long playrooms were empty! the latter-day children at least still spent their nights in sleep. As they went through these, the little officer pointed out the nature of the toys, developments of those devised by that inspired sentimentalist Froebel. There were nurses here, but much was done by machines that sang and danced and dandled.

Graham was still not clear upon many points. "But so many orphans," he said perplexed, reverting to a first misconception, and learnt again that they were not orphans.

So soon as they had left the _creche_ he began to speak of the horror the babies in their incubating cases had caused him. "Is motherhood gone?" he said. "Was it a cant? Surely it was an instinct. This seems so unnatural—abominable almost."

"Along here we shall come to the dancing place," said Asano by way of reply. "It is sure to be crowded. In spite of all the political unrest it will be crowded. The women take no great interest in politics—except a few here and there. You will see the mothers—most young women in London are mothers. In that class it is considered a creditable thing to have one child—a proof of animation. Few middle class people have more than one. With the Labour Company it is different. As for motherhood They still take an immense pride in the children. They come here to look at them quite often."

"Then do you mean that the population of the world—?"

"Is falling? Yes. Except among the people under the Labour Company. They are reckless—."

The air was suddenly dancing with music, and down a way they approached obliquely, set with gorgeous pillars as it seemed of clear amethyst, flowed a concourse of gay people and a tumult of merry cries and laughter. He saw curled heads, wreathed brows, and a happy intricate flutter of gamboge pass triumphant across the picture.

"You will see," said Asano with a faint smile "The world has changed. In a moment you will see the mothers of the new age. Come this way. We shall see those yonder again very soon."

They ascended a certain height in a swift lift, and changed to a slower one. As they went on the music grew upon them, until it was near and full and splendid, and, moving with its glorious intricacies they could distinguish the beat of innumerable dancing feet. They made a payment at a turnstile, and emerged upon the wide gallery that overlooked the dancing place, and upon the full enchantment of sound and sight.

"Here," said Asano, "are the fathers and mothers of the little ones you saw."

The hall was not so richly decorated as that of the Atlas, but saving that, it was, for its size, the most splendid Graham had seen. The beautiful white limbed figures that supported the galleries reminded him once more of the restored magnificence of sculpture; they seemed to writhe in engaging attitudes, their faces laughed. The source of the music that filled the place was hidden, and the whole vast shining floor was thick with dancing couples. "Look at them," said the little officer, "see how much they show of motherhood."

The gallery they stood upon ran along the upper edge of a huge screen that cut the dancing hall on one side from a sort of outer hall that showed through broad arches the incessant onward rush of the city ways. In this outer hall was a great crowd of less brilliantly dressed people, as numerous almost as those who danced within, the great majority wearing the blue uniform of the Labour Company that was now so familiar to Graham. Too poor to pass the turnstiles to the festival, they were yet unable to keep away from the sound of its seductions. Some of them even had cleared spaces, and were dancing also, fluttering their rags in the air. Some shouted as they danced, jests and odd allusions Graham did not understand. Once someone began whistling the refrain of the revolutionary song, but it seemed as though that beginning was promptly suppressed. The corner was dark and Graham could not see. He turned to the hall again. Above the caryatidae were marble busts of men whom that age esteemed great moral emancipators and pioneers; for the most part their names were strange to Graham, though he recognised Grant Allen, Le Gallienne, Nietzsche, Shelley and Goodwin. Great black festoons and eloquent sentiments reinforced the huge inscription that partially defaced the upper end of the dancing place, and asserted that "The Festival of the Awakening" was in progress.

"Myriads are taking holiday or staying from work because of that, quite apart from the labourers who refuse to go back," said Asano. "These people are always ready for holidays."

Graham walked to the parapet and stood leaning over, looking down at the dancers. Save for two or three remote whispering couples, who had stolen apart, he and his guide had the gallery to themselves. A warm breath of scent and vitality came up to him. Both men and women below were lightly clad, bare-armed, open-necked, as the universal warmth of the city permitted. The hair of the men was often a mass of effeminate curls, their chins were always shaven, and many of them had flushed or coloured cheeks. Many of the women were very pretty, and all were dressed with elaborate coquetry. As they swept by beneath, he saw ecstatic faces with eyes half closed in pleasure.

"What sort of people are these?" he asked abruptly.

"Workers—prosperous workers. What you would have called the middle class. Independent tradesmen with little separate businesses have vanished long ago, but there are store servers, managers, engineers of a hundred sorts. Tonight is a holiday of course, and every dancing place in the city will be crowded, and every place of worship."

"But—the women?"

"The same. There's a thousand forms of work for women now. But you had the beginning of the independent working-woman in your days. Most women are independent now. Most of these are married more or less—there are a number of methods of contract—and that gives them more money, and enables them to enjoy themselves."

"I see," said Graham looking at the flushed faces, the flash and swirl of movement, and still thinking of that nightmare of pink helpless limbs. "And these are—mothers."

"Most of them."

"The more I see of these things the more complex I find your problems. This, for instance, is a surprise. That news from Paris was a surprise."

In a little while he spoke again:

"These are mothers. Presently, I suppose, I shall get into the modern way of seeing things. I have old habits of mind clinging about me—habits based, I suppose, on needs that are over and done with. Of course, in our time, a woman was supposed not only to bear children, but to cherish them, to devote herself to them, to educate them—all the essentials of moral and mental education a child owed its mother. Or went without. Quite a number, I admit, went without. Nowadays, clearly, there is no more need for such care than if they were butterflies. I see that! Only there was an ideal—that figure of a grave, patient woman, silently and serenely mistress of a home, mother and maker of men—to love her was a sort of worship—"

He stopped and repeated, "A sort of worship."

"Ideals change," said the little man, "as needs change."

Graham awoke from an instant reverie and Asano repeated his words. Graham's mind returned to the thing at hand.

"Of course I see the perfect reasonableness of this Restraint, soberness, the matured thought, the unselfish a act, they are necessities of the barbarous state, the life of dangers. Dourness is man's tribute to unconquered nature. But man has conquered nature now for all practical purposes—his political affairs are managed by Bosses with a black police— and life is joyous."

He looked at the dancers again. "Joyous," he said.

"There are weary moments," said the little officer, reflectively.

"They all look young. Down there I should be visibly the oldest man. And in my own time I should have passed as middle-aged."

"They are young. There are few old people in this class in the work cities."

"How is that?"

"Old people's lives are not so pleasant as they used to be, unless they are rich to hire lovers and helpers. And we have an institution called Euthanasy."

"Ah! that Euthanasy!" said Graham. "The easy death?"

"The easy death. It is the last pleasure. The Euthanasy Company does it well. People will pay the sum—it is a costly thing—long beforehand, go off to some pleasure city and return impoverished and weary, very weary."

"There is a lot left for me to understand," said Graham after a pause. "Yet I see the logic of it all. Our array of angry virtues and sour restraints was the consequence of danger and insecurity. The Stoic, the Puritan, even in my time, were vanishing types. In the old days man was armed against Pain, now he is eager for Pleasure. There lies the difference. Civilisation has driven pain and danger so far off—for well-to-do people. And only well-to-do people matter now. I have been asleep two hundred years."

For a minute they leant on the balustrading, following the intricate evolution of the dance. Indeed the scene was very beautiful.

"Before God," said Graham, suddenly, "I would rather be a wounded sentinel freezing in the snow than one of these painted fools!"

"In the snow," said Asano, "one might think differently."

"I am uncivilised," said Graham, not heeding him. "That is the trouble. I am primitive—Palaeolithic. Their fountain of rage and fear and anger is sealed and closed, the habits of a lifetime make them cheerful and easy and delightful. You must bear with my nineteenth century shocks and disgusts. These people, you say, are skilled workers and so forth. And while these dance, men are fighting—men are dying in Paris to keep the world—that they may dance."

Asano smiled faintly. "For that matter, men are dying in London," he said.

There was a moment's silence.

"Where do these sleep?" asked Graham.

"Above and below—an intricate warren."

"And where do they work? This is—the domestic life."

"You will see little work to-night. Half the workers are out or under arms. Half these people are keeping holiday. But we will go to the work places if you wish it."

For a time Graham watched the dancers, then suddenly turned away. "I want to see the workers. I have seen enough of these," he said.

Asano led the way along the gallery across the dancing hall. Presently they came to a transverse passage that brought a breath of fresher, colder air.

Asano glanced at this passage as they went past, stopped, went back to it, and turned to Graham with a smile. "Here, Sire," he said, "is something—will be familiar to you at least—and yet—. But I will not tell you. Come!"

He led the way along a closed passage that presently became cold. The reverberation of their feet told that this passage was a bridge. They came into a circular gallery that was glazed in from the outer weather, and so reached a circular chamber which seemed familiar, though Graham could not recall distinctly when he had entered it before. In this was a ladder— the first ladder he had seen since his awakening—up which they went, and came into a high, dark, cold place in which was another almost vertical ladder. This they ascended, Graham still perplexed.

But at the top he understood, and recognized the metallic bars to which he clung. He was in the cage under the ball of St. Paul's. The dome rose but a little way above the general contour of the city, into the still twilight, and sloped away, shining greasily under a few distant lights, into a circumambient ditch of darkness.

Out between the bars he looked upon the wind-clear northern sky and saw the starry constellations all unchanged. Capella hung in the west, Vega was rising, and the seven glittering points of the Great Bear swept overhead in their stately circle about the Pole.

He saw these stars in a clear gap of sky. To the east and south the great circular shapes of complaining wind-wheels blotted out the heavens, so that the glare about the Council House was hidden. To the south-west hung Orion, showing like a pallid ghost through a tracery of iron-work and interlacing shapes above a dazzling coruscation of lights. A bellowing and siren screaming that came from the flying stages warned the world that one of the aeroplanes was ready to start. He remained for a space gazing towards the glaring stage. Then his eyes went back to the northward constellations.

For a long time he was silent. "This," he said at last, smiling in the shadow, "seems the strangest thing of all. To stand in the dome of Saint Paul's and look once more upon these familiar, silent stars!"

Thence Graham was taken by Asano along devious ways to the great gambling and business quarters where the bulk of the fortunes in the city were lost and made. It impressed him as a well-nigh interminable series of very high halls, surrounded by tiers upon tiers of galleries into which opened thousands of offices, and traversed by a complicated multitude of bridges, footways, aerial motor rails, and trapeze and cable leaps. And here more than anywhere the note of vehement vitality, of uncontrollable, hasty activity, rose high. Everywhere was violent advertisement, until his brain swam at the tumult of light and colour. And Babble Machines of a peculiarly rancid tone were abundant and filled the air with strenuous squealing and an idiotic slang. "Skin your eyes and slide," "Gewhoop, Bonanza," "Gollipers come and hark!"

The place seemed to him to be dense with people either profoundly agitated or swelling with obscure cunning, yet he learnt that the place was comparatively empty, that the great political convulsion of the last few days had reduced transactions to an unprecedented minimum. In one huge place were long avenues of roulette tables, each with an excited, undignified crowd about it; in another a yelping Babel of white-faced women and red-necked leathery-lunged men bought and sold the shares of an absolutely fictitious business undertaking which, every five minutes, paid a dividend of ten per cent and cancelled a certain proportion of its shares by means of a lottery wheel.

These business activities were prosecuted with an energy that readily passed into violence, and Graham approaching a dense crowd found at its centre a couple of prominent merchants in violent controversy with teeth and nails on some delicate point of business etiquette. Something still remained in life to be fought for. Further he had a shock at a vehement announcement in phonetic letters of scarlet flame, each twice the height of a man, that "WE ASSURE THE PROPRAIET'R. WE ASSURE THE PROPRAIET'R."

"Who's the proprietor?" he asked.

"You."

"But what do they assure me?" he asked. "What do they assure me?"

"Didn't you have assurance?"

Graham thought. "Insurance?"

"Yes—Insurance. I remember that was the older word. They are insuring your life. Dozands of people are taking out policies, myriads of lions are being put on you. And further on other people are buying annuities. They do that on everybody who is at all prominent. Look there!"

A crowd of people surged and roared, and Graham saw a vast black screen suddenly illuminated in still larger letters of burning purple. "Anuetes on the Propraiet'r—x 5 pr. G." The people began to boo and shout at this, a number of hard breathing, wildeyed men came running past, clawing with hooked fingers at the air. There was a furious crush about a little doorway.

Asano did a brief calculation. "Seventeen per cent per annum is their annuity on you. They would not pay so much per cent if they could see you now, Sire. But they do not know. Your own annuities used to be a very safe investment, but now you are sheer gambling, of course. This is probably a desperate bid. I doubt if people will get their money."

The crowd of would-be annuitants grew so thick about them that for some time they could move neither forward no backward. Graham noticed what appeared to him to be a high proportion of women among the speculators, and was reminded again of the economical independence of their sex. They seemed remarkably well able to take care of themselves in the crowd, using their elbows with particular skill, as he learnt to his cost. One curly-headed person caught in the pressure for a space, looked steadfastly at him several times, almost as if she recognized him, and then, edging deliberately towards him, touched his hand with her arm in a scarcely accidental manner, and made it plain by a look as ancient as Chaldea that he had found favour in her eyes. And then a lank, grey-bearded man, perspiring copiously in a noble passion of self-help, blind to all earthly things save that glaring, bait, thrust between them in a cataclysmal rush towards that alluring "x 5 pr. G."

"I want to get out of this," said Graham to Asano. "This is not what I came to see. Show me the workers. I want to see the people in blue. These parasitic lunatics—"

He found himself wedged in a struggling mass of people, and this hopeful sentence went unfinished.

CHAPTER XXI

THE UNDER SIDE

From the Business Quarter they presently passed by the running ways into a remote quarter of the city, where the bulk of the manufactures was done. On their way the platforms crossed the Thames twice, and passed in a broad viaduct across one of the great roads that entered the city from the North. In both cases his impression was swift and in both very vivid. The river was a broad wrinkled glitter of black sea water, overarched by buildings, and vanishing either way into a blackness starred with receding lights. A string of black barges passed seaward, manned by blue-clad men. The road was a long and very broad and high tunnel, along which big-wheeled machines drove noiselessly and swiftly. Here, too, the distinctive blue of the Labour Company was in abundance. The smoothness of the double tracks, the largeness and the lightness of the big pneumatic wheels in proportion to the vehicular body, struck Graham most vividly. One lank and very high carriage with longitudinal metallic rods hung with the dripping carcasses of many hundred sheep arrested his attention unduly. Abruptly the edge of the archway cut and blotted out the picture.

Presently they left the way and descended by a lift and traversed a passage that sloped downward, and so came to a descending lift again.

The appearance of things changed. Even the pretence of architectural ornament disappeared, the lights diminished in number and size, the architecture became more and more massive in proportion to the spaces as the factory quarters were reached. And in the dusty biscuit-making place of the potters, among the felspar mills in the furnace rooms of the metal workers, among the incandescent lakes of crude Eadhamite, the blue canvas clothing was on man, woman and child.

Many of these great and dusty galleries were silent avenues of machinery, endless raked out ashen furnaces testified to the revolutionary dislocation, but wherever there was work it was being done by slow-moving workers in blue canvas. The only people not in blue canvas were the overlookers of the work-places and the orange-clad Labour Police. And fresh from the flushed faces of the dancing halls, the voluntary vigours of the business quarter, Graham could note the pinched faces, the feeble muscles, and weary eyes of many of the latter-day workers. Such as he saw at work were noticeably inferior in physique to the few gaily dressed managers and forewomen who were directing their labours. The burly labourers of the Victorian times had followed the dray horse and all such living force producers, to extinction; the place of his costly muscles was taken by some dexterous machine. The latter-day labourer, male as well as female, was essentially a machine-minder and feeder, a servant and attendant, or an artist under direction.

The women, in comparison with those Graham remembered, were as a class distinctly plain and flat-chested. Two hundred years of emancipation from the moral restraints of Puritanical religion, two hundred years of city life, had done their work in eliminating the strain of feminine beauty and vigour from the blue canvas myriads. To be brilliant physically or mentally, to be in any way attractive or exceptional, had been and was still a certain way of emancipation to the drudge, a line of escape to the Pleasure City and its splendours and delights, and at last to the Euthanasy and peace. To be steadfast against such inducements was scarcely to be expected of meanly nourished souls. In the young cities of Graham's former life, the newly aggregated labouring mass had been a diverse multitude, still stirred by the tradition of personal honour and a high morality; now it was differentiating into a distinct class, with a moral and physical difference of its own—even with a dialect of its own.

They penetrated downward, ever downward, towards the working places. Presently they passed underneath one of the streets of the moving ways, and saw its platforms running on their rails far overhead, and chinks of white lights between the transverse slits. The factories that were not working were sparsely lighted; to Graham they and their shrouded aisles of giant machines seemed plunged in gloom, and even where work was going on the illumination was far less brilliant than upon the public ways.

Beyond the blazing lakes of Eadhamite he came to the warren of the jewellers, and, with some difficulty and by using his signature, obtained admission to these galleries. They were high and dark, and rather cold. In the first a few men were making ornaments of gold filigree, each man at a little bench by himself, and with a little shaded light. The long vista of light patches, with the nimble fingers brightly lit and moving among the gleaming yellow coils, and the intent face like the face of a ghost, in each shadow had the oddest effect.

The work was beautifully executed, but without any strength of modelling or drawing, for the most part intricate grotesques or the ringing of the changes on a geometrical motif. These workers wore a peculiar white uniform without pockets or sleeves. They assumed this on coming to work, but at night they were stripped and examined before they left the premises of the Company. In spite of every precaution, the Labour policeman told them in a depressed tone, the Company was not infrequently robbed.

Beyond was a gallery of women busied in cutting and setting slabs of artificial ruby, and next these were men and women busied together upon the slabs of copper net that formed the basis of cloisonne tiles. Many of these workers had lips and nostrils a livid white, due to a disease caused by a peculiar purple enamel that chanced to be much in fashion. Asano apologised to Graham for the offence of their faces, but excused himself on the score of the convenience of this route. "This is what I wanted to see," said Graham; "this is what I wanted to see," trying to avoid a start at a particularly striking disfigurement that suddenly stared him in the face.

"She might have done better with herself than that," said Asano.

Graham made some indignant comments.

"But, Sire, we simply could not stand that stuff without the purple," said Asano. "In your days people could stand such crudities, they were nearer the barbaric by two hundred years."

They continued along one of the lower galleries of this cloisonne factory, and came to a little bridge that spanned a vault. Looking over the parapet, Graham saw that beneath was a wharf under yet more tremendous archings than any he had seen. Three barges, smothered in floury dust, were being unloaded of their cargoes of powdered felspar by a multitude of coughing men, each guiding a little truck; the dust filled the place with a choking mist, and turned the electric glare yellow. The vague shadows of these workers gesticulated about their feet, and rushed to and fro against a long stretch of white-washed wall. Every now and then one would stop to cough.

A shadowy, huge mass of masonry rising out of the inky water, brought to Graham's mind the thought of the multitude of ways and galleries and lifts, that rose floor above floor overhead between him and the sky. The men worked in silence under the supervision of two of the Labour Police; their feet made a hollow thunder on the planks along which they went to and fro. And as he looked at this scene, some hidden voice in the darkness began to sing.

"Stop that!" shouted one of the policemen, but the order was disobeyed, and first one and then all the white-stained men who were working there had taken up the beating refrain, singing it defiantly, the Song of the Revolt. The feet upon the planks thundered now to the rhythm of the song, tramp, tramp, tramp. The policeman who had shouted glanced at his fellow, and Graham saw him shrug his shoulders. He made no further effort to stop the singing.

And so they went through these factories and places of toil, seeing many painful and grim things. But why should the gentle reader be depressed? Surely to a refined nature our present world is distressing enough without bothering ourselves about these miseries to come. We shall not suffer anyhow. Our children may, but what is that to us? That walk left on Graham's mind a maze of memories, fluctuating pictures of swathed halls, and crowded vaults seen through clouds of dust, of intricate machines, the racing threads of looms, the heavy beat of stamping machinery, the roar and rattle of belt and armature, of ill-lit subterranean aisles of sleeping places, illimitable vistas of pin-point lights. And here the smell of tanning, and here the reek of a brewery and here, unprecedented reeks. And everywhere were pillars and cross archings of such a massiveness as

Graham had never before seen, thick Titans of greasy, shining brickwork crushed beneath the vast weight of that complex city world, even as these anemic millions were crushed by its complexity. And everywhere were pale features, lean limbs, disfigurement and degradation.

Once and again, and again a third time, Graham heard the song of the revolt during his long, unpleasant research in these places, and once he saw a confused struggle down a passage, and learnt that a number of these serfs had seized their bread before their work was done. Graham was ascending towards the ways again when he saw a number of blue-clad children running down a transverse passage, and presently perceived the reason of their panic in a company of the Labour Police armed with clubs, trotting towards some unknown disturbance. And then came a remote disorder. But for the most part this remnant that worked, worked hopelessly. All the spirit that was left in fallen humanity was above in the streets that night, calling for the Master, and valiantly and noisily keeping its arms.

They emerged from these wanderings and stood blinking in the bright light of the middle passage of the platforms again. They became aware of the remote hooting and yelping of the machines of one of the General Intelligence Offices, and suddenly came men running, and along the platforms and about the ways everywhere was a shouting and crying. Then a woman with a face of mute white terror, and another who gasped and shrieked as she ran.

"What has happened now?" said Graham, puzzled, for he could not understand their thick speech. Then he heard it in English and perceived that the thing that everyone was shouting, that men yelled to one another, that women took up screaming, that was passing like the first breeze of a thunderstorm, chill and sudden through the city, was this: "Ostrog has ordered the Black Police to London. The Black Police are coming from South Africa.... The Black Police. The Black Police."

Asano's face was white and astonished; he hesitated, looked at Graham's face, and told him the thing he already knew. "But how can they know?" asked Asano.

Graham heard someone shouting. "Stop all work. Stop all work," and a swarthy hunchback, ridiculously gay in green and gold, came leaping down the platforms toward him, bawling again and again in good English,

"This is Ostrog's doing, Ostrog, the Knave! The Master is betrayed." His voice was hoarse and a thin foam dropped from his ugly shouting mouth. He yelled an unspeakable horror that the Black Police had done in Paris, and so passed shrieking, "Ostrog the Knave!"

For a moment Graham stood still, for it had come upon him again that these things were a dream. He looked up at the great cliff of buildings on either side, vanishing into blue haze at last above the lights, and down to the roaring tiers of platforms, and the shouting, running people who were gesticulating past. "The Master is betrayed!" they cried. "The Master is betrayed!"

Suddenly the situation shaped itself in his mind real and urgent. His heart began to beat fast and strong.

"It has come," he said. "I might have known. The hour has come."

He thought swiftly. "What am I to do?"

"Go back to the Council House," said Asano.

"Why should I not appeal——? The people are here."

"You will lose time. They will doubt if it is you. But they will mass about the Council House. There you will find their leaders. Your strength is there with them."

"Suppose this is only a rumour?"

"It sounds true," said Asano.

"Let us have the facts," said Graham.

Asano shrugged his shoulders. "We had better get towards the Council House," he cried. "That is where they will swarm. Even now the ruins may be impassable."

Graham regarded him doubtfully and followed him.

They went up the stepped platforms to the swiftest one, and there Asano accosted a labourer. The answers to his questions were in the thick, vulgar speech.

"What did he say?" asked Graham.

"He knows little, but he told me that the Black Police would have arrived here before the people knew—had not someone in the Wind-Vane Offices Learnt. He said a girl."

"A girl? Not?"

"He said a girl—he did not know who she was. Who came out from the Council House crying aloud, and told the men at work among the ruins."

And then another thing was shouted, something that turned an aimless tumult into determinate movements, it came like a wind along the street. "To your Wards, to your Wards. Every man get arms. Every man to his Ward!"

CHAPTER XXII
THE STRUGGLE IN THE COUNCIL HOUSE

As Asano and Graham hurried along to the ruins about the Council House, they saw everywhere the excitement of the people rising. "To your Wards To your Wards!" Everywhere men and women in blue were hurrying from unknown subterranean employments, up the staircases of the middle path—at one place Graham saw an arsenal of the revolutionary committee besieged by a crowd of shouting men, at another a couple of men in the hated yellow uniform of the Labour Police, pursued by a gathering crowd, fled precipitately along the swift way that went in the opposite direction.

The cries of "To your Wards!" became at last a continuous shouting as they drew near the Government quarter. Many of the shouts were unintelligible. "Ostrog has betrayed us," one man bawled in a hoarse voice, again and again, dinning that refrain into Graham's ear until it haunted him. This person stayed close beside Graham and Asano on the swift way, shouting to the people who swarmed on the lower platforms as he rushed past them. His cry about Ostrog alternated with some incomprehensible orders Presently he went leaping down and disappeared.

Graham's mind was filled with the din. His plans were vague and unformed. He had one picture of some commanding position from which he could address the multitudes, another of meeting Ostrog face to face. He was full of rage, of tense muscular excitement, his hands gripped, his lips were pressed together.

The way to the Council House across the ruins was impassable, but Asano met that difficulty and took Graham into the premises of the central post-office. The post-office was nominally at work, but the blue-clothed porters moved sluggishly or had stopped to stare through the arches of their galleries at the shouting men who were going by outside. "Every man to his Ward! Every man to his Ward!" Here, by Asano's advice, Graham revealed his identity.

They crossed to the Council House by a cable cradle. Already in the brief interval since the capitulation of the Councillors a great change had been wrought in the appearance of the ruins. The spurting cascades of the ruptured sea water-mains had been captured and tamed, and huge temporary pipes ran overhead along a flimsy looking fabric of girders. The sky was laced with restored cables and wires that served the Council House, and a mass of new fabric with cranes and other building machines going to and fro upon it, projected to the left of the white pile.

The moving ways that ran across this area had been restored, albeit for once running under the open sky. These were the ways that Graham had seen from the little balcony in the hour of his awakening, not nine days since, and the hall of his Trance had been on the further side, where now shapeless piles of smashed and shattered masonry were heaped together.

It was already high day and the sun was shining brightly. Out of their tall caverns of blue electric light came the swift ways crowded with multitudes of people, who poured off them and gathered ever denser over the wreckage and confusion of the ruins. The air was full of their shouting, and they were pressing and swaying towards the central building. For the most part that shouting mass consisted of shapeless swarms, but here and there Graham could see that a rude discipline struggled to establish itself. And every voice clamoured for order in the chaos. "To your Wards! Every man to his Ward!"

The cable carried them into a hall which Graham recognised as the ante-chamber to the Hall of the Atlas, about the gallery of which he had walked days ago with Howard to show himself to the vanished Council, an hour from his awakening. Now the place was empty except for two cable attendants. These men seemed hugely astonished to recognise the Sleeper in the man who swung down from the cross seat.

"Where is Helen Wotton?" he demanded. "Where is Helen Wotton?" They did not know.

"Then where is Ostrog? I must see Ostrog forthwith. He has disobeyed me. I have come back to take things out of his hands." Without waiting for Asano, he went straight across the place, ascended the steps at the further end, and, pulling the curtain aside, found himself facing the perpetually labouring Titan.

The hall was empty. Its appearance had changed very greatly since his first sight of it. It had suffered serious injury in the violent struggle of the first outbreak. On the right hand side of the great figure the upper half of the wall had been torn away for nearly two hundred feet of its length, and a sheet of the same glassy film that had enclosed Graham at his awakening had been drawn across the gap. This deadened, but did not altogether exclude the roar of the people outside. "Wards! Wards! Wards!" they seemed to be saying. Through it there were visible the beams and supports of metal scaffoldings that rose and fell according to the requirements of a great crowd of workmen. An idle building machine, with lank arms of red painted metal that caught the still plastic blocks of mineral paste and swung them neatly into position, stretched gauntly across this green tinted picture. On it were still a number of workmen staring at the crowd below. For a moment he stood regarding these things, and Asano overtook him.

"Ostrog," said Asano, "will be in the small offices beyond there." The little man looked livid now and his eyes searched Graham's face.

They had scarcely advanced ten paces from the curtain before a little panel to the left of the Atlas rolled up, and Ostrog, accompanied by Lincoln and followed by two black and yellow clad negroes, appeared crossing the remote corner of the hall, towards a second panel that was raised and open. "Ostrog," shouted Graham, and at the sound of his voice the little party turned astonished.

Ostrog said something to Lincoln and advanced alone.

Graham was the first to speak. His voice was loud and dictatorial. "What is this I hear?" he asked. "Are you bringing negroes here—to keep the people down?"

"It is none too soon," said Ostrog. "They have been getting out of hand more and more, since the revolt. I under-estimated—"

"Do you mean that these infernal negroes are on the way?"

"On the way. As it is, you have seen the people—outside?"

"No wonder! But—after what was said. You have taken too much on yourself, Ostrog."

Ostrog said nothing, but drew nearer.

"These negroes must not come to London," said Graham. "I am Master and they shall not come."

Ostrog glanced at Lincoln, who at once came towards them with his two attendants close behind him. "Why not?" asked Ostrog.

"White men must be mastered by white men. Besides—"

"The negroes are only an instrument."

"But that is not the question. I am the Master. I mean to be the Master. And I tell you these negroes shall not come."

"The people—"

"I believe in the people."

"Because you are an anachronism. You are a man out of the Past—an accident. You are Owner perhaps of half the property in the world. But you are not Master. You do not know enough to be Master."

He glanced at Lincoln again. "I know now what you think—I can guess something of what you mean to do. Even now it is not too late to warn you. You dream of human equality—of a socialistic order—you have all those worn-out dreams of the nineteenth century fresh and vivid in your mind, and you would rule this age that you do not understand."

"Listen!" said Graham. "You can hear it—a sound like the sea. Not voices—but a voice. Do you altogether understand?"

"We taught them that," said Ostrog.

"Perhaps. Can you teach them to forget it? But enough of this! These negroes must not come."

There was a pause and Ostrog looked him in the eyes.

"They will," he said.

"I forbid it," said Graham.

"They have started."

"I will not have it."

"No," said Ostrog. "Sorry as I am to follow the method of the Council—. For your own good—you must not side with disorder. And now that you are here—. It was kind of you to come here."

Lincoln laid his hand on Graham's shoulder. Abruptly Graham realized the enormity of his blunder in coming to the Council House. He turned towards the curtains that separated the hall from the antechamber. The clutching hand of Asano intervened. In another moment Lincoln had grasped Graham's cloak.

He turned and struck at Lincoln's face, and incontinently a negro had him by collar and arm. He wrenched himself away, his sleeve tore noisily, and he stumbled back, to be tripped by the other attendant. Then he struck the ground heavily and he was staring at the distant ceiling of the hall.

He shouted, rolled over, struggling fiercely, clutched an attendant's leg and threw him headlong, and struggled to his feet.

Lincoln appeared before him, went down heavily again with a blow under the point of the jaw and lay still. Graham made two strides, stumbled. And then Ostrog's arm was round his neck, he was pulled over backward, fell heavily, and his arms were pinned to the ground. After a few violent efforts he ceased to struggle and lay staring at Ostrog's heaving throat.

"You—are—a prisoner," panted Ostrog, exulting. "You—were rather a fool—to come back."

Graham turned his head about and perceived through the irregular green window in the walls of the hall the men who had been working the building cranes gesticulating excitedly to the people below them. They had seen!

Ostrog followed his eyes and started. He shouted something to Lincoln, but Lincoln did not move. A bullet smashed among the mouldings above the Atlas The two sheets of transparent matter that had been stretched across this gap were rent, the edges of the torn aperture darkened, curved, ran rapidly towards the framework, and in a moment the Council chamber stood open to the air. A chilly gust blew in by the gap, bringing with it a war of voices from the ruinous spaces without, an elvish babblement, "Save the Master!" "What are they doing to the Master?" "The Master is betrayed!"

And then he realised that Ostrog's attention was distracted, that Ostrog's grip had relaxed, and, wrenching his arms free, he struggled to his knees. In another moment he had thrust Ostrog back, and he was on one foot, his hand gripping Ostrog's throat, and Ostrog's hands clutching the silk about his neck. But now men were coming towards them from the dais—men whose intentions he misunderstood. He had a glimpse of someone running in the distance towards the curtains of the antechamber, and then Ostrog had slipped from him and these newcomers were upon him. To his infinite astonishment, they seized him. They obeyed the shouts of Ostrog.

He was lugged a dozen yards before he realised that they were not friends—that they were dragging him towards the open panel. When he saw this he pulled back, he tried to fling himself down, he shouted for help with all his strength. And this time there were answering cries.

The grip upon his neck relaxed, and behold! in the lower corner of the rent upon the wall, first one and then a number of little black figures appeared shouting and waving arms. They came leaping down from the gap into the light gallery that had led to the Silent Rooms. They ran along it, so near were they that Graham could see the weapons in their hands, Then Ostrog was shouting in his ear to the men who held him, and once more he was struggling with all his strength against their endeavours to thrust him towards the opening that yawned to receive him. "They can't come down," panted Ostrog. "They daren't fire. It's all right." "We'll save him from them yet."

For long minutes as it seemed to Graham that inglorious struggle continued. His clothes were rent in a dozen places, he was covered in dust, one hand had been trodden upon. He could hear the shouts of his supporters, and once he heard shots. He could feel his strength giving way, feel his efforts wild and aimless. But no help came, and surely, irresistibly, that black, yawning opening came nearer.

The pressure upon him relaxed and he struggled up. He saw Ostrog's grey head receding and perceived that he was no longer held. He turned about and came full into a man in black. One of the green weapons cracked close to him, a drift of pungent smoke came into his face, and a steel blade flashed. The huge chamber span about him.

He saw a man in pale blue stabbing one of the black and yellow attendants not three yards from his face. Then hands were upon him again.

He was being pulled in two, directions now. It seemed as though people were shouting to him. He wanted to understand and could not. Someone was clutching about his thighs, he was being hoisted in spite of his vigorous efforts. He understood suddenly, he ceased to struggle. He was lifted up on men's shoulders and carried away from that devouring panel. Ten thousand throats were cheering.

He saw men in blue and black hurrying after the retreating Ostrogites and firing. Lifted up, he saw now across the whole expanse of the hall beneath the Atlas image, saw that he was being carried towards the raised platform in the centre of the place. The far end of the hall was already full of people running towards him. They were looking at him and cheering.

He became aware that a sort of body-guard surrounded him. Active men about him shouted vague orders. He saw close at hand the black moustached man in yellow who had been among those who had greeted him in the public theatre, shouting directions. The hall was already densely packed with swaying people, the little metal gallery sagged with a shouting load, the curtains at the end had been torn away, and the ante-chamber was revealed densely crowded. He could scarcely make the man near him hear for the tumult about them. "Where has Ostrog gone?" he asked.

The man he questioned pointed over the heads towards the lower panels about the hall on the side opposite the gap. They stood open and armed men, blue clad with black sashes, were running through them and vanishing into the chambers and passages beyond. It seemed to Graham that a sound of firing drifted through the riot. He was carried in a staggering curve across the great hall towards an opening beneath the gap.

He perceived men working with a sort of rude discipline to keep the crowd off him, to make a space clear about him. He passed out of the hall, and saw a crude, new wall rising blankly before him topped by blue sky. He was swung down to his feet; someone gripped his arm and guided him. He found the man in yellow close at hand. They were taking him up a narrow stairway of brick, and close at hand rose the great red painted masses, the cranes and levers and the still engines of the big building machine.

He was at the top of the steps. He was hurried across a narrow railed footway, and suddenly with a vast shouting the amphitheatre of ruins opened again before him. "The Master is with us! The Master! The Master!" The shout swept athwart the lake of faces like a wave, broke against the distant cliff of ruins, and came back in a welter of cries. "The Master is on our side!"

Graham perceived that he was no longer encompassed by people, that he was standing upon a little temporary platform of white metal, part of a flimsy seeming scaffolding that laced about the great mass of the Council House. Over all the huge expanse of the ruins, swayed and eddied the shouting people; and here and there the black banners of the revolutionary societies ducked and swayed and formed rare nuclei of organisation in the chaos. Up the steep stairs of wall and scaffolding by which his rescuers had reached the opening in the Atlas Chamber, clung a solid crowd, and little energetic black figures clinging to pillars and projections were strenuous to induce these congested masses to stir. Behind him, at a higher point on the scaffolding, a number of men struggled upwards with the flapping folds of a huge black standard. Through the yawning gap in the walls below him he could look down upon the packed attentive multitudes in the Hall of the Atlas. The distant flying stages to the south came out bright and vivid, brought nearer as it seemed by an unusual translucency of the air. A solitary aeropile beat up from the central stage as if to meet the coming aeroplanes.

"What had become of Ostrog?" asked Graham, and even as he spoke he saw that all eyes were turned from him towards the crest of the Council House building. He looked also in this direction of universal attention. For a moment he saw nothing but the jagged corner of a wall, hard and clear against the sky. Then in the shadow he perceived the interior of a room and recognised with a start the green and white decorations of his former prison. And coming quickly across this opened room and up to the very verge of the cliff of the ruins came a little white clad figure followed by two other smaller seeming figures in black and yellow. He heard the man beside him exclaim "Ostrog," and turned to ask a question. But he never did, because of the startled exclamation of another of those who were with him and a lank finger suddenly pointing. He looked, and behold the aeropile that had been rising from the flying stage when last he had looked in that direction, was driving towards them. The swift steady flight was still novel enough to hold his attention.

Nearer it came, growing rapidly larger and larger, until it had swept over the further edge of the ruins and into view of the dense multitudes below. It drooped across the space and rose and passed overhead, rising to clear the mass of the Council House, a filmy translucent shape with the solitary aeronaut peering down through its ribs. It vanished beyond the skyline of the ruins.

Graham transferred his attention to Ostrog. He was signalling with his hands, and his attendants busy breaking down the wall beside him. In another moment the aeropile came into view again, a little thing far away, coming round in a wide curve and going slower.

Then suddenly the man in yellow shouted: "What are they doing? What are the people doing? Why is Ostrog left there? Why is he not captured? They will lift him—the aeropile will lift him! Ah!"

The exclamation was echoed by a shout from the ruins. The rattling sound of the green weapons drifted across the intervening gulf to Graham, and, looking down, he saw a number of black and yellow uniforms running along one of the galleries that lay open to the air below the promontory upon which Ostrog stood. They fired as they ran at men unseen, and then emerged a number of pale blue figures in pursuit. These minute fighting figures had the oddest effect; they seemed as they ran like little model soldiers in a toy. This queer appearance of a house cut open gave that struggle amidst furniture and passages a quality of unreality. It was perhaps two hundred yards away from him, and very nearly fifty above the heads in the ruins below. The black and yellow men ran into an open archway, and turned and fired a volley. One of the blue pursuers striding forward close to the edge, flung up his arms, staggered sideways, seemed to Graham's sense to hang over the edge for several seconds, and fell headlong down. Graham saw him strike a projecting corner, fly out, head over heels, head over heels, and vanish behind the red arm of the building machine.

And then a shadow came between Graham and the sun. He looked up and the sky was clear, but he knew the aeropile had passed. Ostrog had vanished. The man in yellow thrust before him, zealous and perspiring, pointing and blatent.

"They are grounding!" cried the man in yellow. "They are grounding. Tell the people to fire at him. Tell them to fire at him!"

Graham could not understand. He heard loud voices repeating these enigmatical orders.

Suddenly over the edge of the ruins he saw the prow of the aeropile come gliding and stop with a jerk. In a moment Graham understood that the thing had grounded in order that Ostrog might escape by it. He saw a blue haze climbing out of the gulf, perceived that the people below him were now firing up at the projecting stem.

A man beside him cheered hoarsely, and he saw that the blue rebels had gained the archway that had been contested by the men in black and yellow a moment before, and were running in a continual stream along the open passage.

And suddenly the aeropile slipped over the edge of the Council House and fell. It dropped, tilting at an angle of forty-five degrees, and dropping so steeply that it seemed to Graham, it seemed perhaps to most of these below, that it could not possibly rise again.

It fell so closely past him that he could see Ostrog clutching the guides of the seat, with his grey hair streaming; see the white-faced aeronaut wrenching over the lever that drove the engine along its guides. He heard the apprehensive vague cry of innumerable men below.

Graham clutched the railing before him and gasped. The second seemed an age. The lower fan of the aeropile passed within an ace of touching the people, who yelled and screamed and trampled one another below.

And then it rose.

For a moment it looked as if it could not possibly clear the opposite cliff, and then that it could not possibly clear the wind-wheel that rotated beyond.

And behold! it was clear and soaring, still heeling sideways, upward, upward into the wind-swept sky.

The suspense of the moment gave place to a fury of exasperation as the swarming people realised that Ostrog had escaped them. With belated activity they renewed their fire, until the rattling wove into a roar, until the whole area became dim and blue and the air pungent with the thin smoke of their weapons.

Too late! The aeropile dwindled smaller and smaller, and curved about and swept gracefully downward to the flying stage from which it had so lately risen. Ostrog had escaped.

For a while a confused babblement arose from the ruins, and then the universal attention came back to Graham, perched high among the scaffolding. He saw the faces of the people turned towards him, heard their shouts at his rescue. From the throat of the ways came the song of the revolt spreading like a breeze across that swaying sea of men.

The little group of men about him shouted congratulations on his escape. The man in yellow was close to him, with a set face and shining eyes. And the song was rising, louder and louder; tramp, tramp, tramp, tramp.

Slowly the realisation came of the full meaning of these things to him, the perception of the swift change in his position. Ostrog, who had stood beside him whenever he had faced that shouting multitude before, was beyond there—the antagonist. There was no one to rule for him any longer. Even the people about him, the leaders and organisers of the multitude, looked to see what he would do, looked to him to act, awaited his orders. He was King indeed. His puppet reign was at an end.

He was very intent to do the thing that was expected of him. His nerves and muscles were quivering, his mind was perhaps a little confused, but he felt neither fear nor anger. His hand that had been trodden upon throbbed and was hot. He was a little nervous about his bearing. He knew he was not afraid, but he was anxious not to seem afraid. In his former life he had often been more excited in playing games of skill. He was desirous of immediate action, he knew he must not think too much in detail of the huge complexity of the struggle about him lest he should be paralysed by the sense of its intricacy. Over there those square blue shapes, the flying stages, meant Ostrog; against Ostrog he was fighting for the world.

CHAPTER XIII
WHILE THE AEROPLANES WERE COMING

For a time the Master of the Earth was not even master of his own mind. Even his will seemed a will not his own, his own acts surprised him and were but a part of the confusion of strange experiences that poured across his being. These things were definite, the aeroplanes were coming, Helen Wotton had warned the people of their coming, and he was Master of the Earth. Each of these facts seemed struggling for complete possession of his thoughts. They protruded from a background of swarming halls, elevated passages, rooms jammed with ward leaders in council kinematograph and telephone rooms, and windows looking out on a seething sea of marching men. The man in yellow, and men whom he fancied were called Ward Leaders, were either propelling him forward or following him obediently; it was hard to tell. Perhaps they were doing a little of both. Perhaps some power unseen and unsuspected, propelled them all. He was aware that he was going to make a proclamation to the People of the Earth, aware of certain grandiose phrases floating in his mind as the thing he meant to say. Many little things happened, and then he found himself with the man in yellow entering a little room where this proclamation of his was to be made.

This room was grotesquely latter-day in its appointments. In the centre was a bright oval lit by shaded electric lights from above. The rest was in shadow, and the double finely fitting doors through which he came from the swarming Hall of the Atlas made the place very still. The dead thud of these as they closed behind him, the sudden cessation of the tumult in which he had been living for hours, the quivering circle of light, the whispers and quick noiseless movements of vaguely visible attendants in the shadows, had a strange effect upon Graham. The huge ears of a phonographic mechanism gaped in a battery for his words, the black eyes of great photographic cameras awaited his beginning, beyond metal rods and coils glittered dimly, and something whirled about with a droning hum. He walked into the centre of the light, and his shadow drew together black and sharp to a little blot at his feet.

The vague shape of the thing he meant to say was already in his mind. But this silence, this isolation, the sudden withdrawal from that contagious crowd, this silent audience of gaping, glaring machines had not been in his anticipation. All his supports seemed withdrawn together; he seemed to have dropped into this suddenly, suddenly to have discovered himself. In a moment he was changed. He found that he now feared to be inadequate, he feared to be theatrical, he feared the quality of his voice, the quality of his wit, astonished, he turned to the man in yellow with a propitiatory gesture. "For a moment," he said, "I must wait. I did not think it would be like this. I must think of the thing I have to say."

While he was still hesitating there came an agitated messenger with news that the foremost aeroplanes were passing over Arawan.

"Arawan?" he said. "Where is that? But anyhow, they are coming. They will be here. When?"

"By twilight."

"Great God! In only a few hours. What news of the flying stages?" he asked.

"The people of the south-west wards are ready."

"Ready!"

He turned impatiently to the blank circles of the lenses again.

"I suppose it must be a sort of speech. Would to God I knew certainly the thing that should be said! Aeroplanes at Arawan! They must have started before the main fleet. And the people only ready! Surely..."

"Oh! what does it matter whether I speak well or ill?" he said, and felt the light grow brighter.

He had framed some vague sentence of democratic sentiment when suddenly doubts overwhelmed him. His belief in his heroic quality and calling he found had altogether lost its assured conviction. The picture of a little strutting futility in a windy waste of incomprehensible destinies replaced it. Abruptly it was perfectly clear to him that this revolt against Ostrog was premature, foredoomed to failure, the impulse of passionate inadequacy against inevitable things. He thought of that swift flight of aeroplanes like the swoop of Fate towards him. He was astonished that he could have seen things in any other light. In that final emergency he debated, thrust debate resolutely aside, determined at all costs to go through with the thing he had undertaken. And he could find no word to begin. Even as he stood, awkward, hesitating, with an indiscrete apology for his inability trembling on his lips, came the noise of many people crying out, the running to and fro of feet. "Wait," cried someone, and a door opened. "She is coming," said the voices. Graham turned, and the watching lights waned.

Through the open doorway he saw a slight grey figure advancing across a spacious hall. His heart leapt. It was Helen Wotton. Behind and about her marched a riot of applause. The man in yellow came out of the nearer shadows into the circle of light.

"This is the girl who told us what Ostrog had dune," he said.

Her face was aflame, and the heavy coils of her black hair fell about her shoulders. The folds of the soft silk robe she wore streamed from her and floated in the rhythm of her advance. She drew nearer and nearer, and his heart was beating fast. All his doubts were gone. The shadow of the doorway fell athwart her face and she was near him. "You have not betrayed us?" she cried. "You are with us?"

"Where have you been?" said Graham.

"At the office of the south-west wards. Until ten minutes since I did not know you had returned. I went to the office of the south-west wards to find the Ward Leaders in order that they might tell the people."

"I came back so soon as I heard——."

"I knew," she cried, "knew you would be with us. And it was I—it was I that told them. They have risen. All the world is rising. The people have awakened. Thank God that I did not act in vain! You are Master still."

"You told them" he said slowly, and he saw that in spite of her steady eyes her lips trembled and her throat rose and fell.

"I told them. I knew of the order. I was here. I heard that the negroes were to come to London to guard you and to keep the people down—to keep you a prisoner. And I stopped it. I came out and told the people. And you are Master still."

Graham glanced at the black lenses of the cameras, the vast listening ears, and back to her face. "I am Master still," he said slowly, and the swift rush of a fleet of aeroplanes passed across his thoughts.

"And you did this? You, who are the niece of Ostrog."

"For you," she cried. "For you! That you for whom the world has waited should not be cheated of your power."

Graham stood for a space, wordless, regarding her. His doubts and questionings had fled before her presence. He remembered the things that he had meant to say. He faced the cameras again and the light about him grew brighter. He turned again towards her.

"You have saved me," he said; "you have saved my power. And the battle is beginning. God knows what this night will see—but not dishonour."

He paused. He addressed himself to the unseen multitudes who stared upon him through those grotesque black eyes. At first he spoke slowly. "Men and women of the new age," he said; "You have arisen to do battle for the race... There is no easy victory before us."

He stopped to gather words. The thoughts that had been in his mind before she came returned, but transfigured, no longer touched with the shadow of a possible irrelevance. "This night is a beginning," he cried. "This battle that is coming, this battle that rushes upon us to-night, is only a beginning. All your lives, it may be, you must fight. Take no thought though I am beaten, though I am utterly overthrown."

He found the thing in his mind too vague for words. He paused momentarily, and broke into vague exhortations, and then a rush of speech came upon him. Much that he said was but the humanitarian commonplace of a vanished age, but the conviction of his voice touched it to vitality. He stated the case of the old days to the people of the new age, to the woman at his side. "I come out of the past to you," he said, "with the memory of an age that hoped. My age was an age of dreams—of beginnings, an age of noble hopes; throughout the world we had made an end of slavery; throughout the world we had spread the desire and anticipation that wars might cease, that all men and women might live nobly, in freedom and peace. ... So we hoped in the days that are past. And what of those hopes? How is it with man after two hundred years?

"Great cities, vast powers, a collective greatness beyond our dreams. For that we did not work, and that has come. But how is it with the little lives that make up this greater life? How is it with the common lives? As it has ever been—sorrow and labour, lives cramped and unfulfilled, lives tempted by power, tempted by wealth, and gone to waste and folly. The old faiths have faded and changed, the new faith—. Is there a new faith?"

Things that he had long wished to believe, he found that he believed. He plunged at belief and seized it, and clung for a time at her level. He spoke gustily, in broken incomplete sentences, but with all his heart and strength, of this new faith within him. He spoke of the greatness of self-abnegation, of his belief in an immortal life of Humanity in which we live and move and have our being. His voice rose and fell, and the recording appliances hummed their hurried applause, dim attendants watched him out of the shadow. Through all those doubtful places his sense of that silent spectator beside him sustained his sincerity. For a few glorious moments he was carried away; he felt no doubt of his heroic quality, no doubt of his heroic words, he had it all straight and plain. His eloquence limped no longer. And at last he made an end to speaking. "Here and now," he cried, "I make my will. All that is mine in the world I give to the people of the world. All that is mine in the world I give to the people of the world. I give it to you, and myself I give to you. And as God wills, I will live for you, or I will die."

He ended with a florid gesture and turned about. He found the light of his present exaltation reflected in the face of the girl. Their eyes met; her eyes were swimming with tears of enthusiasm. They seemed to be urged towards each other. They clasped hands and stood gripped, facing one another, in an eloquent silence. She whispered. "I knew," she whispered. "I knew." He could not speak, he crushed her hand in his. His mind was the theatre of gigantic passions.

The man in yellow was beside them. Neither had noted his coming. He was saying that the south-west wards were marching. "I never expected it so soon," he cried. "They have done wonders. You must send them a word to help them on their way."

Graham dropped Helen's hand and stared at him absent-mindedly. Then with a start he returned to his previous preoccupation about the flying stages.

"Yes," he said. "That is good, that is good." He weighed a message. "Tell them;—well done South West."

He turned his eyes to Helen Wotton again. His face expressed his struggle between conflicting ideas. "We must capture the flying stages," he explained. "Unless we can do that they will land negroes. At all costs we must prevent that."

He felt even as he spoke that this was not what had been in his mind before the interruption. He saw a touch of surprise in her eyes. She seemed about to speak and a shrill bell drowned her voice.

It occurred to Graham that she expected him to lead these marching people, that that was the thing he had to do. He made the offer abruptly. He addressed the man in yellow, but he spoke to her. He saw her face respond. "Here I am doing nothing," he said.

"It is impossible," protested the man in yellow.

"It is a fight in a warren. Your place is here."

He explained elaborately. He motioned towards the room where Graham must wait, he insisted no other course was possible. "We must know where you are," he said. "At any moment a crisis may arise needing your presence and decision." The room was a luxurious little apartment with news machines and a broken mirror that had once been en _rapport_ with the crow's nest specula. It seemed a matter of course to Graham that Helen should stop with him.

A picture had drifted through his mind of such a vast dramatic struggle as the masses in the ruins had suggested. But here was no spectacular battle-field such as he imagined. Instead was seclusion—and suspense. It was only as the afternoon wore on that he pieced together a truer picture of the fight that was raging, inaudibly and invisibly, within four miles of him, beneath the Roehampton stage. A strange and unprecedented contest it was, a battle that was a hundred thousand little battles, a battle in a sponge of ways and channels, fought out of sight of sky or sun under the electric glare, fought out in a vast confusion by multitudes untrained in arms, led chiefly by acclamation, multitudes dulled by mindless labour and enervated by the tradition of two hundred years of servile security against multitudes demoralised by lives of venial privilege and sensual indulgence. They had no artillery, no differentiation into this force or that; the only weapon on either side was the little green metal carbine, whose secret manufacture and sudden distribution in enormous quantities had been one of Ostrog's culminating moves against the Council. Few had had any experience with this weapon, many had never discharged one, many who carried it came unprovided with ammunition; never was wilder firing in the history of warfare. It was a battle of amateurs, a hideous experimental warfare, armed rioters fighting armed rioters, armed rioters swept forward by the words and fury of a song, by the tramping sympathy of their numbers, pouring in countless myriads towards the smaller ways, the disabled lifts, the galleries slippery with blood, the halls and passages choked with smoke, beneath the flying stages, to learn there when retreat was hopeless the ancient mysteries of warfare. And overhead save for a few sharpshooters upon the roof spaces and for a few bands and threads of vapour that multiplied and darkened towards the evening, the day was a clear serenity. Ostrog it seems had no bombs at command and in all the earlier phases of the battle the aeropiles played no part. Not the smallest cloud was there to break the empty brilliance of the sky. It seemed as though it held itself vacant until the aeroplanes should come.

Ever and again there was news of these, drawing nearer, from this Mediterranean port and then that, and presently from the south of France. But of the new guns that Ostrog had made and which were known to be in the city came no news in spite of Graham's urgency, nor any report of successes from the dense felt of fighting strands about the flying stages. Section after section of the Labour Societies reported itself assembled, reported itself marching, and vanished from knowledge into the labyrinth of that warfare What was happening there? Even the busy ward leaders did not know. In spite of the opening and closing of doors, the hasty messengers, the ringing of bells and the perpetual clitter-clack of recording implements, Graham felt isolated, strangely inactive, inoperative.

Their isolation seemed at times the strangest, the most unexpected of all the things that had happened since his awakening. It had something of the quality of that inactivity that comes in dreams. A tumult, the stupendous realisation of a world struggle between Ostrog and himself, and then this confined quiet little room with its mouthpieces and bells and broken mirror!

Now the door would be closed and they were alone together; they seemed sharply marked off then from all the unprecedented world storm that rushed together without, vividly aware of one another, only concerned with one another. Then the door would open again, messengers would enter, or a sharp bell would stab their quiet privacy, and it was like a window in a well built brightly lit house flung open suddenly to a hurricane. The dark hurry and tumult, the stress and vehemence of the battle rushed in and overwhelmed them. They were no longer persons but mere spectators, mere impressions of a tremendous convulsion. They became unreal even to themselves, miniatures of personality, indescribably small, and the two antagonistic realities, the only realities in being were first the city, that throbbed and roared yonder in a belated frenzy of defence and secondly the aeroplanes hurling inexorably towards them over the round shoulder of the world.

At first their mood had been one of exalted confidence, a great pride had possessed them, a pride in one another for the greatness of the issues they had challenged. At first he had walked the room eloquent with a transitory persuasion of his tremendous destiny. But slowly uneasy intimations of their coming defeat touched his spirit. There came a long period in which they were alone. He changed his theme, became egotistical, spoke of the wonder of his sleep, of the little life of his memories, remote yet minute and clear, like something seen through an inverted opera-glass, and all the brief play of desires and errors that had made his former life. She said little, but the emotion in her face followed the tones in his voice, and it seemed to him he had at last a perfect understanding. He reverted from pure reminiscence to that sense of greatness she imposed upon him. "And through it all, this destiny was before me," he said; "this vast inheritance of which I did not dream."

Insensibly their heroic preoccupation with the revolutionary struggle passed to the question of their relationship. He began to question her. She told him of the days before his awakening, spoke with a brief vividness of the girlish dreams that had given a bias to her life, of the incredulous emotions his awakening had aroused. She told him too of a tragic circumstance of her girlhood that had darkened her life, quickened her sense of injustice and opened her heart prematurely to the wider sorrows of the world. For a little time, so far as he was concerned, the great war about them was but the vast ennobling background to these personal things.

In an instant these personal relations were submerged. There came messengers to tell that a great fleet of aeroplanes was rushing between the sky and Avignon. He went to the crystal dial in the corner and assured himself that the thing was so. He went to the chart room and consulted a map to measure the distances of Avignon, New Arawan, and London. He made swift calculations. He went to the room of the Ward Leaders to ask for news of the fight for the stages—and there was no one there. After a time he came back to her.

His face had changed. It had dawned upon him that the struggle was perhaps more than half over, that Ostrog was holding his own, that the arrival of the aeroplanes would mean a panic that might leave him helpless. A chance phrase in the message had given him a glimpse of the reality that came. Each of these soaring giants bore its thousand half savage negroes to the death grapple of the city. Suddenly his humanitarian enthusiasm showed flimsy. Only two of the Ward Leaders were in their room, when presently he repaired thither, the Hall of the Atlas seemed empty. He fancied a change in the bearing of the attendants in the outer rooms. A sombre disillusionment darkened his mind. She looked at him anxiously when he returned to her.

"No news," he said with an assumed carelessness in answer to her eyes.

Then he was moved to frankness. "Or rather—bad news. We are losing. We are gaining no ground and the aeroplanes draw nearer and nearer."

He walked the length of the room and turned.

"Unless we can capture those flying stages in the next hour—there will be horrible things. We shall be beaten.

"No!" she said. "We have justice—we have the people. We have God on our side."

"Ostrog has discipline—he has plans. Do you know, out there just now I felt—. When I heard that these aeroplanes were a stage nearer. I felt as if I were fighting the machinery of fate."

She made no answer for a while. "We have done right," she said at last.

He looked at her doubtfully. "We have done what we could. But does this depend upon us? Is it not an older sin, a wider sin?"

"What do you mean?" she asked.

"These blacks are savages, ruled by force, used as force. And they have been under the rule of the whites two hundred years. Is it not a race quarrel? The race sinned—the race pays."

"But these labourers, these poor people of London—!"

"Vicarious atonement. To stand wrong is to share the guilt."

She looked keenly at him, astonished at the new aspect he presented.

Without came the shrill ringing of a bell, the sound of feet and the gabble of a phonographic message. The man in yellow appeared. "Yes?" said Graham.

"They are at Vichy."

"Where are the attendants who were in the great Hall of the Atlas?" asked Graham abruptly.

Presently the Babble Machine rang again. "We may win yet," said the man in yellow, going out to it. "If only we can find where Ostrog has hidden his guns. Everything hangs on that now. Perhaps this—"

Graham followed him. But the only news was of the aeroplanes. They had reached Orleans.

Graham returned to Helen. "No news," he said "No news."

"And we can do nothing?"

"Nothing."

He paced impatiently. Suddenly the swift anger that was his nature swept upon him. "Curse this complex world!" he cried, "and all the inventions of men! That a man must die like a rat in a snare and never see his foe! Oh, for one blow!..."

He turned with an abrupt change in his manner. "That's nonsense," he said. "I am a savage."

He paced and stopped. "After all London and Paris are only two cities. All the temperate zone has risen. What if London is doomed and Paris destroyed? These are but accidents." Again came the mockery of news to call him to fresh enquiries. He returned with a graver face and sat down beside her.

"The end must be near," he said. "The people it seems have fought and died in tens of thousands, the ways about Roehampton must be like a smoked beehive. And they have died in vain. They are still only at the sub stage. The aeroplanes are near Paris. Even were a gleam of success to come now, there would be nothing to do, there would be no time to do anything before they were upon us. The guns that might have saved us are mislaid. Mislaid! Think of the disorder of things! Think of this foolish tumult, that cannot even find its weapons! Oh, for one aeropile—just one! For the want of that I am beaten. Humanity is beaten and our cause is lost! My kingship, my headlong foolish kingship will not last a night. And I have egged on the people to fight—."

"They would have fought anyhow."

"I doubt it. I have come among them—"

"No," she cried, "not that. If defeat comes—if you die—. But even that cannot be, it cannot be, after all these years."

"Ah! We have meant well. But—do you indeed believe—?"

"If they defeat you," she cried, "you have spoken. Your word has gone like a great wind through the world, fanning liberty into a flame. What if the flame sputters a little! Nothing can change the spoken word. Your message will have gone forth...."

"To what end? It may be. It may be. You know I said, when you told me of these things dear God! but that was scarcely a score of hours ago!—I said that I had not your faith. Well—at any rate there is nothing to do now...."

"You have not my faith! Do you mean—? You are sorry?"

"No," he said hurriedly, "no! Before God—no!" His voice changed. "But—. I think—I have been indiscreet. I knew little—I grasped too hastily...."

He paused. He was ashamed of this avowal. "There is one thing that makes up for all. I have known you. Across this gulf of time I have come to you. The rest is done. It is done. With you, too, it has been something more—or something less—"

He paused with his face searching hers, and without clamoured the unheeded message that the aeroplanes were rising into the sky of Amiens.

She put her hand to her throat, and her lips were white. She stared before her as if she saw some horrible possibility. Suddenly her features changed. "Oh, but I have been honest!" she cried, and then, "Have I been honest? I loved the world and freedom, I hated cruelty and oppression. Surely it was that."

"Yes," he said, "yes. And we have done what it lay in us to do. We have given our message, our message! We have started Armageddon! But now—. Now that we have, it may be our last hour, together, now that all these greater things are done...."

He stopped. She sat in silence. Her face was a white riddle.

For a moment they heeded nothing of a sudden stir outside, a running to and fro, and cries. Then Helen started to an attitude of tense attention. "It is—," she cried and stood up, speechless, incredulous, triumphant. And Graham, too, heard. Metallic voices were shouting "Victory!" Yes it was "Victory!" He stood up also with the light of a desperate hope in his eyes.

Bursting through the curtains appeared the man in yellow, startled and dishevelled with excitement. "Victory," he cried, "victory! The people are winning. Ostrog's people have collapsed."

She rose. "Victory?" And her voice was hoarse and faint.

"What do you mean?" asked Graham. "Tell me! What?"

"We have driven them out of the under galleries at Norwood, Streatham is afire and burning wildly, and Roehampton is ours. Ours!— and we have taken the aeropile that lay thereon."

For an instant Graham and Helen stood in silence, their hearts were beating fast, they looked at one another. For one last moment there gleamed in Graham his dream of empire, of kingship, with Helen by his side. It gleamed, and passed.

A shrill bell rang. An agitated grey-headed man appeared from the room of the Ward Leaders. "It is all over," he cried.

"What matters it now that we have Roehampton? The aeroplanes have been sighted at Boulogne!"

"The Channel!" said the man in yellow. He calculated swiftly. "Half an hour."

"They still have three of the flying stages," said the old man.

"Those guns?" cried Graham.

"We cannot mount them—in half an hour."

"Do you mean they are found?"

"Too late," said the old man.

"If we could stop them another hour!" cried the man in yellow.

"Nothing can stop them now," said the old man, "they have near a hundred aeroplanes in the first fleet."

"Another hour?" asked Graham.

"To be so near!" said the Ward Leader. "Now that we have found those guns. To be so near—. If once we could get them out upon the roof spaces."

"How long would that take?" asked Graham suddenly.

"An hour—certainly."

"Too late," cried the Ward Leader, "too late."

"Is it too late?" said Graham. "Even now—. An hour!"

He had suddenly perceived a possibility. He tried to speak calmly, but his face was white. "There is one chance. You said there was an aeropile—?"

"On the Roehampton stage, Sire."

"Smashed?"

"No. It is lying crossways to the carrier. It might be got upon the guides—easily. But there is no aeronaut—."

Graham glanced at the two men and then at Helen. He spoke after a long pause. "We have no aeronauts?"

"None."

"The aeroplanes are clumsy," he said thoughtfully, "compared with the aeropiles."

He turned suddenly to Helen. His decision was made. "I must do it."

"Do what?"

"Go to this flying stage—to this aeropile."

"What do you mean?"

"I am an aeronaut. After all—. Those days for which you reproached me were not wasted."

He turned to the old man in yellow. "Put the aeropile upon the guides."

The man in yellow hesitated.

"What do you mean to do?" cried Helen.

"This aeropile—it is a chance—."

"You don't mean—?"

"To fight—yes. To fight in the air. I have thought before—. An aeroplane is a clumsy thing. A resolute man—!"

"But—never since flying began—" cried the man in yellow.

"There has been no need. But now the time has come. Tell them now—send them my message—to put it upon the guides."

The old man dumbly interrogated the man in yellow, nodded, and hurried out.

Helen made a step towards Graham. Her face was white. "But—How can one fight? You will be killed."

"Perhaps. Yet, not to do it—or to let someone else attempt it—."

He stopped, he could speak no more, he swept the alternative aside by a gesture, and they stood looking at one another.

"You are right," she said at last in a low tone. "You are right. If it can be done... must go."

Those days for not altogether

He moved a step towards her, and she stepped back, her white face struggled against him and resisted him. "No," she gasped. "I cannot bear—. Go now."

He extended his hands stupidly. She clenched her fists. "Go now," she cried. "Go now."

He hesitated and understood. He threw his hands up in a queer half-theatrical gesture. He had no word to say. He turned from her.

The man in yellow moved towards the door with clumsy belated tact. But Graham stepped past him. He went striding through the room where the Ward Leader bawled at a telephone directing that the aeropile should be put upon the guides.

The man in yellow glanced at Helen's still figure, hesitated and hurried after him. Graham did not once look back, he did not speak until the curtain of the ante-chamber of the great hall fell behind him. Then he turned his head with curt swift directions upon his bloodless lips.

CHAPTER XXIV

THE COMING OF THE AEROPLANES

Two men in pale blue were lying in the irregular line that stretched along the edge of the captured Roehampton stage from end to end, grasping their carbines and peering into the shadows of the stage called Wimbledon Park. Now and then they spoke to one another. They spoke the mutilated English of their class and period. The fire of the Ostrogites had dwindled and ceased, and few of the enemy had been seen for some time. But the echoes of the fight that was going on now far below in the lower galleries of that stage, came every now and then between the staccato of shots from the popular side. One of these men was describing to the other how he had seen a man down below there dodge behind a girder, and had aimed at a guess and hit him cleanly as he dodged too far "He's down there still," said the marksman. "See that little patch. Yes. Between those bars." A few yards behind them lay a dead stranger, face upward to the sky, with the blue canvas of his jacket smoldering in a circle about the neat bullet hole on his chest. Close beside him a wounded man, with a leg swathed about, sat with an expressionless face and watched the progress of that burning. Gigantic behind them, athwart the carrier lay the captured aeropile.

"I can't see him now," said the second man in a ton of provocation.

The marksman became foul-mouthed and high-voiced in his earnest endeavour to make things plain And suddenly, interrupting him, came a noisy shouting from the substage.

"What's going on now," he said, and raised himself on one arm to stare at the stairheads in the central groove of the stage. A number of blue figures were coming up these, and swarming across the stage to the aeropile.

"We don't want all these fools," said his friend. "They only crowd up and spoil shots. What are they after?"

"Ssh!—they're shouting something."

The two men listened. The swarming new-comers had crowded densely about the aeropile. Three Ward Leaders, conspicuous by their black mantles and badges, clambered into the body and appeared above it. The rank and file flung themselves upon the vans, gripping hold of the edges, until the entire outline of the thing was manned, in some places three deep. One of the marksmen knelt up. "They're putting it on the carrier—that's what they're after."

He rose to his feet, his friend rose also. "What's the good?" said his friend. "We've got no aeronauts."

"That's what they're doing anyhow." He looked at his rifle, looked at the struggling crowd, and suddenly turning to the wounded man. "Mind these, mate," he said, handing his carbine and cartridge belt; and in a moment he was running towards the aeropile. For a quarter of an hour he was a perspiring Titan, lugging, thrusting, shouting and heeding shouts, and then the thing was done, and he stood with a multitude of others cheering their own achievement. By this time he knew, what indeed everyone in the city knew, that the Master, raw learner though he was, intended to fly this machine himself, was coming even now to take control of it, would let no other man attempt it. "He who takes the greatest danger, he who bears the heaviest burden, that man is King," so the Master was reported to have spoken. And even as this man cheered, and while the beads of sweat still chased one another from the disorder of his hair, he heard the thunder of a greater tumult, and in fitful snatches the beat and impulse of the revolutionary song. He saw through a gap in the people that a thick stream of heads still poured up the stairway. "The Master is coming," shouted voices, "the Master is coming," and the crowd about him grew denser and denser. He began to thrust himself towards the central groove. "The Master is coming!" "The Sleeper, the Master!" "God and the Master!" roared the Voices.

And suddenly quite close to him were the black uniforms of the revolutionary guard, and for the first and last time in his life he saw Graham, saw him quite nearly. A tall, dark man in a flowing black robe, with a white, resolute face and eyes fixed steadfastly before him; a man who for all the little things about him held neither ears nor eyes nor thoughts.... For all his days that man remembered the passing of Graham's bloodless face. In a moment it had gone and he was fighting in the swaying crowd. A lad weeping with terror thrust against him, pressing towards the stairways, yelling "Clear for the aeropile!" The bell that clears the flying stage became a loud unmelodious clanging.

With that clanging in his ears Graham drew near the aeropile, marched into the shadow of its tilting wing. He became aware that a number of people about him were offering to accompany him, and waved their offers aside. He wanted to think how one started the engine. The bell clanged faster and faster, and the feet of the retreating people roared faster and louder. The man in yellow was assisting him to mount through the ribs of the body. He clambered into the aeronaut's place, fixing himself very carefully and deliberately. What was it? The man in yellow was pointing to two aeropiles driving upward in the southern sky. No doubt they were looking for the coming aeroplanes. That—presently—the thing to do now was to start. Things were being shouted at him, questions, warnings. They bothered him. He wanted to think about the aeropile, to recall every item of his previous experience. He waved the people from him, saw the man in yellow dropping off through the ribs, saw the crowd cleft down the line of the girders by his gesture.

For a moment he was motionless, staring at the levers, the wheel by which the engine shifted, and all the delicate appliances of which he knew so little. His eye caught a spirit level with the bubble towards him, and he remembered something, spent a dozen seconds in swinging the engine forward until the bubble floated in the centre of the tube. He noted that the people were not shouting, knew they watched his deliberation. A bullet smashed on the bar above his head. Who fired? Was the line clear of people? He stood up to see and sat down again.

In another second the propeller was spinning, and he was rushing down the guides. He gripped the wheel and swung the engine back to lift the stem. Then it was the people shouted. In a moment he was throbbing with the quiver of the engine, and the shouts dwindled swiftly behind, rushed down to silence. The wind whistled over the edges of the screen, and the world sank away from him very swiftly.

Throb, throb, throb—throb, throb, throb; up he drove. He fancied himself free of all excitement, felt cool and deliberate. He lifted the stem still more, opened one valve on his left wing and swept round and up. He looked down with a steady head, and up. One of the Ostrogite aeropiles was driving across his course, so that he drove obliquely towards it and would pass below it at a steep angle. Its little aeronauts were peering down at him. What did they mean to do? His mind became active. One, he saw held a weapon pointing, seemed prepared to fire. What did they think he meant to do? In a moment he understood their tactics, and his resolution was taken. His momentary lethargy was past. He opened two more valves to his left, swung round, end on to this hostile machine, closed his valves, and shot straight at it, stem and wind-screen shielding him from the shot. They tilted a little as if to clear him. He flung up his stem.

Throb, throb, throb—pause—throb, throb—he set his teeth, his face into an involuntary grimace, and crash! He struck it! He struck upward beneath the nearer wing.

Very slowly the wing of his antagonist seemed to broaden as the impetus of his blow turned it up. He saw the full breadth of it and then it slid downward out of his sight.

He felt his stem going down, his hands tightened on the levers, whirled and rammed the engine back. He felt the jerk of a clearance, the nose of the machine jerked upward steeply, and for a moment he seemed to be lying on his back. The machine was reeling and staggering, it seemed to be dancing on its screw. He made a huge effort, hung for a moment on the levers, and slowly the engine came forward again. He was driving upward but no longer so steeply. He gasped for a moment and flung himself at the levers again. The wind whistled about him. One further effort and he was almost level. He could breathe. He turned his head for the first time to see what had become of his antagonists. Turned back to the levers for a moment and looked again. For a moment he could have believed they were annihilated. And then he saw between the two stages to the east was a chasm, and down this something, a slender edge, fell swiftly and vanished, as a sixpence falls down a crack.

At first he did not understand, and then a wild joy possessed him. He shouted at the top of his voice, an inarticulate shout, and drove higher and higher up the sky. Throb, throb, throb, pause, throb, throb, throb. "Where was the other aeropile?" he thought. "They too—." As he looked round the empty heavens he had a momentary fear that this machine had risen above him, and then he saw it alighting on the Norwood stage. They had meant shooting. To risk being rammed headlong two thousand feet in the air was beyond their latter-day courage. The combat was declined.

For a little while he circled, then swooped in a steep descent towards the westward stage. Throb throb throb, throb throb throb. The twilight was creeping on apace, the smoke from the Streatham stage that had been so dense and dark, was now a pillar of fire, and all the laced curves of the moving ways and the translucent roofs and domes and the chasms between the buildings were glowing softly now, lit by the tempered radiance of the electric light that the glare of the way overpowered. The three efficient stages that the Ostrogites held—for Wimbledon Park was useless because of the fire from Roehampton, and Streatham was a furnace—were glowing with guide lights for the coming aeroplanes. As he swept over the Roehampton stage he saw the dark masses of the people thereon. He heard a clap of frantic cheering, heard a bullet from the Wimbledon Park stage tweet through the air, and went beating up above the Surrey wastes. He felt a breath of wind from the south-west, and lifted his westward wing as he had learnt to do, and so drove upward heeling into the rare swift upper air. Throb throb throb—throb throb throb.

Up he drove and up, to that pulsating rhythm, until the country beneath was blue and indistinct, and London spread like a little map traced in light, like the mere model of a city near the brim of the horizon. The south-west was a sky of sapphire over the shadowy rim of the world, and ever as he drove upward the multitude of stars increased.

And behold! In the southward, low down and glittering swiftly nearer, were two little patches of nebulous light. And then two more, and then a nebulous glow of swiftly driving shapes. Presently he could count them.

There were four and twenty. The first fleet of aeroplanes had come! Beyond appeared a yet greater glow.

He swept round in a half circle, staring at this advancing fleet. It flew in a wedge-like shape, a triangular flight of gigantic phosphorescent shapes sweeping nearer through the lower air. He made a swift calculation of their pace, and spun the little wheel that brought the engine forward. He touched a lever and the throbbing effort of the engine ceased. He began to fall, fell swifter and swifter. He aimed at the apex of the wedge. He dropped like a stone through the whistling air. It seemed scarce a second from that soaring moment before he struck the foremost aeroplane.

No man of all that black multitude saw the coming of his fate, no man among them dreamt of the hawk that struck downward upon him out of the sky. Those who were not limp in the agonies of air-sickness, were craning their black necks and staring to see the filmy city that was rising out of the haze, the rich and splendid city to which "Massa Boss" had brought their obedient muscles. Bright teeth gleamed and the glossy faces shone. They had heard of Paris. They knew they were to have lordly times among the "poor white" trash. And suddenly Graham struck them.

He had aimed at the body of the aeroplane, but at the very last instant a better idea had flashed into his mind. He twisted about and struck near the edge of the starboard wing with all his accumulated weight. He was jerked back as he struck. His prow went gliding across its smooth expanse towards the rim. He felt the forward rush of the huge fabric sweeping him and his aeropile along with it, and for a moment that seemed an age he could not tell what was happening. He heard a thousand throats yelling, and perceived that his machine was balanced on the edge of the gigantic float, and driving down, down; glanced over his shoulder and saw the backbone of the aeroplane and the opposite float swaying up. He had a vision through the ribs of sliding chairs, staring faces, and hands clutching at the tilting guide bars. The fenestrations in the further float flashed open as the aeronaut tried to right her. Beyond, he saw a second aeroplane leaping steeply to escape the whirl of its heeling fellow. The broad area of swaying wings seemed to jerk upward. He felt his aeropile had dropped clear, that the monstrous fabric, clean overturned, hung like a sloping wall above him.

He did not clearly understand that he had struck the side float of the aeroplane and slipped off, but he perceived that he was flying free on the down glide and rapidly nearing earth. What had he done? His heart throbbed like a noisy engine in his throat and for a perilous instant he could not move his levers because of the paralysis of his hands. He wrenched the levers to throw his engine back, fought for two seconds against the weight of it, felt himself righting driving horizontally, set the engine beating again.

He looked upward and saw two aeroplanes glide shouting far overhead, looked back, and saw the main body of the fleet opening out and rushing upward and outward; saw the one he had struck fall edgewise on and strike like a gigantic knife-blade along the wind-wheels below it.

He put down his stern and looked again. He drove up heedless of his direction as he watched. He saw the wind-vanes give, saw the huge fabric strike the earth, saw its downward vans crumple with the weight of its descent, and then the whole mass turned over and smashed, upside down, upon the sloping wheels. Throb, throb, throb, pause. Suddenly from the heaving wreckage a thin tongue of white fire licked up towards the zenith. And then he was aware of a huge mass flying through the air towards him, and turned upwards just in time to escape the charge—if it was a charge— of a second aeroplane. It whirled by below, sucked him down a fathom, and nearly turned him over in the gust of its close passage.

He became aware of three others rushing towards him, aware of the urgent necessity of beating above them. Aeroplanes were all about him, circling wildly to avoid him, as it seemed. They drove past him, above, below, eastward and westward. Far away to the westward was the sound of a collision, and two falling flares. Far away to the southward a second squadron was coming. Steadily he beat upward. Presently all the aeroplanes were below him, but for a moment he doubted the height he had of them, and did not swoop again. And then he came down upon a second victim and all its load of soldiers saw him coming. The big machine heeled and swayed as the fear maddened men scrambled to the stern for their weapons. A score of bullets sung through the air, and there flashed a star in the thick glass wind-screen that protected him. The aeroplane slowed and dropped to foil his stroke, and dropped too low. Just in time he saw the wind-wheels of Bromley hill rushing up towards him, and spun about and up as the aeroplane he had chased crashed among them. All its voices wove into a felt of yelling. The great fabric seemed to be standing on end for a second among the heeling and splintering vans, and then it flew to pieces. Huge splinters came flying through the air, its engines burst like shells. A hot rush of flame shot overhead into the darkling sky.

"_Two!_" he cried, with a bomb from overhead bursting as it fell, and forthwith he was beating up again. A glorious exhilaration possessed him now, a giant activity. His troubles about humanity, about his inadequacy, were gone for ever. He was a man in battle rejoicing in his power. Aeroplanes seemed radiating from him in every direction, intent only upon avoiding him, the yelling of their packed passengers came in short gusts as they swept by. He chose his third quarry, struck hastily and did but turn it on edge. It escaped him, to smash against the tall cliff of London wall. Flying from that impact he skimmed the darkling ground so nearly he could see a frightened rabbit bolting up a slope. He jerked up steeply, and found himself driving over south London with the air about him vacant. To the right of him a wild riot of signal rockets from the Ostrogites banged tumultuously in the sky. To the south the wreckage of half a dozen air ships flamed, and east and west and north the air ships fled before him. They drove away to the east and north, and went about in the south, for they could not pause in the air. In their present confusion any attempt at evolution would have meant disastrous collisions. He could scarcely realize the thing he had done. In every quarter aeroplanes were receding. They were receding. They dwindled smaller and smaller. They were in flight!

He passed two hundred feet or so above the Roehampton stage. It was black with people and noisy with their frantic shouting. But why was the Wimbledon Park stage black and cheering, too? The smoke and flame of Streatham now hid the three further stages. He curved about and rose to see them and the northern quarters. First came the square masses of Shooter's Hill into sight from behind the smoke, lit and orderly with the aeroplane that had landed and its disembarking negroes. Then came Blackheath, and then under the corner of the reek the Norwood stage. On Blackheath no aeroplane had landed but an aeropile lay upon the guides. Norwood was covered by a swarm of little figures running to and fro in a passionate confusion. Why? Abruptly he understood. The stubborn defence of the flying stages was over, the people were pouring into the under-ways of these last strongholds of Ostrog's usurpation. And then, from far away on the northern border of the city, full of glorious import to him, came a sound, a signal, a note of triumph, the leaden thud of a gun. His lips fell apart, his face was disturbed with emotion.

He drew an immense breath. "They win," he shouted to the empty air; "the people win!" The sound of a second gun came like an answer. And then he saw the aeropile on Blackheath was running down its guides to launch. It lifted clean and rose. It shot up into the air, driving straight southward and away from him.

In an instant it came to him what this meant. It must needs be Ostrog in flight. He shouted and dropped towards it. He had the momentum of his elevation and fell slanting down the air and very swiftly. It rose steeply at his approach. He allowed for its velocity and drove straight upon it.

It suddenly became a mere flat edge, and behold! he was past it, and driving headlong down with all the force of his futile blow.

He was furiously angry. He reeled the engine back along its shaft and went circling up. He saw Ostrog's machine beating up a spiral before him. He rose straight towards it, won above it by virtue of the impetus of his swoop and by the advantage and weight of a man. He dropped headlong— dropped and missed again! As he rushed past he saw the face of Ostrog's aeronaut confident and cool and in Ostrog's attitude a wincing resolution. Ostrog was looking steadfastly away from him—to the south. He realized with a gleam of wrath how bungling his flight must be. Below he saw the Croyden hills. He jerked upward and once more he gained on his enemy.

He glanced over his shoulder and his attention was arrested by a strange thing. The eastward stage, the one on Shooter's Hill, appeared to lift; a flash changing to a tall grey shape, a cowled figure of smoke and dust, jerked into the air. For a moment this cowled figure stood motionless, dropping huge masses of metal from its shoulders, and then it began to uncoil a dense head of smoke. The people had blown it up, aeroplane and all! As suddenly a second flash and grey shape sprang up from the Norwood stage. And even as he stared at this came a dead report, and the air wave of the first explosion struck him. He was flung up and sideways.

For a moment the aeropile fell nearly edgewise with her nose down, and seemed to hesitate whether to overset altogether. He stood on his wind-shield wrenching the wheel that swayed up over his head. And then the shock of the second explosion took his machine sideways.

He found himself clinging to one of the ribs of his machine, and the air was blowing past him and upward. He seemed to be hanging quite still in the air, with the wind blowing up past him. It occurred to him that he was falling. Then he was sure that he was falling. He could not look down.

He found himself recapitulating with incredible swiftness all that had happened since his awakening, the days of doubt the days of Empire, and at last the tumultuous discovery of Ostrog's calculated treachery, he was beaten but London was saved. London was saved!

The thought had a quality of utter unreality. Who was he? Why was he holding so tightly with his hands? Why could he not leave go? In such a fall as this countless dreams have ended. But in a moment he would wake....

His thoughts ran swifter and swifter. He wondered if he should see Helen again. It seemed so unreasonable that he should not see her again. It _must_ be a dream! Yet surely he would meet her. She at least was real. She was real. He would wake and meet her.

Although he could not look at it, he was suddenly aware that the earth was very near.

The End

A TRIBUTE TO NANCY GREEN, [MARCH 4, 1834 – AUGUST 30, 1923]. NANCY BECAME THE WORLD'S FIRST LIVING TRADEMARK AS AUNT JEMIMA. THIS AD IS FROM 1943. NANCY HAD BEEN BORN INTO SLAVERY IN THE CONFEDERATE SOUTH. MAY SHE GET SOME FRACTION OF THE JUSTICE SHE DESERVES IN OUR REMEMBRANCE OF HER.

THE TREASURE OF THE ISLE OF MIST

BY W.W. TARN

From 1920

A Fairytale for my Daughter

CHAPTER 1
THE GIFT OF THE SEARCH

The Student and Fiona lived in a little gray house on the shores of a gray sea-loch in the Isle of Mist. The Student was a thin man with a stoop to his shoulders, which old Anne MacDermott said came of reading books; but really it was because he had been educated at a place where this is expected of you. Fiona, when she was doing nothing else, used to help Anne to keep house, rather jerkily, in the way a learned man may be supposed to like. She was a long-legged creature of fifteen, who laughed when her father threatened her with school on the mainland, and she had a warm heart and a largish size in shoes. Sometimes they had dinner; sometimes nobody remembered in time, and they had sunset and salt herrings, with a bowl of glorious yellow corn-daisies to catch the sunset.

It was Anne who saw the old hawker crossing the field behind the house, and burst in on the bookroom to inform the Student that he wanted buttons. She was met by a patient remonstrance on her ambiguous use of language:

"For," said the Student, "if you mean that buttons are lacking to me, there may be something to be said for you; but if you mean that I desire buttons, then indeed I do not desire buttons; I desire . . ."

Whereon Anne fled, and went out to meet the hawker. The frail old man, bending under his pack, was crossing the meadow behind the house, brushing his way through the September clover. His white hair was uncovered save for the huge umbrella which he carried alike in sun and rain; but youth still lingered in his eyes, which were bright as the dawn and deep as the sea-caves. Behind him followed a little rough-haired terrier, black as jet, his inseparable companion. At the door he unslung his pack, and, leaving Anne to select her buttons, passed straight through, knocked at the bookroom door, and went in.

The Student wheeled round in his chair and began to grope about.

"Have you seen my spectacles?" he said. "I can't see who you are till I put them on, and I can't put them on till you find them for me, for I can't see to find them myself unless I have them on. Pardon this involved sentence."

The old hawker picked up the missing spectacles and handed them over.

"You wouldn't remember me, in any case," he said. "I last saw you twenty-five years ago, when you were trying to dig at Verria. There was an old man there, do you remember, being beaten by armed Bashi-Bazouks, and you held them up with an empty revolver, and took the old man to your camp and nursed him, and you said things to the Turkish Governor, and . . ."

"My excavations came to an untimely end," said the Student. "I always owed that old man a grudge for being beaten before my tent. Why couldn't he have been beaten somewhere else? I should like to meet him again and tell him precisely what I thought of his conduct."

"You have done both now," said the hawker. "And it is his turn."

"Impossible," said the Student. "He was as old twenty-five years ago as you are now."

"At my age," said the old man, "one grows no older. No one who walks the world as I do need ever grow any older. You can walk thirty miles on Monday when you are twenty years old; good. If you can do it on Monday you can do it on Tuesday; and if on Tuesday, then on Wednesday; therefore, by an easy reckoning, you can do it as well at eighty years old as at twenty. Thus you never age."

"There's a flaw in that somewhere," said the Student. "I know; it's the Heap. How many grains of sand make a heap?"

"How many buttons do you want?" said the hawker. "You saved my life once; you shall have all the buttons you want for nothing."

"I thought you couldn't answer my question," said the Student. "But we are getting on much too fast; we haven't really begun yet. I suppose you came here to sell things? Anne seemed to know you, and she said I wanted buttons. I pointed out to her that her statement was either an untruth or a truism, and equally objectionable in either sense; and now you repeat it, just as I was beginning to consider you quite an intelligent person. By the way, who are you?"

"I have a different name in most countries which I visit," said the old man. "But by profession I sell buttons—and other things."

"What sort of things?" said the Student.

"I have dreams," said the old man, "dreams and the matter of dreams; imaginings of the impossible come true; the wonder of the hills at sunrise; the quest of unearthly treasure among the moon-flowers; the look in the eyes of a child that trusts you."

The Student took off his spectacles, rubbed his eyes hard, and settled his shoulders.

"I desire something very much," he said. "If you can do all that, you can give me what I desire."

The hawker frowned.

"You are a scholar," he said, "and I can do nothing for scholars. You need no ideal, for you have one. You need no dreams, for your life is one. For you, the earth pours out hidden treasure, and the impossible comes true day by day. What you desire just now is a long definite inscription to settle a controverted point in your favor. And if I could give it you, just think how miserable you'd be. Nothing further to argue about, there; and several quite happy and contentious professors would be reduced to such straits that I don't know what crimes you might all commit. You might even take to making money."

"If I wanted money," said the Student, "I should, being an intelligent person, at once proceed to make it. Then I should have to live in the big house again, instead of letting it, and my precious time would be spent in arguing with my gardener and endeavoring to conceal my ignorance from my chauffeur. As it is, we live anyhow, and I am happy."

"Happiness doesn't score any points in the game," said the hawker. "What good do you and your inscriptions do, anyway?"

"That's not my job here," said the Student. "That will come on afterwards. Besides, I don't want to do good. I am old-fashioned; why should I take my neighbor by the throat and say, 'Let me do good to you, or it shall be the worse for you and yours'? Besides, I can't do good. You can't dot the wilderness with prosperous homesteads when half the years the oats don't ripen till the year after. Besides, I do do good; I have let the big house to shooting tenants, and it's excellent for their health. Besides seventeen other reasons, which I can enumerate if you are able to bear them. Besides, Fiona is fond of me."

"Yes," said the old man softly, "that's your real justification. And it's a great deal more than I could give you; my hawker's licence doesn't cover the big things. How many buttons do you want?"

Fiona came scrambling through the open window, and curled herself up on the rug with her head on the Student's knee. The Student stroked her hair.

"Tell me what it's all about," she said.

"This gentleman," he said, "once interrupted a very important piece of work which I was doing, and I was just about to tell him exactly what I thought of him when you interrupted me."

The old hawker had risen and bowed courteously to the girl.

"My dear young lady," he said, "I have been searching my pack for a present for your father, and found nothing suitable. But perhaps I could find something for you."

Fiona jumped up.

"Have you a hedgehog?" was her question.

"I do not carry them with me, as a general thing," said the old man. "No doubt one could be got. But why a hedgehog?"

"I want one for the Urchin," she said. "You see, it's his namesake."

"I see," said the old man, quite gravely. "And who is the Urchin?"

"The Urchin," said the Student, "is a young rascal who is the son of my shooting tenant. He plunders my daughter of all her possessions, and she abets him in every form of villainy."

"I do try to stop him throwing stones at things," said the girl.

"Here are hedgehogs," said the hawker. "Isn't that lucky, now?"

Past the window came five hedgehogs in a solemn row, two big and three little. Behind them, marshalling the procession, walked the black terrier, with an eye of happy drollery.

"There's something wrong about those hedgehogs," said the girl. "They don't do things like that. I don't think I want a hedgehog any more, thank you. How did you make them do that? Is your dog a conjurer?"

"I never harm anything," said the old man, "so that many creatures will come to me when I call. But I have better presents than that."

"Choose for her, my friend," said the Student.

The old man began talking to himself in a low voice.

"Youth she has," he said, "and freedom, and the joy of life. Wonder also, and dim imaginings of unseen things. And of the things which men desire, fame and power are not worth giving, and love is not mine to give. I have it. I give you the Search," he said. "The search for the treasure of the Isle of Mist. Others have searched for it before; and some have found; but the treasure never grows less."

"That's splendid," said the girl. "And when I find the treasure I will buy my father seven great books which no one else wants to read, and he will be perfectly happy."

"But I did not promise treasure," said the old man. "I promised a search."

Fiona's face fell.

"Then am I not to find anything at the end of it?" she asked.

The old man chuckled quietly.

"I did not say that either," he said. "There _is_ a treasure, and you shall search for it; and you will find it if you are able. Many there are who helped to build it up. Cuchulain and the forgotten heroes who fought before Cuchulain; Ossian and the forgotten bards who sang before Ossian; Columba and the forgotten saints who died before Columba; each has added something to the pile. It is their treasure which you shall seek for; that is my gift to you."

"How shall I know where to begin?" asked the girl. "And may I take the Urchin with me?"

"Whether you can take the Urchin with you or not depends on his capacity to go," said the old man. "And as to beginning, I think you will find that the Search will begin itself, independently of you. It always does.

But I can give you something that will help you," and he took out of his pocket a red copper bangle, rudely hammered out with some rough implement, which he slipped over her wrist. "That was made long ago," he said, "made by men to whom metal was a new toy, men who perhaps were nearer to the heart of things than we are."

"You will stay and have some dinner, will you not?" said the Student. "At least, if this is a dinner night. Fiona, is this a dinner night?"

"I have my doubts," said the girl. "Oat cake and honeysuckle, I expect."

"And what better?" said the old man. "But I fear I could not dine with you, were it ortolans and Tokay. For I may never eat beneath a roof. The open moor is my dining hall, and the stars serve me. And the long white road is calling me even now. But I think that before the treasure is found you will see me again."

CHAPTER 2
THE BEGINNING OF TROUBLE

"**M**an," said the Student, "is a weird creature. He dimly remembers that he began his evolution, not as a pair, but as a horde; and to the horde he still seeks, forming huge crowds during his working days, and on his holidays merely transferring the same crowds in their totality to some other place, accompanied by a great deal of purposeless noise. Apart from his crowd he apparently feels chilly, and without noise unhappy. Nothing is more striking to the reflective mind than the abdication of civilization in the face of meaningless noises."

"Daddy," said Fiona, "I want your advice on the matter of treasure hunting. For if two go together, they don't make a crowd, and they needn't make a noise."

"Quote correctly," said the Student. "What Homer said was, that if you and I went to look for a treasure, I, being a mere man, would find it at once by logical processes of induction and deduction, while you, being a superior woman, were losing yourself in the quicksands of the intuitive short cut."

"Sir," said the girl, "your word is law to me. Therefore deduce."

"Persiflage," said the Student, "is not to be encouraged in young children. Remember that if you were to force me to do so I might come with you, and then I should see exactly how you bungled the thing."

"But that's what I want you to do, daddy," said Fiona.

"I don't," said the Student. "Though treasure hunting is quite an ancient and respectable amusement. For treasure, some have descended the crater of Popocatapetl; some have dived at Tobermory; some have dug in Kensington Gardens. Alexander found a treasure at Persepolis, and Essex lost another in Cadiz harbor. The treasure of the Incas lies hid in a Peruvian ravine, known but to two Indians at a time; the plunder which Alaric took from Rome is still beneath the river which he diverted to guard it. No one has ever found the hoard of Captain Kidd, or the gold carried in the Venetian galleon which sailed with the Armada and went on the rocks in this loch. The pursuit of treasure is, therefore, no doubt, for the young, a legitimate pastime."

"Daddy," said Fiona, "did one of the Armada ships really go ashore here?"

"Yes, my dear," said the Student. "She was a great Venetian, called after the Madonna of the Holy Cross, and she carried the doubloons contributed by the Church."

"That's not the treasure the old man meant," said the girl.

"It is not," said the Student. "We know all about the Venetian ship. The crew were mostly knocked on the head, but the captain brought the doubloons ashore and hid them. He himself was saved by my ancestor for the time being, to whom he gave a map showing the place in the cave in which the treasure was hidden. He never came back for it. So far, everything proceeded on approved lines. Unhappily, my ancestor was a careless sort of person, and gambled the plan away. We never heard any more of it. It is, however, a family tradition that there was nothing on the plan to identify the cave; and as this coast, and the islands in the loch, are honeycombed with caves, it would be of little use if we had it. No one knows whereabouts the galleon went ashore. On calm nights her officers may be seen swimming round the cliffs, keeping guard still over their holy gold. Angus MacEachan saw one once, and tried to speak to him; but he turned into a seal, and just looked at Angus with large patient eyes; and Angus' boat was wrecked the week after."

"And did you never search for the gold, daddy?" asked Fiona.

"Never, my dear," he said. "In the first place, it would mean a minute examination of some 170 caves. In the second place, half of the caves are not mine. In the third place, it is not the kind of treasure I want. In the fourth place, I haven't time. In the fifth place, I am morally certain it is not there now. In the sixth place, the Government would claim it as treasure-trove. And in the seventh and last place, I never thought about it till you asked me."

"I'm not getting any further with _my_ treasure hunting, daddy," said Fiona. "Let's go out together and start."

"My dear," said the Student, "it's your search, not mine. It's no use my trying to come with you. And I have a fancy that it won't begin like that."

"Can you tell me how to begin then, daddy?" she asked.

"I suppose by taking no notice of it," he said. "It was to begin itself, wasn't it? And I have an uncomfortable suspicion that you hunt this kind of treasure by turning round and going the other way. So I think you'd better run out and find the Urchin, and I'll get back to my inscriptions."

The Urchin was Fiona's principal ally; a troublesome ally, owing to his propensity for throwing stones. She found him now on the shore, steadily bombarding a shore lark, that would move a little way out of range and then sit down again, affording a splendid target. Luckily the enthusiasm of the persecutor in pursuit was well matched by the inaccuracy of his aim.

"Urchin," she called out, "if you hurt that bird the Little People will take you; I thought I'd knocked that into you all right, even if you _are_ English and slow in the uptake."

"All right," said the Urchin with a grin. "We conquered you, anyway."

"As a matter of fact," said the girl, "it was we who annexed you. If your people were as bad shots as you, Urchin, it must have been quite easy. You can't hit a bird sitting."

"Can't I?" said the Urchin. "You watch." Another fling, and horrors! the shore lark rolled over, twittering helplessly and miserably.

Fiona was across the rocks like a young goat; and when the Urchin, contrite but defiant, arrived, she had the wounded bird in her hands and was holding it to her breast, feeling gently for its hurt. It lay quite still, panting, and watching her with quick bright eyes.

"Broken wing," she said. "I believe it will mend. Urchin, you are a mere beast. You'd better go home; I don't want ever to see you again."

The Urchin turned scarlet.

"That's just like a girl," he said. "First you tell me I can't hit the old bird, which is the same thing as telling me to hit it; and then when I do hit it you turn round on me and call names; and all the time you're just as bad as I am." And the Urchin turned and stalked off, an heroic figure with the mien of a Marcus Curtius about to save his country by leaping into the gulf. Unhappily there was a real gulf, and the boy, head in air, rolled neatly into it, and emerged from between two rocks, dripping and no longer heroic, rubbing a torn stocking and a scraped shin.

It was too much for Fiona's gravity.

"Urchin," she called, "come back here, _quick_." And as the unhappy Urchin stood in doubt, hither and thither dividing the swift mind, she slid over the rocks and caught him. "My fault," she said, "and I'm sorry all the way through. Now I'll mend you first, and then we must mend the bird."

"And then what'll we do?" said the boy. "Let's do something harmless for a bit, hunt for shells or shrimps or . . ."

"Treasure," suggested Fiona, rather shyly. And by the time they had reached the house, and she had repaired the Urchin, and disposed the wounded bird as comfortably as possible, the boy had been put in possession of the essential facts of the case.

"Mar-vellous," was the Urchin's comment. "Now, don't you see, Fiona? you can have your treasure when we find it, and I'll have the Spanish treasure when we find it, and there we both are. I want lots and lots and lots of those doubloons."

"What for?" said Fiona.

"Gun," said the Urchin. "Donald Ruadh has an old gun which he would sell me for two pounds. He says one barrel shoots all right sometimes. And I would use the rest of the doubloons to buy cartridges, and then I could kill curlews."

"You little wretch," said the girl. "You won't kill my curlews while I'm about. And anyhow your old gun would probably blow you up first. And anyhow you haven't got the doubloons yet. And they're not yours if you do find them."

"Whose would they be?" asked the Urchin.

"I suppose my father's," said Fiona. "But it depends on which cave they were in."

"Come on, then," said the boy. "I'm going to ask him for them."

The Student took the interruption good-humoredly.

"I am in the second century," he said. "Doubloons have not yet been coined. As to these doubloons, I am quite sure they are not there, wherever 'there' may be; but if they are there, I have no objection to the Urchin fighting the Government for them. Urchin, would you like a deed?"

And, to the delight of the Urchin, the Student proceeded to make out a document, which called on all men to know that the said Student thereby assigned to the said Urchin all the estate, right, title, and interest, if any, of the said Student in and to a certain treasure of doubloons or other coins once carried in the galleon called _Our Lady of the Holy Cross_ were the same a little more or less ("all good deeds get that in somewhere," said the Student) to hold to the said Urchin and his heirs ("but I don't suppose the heirs will see much of it") to the intent that he might become a wiser and a better Urchin and not interrupt the said Student any more when he wanted to work. This being done, the Student signed his name at the end, made a beautiful blot of hot red sealing wax and put his signet ring on it, and made Fiona sign her name as witness ("which is probably not legal," he explained cheerfully); then he handed over the deed to the rejoicing Urchin, with the remark that it was quite as good as many lawyers' deeds, and drove the pair of them out of the bookroom.

"Good," said the Urchin. "Now I've a treasure just the same as you."

"If we find them," said Fiona.

"Well, let's go and start hunting for them at any rate," said the boy.

"Pardon me," said the shore lark, "if I interrupt; but you might be the better of a few hints."

Fiona dropped on her knees and took the little bird in her hands again.

"So you can talk," she said. "That's jolly. You've a first-rate chance of returning good for evil, and making us feel worms."

"Don't talk of worms," said the shore lark, "you have entirely omitted to provide me with any. Send him to get some, and I'll tell you something. He can't understand what I'm saying, anyhow."

"Urchin," said the girl, "he's asking for worms. Go and get him some."

"One would think you and he could talk to each other," said the boy. "Silly, I call it, going on like that. I suppose that's what girls do."

"Urchin," said Fiona, "when you and I have a row, what happens?"

"_You_ happen," said the Urchin. "You've three years' pull; 'tisn't fair; just like a girl, to go and have three years' pull of a chap."

"Stop grousing," said the girl, "and get me the worms, there's a dear little boy."

The Urchin flung the nearest book at her, missed as usual, and, having thus made his honor white, departed, declaring in simpler language that the love of worms was the root of all evil.

"I can't tell you much," said the shore lark, "but one sometimes picks up things, hopping about, and I heard you say treasure. If you mean the Venetian ship, don't start without consulting the finner. He is very old, and I believe that he knows everything that happens in this loch."

"I don't really mean that," said Fiona. "That's half a jest. I mean my own search, the search for the treasure of the Isle of Mist."

"We have all heard of it," said the shore lark, "and we all know that you cannot find it by looking for it. All I can tell you is this: the curlews have a tradition that the last man who found it went up a hill. That is what they tell each other when they call in the spring; and I believe they know."

"They are like the spirits of the hills themselves," said Fiona. "Tell me why it is I can understand you."

"I have no idea," said the shore lark. "I am only a little bird, and I don't know very much. I chanced speaking to you because I wanted worms."

The girl slipped across into the bookroom.

"Daddy," she said, "come back out of the second century, and tell me why I can understand the shore lark."

The Student looked up with a patient smile in far-away eyes.

"It isn't time to come back yet," he said. "And I have not fully grasped your meaning. You appear to refer to some conversation with some bird. There are precedents, of course. For instance, the philosopher Empedocles, having been a bird himself in a former life, remembered their speech; he ended by leaping into Ætna. Siegfried also, having bathed in the blood of Fafnir, followed the voice of a bird of the wood; he ended by losing his love and his life. There was once a sailor who took the advice of a parrot, and was hanged. Birds are light-minded, as the poet Aristophanes discovered; and it would seem that little good comes of talking to them."

"My shore lark is a darling," said Fiona. "And I don't intend to be hanged."

"That," said the Student, "is as Providence pleases. One never knows, as my poor ancestor said when he fell into a bear-trap and found the bear there before him."

"O daddy," said the girl, "did he really? And what happened?"

"This ancestor of mine," said the Student, "was a very strong man. If he had not been, someone else would have killed him first, and he would not have been my ancestor; the other man would have been someone else's ancestor, so to speak. Being a very strong man, he naturally killed the bear. He must have, or he would not have lived to be my ancestor. In those days everyone lived in caves, and he lived in a cave too; and he always killed the other man, sometimes fairly, sometimes, I regret to say, otherwise. He courted my ancestress by knocking her down from behind with the blunt end of a stone ax, a method which I do not defend; but when her senses returned she told him he had acted like a man, and they became a most devoted couple. This was partly due, no doubt, to the fact that he never saw the meaning of the things she said; she took good care that he shouldn't, for though slow of wit he was handy with his ax. Their life I think must have been very happy till one day he found a red stone which he could heat and shape with his ax, and he hammered out that copper bracelet you're wearing; and then came the deluge, for metal meant magic then, as you know. Next day my ancestress found him conversing with the local vulture; within a week he was giving exhibitions in the other caves with the vulture's assistance; in a month he had become the tribal god; and about two years after, owing to the persistent failure of some of his magic to come off, he was, for a brief moment, the tribal banquet. Now you know what comes of talking to shore larks."

"Daddy," she said, "you can't know if that's true or not, can you?"

"It may not all be what _you_ call true," said the Student, "but it's true in quite a lot of ways. It's true psychologically, and anthropologically, and palæethnologically; and that does to start with. And I certainly _had_ ancestors. And there _is_ a bracelet. And you _were_ talking strange words about a shore lark. And you must really take care, my dear daughter; for you _ought_ now to become a tribal priestess, and be hurled from a high place into the sea the first season that the herring fail."

CHAPTER 3
THE HAUNTED CAVE

A sunlit sheet of sea, violet and azure, clothed in slender cloud shadows and heaving gently to the long Atlantic ground-swell. Up through the calm water, to meet the eye of the gazer, came the green clearness of stone, and blinks of unveined sand showing white between the brown tangled blades of the great oar-weed; and you might see a school of little cuddies, heads all one way, playing hide and seek in the sea forest, and caring no whit for the clumsy armored crab beneath them, who crawled sideways, a laborious patch of color in the shimmering transparency. Up out of the deep water the gray rocks rose clear and fine, a mass of platforms and pinnacles, roughened with barnacles and tufted with dulse, whose crimson leaves floated and swung in the white foam of the lisping swell; and above the rocks and beyond the sea's reach the cliff stood up black, showing all the strata that had gone to the making of it outlined with little patches of coarse grass. On one such patch grazed without concern a sheep which had slipped over, happy in her ignorance of the fact that she could never be drawn up again alive; the wiser raven overhead was clanging away with short barks to tell his mate. On a ridge on the cliff side sat a pair of young scarfs, almost invisible save when they twisted their long necks about like two snakes, trying to make up their minds to follow their mother, who had just flopped clumsily into the water, feet first, and had turned there and then into a miracle of easy grace, as she used her head to dash the spray over her back. Out at sea a solan rose steadily in a sweeping spiral, the white and black of him glittering in the sun; suddenly he checked, reversed engines, and fell plump like an inverted cross, his long raking wings clapping to as he struck the water; a moment, and he was up, and there sat, choking and gobbling over his fish, ere he rose again in his majestic rings.

The two children had grounded their boat on a little pebble beach between the rocks, and were sitting on a big tuft of sea pinks, munching handfuls of the sweet dulse and watching the solan at his fishing. They were by way of fishing themselves, but the afternoon was as yet too early and too clear for them. The Urchin had a pile of stones beside him, and was apparently trying to see how many times in twenty he could miss a large and obvious spur of rock. Fiona had a book of poetry, and was making intermittent efforts to read; but the world was too full of things to give poetry a fair chance.

The Urchin threw his last stone away.

"Silly sitting here," he said; "come and explore."

So, scrambling and sliding, the two made their way across the rocks, stopping at every rock pool to raise its fringe of weed with careful hands and investigate the wonder of the little world below; sea flowers of every hue, white and green, gray and orange, purple and white and gray and purple again, some smooth and satisfied, others with tentacles greedily awash, that could be induced to suck at a small finger dexterously inserted; sea shells of every contour, some living and clutching at the rock, some cast off and dead, others again protruding alien claws, resurrected to a life of artificial movement by the little hermit crabs whose tails they sheltered; here and there the spiky pink globe of a sea urchin, waiting for the tide to float him off. And in one deep little pot, with sides green like a grotto of ferns, they found a miniature battle. A small green crab, who had cast his shell, sat humped in a recess of the grotto, a thing soft and vulnerable, a delight to the enemy; and in front of him, excited and transparent, were half a dozen shrimps, the horn on each forehead pointed at him; from time to time some young gallant would dash in to prod the helpless monster, and at once backwater again into the ranks of his friends. The crab bore his torment with a patience born of the knowledge that each minute his new carapace was hardening; the shrimps had no wit to count the cost, or reckon the odds that the rising tide might bear them away in safety from the day of vengeance.

On hands and knees, not daring to breathe on the limpid surface of the pool, the children watched the little drama. From the cliff top the heated air rose dancing into the sky. So still were earth and air and sea that the old finner's rise sounded as though the cliff were falling. He had worked nearer in to the rocks than seemed possible for his ninety feet of blubber and muscle, and as his black side rolled over, the water about him boiled like a pot; but he did not splash, for he had been well brought up and always knew what his tail was doing, though it was so far away.

"Shiver these rocks," he began in a rage, as he flung two fountains out of his nose. Then he caught sight of Fiona and the gleam of the red bracelet.

"Oh my fins and flippers!" he spouted. "I ask pardon, young lady; I haven't the manners of a grampus. And they told me about you."

"Who's they?" asked Fiona, ungrammatically.

"Friends at Court, friends at Court," said the finner. "What a thing to have. 'No need of the old sailorman,' said I. But they said I must go. And I've scraped the barnacles off my precious tail. Will it run to some tobacco?"

"Will what run?" said the girl. "Your tail? What is it you want?"

"Hints are wasted, I see," said the whale. "'One question,' said I. Only one. But magic is magic, you know, even for a tough old sailorman. Come now, one question. I'm too far inshore for my liking."

Fiona understood.

"Is it about my treasure?" she said.

"Yours, or that boy's there, whichever you like," said the whale. "But only one, only one."

For about two seconds Fiona did some hard mental drill. Then she said:

"Will you please tell me where the Urchin can find his treasure?"

"You do have luck," said the finner. "Think of it, then. O you little fishes, think of it. If you'd asked the other, I didn't know the answer. Wouldn't have got an answer, and my tail all scraped for nothing. And this one, my great-great-grandmother saw it all, and nobody knows here but me and the seals and one man, and he's too fat to count. West cave, Scargill Island; and bring you luck, my dear. Will it run to some tobacco?"

"Thank you so much," said Fiona politely. "And I'm sorry I haven't any tobacco with me. But if you could wait a few minutes . . ."

"Shiver it, I'm scraping again," said the whale. "No tobacco and very few barnacles in this world. O my grandmother's flukes, I might as well be a bottlenose!"

Once more the water boiled, and beneath it the huge black body shot away for the open sea.

"Fiona," said the boy, "do you really think it's cricket?"

"What isn't cricket?" she asked.

"Fiona," he said, "I've been a brother to you. I have done all the things a brother ought to do. I have taught you to throw like a boy. I have pinched you for new clothes. I have called you names, to make you good-tempered. I have made remarks on your personal appearance, to prevent your being vain. I have even fought with you, solely for your good. And this is how you repay me. The other day you pretended to be talking to a shore lark; to-day it was an old whale, who spouted and banged his tail on the rock. If it's a joke, I don't see it. If it's not a joke, do go into a lunatic asylum, and let me find a simpler job."

Fiona tossed up mentally between hitting him and laughing; it came down laughing.

"Urchin," she said, "it's all right. I don't understand it much better than you do, but it has something to do with this bracelet of mine. I can really understand them and they can understand me. If you doubt my word, we will fight a duel with the boat stretchers, and I will bury you in the sand here afterwards."

"Oh, I believe you when you talk like that," said the Urchin; "only it's worse than the Latin grammar. _Psittacus loquitur_, "the parrot talks"; but this thing seemed to be a whale; it was very like one."

"It was a whale," said Fiona. "He said his great-great-grandmother had seen the Spanish captain land his doubloons, and that it was in the west cave on Scargill Island."

"That means the big cave at the end facing the sea," said the boy.

"The cave that no one has ever got to the end of," said Fiona.

"The cave that's haunted," said the boy.

"But of course it's haunted; it's the ghosts of the Spaniards. Silly of us not to have guessed."

Fiona had a hazy recollection of things her father used to say.

"I expect the haunting is thousands of years older than the Spaniards," she said. "Urchin, are you afraid of ghosts?"

"Not a bit," said the Urchin stoutly. "They would be splendid to throw stones at. It wouldn't hurt them."

"Come on then, let's go," said the girl. "There's lots of daylight."

"None of the people here will go into it, you know," said the Urchin.

"I know," said Fiona. "All the more reason for going on our own. There might really be something there, if no one ever goes to take it away."

So the boat was launched, and the adventure also. Fiona pulled stroke; the Urchin was a clumsy and unpunctual bow, and the girl had to steer from the stroke oar, which needs more doing than you may think if you haven't tried it. But they made the end of Scargill in time, and then Fiona took both the oars and coasted, while the Urchin got out a couple of bamboo poles, garnished with white flies, and let the casts trail, occasionally getting one of the beautiful little scarlet lythe, that came at the fly with the spring and dash of a sea trout. For even adventurers need supper. And so they came, past many a smaller cave mouth in the black side of the island, to the huge bluff that fronts the full Atlantic, and the great west cave.

Atlantic was half asleep to-day, and muttered drowsily to the quiet rocks outside. But the great cave was seldom quiet. In the winter, when Atlantic turned himself restlessly and spoke aloud, the sound of his speaking came back from its depths like the roar of a heavy gun; and even in the stillness the lisp of the swell in it echoed as from the roots of the island in a low intermittent boom. Outside, on the calm water, floated the whiskered head of a seal, watching the boat with gentle, fearless eyes,—"the officer on guard," Fiona whispered;—and from the black cliff's face, like a hanging fringe over the mouth of the cave, the water splashed down, trickle by trickle, in quick, heavy drops. The children rowed in through the little shower, and Fiona paddled gently up the cave. Its huge limestone walls stood up stark on either hand, rising into the darkness above, and sinking below into the green water, as far as eye could follow them. Near the water-line grew a little seaweed, and some white whelks clung; but as they went down the waterway these vanished, and gray cliff and green water alike began to turn black. Looking back, Fiona could see a bright patch, a patch of sky and sky-reflecting sea, framed in the narrow slit of the cave's mouth. The waterway was narrowing now; she shipped her oars and stood up, using one as a paddle, and instructing the Urchin how to fend off the boat's stern with his hands. In front, on a ledge in the cave's roof, it was just possible to make out a row of blue dots in the growing darkness; as the boat drew nearer, the blue dots fluttered, detached themselves from the cliff, and a swarm of pigeons came whirring over the boat and down the cave toward the sunlight;—"Your ghosts, Urchin," said the girl. Henceforward the cave was void of life, unless some strange, eyeless fish lurked in its inky depths. Darker and darker grew the waterway, and the last gleam of light vanished. Fiona was feeling her way now, aided by the phosphorescent drip from her oar blade; the Urchin, with unusual sense, splashed his hands in the water to increase the pale glow, which just revealed the line of the cliff. Neither dare speak now; possibly, had Fiona not had some idea of what was coming, she would have turned. But already there was a faint gleam ahead, faint as a glow worm, but still a gleam; and as the boat slid forward, and the low boom in the depths of the cave grew closer, the cave walls very slowly began to grow gray again out of the blackness. A few minutes more, and the walls were an outline, and before them, a fringe of white on round wet stones, the end of the waterway. And as the boat grounded, Fiona pointed up, and the Urchin, looking, saw a little round hole; a natural shaft ran down into the cave from the surface of the island, giving light enough for their eyes, now accustomed to the darkness, to distinguish outlines.

They drew their boat up on the stones far enough for the swell not to dislodge it; then the same impulse seized them both and they burst out laughing, not aloud, for something in the place made it impossible to laugh or talk aloud, but in a kind of mirthless whisper.

"We've come without any lights," said Fiona in an undertone.

"We have," said the Urchin. "But probably the stuff is only a few yards above high-water mark; they wouldn't go far in."

"They might have," said Fiona; "they'd have had torches or something."

"Let's go as far as we can, anyway, as we are here," said the Urchin.

So they started scrambling over the stones in the gray half-light. Presently there rose before them a great mass of rock and earth, half blocking the cave; it looked like some old landslip.

"It's easy at this end, Fiona," said the boy; and up they went, to find that the rock barrier blocked most of what little light remained. Beyond was darkness.

"We must go back and get light," said Fiona. "I can't even see the stones below." A pause; then, "Stop swinging your feet, Urchin; I want to listen."

"I'm not," said the Urchin.

Another pause, and then the Urchin spoke again, in a kind of stage whisper, "I'm frightened." The words seemed squeezed out of him.

"We may as well go back, anyhow," said Fiona, in a strained voice. "Down you go, Urchin."

The Urchin did go down at a considerable pace, and ran for the boat. Fiona managed to walk, by repeating to herself all the time under her breath, "You mustn't run, you mustn't run." But once in the boat she did not rebuke the Urchin for standing up and taking the other oar; and the pair paddled out, with many bumpings and scrapings, in a more speedy and less scientific manner than that in which they had entered.

Once out in the sunlight they felt better. They started automatically to fish home, and presently were talking again. But neither of them referred to the thing that was uppermost in each mind, though each was wondering if the other knew. For as they had sat on the wall of rock, each had heard clearly, in the utter darkness of the unvisited cave, the sound of heavy footsteps.

CHAPTER 4
THE URCHIN VANISHES

To most people there is some corner of the earth which means more than all others; and there are two or three in the world whose holy place is the old house on the sea-loch which the Student's humbler neighbors called the "big house." An old square building of gray stone, that matches the gray sky and the gray sea, it has small claims to beauty; it was built in the days of blank windows, and every wind in the island meets and screams round the battered iron balustrade which leads up its steps to the door, and strives to tear down the tendrils of ivy that cling to the east front. To the south front, lashed by the full Atlantic gales, not even ivy can cling; only a few twisted elders and stunted planes grow there, and take the first force of the winter wind; but the old lawn to the north bursts in summer into a cloud of white marguerites, whose ethereal beauty at sunset is like the ghosts of the dreams that haunt the place. For to some of us the old house is full of dreams, that cling to the dark passages and the uneven floors, and play in and out of the little windows that are still propped open with wood, as they were a hundred years ago; dreams of the bright lights and the bright voices that greeted us, coming in out of the blinding rain; dreams of the dance and the song, songs of old lost causes from which all bitterness has died away, leaving to-day nothing but beauty behind them; dreams of faded joys and forgotten sorrows, of loves that have passed elsewhere and of memories that abide; dreams of faces that are seen no more. Some day it will change ownership; it will be sold to someone from whom understanding of these things has been withheld, and who will see only the darkness of the old corridors, the shabbiness of the old doorway; and he will build new doors, and porticoes and a wide verandah, and make it fair within and without, levelling the floors and trimming the lawns; and he will have destroyed the old house and the fragrance of it, and it will never return. But to-day it still stands as it has stood for many a long year, clothed in the memories that never leave it and rich in all that the past has built into it; and to some who may never dwell there again it is yet ever present as the home of their hearts' desire, a true house of faery.

The Student had let the old house to the Urchin's father. He was a tall, thin man with a hooked nose, and he knew more about one particular family of Coleoptera than anyone living. He had taken the place, not because he wanted it for its shooting, but because one of the beetles of his family was reputed to be plentiful in the neighborhood. He was never there long; he was never anywhere long. For thirty years he had pursued his beetles over five continents; his measurements of their wing cases alone filled nine enormous MS. volumes. His great work on the variation of the length of the wing case in beetles kept in captivity had become a classic. Scientific men had nothing but praise for the book; several even read it. The majority believed that he had re-founded Neo-Mendelism past any overthrowing; a small but persistent minority argued that, on the contrary, he had utterly overthrown the Neo-Mendelians. All, however, agreed that the book was epoch-making, even though they differed utterly as to the sort of epoch which it made. The author himself was a shy and modest person, who never lost his temper except when people sent him unpaid parcels from Timbuctoo or Khamchatka containing beetles of other families in which he took no interest. On the rare occasions when he could be induced to go into society, kind-hearted hostesses, who saw no reason why one crawling thing should not do as well as another had been known to try to please him by starting a conversation about ladybirds or earwigs; and it was said to be worth foregoing one's cigar to hear him explain, with a chuckle, that though earwigs or ladybirds were no doubt meritorious creatures in their several spheres, and possibly legitimate objects of study to others, they were not his subject; his subject was a particular family of

Coleoptera. He and the Student had become great friends, and when he was in the island he would often drop in to see the Student's bookroom after dinner and there the two would sit, one on either side of the fire, each smoking at a tremendous pace and talking hard on his own subject. Neither ever expected an answer from the other; neither ever got one. But they had silently established an unwritten law that when one had talked for three minutes by the clock on the mantelpiece he was to stop and let the other have a turn; and when at last they said good night, each felt that they had both had a thoroughly enjoyable evening. And so they had.

Unlike to unlike. The Urchin's father had married the daughter of a stockbroker, who, on her death, had left him two legacies; one was the Urchin, and the other was an occasional visitation from her brother Jeconiah. Mr. Jeconiah P. Johnson, the well-known promoter of companies, was a short, stout man with a red face and a shifty blue eye, always immaculately dressed in broadcloth with a huge expanse of white waistcoat, over which sprawled his double watch chain and his triple chin. There were possibly some good points even about Jeconiah, if anything so rotund could be said to have points; but there were certainly not many. He was supposed by some to possess what is called "a high standard of business morality"; it would be truer to say that his code was prehistoric. He had so far kept himself right with the law, because he had mastered the sordid maxim which proclaims that honesty is the best policy; no other reason was likely to occur to him. With some effort he had succeeded in formulating a rule of conduct of which he was rather proud: Do good to yourself and your friends and evil to those who stand in your way. If anyone had told him that the philosophy of ethics took its rise, some twenty-two centuries ago, in a reaction against a similar rule, he would have remarked jocosely that he never studied back numbers. Of anything more exalted than "policy," anything not to be reckoned in terms of £.s.d., he was as ignorant as a hippopotamus.

He was never very fond of his right hand's knowing what his left hand did; for while the right hand promoted companies, the left hand, by means of a manager and a registered alias, carried on a very useful little money-lender's business. He was never averse to putting the screw on, if there was anything to be got by it; and sometimes he got rather funny things. Recently he had had a broken debtor on his hands, and had taken what he could get; among other things, an old bureau full of papers. Jeconiah, being a methodical soul, had turned a clerk on to sort the papers; and the clerk had presently brought him the long lost map of the Scargill cave, and a sheet of paper containing somebody's rough explanation of what it was supposed to be. Jeconiah, who had heard the story, scented possibilities, and, it being a slack time in the City, promptly invited himself to his brother-in-law's house to recover from an attack of influenza. That is how Jeconiah comes into this story. It could not be helped, for he had the map. The finner had said he was too fat to count; but that is where the finner was wrong.

Jeconiah forthwith gave his mind, such as it was, to the subject of caves. Diffidence was not his failing, and he cross-examined every person he could find, concealing, of course, his real object. He collected a splendid amount of rubbish; but he was acute enough where his pocket was concerned, and out of the rubbish he presently dragged forth the fact of the haunted cave which no one would enter. Whereon Jeconiah went over to Scargill to fish, and had a look at the lie of the island; settled with himself that it seemed a good enough place for a wreck, and told the keeper to row him into the west cave. But the keeper, who had no particular liking for Jeconiah, refused point-blank, and told him he would not find a man in the island who would do it; and Jeconiah, who had suddenly lost interest in the fishing, went home in a bad temper. This happened the day after the two children were in the cave; and the day after that the Urchin's father received an excited cablegram from Brazil on the subject of his beloved beetles. He rushed down at once to see the Student.

"I am going to Brazil, I don't know for how long," he said. "And my boy can't go back to school for a month or more, as they have scarlet fever in the village there. And I don't like to leave him with the housekeeper, and I start in two hours. Will you take him?"

"Delighted," said the Student. "Fiona will look after him."

So the Urchin came, and with him came to Fiona a sense of responsibility for him. She couldn't help it.

But Jeconiah showed no intention of moving. On the contrary, the after-effects of influenza were still troubling him sorely, it seemed. At last the Urchin's father had to tell him to stay a week or two longer, if he wanted to; the servants would be there anyhow. And Jeconiah thanked him and settled down to stay, as he had meant to do all along. But as soon as his brother-in-law was gone he took the car and went off for the day. The chauffeur said that he went to a lot of places and talked to a lot of people; and a couple of days later two strange men in a boat entered the bay and proceeded to camp out on a part of the shore which was not the Student's property. Jeconiah had, in fact, hired the boat, and found a couple of ne'er-do-wells from the mainland who knew nothing of him and were ready to row him anywhere in pursuit of his business, which was understood to be photographing wild birds for an illustrated paper.

Jeconiah had, however, made one great mistake. He was aware that you must not neglect little things, and he had neglected quite a big little thing—the Urchin. He had never spoken to him about caves, or taken the least notice of the boy's movements. And the Urchin on his side had been hard at work. He had confessed to Fiona on the subject of the footsteps, and she to him; and they had agreed, under the broad healthy light of day, that probably they had been mistaken and afraid of the dark, and that with lanterns it would be all right. They agreed, however, that it was necessary to have a really good light, and the difficulty was to find one. It was the Urchin who came forward as the saviour of society by proposing to win over Jones, the chauffeur, and get the loan of one of the big acetylene head-lamps from the car. Jones, a newcomer, had not yet heard about the cave, and, being English, he had not yet found his feet among his fellows and was glad of any sort of diversion. The Urchin wound up a triumphant half hour of diplomacy by making Jones promise to lend him one of the headlights and show him how to work it. Then the Urchin fell, as many greater men have fallen; he was lifted up with pride, and told Jones that Fiona and he were going treasure-hunting. Jones grinned; but that evening he talked; and in due course Jeconiah heard.

Fiona was digging in her garden, or rather in the Urchin's, for she had assigned him one bit of it, which she had to cultivate for him; otherwise it would have run waste, for all the work the Urchin put into it. Her garden was one corner of the old walled garden of the Student's house, which was not very well kept now. Once it had been gay with flowers and rich with fruit; but now few flowers grew there save such as could look after themselves, and the fruit had come down to two gnarled old apple trees, in which Fiona had made her earliest experiments in climbing. Most of the ground, so far as it was in use, was now given over to cabbages and potatoes; but in June the borders were sweet with double white narcissus, and now in September there was a revel of unpruned roses, their blooms growing smaller year by year, and a mass of the dark-red blossoms of the little west coast fuchsia, which knows how to live through the winter. One deserted corner was gay with Turk's turban, which still had strength to push up through the ever-thickening tangle of weeds; and groups of winter crocus were coming up in the borders, and among them a few Shirley poppies which Fiona had sown herself. Fiona had had thoughts of taking the garden in hand, but the space enclosed by the old walls was far too large for her to manage unaided; and as there was no money to pay a proper gardener, she had had to content herself with clearing one corner. Here she had achieved a riot of color. She had made a little rockery of oak-leaf and beech ferns brought down from the hill, sentinelled by tall pink foxgloves; the worn-out plum trees against the wall behind were threaded and festooned with thick trailers of yellow and scarlet nasturtium; and in front of the rockery, her especial pride, was a great bed of velvet pansies, rich with every hue of the rainbow. They were flanked by simple annuals, filmy pink poppies, orange escholtzias and sweet-scented mignonette; and in a bed by themselves were the gold and crimson snapdragons which the Urchin had begged for her from the gardener at the big house.

She must needs dig up a centipede, one of the small yellow ones. They were her special dislike. The centipede did not like being dug up either, and writhed himself into seven different sets of tangles at once, as is the way of the smaller centipedes.

"You horrid little yellow beast," she said, forgetting that he could understand, and made a dab at him with her spade, which, to her relief, missed him. She felt she had done her duty by hitting at him, but did not hide from herself that she had really missed him on purpose.

"Little's all right," said the centipede, "and yellow's all right; and though I'm not really a beast, we will let it go at that. But I'm not a bit horrid."

"But I don't like you," said Fiona, "and you wriggle so."

"In the circles in which I move," said the centipede, "my wriggling is much admired. And the mere fact that you do not like me—which, I may remind you, is only a subjective impression and has neither objective validity nor permanent value—does not entitle you to call me names. You ought to have learnt better, with that bangle of yours. For all you know, I may be a model of the more unselfish virtues."

"But you eat the roots of my flowers," said Fiona.

"That is the first I have heard of it," said the centipede. "But one lives and learns. It need not be the same one, though, who does both. So in the present case I propose that I should live and you should learn."

"I wasn't going to kill you really," said Fiona.

The centipede bowed.

"A little courtesy does oil the creaking machinery of life, doesn't it?" he said. "Please lift me up, for I have something to tell you, and your head is so far away. Shouting at you hurts my throat."

Fiona stooped down and took up the little yellow creature in her hand.

"Congratulations," said the centipede. "We _are_ getting on. You wanted badly to shudder, and you didn't. We shall make something of you yet. My old friend the bookworm—who lives in your father's library, by the way—has recently supplied me with a new quotation from the great poet Virgil, who had once, you may remember, quite a reputation as a magician. It was to the effect that if you couldn't get what you wanted by beginning at the top, you should start again at the bottom. I am the bottom. I am not the _very_ bottom, but I am near enough to it for your purpose. Now you see what you have gained by not killing me."

"I don't see anything yet, I'm afraid," said Fiona.

"One must have patience with weaker vessels," said the centipede. "So I will explain. My friend the bookworm, who supplies me with my quotations, has a cousin of the same profession in the library at the big house. It was through him that I got the story I am going to tell you about the fat man."

"Mr. Johnson!" exclaimed Fiona. "He has nothing to do with me." She disliked Jeconiah heartily, so far as she had given any thought to him.

"Oh, yes, he has," said the centipede. "This is where I come in. My bookworm's cousin, who is a great linguist and understands English perfectly, was at work in the library the other evening, and the fat man was having his coffee there. After coffee he lit a cigar and began to walk up and down, and presently he started talking to himself out loud, as my informant says he often does when he is excited. And by piecing his talk together, my informant made out that he had the map of the Scargill cave, which one of your ancestors once gambled away, and that somehow or other he had found out that the cave of the map _was_ the Scargill cave, and that he was only waiting for a smooth day to go and locate the treasure."

"Well?" said Fiona.

"Oh, come now," said the centipede, "it's no use pretending. We all know that you are treasure-hunting—remember we can all understand everything _you_ say, whether we are linguists or not—and my advice to you is, to be quick about it, before the fat man can get his oar in."

"Thank you so much," said Fiona. "And I am so sorry I began by being rude. Tell me, why have you told me all this when I began by being rude?"

"Because I am a model of the more unselfish virtues, of course," said the centipede with a suppressed chuckle. "As a fact, I had an earth-phone from headquarters. But we are all backing you, you know. And now will you put me down, please; the upper air is chilly."

He wriggled into a crack in the ground, and was gone.

That evening Fiona and the Urchin made their final preparations, in case the morrow should fall calm. That evening also Jeconiah heard that he had rivals in the field. His language, as he walked up and down the library, would have been very bad for the bookworm's morals had that intelligent insect been able to understand it all; but the bookworm's English, though good, was literary, and much of the modern idiom employed by Jeconiah slid off its back. Jeconiah's plan had been to make sure that the gold was there, and then charter a launch from Glasgow and take it straight to railway-head; he saw now that he could not afford the time, and that unless he could deal with the children in some way he might have to take the gold off in his boat, which would entail some risk, as well as cost him a heavy sum to buy his two boatmen. Also he made up his mind that he must go the next morning, whatever the weather, if it were possible to launch the boat; he knew that the children, with their little skiff, could only go to sea on calm days.

Unfortunately for Jeconiah, the night fell calm, and though he rose early, he had no notion of starting without a good breakfast. By the time his boat was launched and he himself aboard, he had the pleasure of seeing through his glasses the children's boat off the east or nearer end of

Scargill. The wealth of adjectives which he employed in the circumstances filled his two loafers with awe and admiration.

Fiona, having the Urchin securely under her roof, had breakfasted before dawn, and as soon as it was light enough the children launched their little boat. The Urchin had the precious headlight, ready charged, tied up in an old sack which would also serve to bring away the plunder; and round his waist he had twisted a length of cast-off rope. Its use was not apparent, but he thought it looked business-like. They saw that Jeconiah's boat was still drawn up ashore, and in good heart they started on their long pull. They had reached the island before Jeconiah had his boat out; having no glasses, they could not see if it was being launched or not. But off the eastern end of the island, which is low and grassy, they had a fright, for an empty boat was drawn ashore there. However, when they rowed close in to look at it, Fiona recognized it.

"It's Angus MacEachan's boat," she said. "He has come to see after the sheep he has on the island. There he is, I can see him; he has got a sheep that has hurt its foot." And indeed they could see Angus tending a sick sheep.

"Fiona," said the boy, "we are too silly for anything. Of course the footsteps we heard in the cave were Angus's. There is another way in somewhere, and he would be looking for a sheep."

Fiona said nothing. As they neared the cave, the problem of the footsteps kept intruding itself more and more vividly upon her; but the Urchin was happy in his theory, and she did not think it necessary to remind him that the footsteps could not possibly have been those of Angus, who walked with a limp. She began to feel a vague sense of disquiet, which she tried in vain to put aside.

They entered the cave, and the Urchin, with much pride, lit his great lamp. The powerful burner threw a wonderful circle of light on to black water and black walls, making them glow and sparkle with a soft radiance till they looked like the very gateway of fairyland. Outside the circle everything became black as pitch. They paddled quietly up the bright waterway, and grounded on the stones at the end. The Urchin was hot after his long row, and helping to draw the boat up on the stones did not make him any cooler; he took off his jacket and pitched it on to a thwart.

"Yes, it is hot, and stuffy," said Fiona. She recollected some story she had read about a coal mine, and sniffed. "I hope there is no gas here," she said.

The Urchin grinned.

"Oh, you girls!" he said. "Who ever heard of gas in a sea cave. What you are smelling is the lamp."

Fiona took the lamp up.

"I'm going to take charge of this myself," she said. "You can carry the treasure."

The Urchin picked up the sack and threw it over his shoulder.

"Go ahead, lady with the lamp," he said, and grinned again. He felt very adventurous. He would rather have liked to be photographed.

With considerable caution, necessitated by the heavy lamp, they climbed the rock barrier and descended into the darkness of the inner cave. The walking was better here; the rounded slippery boulders had given place to a floor of pebbles and sand. Quite a short way from the barrier the wall of the cave curved away in a semicircle on the right, its smooth surface forming a kind of small recess. Fiona swept the recess with her lamp, and on the sandy floor something gleamed back; the Urchin pounced on it and picked it up. It was a gold coin, not the least like any which the children had ever seen. It was, in fact, a doubloon.

"This must be one of them," said the boy exultantly as he pocketed it; "one that got dropped. Come on, it can't be much farther."

But Fiona held the lamp steady and stared at the sand.

"Look at the marks on the sand," she said. "They are like the marks of heavy boxes. The treasure has been here, Urchin, and it's not here now. Someone has been here and taken it, and dropped one piece."

"I don't think so," said the Urchin. "We shall find them a bit farther on."

So they went on, but not very far. For the light of the lamp suddenly fell on a rock wall before them, the end of the cave. And it had ended, not as the other caves do, by the roof growing lower and lower till it meets the floor; it had ended in this huge chamber of high rocky walls.

"So this is the cave that no one has ever reached the end of," said Fiona. "Why, it goes no distance at all."

They retraced their steps to the recess, and then back to the end again, looking on this side and on that for openings, but it seemed quite clear that there were none.

"The boxes must have been carried off by sea," said Fiona.

But the Urchin had an idea.

"No one would try to carry great heavy boxes over the rock barrier," he said. "They'd just take the gold out in sacks."

"The barrier may be a rock-fall," said Fiona. "The treasure may all have been cleared out long ago."

And then there came to the Urchin the realization of the fact that he had lost his gun. He turned very red.

"It's a shame," he said angrily, "an awful shame. It was given to me, and someone has taken it. Can't you think where it could be, Fiona? I'd go _anywhere_ to find it."

Whatever Fiona may have been going to say, her words tailed off into sudden silence. For from beyond the cave wall, as it seemed, sounded again the footsteps which they had heard before; and this time they knew that there was no cave there, and that It was walking through solid rock as if along a road. There was no question this time of any concealment or pretence; both frankly turned tail and made for the rock barrier. Halfway there the Urchin tripped and fell heavily on his head. Fiona put the lamp down and helped him up, dizzy and shaking.

"Can you go on, Urchin?" she said. "If not, I'll try and carry you."

The Urchin looked back into the blackness, unrelieved by any ray of the lamp, which faced the other way. The footsteps were steadily drawing nearer, neither hasting nor staying. What the Urchin may have thought he saw Fiona could not guess; he gave one shriek, slid out of her grasp, and bolted for the rock barrier as fast as his trembling feet would carry him.

For one moment Fiona all but followed him. Then it suddenly came to her that she was responsible for the boy's safety. She never knew afterwards how she managed to do what she did; but she turned, and with the courage of utter desperation—the courage which enables the hen partridge to face the sparrow hawk—stood at bay, swinging up the heavy lamp to see and face whatever should come.

And into the circle of lamplight quietly walked the figure of the old hawker.

The revulsion of feeling was too much for Fiona. She sprang forward and caught the old man's hand and clung to it.

"Oh," she said, "I'm so glad it's you. We heard the footsteps and we were so frightened." The relief of it all was overwhelming; she was almost crying, and went on saying anything, hardly knowing what she said, just for the mere human companionableness of it. "How did you come here? I suppose you came over with Angus in his boat. Of course you would. Then there must be another way into the cave after all, and we couldn't find it."

"And so I frightened you?" said the old man gently, making no effort to withdraw his hand. "Yes, there is another way in." He made no attempt to answer all her questions.

"Urchin," called Fiona, raising her voice. "Urchin, come back; it's all right."

But there was no answer.

"Urchin," she shouted; "Urchin."

But there was no answer save the echoing of the empty cave.

"He was going down to the boat," she said, loyally repressing the fact that the Urchin had bolted. "We must go after him, for he had hurt his head, and I am afraid of his falling again."

They climbed the rock barrier, and made their way to the boat. The boat lay there as it had been left, half ashore, with the swell rippling against the stern, and over one thwart the Urchin's jacket, just as he had thrown it down. And the boat was as empty as the cave.

Into Fiona's eyes came a sudden fear.

"He must have fallen again, and be lying somewhere," she said.

They went back, searching every nook and corner of the cave, turning the light into every crevice, under every rock, making a minute examination of the rock barrier; and there was no sign.

And then Fiona broke down.

"He is drowned," she said, and just sat and sobbed.

After a few moments the old man came and sat down beside her. In his gentle voice he said that the Urchin could not possibly be drowned. The water was quite shallow at the edge, and he was a good swimmer, was he not? And even if he had not been, the swell would have rolled him ashore. He himself had no doubt that all would come right.

Fiona ceased sobbing and turned on him.

"Do you know where he is?" she demanded bluntly.

"How would I know when you do not know?" said the old man. "Could I see what you could not see?" And then "Listen."

Down the waterway came voices, and the sound of oars. It was in fact Jeconiah's boat entering the cave.

Fiona caught at the straw.

"He may have swum out to the other boat," she said.

But there was no one in the other boat but Jeconiah and his two men. They had powerful lanterns, and the boat was full of sacks. Jeconiah himself was purple with suppressed rage and impatience. The moment he could get ashore, he waddled up to Fiona and shook the map of the cave in her face, exclaiming, "Remember, if you have found anything it belongs to me and I claim it."

Fiona had only one thought in her mind at the moment, and the foolish impertinence of the little fat man was to her merely so much unnecessary sound. Her answer was "Have you seen the Urchin? We have lost him. Did he not swim out to your boat?" She was almost sobbing again.

"Confound the brat!" said Jeconiah roughly. "I've not come here to play hide-and-seek with a parcel of children. Tell me at once what you've found."

Fiona straightened herself, and looked at Jeconiah as though he were some noxious reptile.

"There was nothing here to find," she said. "And this cave belongs to my father. And anything in it he gave to the Urchin."

"Well, he's not here," said Jeconiah brutally, "and I am. Who finds, keeps."

And calling to his men to bring the lights, he set off, between stumbling and crawling, for the rock barrier. One of the men had the decency to stop a moment and tell Fiona that they had seen nothing of any boy; Jeconiah turned and abused him for a laggard.

With a good deal of difficulty the two men hoisted and shoved Jeconiah over the rock barrier. Once over, he took a light himself, told the men to wait where they were, and after a good look at the map set out for the recess where the Urchin had found the doubloon. Fiona followed him; there was some vague idea in her mind of protecting the Urchin's property; behind that there was still a faint subconscious hope that in some way or other the Urchin would suddenly reappear, and laugh at her terrors.

Jeconiah reached the recess. He saw and understood the marks of the boxes on the sand. He swung round on Fiona with a snarl like that of a hungry wolf.

"You think you're clever, don't you, you and your father," he said. "I suppose you've had the stuff moved. But I'll have it if I go to the middle of the earth for it."

It was the old hawker who shouted. He had stood apart, a silent spectator of the scene. And at this moment he called out, in a voice of surprising power for so frail a body:

"Look out above you. Jump."

Fiona, who had learned to obey, jumped back just in time. But Jeconiah had never learnt to obey any orders but his own. He stood, stupidly staring, as a bit of the roof of the cave bowed downward, gave way, and came cascading about him in a shower of earth and big stones, that filled the air with thick dust. When the dust cleared again, they saw Jeconiah lying on his back in the middle of the cliff fall, motionless, and to all appearance dead.

But Fiona was not looking at Jeconiah. She was looking at the place where the roof of the cave had bowed itself before falling; and into her mind came crowding dim forgotten legends, legends of fear and hope. And she was saying over and over again to herself, as though she might miss its purport, that behind the cliff fall, as if impelling and directing it, she had seen a small brown elfin hand.

It was the old hawker who took charge of the situation. The two men, who at first had looked as if they would run, became amenable when he spoke to them. They carried Jeconiah's body to his boat, and laid it in the stern-sheets. One of the men pointed out that there was no mark at all on his face or head, and that he did not believe he had been struck.

"Died of fright, I expect," he said curtly.

"Lucky we stood out for wages in advance," said his companion. It looked as if this might be Jeconiah's fitting epitaph.

The old man himself went with Fiona in her boat. But he was too feeble to row far, so he landed on the island and went in search of Angus.

In due course Angus came down and rowed Fiona home, saying that the old man was going to look after his sheep for him till he returned. It did not occur to Fiona, until they had gone too far to turn back, that it looked as though the old man wished to avoid questions. Her mind was in a helpless whirl in which everything seemed unreal, except the Urchin and that small brown hand. She could not give her father any very coherent account of what had happened; but he went out at once to find a boat and men to search the cave.

Jeconiah was laid on his bed in the big house, and there was much commotion there; this one must go for the doctor and that one for the Student; scared maids stood and whispered in the corridors; the two loafers, heroes of the hour, feasted happily in the kitchen. Then the doctor came, and went upstairs with a grave face, as befitted the occasion; but he did not come down again, and surmise grew. Half an hour passed before the door opened, and the doctor, smiling and rubbing his hands together, came into the library, where the Student had just entered and was talking to the housekeeper.

"He's not dead at all," said the doctor. "It's catalepsy—suspended animation, you know. Like the frog in the marble. Had a shock, you tell me? Just so, just so. How long? Oh, he may be an hour, and he may be a month; no one can ever say. Never had the good luck to see a case before. Not _very_ uncommon, no. Mustn't try to rouse him, you know; might be dangerous. Just wait. Send for me at once if he comes to. Can get two nurses to watch him, if you like; just as well perhaps. Sometimes they are odd when they wake; think they are someone else for a bit, you know, change their habits, and so on. Dual personality? Oh, yes, several well-attested cases; but I don't mean as much as that. Might arise this way, of course; but what I mean is more just queer. But of course he need not be; might wake up as if he'd been asleep. If it lasts long, take away all the almanacs and things, in case he gets a shock. Well, good day, good day."

And the doctor went; and Jeconiah's body lay still on the bed, waiting till his soul, if he had one, should return to it.

So the Student went home again; and on his way he met the old hawker, who stopped and spoke to him; and for a few moments the two walked together, the old man talking rather quickly. Fiona, watching from the window of the bookroom, could see that her father first looked puzzled and then grave and then considerably relieved; in a dim kind of way she found herself thinking that Angus must have rowed back very fast to Scargill, if the old hawker were already landed. She was wondering who he really was and why her father talked to him.

"Tell Anne to get us something to eat—anything," said the Student. "The boat will be here directly."

The Student, by straining what remained of old loyalty as far as he dared, had found half a dozen volunteers, good men, to face the haunted cave, provided he went himself.

"Do you want to come, Fiona?" he said. Of course Fiona meant to come.

And while they waited, the Student questioned Fiona, and had the whole story coherently, except the hand. That part Fiona felt she could not tell; there, in the cheerful bookroom, it seemed so impossible. Once or twice he nodded, and said, "That would be so"; and at the end he pointed out that whatever had happened had happened when her back was turned, as she faced the coming footsteps. She had not thought of that. What puzzled her, and hurt her a little, was that, though her father seemed to feel for _her_, he did not appear to be particularly concerned about the Urchin. "I believe it will come right," was all he said.

The boat arrived, rowed by strong hands; the men worked with a will, and the distance to the cave seemed short. They had brought good lights, and the Student had a powerful electric torch. High and low they searched the cave, and found nothing. One man, who was a good swimmer, dived several times and found nothing there either. Tracking footsteps was impossible; the sand, where there was any, had been hopelessly trampled.

When nothing more could be done, the Student said that he wanted to look for a thing himself which he had an idea of. He went down to the end of the cave with his torch and tapped the wall with a geological hammer. Fiona sat on the rock barrier and watched him; what he was seeking she had no idea. He came slowly back down the cave, tapping the wall, till he reached the recess where the Urchin had picked up the doubloon. He went straight to the back of the recess and tapped the wall there; and even as he did so a large piece of stone fell from above, and smashed the electric torch in his hand. He came back to the rock barrier quite unperturbed, looking as if he had found what he sought.

"Not very safe, this cave," he said calmly; and told the men to push off the boat. "There is nothing more we can do," he said; "the boy is certainly not here."

The men's courage was fast ebbing away; they were glad to get out of the haunted place.

Fiona sat in silence all the way home. It was dark before they reached the house. She waited while Anne bustled over supper; she thought she would never see her father alone. At last supper was over, and he went into the bookroom and began to light his pipe; she followed him. Her words came out in a torrent.

"Daddy," she said, "what does it all mean? and why are you so strange and unconcerned? What did that old man tell you? If I couldn't see, _he_ must have seen, for he was facing. What is it you know? And why have you told me nothing?"

"Sit down, little daughter," said the Student. He drew her beside his knee, with her head on his arm. "I will tell you now what I can. The old man gave me a sort of hint. He did not really see, for the lamp was the other way; I fancy he guessed. I wanted to test what he said to me. I have tested it now with my hammer; it all agrees. I am absolutely certain that no harm has come to the Urchin. But I can do nothing for him myself. And I must not even tell you what I think; for if I do it ruins everything. All I may tell you is this, that you are the only person who can do anything. You will have to do it all yourself and by yourself, little daughter. I believe you have ways and means of your own of finding out. Are you going through with it, Fiona?"

"Of course I am, daddy," she said. "How can I do anything else? If only I knew what it is I have to do to find him—how to begin even."

"I cannot even tell you that," said the Student. But his fingers played with the copper bangle on her wrist. And out of some dim corner of subconsciousness she seemed to hear a small voice which said "If you can't get what you want by beginning at the top you must start again at the bottom." Her father, with his learning, was the top; the bottom . . . ?

Fiona went to bed less miserable than she had expected.

CHAPTER 5
THE OREAD

Fiona was out long before breakfast next morning, digging furiously in her garden. Not many minutes passed before she was rewarded by a glint of something yellow in a shovelful of earth, and there was the centipede.

"You dear creature," she said, and caught it up quickly before it could wriggle away.

"How polite we are this morning," said the centipede, swelling with conscious pride. "I suppose we want something."

Fiona's mind was far too completely taken up with her one object to notice or resent any insinuations.

"Yes, I do," she said. "You told me that if I could not get what I wanted by beginning at the top I must start again at the bottom. I can do nothing from the top this time, so I've come to you."

"Flattered, to be sure," said the centipede. "How frank we are."

"Please don't be cross," said Fiona, humbly. "I am only doing what you told me to do."

"Bless you, child, I'm not cross," said the centipede. "I'm a philosopher."

"Don't philosophers get cross?" asked the girl.

"Never," said the centipede. "And when they do they call it something else. What's the matter with me is, that I've sprained my seventh ankle on bow side, counting from the tail. Don't say you're sorry, for you're not. Anyone can see you're not."

"You are horrid to-day," said Fiona. "And the other day you were so nice."

"That's what makes me such a charming companion," said the centipede. "You never know what to expect. So I never pall."

"I want to know where the Urchin is, and how I am to find him," said Fiona.

"Is that all?" said the centipede. "Fancy interrupting my breakfast on account of that boy. Well, one question at a time. We'll have the last one first; I'm in that sort of mood to-day."

"How can I find the Urchin, then, please?" asked Fiona.

"Well, you've been told _that_ already," said the centipede. "Haven't you a memory?"

Fiona thought and thought, but could make nothing of it.

"My friend the bookworm was there at the time," said the centipede, "and heard the shore lark tell you that the last man went up a hill. Very well. Go up a hill."

"But that was for something quite different," said Fiona. "That was for my treasure. I am not thinking of any treasure now."

"Silly of you, then," said the centipede. "I would be. Ever studied philosophy?"

"No," said Fiona.

"That's a pity," said the centipede. "Then you've never heard of Hegel and the unity of opposites? Black and white are only different aspects of the same thing, you know. And as soon as you begin to think about it, you see at once how sensible it is. Well, a treasure-hunt and a boy-hunt are only different aspects of a hunt, aren't they? Therefore they are the same thing. Therefore what does for one does for the other. Therefore you go up a hill. There's logic for you," and once more he swelled proudly.

"Thank you very much," said Fiona. "And now will you please tell me where the Urchin is?"

"Tell you!" exclaimed the centipede. "Why, it was you told me. You prophesied the whole thing."

"I'm sure I don't remember it, then," said Fiona.

"What's the matter with _you_," said the centipede, "is that you refuse to exert your intelligence, such as it is. You should take a lesson by me. You humans are all forgetting nowadays that the spoken word is an instrument of great power, and that once it is launched it goes on and on, and can work magic on its own account, quite independently of you. If you say a thing will happen, it frequently does happen."

"But what did I say?" asked Fiona.

"You told the Urchin that if he hurt the shore lark the Little People would take him. Well, they've taken him. That's all."

And the centipede slid down on to the ground, and with something like a chuckle vanished. He had evidently learned from his philosophy to bear with resignation the misfortunes of others.

But Fiona did not set off up a hill at once. After breakfast she went to the bookroom and spoke to her father.

"I have found out where the Urchin is, daddy," she said. "He was carried off by the fairies."

The Student showed no surprise.

"You have not been long finding out, Fiona," he said. "I thought you had ways and means of your own."

"But, daddy," she said, "I don't _really_ believe it, you know. It sounds so absurd nowadays. Do you believe it?"

"I believe it, yes," said the Student. "I knew yesterday. Now that you know, I may talk to you about it, so far."

"I don't know that I do really know," she said. "Things like that don't _really_ happen, do they? Whoever heard of it?"

"You and I have heard of it," he answered. "And that is enough. The proposition that people are not carried off by fairies is a mere working hypothesis, liable to be overthrown by any one case to the contrary. Well, we've got a case to the contrary, and that's the end of the hypothesis."

"I'm arguing against myself, daddy, you know," she said. "I want to believe that we do know where he is."

"No difficulty at all," said the Student, "to anyone with a properly trained mind, like yours and mine. Take it this way. No one has ever crossed the South Arabian desert or explored the snow ranges of New Guinea, have they? Well, for all anyone can say to the contrary, people may be carried off by fairies every day of the week in New Guinea or South

Arabia, mayn't they? It may even be the rule there. It may be a working hypothesis among the pygmies of New Guinea that such a thing _always_ happens—at death, for instance. It would be just as good a working hypothesis as it is that it _never_ happens."

"But, daddy, it would be so extraordinary, wouldn't it?"

"Not a bit more extraordinary," he said, "than the inside of a bit of radium, or the inside of an egg, for that matter. It is probably simpler for the Urchin to become a fairy than for an egg to become a bird, or a caterpillar a butterfly. It would not be nearly as strange as it is that there is a water beast which can shed its gills and become a land beast, or that Uranus moons go round the wrong way. You can't knock it out by any reasoning of that kind, Fiona. It's merely a matter of fact; and if we have found a case we _have_ found a case."

"Then you knew yesterday, daddy?" she said.

"I had a very fair idea," he answered. "That is why I was tapping in the cave with a hammer. Can you guess why?"

Fiona saw.

"To find the rest of the cave," she said. "That is where he would be."

"Just so," said the Student. "These caves cannot end in a wall, as that one seems to. I thought the wall must ring hollow somewhere, and the hollow is in the recess where the stone nearly fell on me. The apparent end of the cave is not in the line of the true cave at all."

"It is the same place where the stones fell on Mr. Johnson," said Fiona.

"That is strange," said the Student.

And then Fiona told about the hand she had seen.

"Of course, of course," said the Student. "That explains the whole thing. They threw the stone down on me too. They did not wish me to know that the wall was hollow just there. They must use it as a doorway. They will have carried the boy through at the moment that you turned your back, of course. I suppose he invited them in some way; they could have no power otherwise."

"He said he would go _anywhere_ to find his treasure," said Fiona.

"That would be quite sufficient for them to act on," said the Student.

"Then the stories about the cruelty of the Little People are true," asked Fiona.

"Only in part," said the Student. "I take it that they are all sorts, like ourselves. They are, as you know, the vanished débris of all the peoples that have helped to make this planet what it is. Good people, many of them. But they cannot altogether love those who have driven them under the ground."

"And who is the old hawker, daddy," she asked, "and what has he to do with it all?"

"I can't talk about anything except what you already know," said the Student. "Have you found out yet how to start?"

"I am to go up a hill," said Fiona. "And I am going up Heleval now. And I came to see if you would come with me."

"I wish I could; I wish very much I could," said the Student. "I do not know what you may find; but I know well that if I went with you, you would find nothing but grass and rock. I am too old to see the things you can see, you know. You have to do it alone, little daughter."

So Fiona filled her pocket with bread and cheese, and started; and the Student, after a useless attempt to settle down to his inscriptions, set up a little three-inch telescope with which he sometimes entertained Fiona on fine nights, gazing at Jupiter's moons or Saturn's rings, and followed her across the moor as far as he could. It was the only way he could go with her.

THERE ARE MANY WORSE THINGS IN THE WORLD THAN SETTING OUT TO CLIMB Heleval on a beautiful morning on the first of October, when the grass in unsunned corners is still pearly with the frost of the night, and the whole earth is touched with the wonderful caress of the cool autumn sunshine. Fiona's way lay along the shore road, past the bank of heather and fern which in August had been gay with flowers, napperd and potentilla, blue milkwort and starry eye-bright, and alive with butterflies, blues and small heaths and pearl-bordered fritillaries; but the flowers were faded now, and in their place, in the little burn where the hazelnuts grew, was a tapestry of purple burrs and scarlet hips. The shore road ended at a little burn; here an old stone bridge, grown over with grass, crossed the pool which in times of spate would hold a fat, white sea-trout, and here Fiona and the Urchin had used to come in summer to gather globe flowers. From this point a sheep track led up the valley beside the burn, through great spaces of yellowing bracken, by little swampy springs where late forget-me-nots still lingered and an early snipe might rise with a skeep, and across low-lying wastes of bog-myrtle, perfuming all the air with its dying leaves; then the ground began to rise, and fern and bog-myrtle gave place to short, hard grass tufted with bulrushes, and beds of matted unburnt heather, seamed with rabbit tracks.

After a time Fiona left the valley and began to climb the hillside, rising steeply through heather and red grass and heather again, most of it dying by now, but with patches still in full flower, worked by the wild bees and making the moorland smell like a honey-pot. Then more grass, and limestone ridges, and she stood on the crest of the moor, which billowed away on her right, wave after wave, till it ran down to the low ground and the sea, and rose up on her left till it ended in the great mass of Heleval, standing up into the cloudless sky. The ground before her was scarred with deep peat-hags, their gray banks touched with the tiny scarlet blossoms of the trumpet-moss, while from their crumbling sides projected bits of the whitened trunks of trees long since dead, last vestiges of the forests that had clothed the island ere ever the Gael first fought his way in. Walking became impossible, and she jumped from gray bank to gray bank, occasionally floundering across a little lake of soft peat, where the wild cotton grass still bloomed, and the mountain hares had left telltale tracks. Now and again a hare itself would scurry away before her up one of the peat ditches, rising to the moor level as soon as he thought he was out of gunshot and sitting up on his haunches to watch; now and again an old grouse, his head and hackles red as a berry in the sunlight, would rise, crow, and swing away over the brow of the moor. And presently from behind Heleval came drifting a gray bird with a long bill who on hovering wings wheeled three times in the air above her and gave his full spring call, the most wonderful sound that the hills ever hear; then he stooped close over her head and with wings spread sickle-wise shot away for the sea. One may see a curlew on the moor in October, but he will not give his spring call; and Fiona felt of good courage, for she knew that the bird had called for her, to tell her she was in the right way.

So she came to the foot of Heleval itself, and started to climb the steep slope of short grass, slippery as polished board, which led up to the rock pinnacle above; the hillside twinkled with the white scuts of rabbits racing up before her to their holes, as round the side of the mountain came their enemy, perhaps the last kite in the island, glittering in the sun as only a glede can, till the beautiful cowardly creature caught sight of Fiona and swept away across the valley. She passed the great cairn where the hill foxes live, and began the last climb to the pinnacle of rock that fronts the flat crest of the mountain. And now something white on the rock, which she had noticed from below without taking account of, began to become insistent. It could not possibly be a patch of snow yet, she thought. Perhaps the shepherd had hung a sheepskin there. But no sheepskin was ever so white.

Then she came up near the pinnacle, and saw. Standing upright against it was a girl, not much older than herself. Her long dark hair blew back over the rock; her white body was half hidden in a trembling veil of white light, which shimmered and played all about her, waving with every breath of the wind. Her face was beautiful and cold, like a frosty moonrise; her eyes shone like the drip of phosphorescent water under the stars.

"You have come at last," said the girl. "Every day for many days I have watched for you."

"Who are you, you beautiful girl?" asked Fiona.

"I am an Oread," said the girl. "I am the spirit of Heleval."

"I have heard," said Fiona, "that long ago people used to believe that everything had a spirit of its own, mountains and rivers and trees. Is it true then?"

"It _was_ true," said the girl. "The world was full of my sisters, once. There were the Naiads in the streams, and the Hamadryads in the woods, and we, the Oreads, in the mountains. Men were wiser and simpler in those days. But now my sisters are nearly all gone. When a tree has become so many cubic feet of timber, how can it shelter a Dryad? When a stream is merely so many units of waterpower, how can a Naiad dwell there? Only the barren mountains, if they contain neither gold nor iron, have been left unappraised and unexploited; and a few Oreads still linger here and there. Once in a while a man fancies that he sees one of us; then he must climb and climb till the day he dies, hoping to see her indeed; down in your world people call him mountain mad."

"How is it then that I have seen you?" asked Fiona.

The Oread touched her bracelet.

"Partly because of this," she said. "But chiefly because you are a child, and can still see. What is it you have come to ask me?"

"How to find the Urchin," said Fiona.

"You know of course where he is?" the girl asked; and Fiona said, "Yes, he is in Fairyland; but I do not know the way to go."

"That is easily told," said the Oread. "The King of the Woodcock will let you in, and any of his people can tell you where to find him. But do you know the danger? If you do arrive, which is very doubtful, the fairies will make you wish a wish; and if your wish be one that does not find favor with them, they will keep you there forever, till you lose your memory and yourself and become even as one of them."

"I will take the risk," said Fiona, "for I must go and try to bring him back."

"Why do you want to bring him back?" asked the Oread. "He is much better where he is. Will he thank you for bringing him back? Not a bit. You will have the labor and the danger, and he will take it all for granted. And then he will become a man, and what use is that? He may be a financier, and cheat somebody; or a politician, and slander somebody; or a learned man, and hinder wisdom. He is much better in Fairyland. Why are you going?"

"I can't help it," said Fiona. "You can't leave people in the lurch, you know."

"Of course you can," said the Oread. "Be sensible and go home; eat, drink, and be merry."

"O, don't you understand?" said Fiona. "Don't you see that there are some things you _can't_ do, whatever anybody says? It's not the reason of the thing; it's only just because I am I, and he is lost. You are so beautiful; haven't you any heart?"

"Neither heart nor soul," said the Oread. "So I ought to be perfectly happy. You have a heart and a soul, and you are not. Which of us is the better off?"

"I wouldn't change, anyhow," said Fiona.

The Oread laughed.

"Of course you wouldn't. It is I who would change if I could. But as I have no soul, and cannot get one, and do not know what it would mean to get one, it is no use worrying; it is best to be happy as I am. In any case,

I would not care to be like men and women. I would not mind having a child's heart, like you. I had a heart once, but it is so long ago that I have almost forgotten what it was like. How old do you think I am?"

"You _look_ about seventeen," said Fiona.

"I am exactly as old as Heleval," said the girl. "And that is more hundreds of thousands of years than you or I could ever count. I am older than any of the fishes or birds or beasts; far older than men or fairies. Look at that," and the Oread swept her arm over the glorious prospect around her; the two great wings of the Isle of Mist stretched far out into the sea, the Atlantic throbbing and sparkling under the blue sky, and across the loch the jagged gray range of the Cuchullins, peak upon peak. "Isn't it all beautiful? We came into being together. Heleval was a giant in those days, a king among other kings; and there was no sea there, and the Cuchullin Hills stood right up into the sky, and twisted and bubbled while the Earth cooled and cracked, and my sisters of the Fire came out of the cracks and taught us mountain spirits the fire dance, and we danced it all night on the great peaks till the stars reeled to watch us. And then the fiery summits cooled and sank down, and my sisters of the Fire sank with them, and a mighty river went foaming out down the valley yonder to a distant sea; and every evening my sisters the Naiads came floating up in a circle with garlands of green on their hair, and they taught us mountain spirits the water dance, and we danced it all night on the moonlit water, while the Ocean crept nearer and nearer to gaze. And then the sea came up, and the river carved Heleval out as you see it, and shrank away, and my sisters the Naiads shrank away with it; and the island was covered with great forests, and my sisters the Hamadryads came out of the tree-trunks and taught us mountain spirits the tree dance, and we danced it all night in the forest glades, till one night men saw; and men felled the forests to capture my sisters of the trees and enslave them, but they vanished as the trees vanished. And to-day only the hills are left, and we, the Oreads, a people few and fading away; and we no longer dance, for we have lost all our sisters, and we no longer have hearts."

The girl's face had filled with color as she spoke, and her eyes had become soft, and her voice sounded like the music of waters far away. Fiona looked at her in wonder.

"Indeed, indeed, you have your heart still," she said. "And you are far more beautiful even than I thought you were. Come home with me, and I will love you as you loved your sisters."

"It is not possible," said the Oread. "It is not free to me to leave Heleval. I _am_ Heleval. And I shall be here till one day men find iron or copper in my mountain, and come up with great engines to carve it and tear its flanks and carry it away; and then I shall go too, as my sisters have gone."

"Will you die?" asked Fiona.

"I do not know what death means," said the girl. "I shall just go back, like a drop of water when it falls into the sea. But do you know what you have done to-day? For a few moments, because you are brave and loyal, you have given me back my heart, which was lost thousands of years ago. It will all fade away again; but before it fades, will you kiss me?"

So Fiona took her in her arms and kissed her, and then turned and went down the hill. Once she faced round, and saw the Oread standing, frosty and white, against the pinnacle of rock, holding out her arms; and she started to go back to her. And even as she moved the whiteness vanished, and there was nothing there but the rocky pinnacle, shining in the slanting sunlight. Rather sadly she went home.

CHAPTER 6
THE KING OF THE WOODCOCK

That night Fiona told her father that she believed she had found the way to go. They also discussed the question of catching a woodcock; with the result that Fiona was up at dawn and off to the kennels behind the big house, where the Urchin's father kept his dogs. She understood that she must take advantage both of the night frost and the habits of the keeper, who was apt to lie in bed awhile when no one was about.

The two setters stood on their hind legs to greet her, and pawed at the bars, whining and dancing with joy. Artemis was white and brown and Apollo was white and black. Fiona threw open the door, and they were out in a moment, tumbling over each other as they made wild rings round the grass, and dashing back in between to lick her hand. She had to sit down and wait till the first exuberance was over, and they came and lay down at her feet with their tongues out.

"It is good to be out so early," said Apollo.

"It's so slow in the kennel," said Artemis. "And we can't even talk to each other, because Apollo was broken in English and doesn't know any Gaelic, and I was broken by another man in Gaelic and don't know any English."

"You'll interpret, won't you?" said Apollo. "Of course we've the international code, but it doesn't take one much further than the passwords."

So for the rest of the morning Fiona had not only to interpret but to make every remark twice over, once in each language. But it will do if the reader takes this for granted.

"What are we going to do?" asked Apollo.

So Fiona explained to them that she wanted to catch a woodcock and ask him a question, and she hoped they would help her.

"Of course we will," said Artemis. "We know all about woodcock. When we go out with himself, we find them for him and stand still, and then he makes a noise and they fall down dead."

"Sometimes," said Apollo.

"Generally," corrected Artemis, loyally. "Will you make them fall down dead?"

Fiona explained that she only wanted to catch one and talk to it.

"We never saw that done," said Apollo. "But we will find one, and then you can catch it."

"It's very early for woodcock," said Artemis. "There won't be any in the heather on the second of October. But there may be an early pair in the ferns."

"The first ones always pitch in the ferns on Glenollisdal," said Apollo.

So to Glenollisdal they went, down the shore road and across the little bridge and then by the shepherd's track along the top of the black cliffs, over grass and stones all rough and white with the frost. The cold morning air was like new wine, and Fiona had to shade her eyes from the low sun. Then the track left the cliffs and began to climb up a sunless valley, across little burns beautiful with fading ferns, till between two great moorland crags it reached the pass, more a watercourse now than a track; and then came the cairn at the summit of the pass, with its glorious view of sea and mountain, and down at one's very feet the deep narrow valley that was Glenollisdal, seamed from crest to foot by its deep burn, which ran half its length through faded brown heather and then out to sea through a huge bed of dying bracken, the whole bathed in the bright morning sun.

"We always come here the first day," said Apollo. "Oh, we are going to have fun."

The three followed the track down to where it passed the top of the fern bed. There was a good deal of grass there, dotted with sheep, and in one place, looking well out to sea, a curious little hard circle in the grass, where no sheep ever came.

"That is the fairy ring," said Artemis. "Where they dance, you know."

"They dance on All Hallows E'en," said Apollo. "But no one ever sees them."

"Because everyone's afraid to go and look," said Artemis.

"Please, may we start?" said Apollo.

"All you have to do is to wait till we point," said Artemis, "and then come to us."

And the two dogs dashed off into the great fern bed, crossing each other backwards and forwards like a pair of scissors as they quartered it.

They were not long about it. Apollo's gallop became a sort of run, a yard or two of stealthy crawl, and he stopped dead, tail stiff and throat distended, like a dog of marble, and looked round for Fiona. Artemis was just crossing him; she whipped round in her stride as if shot and became a second marble image where she stood.

Fiona walked down to Apollo. But the ferns rustled a good deal as she made her way through, and as she reached the dog's side the cock rose, five yards away, with a lazy careless flap as if it felt only the bother of being disturbed. For a moment she had a vivid impression of the white patches at the end of its fan of tail feathers, and then it gradually gathered speed and swept away over the side of the valley; for an instant it showed black as it crossed the sky line, and then it was gone.

Apollo turned to Fiona with unhappy eyes and licked her hand. But Artemis never moved a muscle.

"Come to me," she said in a low whisper.

Very quietly Fiona reached her side.

"The other bird is here," whispered Artemis, "just under my nose. Stoop down."

Fiona bent down between the stalks of the bracken. The woodcock was sitting with its back to her, a little brown bunch of feathers. Very gently she put her hand out, and even as she did so she became aware of a wise black eye looking at her, though the bird faced the other way. Her hand closed on the empty air, and the woodcock, with a wonderful spring, was well on its way to seek its mate.

"I believe I could have put a foot on it," said Artemis regretfully. "But of course we are not allowed to."

"I don't know how I came to be so foolish," said Fiona. "I ought to have spoken to it instead of trying to catch it. But I forgot."

"Better luck next time," said Apollo; "we must try again."

But though the dogs worked the whole of the ferns carefully, there was no other bird there.

They came back and lay down beside Fiona, tongues out and panting.

"It's no use trying the heather yet, I know," said Artemis. "Birds are never in it at this time of year."

"There are some more ferns two miles on," said Apollo doubtfully. "I saw a bird there once, three years ago."

"I wish I knew what to do," said Fiona.

"We can leave it for a day or two and come back," said Artemis. "Those two birds will be back again to look for each other."

"But they won't be so confiding again," added Apollo.

They were all so preoccupied that they never noticed the shepherd till he was quite close to them. He was striding down the track, a big, raw-boned man with red hair; a plaid was thrown loosely across his shoulder; at his heels followed a jet black collie.

The dogs saw him first. It would seem that they did not like him. Every hair on their necks bristled; they shrank close to Fiona, making little moaning noises in their throats, and flattening themselves as if they were trying to burrow into the ground. Their eyes were full of terror.

"Why, Artemis, Apollo, what's the matter?" said Fiona. Then she looked up and saw the shepherd. "Why, it's only the new shepherd and his collie. There's nothing to be afraid of."

"Collie!" said Apollo. "That thing's not a collie. Can't you see?"

"Shepherd!" echoed Artemis. "That thing's not a shepherd. Oh, can't you see?"

The shepherd came up to Fiona, and said that Miss Fiona was out early and was there anything he could be doing for her. He spoke in the soft correct English of the Gael.

"I came out to catch a woodcock to talk to it," said Fiona, "and we can't catch one."

It occurred to her, even as she spoke, that the statement sounded a little out of the ordinary. But the rough shepherd never let the least sign of this show on his face. He answered in the most matter-of-fact way, with the gentle courtesy of the west coast, that there would not be many woodcock in yet, and would he try to catch one for Miss Fiona?

"Oh, do you think you could?" said Fiona eagerly. "I should be so grateful."

Then the shepherd saw the trouble of the dogs. He said something to them in a language that was neither English nor Gaelic, and waved his own dog to go. The collie went straight off up the moor, and sat down on the top of the nearest rock ledge, an odd little blot of black on the brown and yellow moorland. Apollo and Artemis got up and shook themselves violently.

"It was the international password," said Apollo. "Goodness knows where he got it from. But we have to recognize it."

"I'm not happy," said Artemis. "I was well brought up. I never associated with this sort of thing before."

Fiona, who knew that a new shepherd had been coming, could make nothing of their trouble, and did her best to smooth them down. The shepherd led the way up the hill, and on to a little rough plateau broken with rocks and bits of heather, lying under the main rise of the hill where it rounds away toward the Glenollisdal burn. "I am thinking that there should be a woodcock about here," he said.

"This is one of the earliest places in all the heather," whispered Artemis to Fiona. "He must know this moor very well."

"It's too early yet, all the same, even for here," said Apollo.

It looked as if Apollo were right. For when at the shepherd's request Fiona threw the dogs off, they quartered the whole plateau and found nothing.

But the shepherd stuck to his guns.

"I am thinking that there should be a bird here," he said. "Will Miss Fiona give me leave to try my own dog?"

Fiona nodded and called the setters to heel; the shepherd waved his hand, and the black collie came racing to him. Some collies will work a ground like a spaniel, and some will even do a little pointing, but the black collie troubled himself neither with one nor the other. When the shepherd spoke to him, he just cantered straight forward to a small patch of heather on the sunless side of a rock, where the frost still lingered, and there sat down quite unconcerned, as though the matter in hand were altogether beneath the scope of his talents.

"I think he has a bird," said the shepherd.

"I tried that place," said Apollo. "There's nothing there."

But the shepherd had gone up to his dog and was peering carefully into the heather. Then he beckoned Fiona.

"Does Miss Fiona see the bird?" he asked, pointing.

Fiona looked long before she saw. The woodcock had squeezed himself right into the roots of a frost-covered clump of heather, and even when the heather was parted nothing showed but his little orange tail, with its white and black points.

"Shall I catch him for Miss Fiona?" asked the shepherd; and Fiona said, "Oh yes, please, if you will."

The shepherd knelt down and brought his two great hands slowly to either side of the tuft of heather; then he closed them with a snap, and drew out the largest woodcock Fiona had ever seen. It struggled and thrashed at his wrists with its powerful wings.

"Will Miss Fiona take the bird now?" he said. "Just behind the wings, with her thumbs on its back."

So Fiona took her bird, and as she did so its back-seeing eye caught the glint of her copper bangle. It stopped thrashing with its wings and lay quite still in her hands.

"Oh, I say," he said, "why didn't you say before, instead of employing these people and frightening an honest bird out of his senses?"

"My dogs couldn't find you," said Fiona. "And I think it was so good of the shepherd to find you for me."

"Shepherd!" said the woodcock. "That wasn't a shepherd. And it wasn't a collie either."

Fiona suddenly recollected that she had not yet thanked the shepherd, and turned to do so. But the shepherd and collie were gone. They must have walked very quickly to have turned the corner of the hill already.

"Where did he go?" she asked Artemis. Artemis shivered.

"To his own place, I hope," said Artemis severely. "Well brought up dogs should not be asked to associate with things like that."

"But it was only the new shepherd," said Fiona.

"There's the new shepherd," said Artemis, nodding toward a distant slope, where a figure with a brown collie could be seen gathering sheep.

"What were they, then?" asked Fiona.

"Two of the Little People, of course," said Apollo. "Oh dear, oh dear, I'm afraid you'll have trouble."

"One generally dies," said Artemis, with cheerful consolation.

"But they were very nice to me indeed," said Fiona.

"Of course they were," said the woodcock. "You're privileged, you know. _We_ all know it. And don't you mind the dogs, my dear. They are good creatures, but they and their forbears have lived so long with humans that they have forgotten most of the things we know. They are nearly as blind as humans now, saving your presence, my dear. And now what is it you want with me?"

"I want to find the King of the Woodcock," said Fiona.

"Bless your heart," said the bird, "and who do you suppose We are? You never saw a woodcock Our size before, did you?" And indeed Fiona never had; for he was as big as a young grouse.

"Eighteen and a half ounces, if I'm a pennyweight," said the woodcock. "I am the heaviest king that we have ever had. Will you please put me down if you want to talk to me? It is hardly consonant with my royal dignity to be held. I shan't fly away; _noblesse oblige_, you know."

So Fiona put him down, and he arranged himself like a bunch of feathers on the ground, his head well back between his shoulders and his beady black eyes looking all round him at once.

"Why didn't Apollo find you?" asked Fiona.

"No scent," said the woodcock, proudly. "I am not like a common bird. No dog can find a king woodcock; and no dog ever has. We can be beaten out of a wood, of course; my great-great-grandfather was shot like that when the family lived in Norfolk, many years ago. So we came up here to the open heather, and have been quite safe ever since. And now what do you want, my dear?"

"I was told you could let me into Fairyland," said Fiona.

"I can let you in by the back door," the bird said. "But are you really going to Fairyland? You'll need some courage, you know, if you are going the back way."

"Is there another way?" asked Fiona.

"There's the front door, of course," said the bird. "But no one can go that way without an invitation. Have you an invitation?"

"No," said Fiona.

"A pity," said the woodcock. "There is no danger that way. But without an invitation you could not even find the door. As it is, you'll have to go in by the back way and take your risks."

"I have to go, whatever they are," said Fiona.

"_Noblesse oblige_," said the woodcock. "Quite so, quite so. Have you been told about the wish?"

"Yes," said Fiona. "I know about that."

"The other thing," continued the bird, "is that you must stick to the main path. Remember that. You must not turn out of it for any reason of any kind. You'll see lots of side paths, and you'll see other things too; but if you once leave the main path by so much as one step you'll never get home again. There are no short cuts to Fairyland."

"Thank you so much," said Fiona. "But how shall I know the main path?"

With his long bill the woodcock tweaked the point feather out of one of his wings and gave it to her.

"This will take you through," he said. "It will point the right way for you; that's why it is called the point feather. Just follow it. If you are frightened and want to leave your search and come home, tap on the ground with it and you will be back in Glenollisdal. But somehow I don't think you will. And whatever you do, don't lose it. When you reach the fairy grove, show it to the guardian, and he will let you in; and mind you don't go in unless he shows you its fellow. Oh, I'm all right, thank you; I'll have grown others long before they are needed. There is no great rush to Fairyland on the part of people who haven't _got_ to go, my dear."

"It all sounds so much more difficult than I thought," said poor Fiona.

"Nothing worth while is ever easy," said the woodcock. "And now I'll show you where to start. By the bye, you can't take the dogs with you."

"This dog wouldn't go," said Artemis, shivering. "That black collie's there somewhere."

"Don't bother about us," said Apollo. "We'll be home long before the keeper is out of bed."

So Fiona took a warm farewell of the two dogs, who lamented her sad fate and wished her luck all in one breath, and then set off homeward with their long swinging gallop.

"And now, if you want to be in time for the great gathering, which you humans call Hallow E'en, you'll have to hurry," said the woodcock.

"But it's nearly a month to Hallow E'en," said Fiona.

"You'll want every minute of it," said the bird. "Come on."

And they started off for the fairy ring, the woodcock pattering along on his little feet at a pace which would have surprised anyone who had never seen a woodcock do it.

"How come you to be doorkeeper?" asked Fiona, as they went.

"Hereditary," said the bird. "We used to go to all the lost lands, you know, like Lyonesse and Lemuria and Bresil and Atlantis. We still cross Ireland once a year and pass on into the Atlantic to salute the site of Plato's island, before we settle in Britain. And Fairyland is only another of the lost lands. Here we are."

They had come to the fairy ring.

"There's nothing more I can do now," said the woodcock. "A straight step and a stout heart, my dear."

Fiona took the feather in her hand and stood in the fairy ring.

CHAPTER 7

FIONA IN THE FAIRY-WORLD

It was very, very dark. Fiona could not see her hand if she held it close before her eyes. It was just blackness. Only one thing broke it; far away—many miles it might be—was a tiny speck of white, like the point of a pin. All round her in the dark were little soft sounds; they brushed against her feet, and passed before her face; little soft sounds, apparently without bodies. She held the tiny point-feather firmly in the fingers of her left hand, and touched it from time to time with her right, as she felt her way, one foot before the other—she could not walk—towards the point of light. And with her and about her went the small soft sounds; one would have said that they whispered and chuckled in the darkness.

How far and how long she went she could never guess; there was nothing by which to measure time or distance, and evidently she was not going to feel hunger or fatigue.

At last she became conscious of a change. The white speck of light was growing brighter and larger; and the small soft sounds were becoming tangible. One brushed past her face, and she felt it; she put out a hand, and there was a scuffing and chuckling, as if they were playing blind man's buff with her. Then the light began to take shape; it was a circular pool lying on the floor and wall of the avenue of blackness down which she was passing; and it came from something on the other side. And the little soft sounds crowded round her; they laughed, they whispered, they clutched at her dress; they were trying to guide her in a certain direction. She tried to shake them off, and found that, though they could touch her, she could not touch them. And then she came into the pool of light.

The light came down a sort of short passage between rocks, with a well-trodden floor; and at the end of it, not twenty yards from where she stood, she could see the fairy grotto. One grand white carbuncle, as big as an arc lamp, hung from the roof, filling the grotto with dazzling white light; and the radiance of the carbuncle was flung back in a million points of new splendor from the walls of the grotto, shifting and shimmering like the rainbow across a waterfall, ruby and orange, yellow and emerald, sapphire and violet, changing as each new facet came into play; for the walls of the grotto were set thick with cut jewels of every hue and color. A glorious sight it looked; and Fiona suddenly became aware that the soft things that clutched at her dress and the soft things that whispered in her ear, were all trying to draw her toward the beautiful grotto. But she felt her feather, and it pointed straight on into the dark. So she moved forward; and with the first step she saw the trap. The floor of the beautiful grotto yawned wide, showing the horrible abyss beneath it; and the darkness was full of soft flutterings, and the chuckling of mocking laughter. But they touched her no more at the time; and suddenly the darkness fell away on each side like a wall, and she stepped out into daylight.

She was in the desert. The yellow burning sand stretched all round her, a mass of glittering particles that made the eyes sore; wave after wave, it went billowing away to the red burning hills that faced and flung back the burning sun. Mile after mile she stumbled along in that aching heat; and then, as she topped a great hillock of sand, she suddenly saw the fairy city. Very beautiful it looked, rose-pink on a wooded island in a fair lake of water, whose blue mirror gave back every trembling cupola and minaret; and toward it, down a broad track marked by tamarisk bushes, went a goodly company of merchants, with tinkling bells on their camels' necks and golden ornaments on their camels' heads, the company of a chief who rode ahead on a white Arab steed with his long jezail laid across his saddle-bow. Here could no doubt be; and Fiona all but stepped on to the broad path in the track of the caravan. But even as she turned she caught sight of the feather and checked herself just in time; and the beautiful city of mirage melted away, and there was no caravan there, but only sand marked by the bones of men, and in place of the tamarisk bushes were gray vultures feasting in a row. She followed the feather straight on across the burning desert; and on a sudden she walked out of the sand into shade.

She was out in the forest. Huge trees rose like the pillars of a cathedral nave, branching far above her head and shutting out the daylight; and up their trunks ran starred creepers of every hue, fighting their way up to the sun. Down from the branches hung orchids of all fantastic shapes, in long still streamers, and great moon moths fluttered round them, taking their joy in the dim light. And the farther she went the thicker grew the forest, and the more oppressive the airless heat. Trailing plants ran across her feet and tried to trip her up; the great trunks closed together till there was barely room to force a way between; the thorns of the creepers tore at her flesh, and instead of the beautiful orchids there came on the trees huge funguses red as blood. And the small soft voices began again; they had caught her up; the forest was full of the same little sounds which she had heard before, whispering and chuckling and fingering her dress. And then, just as it seemed impossible to fight a way farther through the dense jungle, she came to the open glade. Full of grass and flowers and sunshine it was, and across it ran a gurgling brook, crossed by a little plank bridge; a sweet breeze moved the grass, and beyond the brook two little spotted deer were feeding; far in the distance were tiny peaks of snow. The soft fingers were all tugging at Fiona's dress, impelling her down the glade; but she had had ample warning of those soft fingers, and she saw that the feather pointed straight on through the tangled forest. And even as she moved she saw that the little bridge was the back of a great water-python; and the fingers loosed their hold of her dress, and the air was full of soft whisperings and laughter. And she walked straight on into the tangled thicket before her; and the forest parted to right and left, and she walked out.

She was in a fair country of green grass and temperate airs, where the path lay true and straight before her through vineyards and groves of oranges. Here and there a cherry tree swung its crown of white blossom above her head, or a cypress stood up tall and straight as a sentinel on duty. Purple flags bloomed under the rocks, and on a clump of brown orchises sat two little jewelled butterflies, burnished green as old copper; up the path of the sunlight came a swallowtail with its stately glancing flight. Everything spoke to her here of fair peace and security; and when she heard the air still rustling with little soft sounds and chuckles, and knew that they had followed her, she began to wonder how it was that, now that she knew their ways, they should think it worth while. And they were becoming most active. The soft sounds brushed all round her; the soft fingers grasped her arms; tiny weightless bodies behind her seemed to be impelling her forward.

And then before her she saw the inevitable two paths: the broad flat path that passed through a fair orchard of lemon trees, where the sunlight threw chequers on to the grass beneath, starred with scarlet and purple anemones; and the narrow stony track, terribly steep, which toiled away up the bare hillside in heat radiated from the rocks. Never had the soft sounds been so insistent; a myriad gentle hands were trying to steer her, even to push her by force, toward the lemon trees. She saw the folly of them so very clearly; and her foot was actually raised to take the first step up the hill path, when she felt the feather turn of itself in her hand, and she became ice from head to foot as she realized that she had all but destroyed herself by despising her opponents. They had striven this time to force her into the _true_ path, believing that she would certainly take the opposite one.

She saw now the end of the fatal hill path, the sudden crumbling precipice which flung men on to pointed rocks far below; and the air behind her became full of woe, voiceless wailings and silent howls of rage, and she saw what she had fought against; a troop of small formless black things, like immature bats, with pale fingers, that fled moaning down the path of the sunlight. She knew now that they would not vex her again.

She passed on through the lemon orchard, and out on to a bare hillside, rough with stones and dotted here and there with great oak trees; plants of asphodel were thrusting their blossoms up among the coarse tufts of grass, and far below, in all its laughing splendor, lay the sea. And as she turned the shoulder of the hill she saw the temple, a fair Doric temple of gray marble, standing in lonely beauty among the scattered oak trees. Its metopes were carved with the figures of gods and heroes of an older day, and round it ran a frieze of warriors who fought with Amazon women. The singing was just over, it seemed; and the double choir of white-robed girls, who had been giving strophe and antistrophe of some festival ode, had broken into groups, these playing at ball, those reclining in the shade or strolling about with their arms round each other's waists. In her chair in the cool portico sat the fair-faced matronly priestess, still crowned with red roses, and before her two little boys poured wine into a crystal goblet. And as she saw Fiona she rose from her chair and greeted her by name, calling her happy that she had now come safely through the path of danger and that her troubles were ended.

"Come here to us," she said, "and rest, for it is but a little way now that you must go, and there is ample time; slake your thirst at this crystal goblet, and lie awhile in the shade, while these maidens crown you with flowers."

But Fiona had learnt her lesson, and she looked at her feather; and the feather pointed straight along the hillside. So she passed on without a look or a word; and as she passed came a noise as of the earth opening; and the pillars of the temple bowed themselves, and the middle of the building collapsed stone by stone, till only the outer columns remained among a mass of fallen blocks, and triglyph and metope and sculptured frieze lay in fragments about them. And among the ruins a red fox with two cubs sat and snarled, as she watched a company of toads crawling in the dust; and of that fair scene all that had not changed was the pallid asphodel, the asphodel whose home is in those other meadows where walk the pallid dead.

And as Fiona passed on, the hillside itself dissolved in mist, and there before her lay the fairy grove. And the guardian of the grove, with white beard sweeping the ground, and old trembling hands, came out to meet her. And she showed him her feather, and from his belt he drew out and held up its fellow; and she knew that the path of danger was over.

"No one has come through by the way you have come for more years than my old memory can follow," he said. "They always fail at the lemon orchard. How did you escape?"

And Fiona told him how the feather had turned in her hand of itself.

The old man bowed almost to the ground.

"That was the direct grace of the King," he said. "You must be a person of the greatest consequence."

And when Fiona said, "I am just an ordinary girl," he again bowed low and said: "Young lady, I take leave to doubt it."

Then he gave Fiona her directions for finding the King, and warned her that she must not loiter in the fairy grove, for the fairies were already gathering for All Hallows E'en.

So Fiona walked swiftly through the grove, not seeing one half of its beauties, though she would have loved to have lingered among the trees. For in the grove grew every tree and plant famous in legend or in history, of which not the tenth part can be told here. There was the Norse ash, whose roots bind together the framework of the earth; there the Irish hazel, of whose nuts could a man but taste he would know all knowledge and all wisdom; there the African pomegranate, but for whose sweetness the Corn-spirit would have disdained to stay beneath the earth, and the race of men would have perished. There stood Deborah's terebinth and Diotima's plane, and the Bô-tree beneath whose branches Gautama Buddha sought and found the path of Enlightenment. There grew the paper-reeds of Egypt, the repository through many centuries of a whole world's learning, the paper-reeds that grow no longer in their old home, even as the prophet Isaiah foretold; and there the clove, for whose perfumed pistils great nations had warred together and brave men died under torture. There stood the English trees, the oak and the white acacia, which had built the three-deckers for the greatest sea captain the world has seen. There was that great traveller, the mulberry, which had left its home on the Yangtse to follow the old Silk Route across Asia; which had crossed the stony Gobi, where wild camels run and the Djinn light their lamps at night to decoy travellers; which had seen the Khotan girls wading knee-deep in the Khotan River, searching for the previous white jade which should make gods for China, as erstwhile for Nineveh and Troy; which had skirted the wandering lake of Lop-nor, and had tarried awhile in old dead cities, now buried under the sands of the dreaded Taklamakan; which had seen the turquoise mines of Khorassan, and voyaged on the broad Oxus stream, till from Iran its way lay clear to the west. There grew the cedars of the Atlas, which had aided their great mountain to support the sky, and had sailed south with Hanno to the Guinea Gulf, to bring home those gorilla hides which lay on the altar of Melcarth at Carthage; and there the most famous of all the trees of the forest, the proud cedars of Lebanon, which had once exulted with their voices over the fall of the king of Assyria, which had built for Solomon his temple and his house for the daughter of

Pharaoh, and which had given to the princes of Tyre the ships in which, greatly daring, they had ranged the three seas, bringing home the gold of India and the silver of Spain and the tin of Cornwall, the wealth of the east and the west, myrrh and frankincense and purple dye, ivory and apes and peacocks. And last of all was the twisted gray olive, beloved of gray-eyed Pallas Athene, the symbol of all that raises man above the savage, the tree in whose train, as it moved out from its home in Asia, had grown up all the civilizations that ringed the Mediterranean.

So Fiona passed through the grove and came out on a broad place of grass, and right before her stood the fairy ring. But not such a one as the ring on Glenollisdal which she knew. This ring was of vast size, and round it grew in a circle huge red toadstools splotched with white, the red toadstools from which the witches of Lapland had used to brew philtres of love and death. But vast as it was, it could not hold all the creatures that swarmed round it. It was a gathering such as Fiona had never dreamt of. On the outskirts stood an innumerable host of little strange beings, of every sort and shape, elves and brownies, gnomes and pixies, trolls and kobolds, goblins and leprechauns; and the babel of them as they whispered together was like the noise of a flock of fieldfares. And within them and around the ring itself stood the fairies.

All the lost peoples and nations and languages, it seemed, were there in miniature; everyone that Fiona had ever heard her father speak of, and many another of which even he knew nothing. There were fairies of the Old Stone peoples, brave-eyed, clad in pelts of the saber-tooth, bearing the blade-bones of bisons on which were carved pictures of the mammoth and the reindeer. Fairies from Egypt, clad in fine white linen with girdles of topaz and aquamarine, with fillets round their brows from which the golden uræus lifted its snake's head, bearing blossoms of the blue lotus. Fairies from Babylon, glowing in coats of scarlet or of many colors, their eyes deep with immemorial learning, bearing clay tablets on which were signs like the footprints of birds. Fairies from Crete, light of foot in the dance, in flounced skirts adorned with golden butterflies, crowned with yellow crocuses and bearing vases on which were painted the creatures of the sea, nautilus and flying fish and polyp. Fairies of the Iberians, black-haired and black-eyed, clad in black cloaks, small and shy and dusty, bearing ingots of tin. Fairies from Cappadocia, in peaked shoes, and pelisses of lion's skin trimmed with the fur of hares, moving to the clash of cymbals, bearing grapes and ears of corn. Fairies from Mexico, with heavy cheek bones, resplendent in mantles woven of the plumage of the quetzal bird, carrying bricks of gold. Fairies from Ethiopia, black as the black diamond, clad in leopard skins and plumed with the feathers of ostriches, carrying tusks of ivory. Fairies from the land of Sheba, well skilled in riddles, in cloaks of camel's hair buckled with clasps of onyx, bearing caskets of agate filled with spices. Buddhist fairies of the Naga race, with the sevenfold cobra's hood springing from their shoulders and shadowing them, languorous and heavy-eyed, carrying crimson water lilies. Fairies from Cambodia, in stiff dresses of cloth of gold, with gilded faces and scarlet eyebrows, bearing pagoda bells which tinkled. Fairies of the Golden Horde, bandy-legged, with pug noses and slits of eyes, clad in dyed sheepskins and carrying the tails of horses. Fairies of the Picts, tattooed to the eyelids, their plaids dyed with crotal and the root of the yellow iris, wearing badges of mountain fern or bog-myrtle and bearing jars of heather ale. Fairies of Britain, in deerskin cloaks fastened with brooches of enamel, with golden torques circling their throats, bearing sprays of mistletoe. Fairies of the Tuatha-dé, with all the youth of the world in their eyes, clad in robes of saffron, crowned with rowans and bearing harps. Fairies from Greece, erect and lissom, beautiful as a sculptor's dream, crowned with wild olive and bearing each the roll of a book. Fairies of old England, in Lincoln green, with feathers of the gray goose in their caps, bearing bows of yew and branches of the may. Fairies from Baghdad, radiant as visions of the night-time, their turbans and their crooked scimitars jewelled with rubies of Badakshan, bearing magic lamps. Fairies from Quinsay, dainty as porcelain, their silken robes embroidered with blossoms of the almond and the peach tree, bearing jars of coral lac wrought in the likeness of dragons, and on their heads the poppy flowers that bring sleep.

And in the middle of the ring stood a throne carved out of a single beryl, green as the sea; and on the throne sat the King of the Fairies, with eyes bright as the dawn and deep as the sea caves, in a cloak of Tyrian purple with clasps of amethyst. His crown and sceptre were of white gold, white gold which has long since perished out of the upper world, and in the end of his sceptre was set a double pentacle of clear crystal brought from the Island of Desire. And in the beryl throne, if he looked at it through the crystal, were shown to him the reflections of all things that he might wish to see. If he looked directly, he saw all that had happened in the world in the past; and if he reversed the crystal, he saw all that should happen in the future; but if he held the pentacle edgewise, then he saw the present, which no man ever sees, and was the greatest magic of all. Round the throne stood his guards, black as Moors, in jackets and trousers of emerald green clasped with orange zircons; half of them bore trumpets of silver, and half of them carried spears with heads of green obsidian as sharp as steel. And on either side of the throne, on a stool, sat a strange creature, a little wizened elf with a large book on his knee. One wore a white cap, and he bore an inkhorn and a bundle of long quills; the other wore a black cap, and he bore a penknife.

Fiona edged herself as far forward as she could into the ring of strange beings, and found herself next an old Leprechaun with a face like a wrinkled apple, who seemed quite inclined to be friendly.

"A human!" he said. "We do not see as many as we used to. But they say there are two to be tried to-night. As you see, we have attempted something out of the ordinary in the way of a welcome." And he waved his arm proudly round the enormous assembly. "Had far to come?" he asked.

Fiona told him how long it had taken her.

"That's nothing," he said. "There are people here to-night who, as soon as the dance is over, will start travelling as fast as they can, and will only just arrive in time for next year's meeting. Good for the shoemaking trade!"

"Where do they try the prisoners?" she asked him.

"Here, in the ring," said the Leprechaun. "The King tries them. There's the Public Prosecutor," and he pointed to a fairy of pompous aspect, with a hooked nose and a Roman toga, and a roll under his arm. "He's a terrible fellow. And there's the King's Remembrancer, those two with the books."

"Why are there two?" asked Fiona.

"One to remember and one to forget, of course, stupid," said the Leprechaun. "Whereever were you educated? Do you think kings want to remember _everything_?"

"It must be very easy forgetting," said Fiona.

"Hardest job in Fairyland," said the Leprechaun. "I suppose you know lots of people with perfect memories; but you never knew one with a perfect forgetfulness, eh? Whitecap there only has to write his book up; but poor Blackcap—he's the one that forgets—his book is written up to start with, and he has to get the pages clean again with his penknife. He never gets them _quite_ clean. They say he has nightmare every night over the things he can't forget altogether."

The King had been talking to one of the officers of his guard. He now rose and held out his sceptre, and there was a great silence round the Fairy ring.

"Before we dance to-night," he said, "we have, as you know, to try two prisoners." He turned to the officer of the guard, and said, "Let them be produced."

The officer at once produced the Urchin from nowhere in particular, as a conjurer produces half-crowns. The boy looked rather large among the Little People, but otherwise he was much as Fiona had last seen him; his shirt and knickerbockers were covered with earthstains and he still had the same length of useless rope coiled round his waist.

But Jeconiah? Was this the prosperous financier, this wretched apology for a living being which the officer held out on the palm of his hand? Not two inches high, its white waistcoat hanging in loose flaps, speechless, and wide-eyed with terror and abject entreaty, it was like the ghost of a parody; the officer had to set it on one of the great toadstools, and mark the place with a stick, lest it should be lost. The King regarded it with interest.

"I understood that the elder prisoner was a very stout man," he said.

"That was so, your Majesty," said the officer. "He was so stout that we thought it useless to attempt to take him through the doorway as he was, so we left his body behind and only brought away the essential part of him. This is all that there really is of him, sire; the rest was wind. When we began to sift him we were afraid that he had no real existence at all, and that there would be nothing to bring before you."

"Well, well," said the King, "there's enough of him to be tried, anyhow. Are the prisoners provided with counsel?"

The Public Prosecutor was understood to say that they were not yet represented.

"Counsel had better be assigned them in the usual way," said the King. "Catch, somebody."

He took a guinea from his pocket and flung it, apparently without looking, into the crowd. But thick as the crowd was, the guinea passed straight through the forest of hands held out for it, and fell into a tiny brown hand behind them. Fiona knew where she had seen that hand before.

The owner of the hand at once stepped forward into the ring. He seemed to be the most singular being in Fairyland. Fiona's first impression was that he was just a large bald head, the color of parchment and wrinkled all over; and this impression remained, even when she realized that he did possess a small body, with the usual allowance of arms and legs. Out of his great head looked a pair of quite incongruous eyes, bright as beads, and full of happy drollery. Behind him came a couple of stout goblins, each laden with dusty law books. They piled the books up in a stack on the ground, and the singular creature with the head proceeded to climb to the top of the stack, where he sat down, cracking his fingers and laughing hugely at some jest of his own, evidently on the best of terms both with himself and his audience. Then he caught Fiona's eye, and deliberately winked at her; but somehow it carried no offence, for the creature seemed absolutely free from malice.

"Privilege honorable profession defend oppressed," he remarked; "duty clients submit large number points," and he patted the books he sat on. He had a habit of clipping his words as he spoke which was totally destructive of the smaller parts of speech, and made his remarks sound like a series of unedited cablegrams.

"We will take the younger prisoner first," announced the King; whereupon the Public Prosecutor proceeded to read, all in one breath, the indictment against the Urchin, to the effect that he did on or about the 20th day of September then last past in despite of the peace of the realm and the safety of the lieges with a stone or some other missile or thing throw at and break the wing of or otherwise hit, cut, hurt, maim, destroy and do wrong to one of the said lieges, to wit, a shore lark, and so forth. When he had finished, instead of evidence being taken, the King merely glanced into the beryl throne.

"True in fact," he said. "Any defence?"

The creature on the bookstack began at once.

"Please Majesty duty client submit series points. First point no intention."

But Fiona did not wait to hear what it had to say. Forcing her way into the ring, she said:

"Please, your Majesty, it was my fault. I told him he couldn't."

The King turned to look at her.

"So this is the young lady," he said. "Very good of you to come, you know. We rarely receive visitors now. We shall try to make you welcome when the trial is over." He turned again to the bookstack, and said: "I will hear the defence."

"It was my fault, your Majesty," said Fiona again.

With grave patience the King started to explain to her.

"Your part of it was your fault, of course. But we are not trying you, for you have come here of your own free will, so we can neither try nor punish. But his part of it was equally his own fault, and unless there is a good defence he will have to be punished."

The creature on the bookstack was nodding and signing to Fiona, but she was too engrossed with a single thought to notice him.

"Then I claim my wish, your Majesty," she said.

"Quite in order," said the King. "The trial will be suspended while the young lady wishes. Officer!"

And immediately the fairy ring was strewn with a strange collection of objects, looking rather like the contents of an old curiosity shop that had gone bankrupt. The officer held them up one by one for Fiona to see.

"When we heard you were coming," said the King, "we collected a few little things for your inspection. It is so long since we had any use for any of them that many of them seem to have developed serious defects, which we regret; but they are the best we could find at short notice. This," he pointed to an old ring, "is a common wishing ring. It used to do all the usual things. The genie attached to it has unfortunately become very deaf with age; but if you can make him hear, we believe he is still in fair working order. This," as a frayed girdle was held up, "is the famous cestus of Aphrodite, which she lent to Helen of Troy. Its wearer used to become the most beautiful and unpopular creature in the world. It will still confer beauty, though hardly suited to the modern style; the unpopularity we guarantee. This," pointing to a huge book, "contains the truth of that which in your world passes as knowledge. It would delight your father. He might publish selected chapters, and watch the critics cut them to pieces. This," as a battered trumpet was exhibited, "is Fame. Your praises would be sung all over the world; and the world would say, 'Never mind what she has _achieved_; tell us about her faults.' This," and he contemplated an old iron sceptre, "is Power. You would become a great ruler, and would probably die in exile. And under this," and he pointed to a sheet of black velvet, thrown loosely over some object, "under this is the treasure of the Isle of Mist, which I am told that you have heard of. Do any of these please you? If not, we have others."

Fiona never thought about it for a moment, of course. She had not done all that she had done to hesitate now. She did not look at the King's face, and she took not the least notice of the creature with the head, who was dancing about in a perfect agony, trying to attract her attention.

"Please your Majesty," she said in breathless haste, "I came here to find the Urchin and take him home with me. That is my wish."

She had hardly spoken the words when her instinct told her something was wrong. A sort of chill seemed to run through the air, and the color seemed to go out of the fairy world. The creature with the head stopped dancing about and began to wring its little hands. She looked up at the King's face, and read there, was it disappointment? was it regret? She hardly knew.

"A very natural and proper wish," said the King gravely. "We shall of course accept it as such, and grant it with great pleasure. The younger prisoner is discharged. Take the next case."

And then Fiona saw. She saw the thing which had once been Jeconiah, with that look of abject terror and entreaty in its eyes; and she realized that it would have meant nothing to her to have included Jeconiah in her wish, and that for Jeconiah it would have meant everything. And she realized also that, worthless and evil as he had been in life, selfish, mean, a thief and a liar, he was still a human being, and had a soul and possibilities of which the fairy world could know nothing. She felt a wave of humiliation pass over her; and she resolved that, whatever he was, and whatever happened, she would not go home without Jeconiah.

The charges against Jeconiah were then read: stealing a treasure, and being a worthless character.

"Any defence?" said the King.

The creature with the head got to work.

"Please Majesty," he said, "admit second count. Character worthless. Object pity however not vindictive punishment. Behalf client offer submit State cure. First count plead not guilty; intention steal treasure admitted but did not succeed."

Fiona, in her new-found humility, had been listening to what the creature with the head was saying. And suddenly it dawned on her that, all through, both he and the King had been trying to help her, so far as was consistent with their own rules; and that perhaps the creature with the head, for all his oddity, knew what he was doing. She asked the Leprechaun who he was.

"You might have asked that with advantage before you interrupted him," said the Leprechaun severely. "He is our Chancellor here. He is the King's most intimate friend, and far the ablest lawyer in Fairyland."

"Defence to first count not admitted," the King was saying. "Your client cannot plead his own bungling of the theft in mitigation of his wrongdoing. Only the intention counts here."

The Chancellor looked immensely relieved at the King's words, though it passed Fiona's wit to see why.

"Apply formal ruling," he said. "Take down," this to Whitecap.

"I hold that nothing counts here but the intention," said the King.

"Majesty pleases," said the Chancellor. "Settles point. Retire defence this prisoner. Submit excellent point younger client."

"We will pass sentence here first," said the King. "Jeconiah P. Johnson, your counsel has very properly thrown up his brief. You are convicted of stealing a treasure, and it is admitted that you are a worthless character. On the first count, I sentence you to be handed over to the executioner to be extended until you become a proper size. If you survive, you will then undergo, as offered by your counsel, the State cure at the hands of the State hypnotizer." He turned to the Chancellor. "Any further submission?"

Fiona had gone over to the stack of books, and bent down over the little creature with the head.

"I have made a most terrible mistake," she said, in a low voice. "I have spoilt everything. I see that you are kind; can you help us?"

"Should have come me first," said the creature, quite gently. "Tried attract attention. Never neglect anyone merely because odd and ugly. May have good heart. Sad mess now; but think see daylight. Any influence that boy?"

"Oh, yes," said Fiona eagerly.

"Right," said the creature. "Make boy wish. Now follow my argument." And he turned to the King.

"Please Majesty submit good point. Majesty just ruled nothing counts here but intention. Younger prisoner no intention hurt shore lark; therefore on Majesty's ruling same as if did not hurt it. Therefore never was guilty. Human prisoner adjudged not guilty is just same as if came here own free will; so held Majesty's father"; and by some extraordinary trick he got the top book open and flopped down among the leaves, from which position he read out bits of an ancient judgment. "Consequently younger prisoner both entitled and bound wish."

The King consulted Whitecap.

"It seems a sound chain of reasoning," he said. Then he turned to the Public Prosecutor. "Have you anything to urge against it?"

"Only that, if he wishes wrong, we can't detain him, because of the young lady's wish," said that official.

"Daniel come judgment," cried the Chancellor triumphantly. "Heads win, tails can't lose. Younger prisoner wish."

He turned to Fiona and whispered to her, "Mind he wishes right."

Fiona started to go over to the Urchin; instantly the guard crossed their spears before her.

"No interference allowed with anyone who is going to wish," said the officer.

Then she tried to call to him, and found that she could not speak. It was like a nightmare. She looked helplessly at the Chancellor; he nodded, and spelt on his fingers the word "think."

Then Fiona understood what he had meant by asking her if she had any influence over the Urchin. She knew that she had a good deal; and bits of conversations with her father came back into her mind. She had made one bad blunder, and she had to correct it as best she could; and without more ado she concentrated her whole mind on taking possession of the mind of the Urchin. Could it be done at all? And if so could it be done in time?

The King stretched out his sceptre, and there was silence.

"The younger prisoner is going to wish," said the King. "Officer!"

And immediately there appeared in the middle of the ring six great boxes, old sea chests made of Spanish chestnut, battered and stained and clamped with bands of iron; and on each was the picture, half obliterated by time and salt water, of the Madonna of the Holy Cross. The officer flung back the lids, and showed each chest full to the brim of glittering golden doubloons.

"That is the treasure from the Venetian galleon which you were seeking," said the King. "We removed it long ago into our safe custody, lest it should tempt men; but it would seem that it tempts them none the less. Now wish."

The Urchin, his eyes bulging out of his head, stared at the shining gold. He murmured "gun," but fortunately so low that the King did not hear him.

Fiona kept her eyes fixed hard on the boy, and bent every effort of mind and will to the one thought, that he must wish as she wished. If only he would turn round. She had already lost sight of the fairies; she now lost sight of the King; she was conscious only of the abject wretched creature that was Jeconiah, and of the back of the Urchin's head. He was still staring at the gold, but he had not yet spoken; that was to the good, and—no, it was not fancy—his ears were turning pink, as they always did when he was in a difficulty. Then he began to shuffle his feet uneasily. Fiona felt that every atom of life and force in her was being concentrated on that one act of will; she did not think she could go through with it many seconds longer, or she would collapse. And then the Urchin turned his head toward her; his face was scarlet, and his eyes were wavering before the fixed gaze of her own; he _must_ do as she wished. She flung everything into one supreme effort—the last reserves which no one thinks they possess till utter necessity teaches them the contrary; and then the Urchin spoke, in a strange voice and all in one breath:

"I want my uncle to go free."

Fiona's will let go with a snap; she felt so dizzy that she had to lean against one of the great toadstools or she would have fallen. Round the assemblage ran a sound like the wind through the tree tops, the noise of thousands drawing in breath at once; and the Chancellor started a war dance on his stack of books, and nearly fell off on his head. The King rose from his throne, but he took no notice of the Urchin; he turned straight to Fiona and bowed to her.

"My compliments, young lady," he said; "the prettiest piece of thought-transference it has ever been our privilege to see. Where did you learn to do it?"

"I never learnt," stammered Fiona. "I made a great mistake, as your Majesty saw, and something had to be done, and your friend suggested this way."

"You needn't mind having made a mistake," said the King. "If you don't make mistakes sometimes you'll never make anything else. And you have made something else this time with a vengeance. As for you, sirrah . . ." and he shook his fist at the Chancellor.

The creature snapped all its fingers in reply.

"Majesty pleases," it began triumphantly. "Duty younger client submit new point arising young lady's action. Client entitled wish. Did not wish himself; young lady wished. Therefore client still entitled wish. Propose develop point considerable length with authorities."

The King raised his hand.

"I think I shall have to intervene," he said. "I believe you would submit points till cockcrow."

"Submit points till next year, if Majesty pleases," said the creature, gleefully.

"If these proceedings don't end soon," said the King, "there will be no time to dance; and if we didn't dance no one knows what would happen to the world above. Even I don't know that. So as we do not generally have three human beings here at once, and as substantial justice has been done, I propose now to exercise the royal prerogative of generosity. Jeconiah P. Johnson, you will, as requested, go free, so far as we can set you free. We cannot set you free from your own worthless character. In order, however, to do the best for you that can be done, before you leave us the State hypnotizer will take you in hand and instil into you a few decent feelings. He won't hurt you, and you won't remember. The effect, I fear, will not be permanent, but it will ease our conscience. And as a sign to the world above that we have treated you liberally, you will find that you will be unable to attend to business until you have told your nephew a fairy tale. Urchin! A doubt exists as to whether you have had your wish or not. You shall have the benefit of the doubt, so far as is good for you. You will find that you will get your gun."

And then the King turned to Fiona.

"Young lady," he said, "you have given us a display of courage which we are not likely to forget. You have rescued your friend; you have, which is much more to the point, rescued your enemy. You have got _two_ wishes out of us, which no one ever did before; and you have asked nothing for yourself. And now what are we to do for you?"

"I think I have everything I want, now, thank your Majesty," said Fiona.

"Did we not hear talk of a treasure?" said the King.

"Yes," said Fiona; "but—I was not thinking about a treasure, your Majesty."

"I know," said the King. "But I was; all the time."

"I must leave it all in your Majesty's hands," said Fiona.

"It is not here," said the King. "What you saw was only a pretence. And we cannot send for it to-night. But if you will honor us sometime by returning to our kingdom, we will see what can be done in memory of your visit. Any time you like. And by the front door, please. You will run no risks that way."

"And now," said the King, stretching out his sceptre over the great throng, "we will dance." He turned to Fiona and the Urchin. "It will be a little while before Mr. Johnson is ready to accompany you home," he said. "Perhaps you will honor us meanwhile by attending the dance also."

So the fairies danced before the King; and the fairy ring whirled and blazed with the color of them, till it was gayer than a gorse-bank in blossom, and brighter than a swarm of dragon-flies on a June grass-field, and more vivid than a fall of shooting stars; and the music that they made was wilder than the wind in the strings of a harp, and sweeter than the blackbird's song, and dearer than all the burns on the moor murmuring in unison. And the two children sat at the King's feet on the steps of the beryl throne and watched the dancers; and the Chancellor sat between them, and held Fiona's hand, and told them such stories as they had never heard before, till between laughter and tears they nearly fell off the steps of the throne, and the Chancellor laughed and cried with them for sheer joy in his own story-telling; and if there were three happier people in the world that night I do not know where they were. And the night itself passed away as a dream that men dream, and its hours seemed to them but as a few minutes—and then across the music and the dance cut the shrill harsh scream of a peacock as he greeted the day. The children saw the King rise from his throne and stretch his sceptre out over the ring; and the ring and the dancers were shrouded in a white mist which rose from the ground and wreathed its arms about them; and the beryl throne dissolved in mist, and the figure of the King above them, pointing, grew dim and huge, and spread and grew, a purple shadow that hung over them, . . . and they were standing alone in the fairy ring on Glenollisdal, under the purple sky, with the white mist wreathing itself about their feet, and the pale November dawn coming slowly up out of the sea.

Did the Urchin fling himself on the grass at Fiona's feet and thank her in broken accents for all she had done for him? I regret to state that the first thing which the Urchin did was to feel in his pocket and draw out the doubloon which he had found in the cave.

"I've got this one, anyhow, Fiona," he said. "But I wonder how I'm going to get that gun."

Then something seemed to prick him; he began to look uncomfortable and shuffle his feet, while his ears turned pink; and at last he managed to blurt out:

"I say, Fiona, it was jolly decent of you, you know."

Fiona only smiled, the wise smile of perfect understanding.

THAT MORNING THE DOCTOR WAS HASTILY SUMMONED WITH THE NEWS THAT Jeconiah was awake. The nurse met him in the passage, wide-eyed and rather frightened.

"He's so strange," she said.

"Tut, tut," said the doctor; "told you he might wake like that. Kind of change in personality? Just so. Often happens. Seldom permanent though. What's he done?"

"Well, doctor, of course we all know Mr. Johnson's reputation," said the nurse. "He's thanked me three times, and hoped I didn't tire myself; and he had all the servants up and said he'd see their wages were raised, and the cook gave notice on the spot because she said she didn't like practical jokes; and he says he wants to go out and gather buttercups and daisies, and play with the little frogs; and he's sent for some old gun that he says he's got to buy for his nephew; and he hasn't opened any of the telegrams that have been waiting for him; he says he mayn't attend to business till he has learnt a fairy tale, and he's had the library ransacked, and he's tearing his hair because there's no such thing in it."

"Oh, well," said the doctor, "we must just have patience, nurse. I expected something of the sort. Just humor him; if you can't find a fairy tale, try him with a history book; he'll never know the difference; and I'll send him up a nice soothing mixture. Very interesting case; ve-ry interesting."

And the doctor, calling up his best professional smile, bustled into Jeconiah's room.

I T WAS THE SAME AFTERNOON, A STILL AFTERNOON OF INDIAN SUMMER, THAT the old hawker, accompanied again by the black terrier, was going down the shore road. He must have had business at the cottage on the beach. But his business was probably not urgent; for he stopped to watch with interest a group on the shore. It consisted of Jeconiah and the Urchin, and they sat on the little patch of sand at the mouth of the burn. The Urchin had across his knees the rusty old gun bought for him by Jeconiah, who had nevertheless exacted the doubloon from him in exchange. He fingered the gun lovingly, while he gazed with undisguised impatience at the proceedings of his uncle. Jeconiah's coat lay on the grounds beside a sheaf of unopened telegrams, and he was putting the finishing touches to a noble castle of sand; its drawbridge was supported by his double watch chain, and its turrets bore a suspicious resemblance in contour to the inside of his hat. He patted his work and gazed at it with pride.

"Fine, isn't it?" he said.

"You'd better hurry up with that fairy tale," said the boy. "If you've got to, you've got to, you know; and you won't keep me much once I get some cartridges."

Jeconiah began to look alarmed.

"But I haven't found one yet," he said, and glanced anxiously at the pile of telegrams.

"Make one up, then," said the boy. "Anybody can do it."

Thus adjured, Jeconiah started.

"Once upon a time there was a very grizzly old bear, and he lived in a beautiful place called Capel Court, and he used to hunt the wild bulls and the stags and the poor little guinea pigs that abounded in that salubrious locality. And there were two young ladies there, called Cora and Dora. . . ."

"Are those the princesses?" asked the boy.

"No, I think not," said Jeconiah. "They were of quite ordinary stock. Well, the old bear thought they were too high and mighty, and that he would like to take them down a point or two. . . ."

"Oh, this won't do," said the Urchin rudely. "This isn't a _real_ fairy tale at all. You must do something better than that."

The wretched Jeconiah groaned, and looked again at his telegrams. Then he started afresh.

"Once upon a time there was a great dragon with seven heads, and he ate seven princesses every day for dinner. . . ."

"That's better," said the boy, encouragingly, as he settled himself to listen.

The old hawker resumed his walk.

"They haven't made a very good job of him, after all," he remarked aloud, apparently to the terrier. "But I expect that sort is incurable."

Was it a flicker of sunlight? Or did the black terrier really wink?

CHAPTER 8

FIONA FINDS HER TREASURE

And Fiona?

Fiona sat on the hearthrug in the bookroom, and told her father the whole story from beginning to end, as it has been told here. And sometimes he asked a question, and sometimes he said, "Yes, that would be so," and sometimes he stroked her hair and said nothing. And when she had ended, he said, "So you never found your own treasure after all, Fiona?"

She said, "I suppose I can have it now, if I go back."

"Do you think you will go back?" he asked.

She replied with another question.

"Have you found out what my treasure is, daddy?"

"I believe I could guess," he answered. "But you have found a good many things already, apart from treasure, haven't you, little daughter?"

She sat silent and looked into the fire.

"I suppose I have," she said.

"We won't enumerate them," said the Student. "It spoils things entirely, sometimes, to put them into words. But I will tell you something an old writer once said. He was talking of that particular kind of treasure which men call Truth; and he said that if he were offered Truth itself on the one hand, and the everlasting search for it on the other hand, he would choose the search. I expect you can understand that now; for you have seen what has happened to you over your own search."

"I think I can understand," said Fiona. "I must be growing older, daddy."

"You'll be too old soon to go back to Fairyland at all, little daughter," said the Student. "If you are going, you will have to go at once."

"What do you think, daddy?" she questioned.

"I can only tell you that, in my case, I went back," the Student answered.

"Why, daddy, have you been in Fairyland too?" cried Fiona. "And you never told me."

"Yes," said the Student. "Even a musty old scholar like myself was young once, you know," and he looked into the fire with eyes which seemed to see things very, very far away. "It was not quite the same as the Fairyland you have been in, Fiona; but we called it Fairyland."

"Can't you come back with me if I go daddy?" asked the girl.

"I'm too old now, little daughter," he said. "For good or for bad, I could never find the way again. I can only see it now through your eyes. I'll come as far as the door with you, and that's all that an old man can do. I suppose you know where the door is?"

"I never felt there was any doubt," said Fiona.

"Then we'll start first thing to-morrow, if it's calm enough," he said.

But that evening was the last of the golden autumn; and when Fiona woke in the morning, the Isle of Mist was justifying its name. The southwest gale was raging round the house like a live animal, seizing it and shaking it, and wailing in the chimneys pitifully, like an unburied ghost; and before the gale the long lead-colored rollers were racing in from the Atlantic, smashing themselves on the crags and shooting up heavenward in columns of spray thrice the height of the cliffs, while the noise of the surf in the Scargill cave came booming across the water like the roar of a battleship's guns. The hills were all shrouded in mist, and the mist was fine salt rain that rolled in from the sea, driving in billows over the moor and across the fields; the gulls were tossed about in it like little bits of waste paper, and every green thing on the island opened its heart to the rain and drank till it could drink no more. Toward evening Fiona and the Student, in oilskins and sou'-westers, went down to the rocks and out seaward as far as was possible, and there stood, unable to speak for the noise. They balanced themselves against the gusts, and felt the tingling drops of salt spray rattle like hail off their coats, while they watched the cliff waterfalls, unable to fall for the wind, go straight up heavenward in clouds of smoke, and the sea foam and tear at the rocks below; and once for a moment the cloud-mist parted, and the hills started out, their dark sides all gashed and seamed with white streaks where every tiny runlet and burn was rushing in spate down toward the sea. Fiona managed to shout, with her clear young voice, "No one can really love this island who only knows it in summer;" and then they went home, out of the dusk and the lashing of the wet wind, to the quiet bookroom and tea things, and lamps, and books; for man may love Nature, but he loves still better the contrast between Nature and the things which he has fashioned for himself.

For three weeks the wind blew; and though there were days when the sea-mist lifted, there was no day on which the sea was calm enough for the launching of their small boat. Then one afternoon came change. The warm air turned chill, and the warm rain became sleet; that night the wind backed to the north, and next day was a blizzard of snow. And the night after the wind fell away, and the snow ceased, and Orion and his two dogs shone huge in a frosty sky; and Fiona woke to the glories of a scarlet sunrise on a great field of white.

"We must hurry, daddy," she said. "It's perfectly calm."

"It's a pet day," said the Student, sniffing the air. "It won't last; the wind backed too suddenly. But it's all right till sunset."

Directly breakfast was over they launched the little boat, and started. The snow shone white in the sunshine, and the calm sea against the snow was as blue as a blue lotus; but the shadows on the snow were a wonder, and the woven complexity of their colorings would have taxed every hue on an artist's palette. So they pulled down and into the cave, at whose mouth the great bluff looked barer and blacker than ever against the world's whiteness; and they grounded their boat and climbed the rock barrier. There the Student sat down and filled and lit his pipe.

"This is as far as I can go," he said. "If I mistake not, you will find that they have opened the door for you."

So Fiona went on to the recess where the Urchin had found the doubloon, and where the torch had been smashed in her father's hand; and the solid wall of the cliff had opened, and there was an archway leading into the black vaulting of the long cave behind. Fiona passed through into the darkness . . . and the darkness parted to right and left of her, and she stood again in the fairy ring where she had stood on All Hallows E'en.

But how changed. Of all the bright throng of fairies that had clustered round it, not one stood there to-day. The circle of scarlet toadstools was broken down and shattered, as though by a great storm; and the ring itself was no longer grass, but was covered deep in snow. Of all the things she had seen there that evening, only one remained. The beryl throne still stood lonely in the midst of the bare ring; and on the throne sat the King of the Fairies. His face rested on his hand, as though he were deep in thought; his eyes were looking at something far away. On the steps of the throne sat the Chancellor, the King's inseparable friend; and he, too, was deep in thought. It was a view of the fairy world which Fiona had never expected.

The King must have heard her step, for he rose from his throne and came down to meet her.

"Have you come for your treasure, Fiona?" he said.

And she said, "I have come because you asked me to come back."

The King held out his sceptre to her; and again the mist came up from the ground and enwrapped the beryl throne, and the figures of the King and the Chancellor wavered and became dim before her. _Were_ they the King and the Chancellor? Was not what she saw, so dim through the mist, the figures of the shepherd who had helped her on Glenollisdal and his black collie? But the mist was wavering again about them, and again all was a blur; and then the mist suddenly cleared, and there was no one there at all but just the old hawker and the little terrier which followed him.

"So you were the King of the Fairies all the time," said Fiona.

"All the time," said the old man gently. "We go about in the world as you see us. And some still entertain angels unaware. Have you come for your treasure, Fiona?"

And this time Fiona answered, "Yes."

"You have earned it," said the King. "And you have found much more than any treasure. Your father has told you that?"

And again Fiona said, "Yes."

"I cannot really give you your treasure," said the King, "for you have it already. I think you have had it all the time; but you did not know. But now you have learnt."

"What is it?" asked Fiona. "But I think I can guess now."

"It is the spirit of the island which you love," said the King, "and which henceforth loves you. You have spoken face to face with bird and beast and with the beings who knew and loved the land before your race was. To-day you have the freedom of the island, and of all living things in it; they are your friends forever. And to the dead in its graveyards you are kin. All that is there has passed into your blood, the old lost loves, the old impossible loyalties, the old forgotten heroisms and tendernesses; all these are yours; and yours are the songs that were sung long ago, and the tales which were told by the fireside; and the deeds of the men and women of old have become part of you. You can walk now through the crowded city and never know it, for the wind from the heather will be about you where you go; you can stand in the tumult of men and never hear them, for round you will be the silence of your own sea. That is the treasure of the Isle of Mist; the island has given you of its soul. You have found greater things already; you will find greater things yet again. But such as it is, it is the best gift which we of the fairy world have to give."

"And now," continued the King, "you will not see us again. And I will take back the bracelet. It would be no further use to you, for you are no longer a child. You are too old for Fairyland."

"But my father could see you," said Fiona.

"He could only see me as I really am through your eyes," said the King. "It may be that some day you too will see me again through the eyes of a child. But for the present it is farewell."

So Fiona stooped down and stroked the little dog, who looked at her with wistful eyes, and took her farewell of the King; and the King raised his hand, and the mist rose again and enwrapped the fairy ring and those in it . . . and Fiona walked out through the archway into the cave, and there sat the Student on the rock barrier, just as she had left him, knocking the ashes out of his pipe. And even as she came to him there was a noise behind her, and when she looked round it was to see the archway blocked by a great fall of rock.

"You will not use that way again, little daughter," said the Student.

"I shall not use any way again now, daddy," she said. "I am too old. But oh, daddy, it has been worth it."

Then they launched their boat and paddled slowly out of the cave, out of the dark into daylight; and before them lay the quiet sea bathed in the winter sun, and the Isle of Mist dreaming under its mantle of white.

The End

ACTRESS GENA ROWLANDS (1930-2024)

PHOTO FROM 1920, DURING PROHIBITION. A WOMAN SITTING IN A WASHINGTON D.C. CAFE, TIPPING HER CANE FLASK.

Thank you for reading another issue of Adventures BookZine!

3	6	8	7	4	9	2	5	1
4	5	1	6	8	2	3	7	9
9	2	7	5	3	1	4	8	6
7	1	3	8	2	6	9	4	5
5	8	2	3	9	4	6	1	7
6	9	4	1	7	5	8	2	3
8	7	5	2	6	3	1	9	4
1	3	9	4	5	8	7	6	2
2	4	6	9	1	7	5	3	8

Next issue will be out this summer.